WE SHALL NOT SHATTER

ELAINE STOCK

ISBN: (ebook)

ISBN: (paperback)

ISBN: (hardcover)

Publisher: Amsterdam Publishers, The Netherlands

info@amsterdampublishers.com

Author Website: https://elainestock.com

We Shall Not Shatter is Book 1 of the Trilogy **Resilient Women of WWII**

Copyright © Elaine Stock, 2022

Cover image: ...

All Rights Reserved. No part of this publication may be reproduced or transmitted in any form or by any means, electronic or mechanical, including photocopy, recording or any other information storage and retrieval system, without prior permission in writing from the publisher.

AUTHOR'S NOTE

Postcard of Górki Street in Brzeziny (date? copyright?)

We Shall Not Shatter was inspired by my paternal family history in Brzeziny, Poland. Although my goal was to make the characters, setting, and world events as accurate as possible based upon many hours of research, the story and its characters are entirely fictitious. Brzeziny, once a town known worldwide for its tailors and craftsmanship, was destroyed during the Holocaust. Rising from this tragic time, like the rest of Poland, Brzeziny is still on the map, but it is a changed town.

I have tried my best to write this story as a tribute—a love song, if you may—to what once was this town and its people. Any inaccuracies are fully my own and are unintentional. If you would like to read more about Brzeziny, please consider the nonfiction book *Brzezin Brzeziny Memorial Book* published by JewishGen, Inc., a true treasure of information.

Dedicated in the Memory of my Great Aunt, Katie Pakula, and her brother, my grandfather, Chaskel (Charles) Pakula of Brzeziny, Poland. You have passed on way too early. May we one day meet in the glorious afterlife.

And also, in memory of all those who lost their lives in Brzeziny, in all of Poland, and all those who fought against Nazism during World War II.

PROLOGUE

Birch and linden trees thick with spring-green leaves lined the dirt road from home. From a cloudless blue sky the warmth of the sun reached five-year-old Zofia like an embrace. After a stretch of chilly days this new one promised goodness. Last night Mamusiu told her a story about the forest fairies and how they pouted and said bad things about the unusual cold weather they suffered through one spring. It was as if they'd lost hope of a better tomorrow, she said. Zofia turned at the willow and headed down the bank to the water, seeing her mama's smiling face in her mind. Her mother was smart. Of course a nice day can follow a nasty one. And today was lovely. The blooming flowers filled the air with a sugary smell. She breathed deeply, and it felt like a promise.

Giggles of delight rushed from her throat as a family of quacking ducks waddled into the water. Movement toward her right stole her attention away from the noisy birds. A girl she'd never seen before stood on the opposite side of the river. Was she new to town? The stranger scampered toward the water, her feet carrying her so fast it seemed she flew. Her strawberry-colored curls bounced.

Those poor ducks. "Stop!" Zofia called. "You'll scare them. Then they'll never come back."

Now on the riverbank, the girl followed the ducks' path.

Zofia tried again. "Please don't hurt them. They're cute and happy. They're a family."

The girl, who must have been about the same age as Zofia, stopped running and glanced her way. She remained quiet. How odd. The ducks continued downstream. The girl studied Zofia, as if she too were curious why they'd never seen each other before.

"I'm Zofia. Who are you? Did you just move here?"

No response came.

Zofia stamped her foot in the tall weedy grass. "How come you won't talk to me?"

The girl bunched her frock, the color of the wheat Zofia's papa grew. She smiled big, her little white teeth shiny in the sunlight. Then she tiptoed through the water, shallow at this narrow part of the river, and trotted toward Zofia. With one little swoop she bent down, plucked a daisy and offered it to Zofia.

This girl was both silly and brave. She could have slipped in the water—the water her own mama warned her not to enter. But she was courageous to have taken a chance.

Zofia took the flower and smiled. "What's your name?"

The girl stared blankly.

Zofia didn't like this game. She jammed her thumb at her chest. "My name is Zofia," she said, this time louder. "Who are you?"

The girl's smile faded. She cupped her ears and shook her head.

"Are you deaf?" Hot shame spread through Zofia, like when she disobeyed her parents even when she knew she shouldn't.

What was this girl's name? If Zofia wrote down her question would that help? She might have been five, but she already knew how to write her name and a few other words. She found a twig. With her foot she brushed away the grass and loosened the soil. She scratched her name into the ground and pointed at the word and then at herself. She offered the twig to the girl, gesturing for her to scrawl her name into the soil.

Aanya.

Zofia nodded. She knew about deafness, had heard about several deaf families who lived in Brzeziny but kept to themselves. Until this day, though, she'd never met a person robbed of hearing. Aanya looked like the other children she knew. Too bad her ears were broken. But it wasn't her fault. She'd find a way to communicate. She held five fingers up and thumped her chest with them. She pointed at Aanya. "How old are you?"

Aanya lifted a hand and wiggled each of her five fingers. They smiled. Drawing houses and stick figures of people, they discovered that though Zofia lived outside of town, and Aanya in Brzeziny, it was an easy walk to each other's houses. They also learned that they both had a mama and papa, but no sisters or brothers. That didn't matter. They could be sisters to each other.

"Let's pick flowers for our mamas," Zofia said, pointing to the figures of their mothers and rattling the daisy Aanya had given her. Aware she was talking aloud only for her own ears to hear, she didn't stop. She didn't want to treat Aanya differently from anyone else.

With an enthusiastic nod, Aanya agreed.

Zofia felt a smile grow throughout her insides. Although Mamusiu had explained that Polska had seen troubles in the past, especially since it hadn't been its own country for over a hundred years—a number bigger than life itself—she sensed it was important to have a friend. No one knew what tomorrow would bring.

Later, after a promise to see each other again, she went one way home and Aanya the opposite way. When Zofia gave her mama the bouquet of daisies mixed with red and orange poppies and told her about her new friend, Mamusiu shook the flowers. She made a horrible face, like she was both afraid and angry.

"She might have been hurt. You must be careful around the deaf. You, darling Zofia, know better than to play with a feeble girl by the water."

"What's feeble?"

Mamusiu wrinkled her nose. "Poor Pan Kaszynski is a fine example. Remember just last week when you asked about his swollen left leg, his red ankle, and why he walks stiffly? His illness has made him into a weak man. He can barely help his family."

"Mamusiu, Aanya isn't feeble. Her ears don't work, but that's all. She's like me—there's nothing wrong with her."

And they were alike in oodles of ways. Other people failed to understand but that didn't matter. Zofia and Aanya became such close friends that through the years they were amazed when others were curious over how one Catholic hearing woman and one Jewish deaf woman were sisterly companions.

1

The French marble clock in the bedroom chimed five o'clock at the same time a pounding came to the front door. The abrupt noise, loud and demanding, rattled Zofia Badower that early January evening. In ordinary times she wouldn't have worried about her son downstairs playing with his toys but ever since 1939 arrived, trouble brewed daily. Every part of Zofia swung into guarded alert. Another set of urgent knockings propelled her downstairs. This harbinger at the door, with unrelenting fists insisting on a response, wouldn't be bringing good news.

She had almost reached the front door when Eban called out, "Mamusiu, the door. I'll stay here."

This shouldn't have been a typical reaction from a curious boy about to turn seven, but her sweet son no longer questioned his parents' orders to keep away from the entrance unless one of them stood by his side. A well-behaved child, he accepted that he needed to remain out of listening range when a caller visited.

"Good boy," she called over her shoulder. At the door she asked the caller's identity, a new practice Jabez, sympathetic toward the Jews suffering under Hitler's changing laws, had insisted upon in a firm husband-tone last November when the world saw how Germany obeyed its leader when he ordered that awful disturbance of *Kristallnacht*.

"Zofia, let me in."

Confusion replaced fear. Jabez's best friend, fully aware her husband was at work in Germany and not due home for two more days, wasn't paying her a social visit. Of that she felt certain.

Zofia opened the door. "Herszel, come in. What's wrong?"

The silver-haired man stepped into the house. His gaze darted about. "Who's home?"

For once she was relieved her mother-in-law and Jabez's aunt were absent. "Just Eban. Lena and Inga are at work."

"Listen carefully," he said, with more assertiveness than she'd ever heard from this grandpa-like man. "I have word that Jabez disappeared while traveling home, along with a handful of our Brzeziner men."

"Disappeared?" The back of her neck and under her arms pooled with sweat. Among the Polish workers who sought work in Germany to make up for the scarce zloty, disappearances were becoming commonplace. But with men like her Jabez, who were trained to keep an eye out for each other, it hadn't occurred. Yet. She hated to think this way, but unlike the majority of Brzeziners who were Jewish, Jabez was Catholic. That social distinction worked in his favor while he was in Germany. In his absence she'd clung to the positive, praying daily that he would be far from harm's way. Perhaps it had not been a question of if bad news might come, but when.

"Did he go missing while in Germany?" Jabez's chances were better if he'd made it across the border into his native country.

"We're uncertain." Herszel slipped off his hat, fumbling the solid black brim with shaking hands. "We think the Germans cornered the men and deported them to a camp."

Tightness squeezed Zofia's throat. Needing details, she forced the words out. "Which camp? Where?"

"We don't have all the specifics yet, but likely a work camp in Germany."

"But Jabez isn't Jewish!" Her declaration, weak and verging on unintended prejudice, made her cringe in shame. She thought about

Aanya. And Herszel was also Jewish. No wonder he lifted a brow. "I didn't quite mean it that way."

"I understand. Jabez and you have close ties to Aanya Gerszon and her family. The Nazis don't care. Association with a Jew is almost as bad to their way of thinking as being a Jew." Herszel paused. His brown eyes darkened to charcoal black. "I was told to alert you. If there are developments, I—or one of our men—will let you know."

Despite her gratitude that her husband and several other men in Brzeziny—a town tucked between Łódź and Warsaw—had formed a network of watchers over developing changes and threats to Poland as Hitler spread his control, Zofia battled weariness. It was increasingly difficult to drag herself out of bed each morning and face the world.

This past year had proved daunting. For the first time in her 32 years of life, Zofia had questioned the collective sanity of the world. When Hitler annexed Austria in the *Anschluss* last March she'd worried about the Austrians and how their lives had changed when German troops entered their country under the guise of restoring law and order. Then the world shifted yet again that September as Hitler manipulated Italy, Great Britain, and France into signing the Munich Agreement to supposedly stave off war. Zofia tried to visualize those living in the Sudeten territory wanting to be part of Germany and being more than content with the change. She struggled to understand how a change forced by the hand of another person could be beneficial, especially if that person was the leader of a separate country.

When *Kristallnacht* followed in November, it became apparent that to obey Hitler's orders meant to enthusiastically enjoy corruption and wickedness. It was as if a dam had broken open and measures of control and self-constraint no longer mattered. Zofia and Aanya couldn't believe the destruction of Jewish-owned businesses, homes, schools, and synagogues unleashed that night. Zofia had turned to her friend and signed, "Why were no questions asked about how this horror came to be?" Aanya had bit down on her lip. "For the sake of survival it's easier to be both blind and deaf."

Now Zofia peered into Herszel's eyes, aware that he wouldn't purposely misguide her. Jabez trusted him for this reason. Reminding herself that the watchers had formed so men like her husband could work more comfortably outside of Brzeziny because they kept an eye out for each other's safety, she tried to smile. Instead, her mouth became dry as she remembered her promise to Jabez. All this time later, it still seemed severe for him to demand that she and Eban leave the country if a threatening development occurred for him at work.

With one hand on the doorknob, Herszel looked down. "I hope to bring better news soon. I must go and inform the others."

The other wives, the other mothers and daughters. Women who wouldn't sleep that night in fear for their beloved men.

"Thank you," she murmured, unable to think of alternative words for the bearer of news she never wanted to hear.

Zofia watched Jabez's longtime friend step back into the snow prints he'd made on his way to her front door. Once on the main road he swung left and headed toward town, his black coat a sharp contrast to the white-blanketed ground that still shone despite the dusky evening.

The frosty cold crept around Zofia's ankles and up her legs, jolting her into action. With Lena and Inga due home from work in an hour, she faced telling them Herszel's news. Again, her heart hammered, due to not only her husband's disappearance and needing to communicate it to the two women, but also Jabez's odd but forceful directive for her to flee Poland if he ever went missing. All this she had to carefully arrange around her promise to her husband not to tell anyone of his involvement with the group of watchers.

There was one exception concerning this vow to Jabez. Then, in need of baring her troubled soul to someone she could trust, she couldn't bring herself to keep this kind of news from Aanya. She'd pushed aside worries over the consequences of breaking her word—and shared the little she knew with her friend. Now, she again needed Aanya's advice.

"Eban," she said, careful to tamp down the sharp sound of alarm from his young ears. She strode through the parlor, crowded with a sofa, chairs and tables covered with framed photographs and plants, and past Jabez's hanging cabinet full of his prized pocket watch collection. She stopped short at the kitchen entrance, aware her little one hadn't replied. "Eban?" she called again and rushed into the small room that also served as her son's bedroom.

Her golden-haired child sat on the bare kitchen floor, his back against his bed squeezed between the table and the small rack of shelves lined with dishes and pots. His toy hippo and horse were spread out before him. An old bedsheet, draped over a chair, most likely served as an elaborate zoo in his creative young mind. Three months ago, the poor child grieved, and rightly so, the loss of his grandpa Oskar. The resilient boy he was, he'd bounced back after a few weeks. She could only hope that if his papa failed to come home in two days, he wouldn't be thrown back into despair.

"There you are," she said gently. For a little boy, Eban's concentration was big and steady. She didn't want to startle him.

He glanced up, his usual smile replaced by pursed lips. "Was Aanya at the door?"

Acid churned Zofia's belly. The stress—from both the truth and the deceit—niggled at her like a sore that wouldn't heal.

She'd be strong for her beautiful boy, for Eban. She had no other choice. "No, my love. But let's go visit her."

"What about supper? I'm hungry."

Her healthy son always had an appetite, and she would have smiled if it weren't for the news she'd just learned. "Dinner's not ready yet. Pack up your toys to bring to Aanya's. I have matters to discuss with Babcia and Aunt Inga, and then I'll bring you home."

He held up the hippo, his favorite toy as of late. "Mamusiu, sing the bird song for my animals. The bird that flies over the forest."

"I just sang it to you at breakfast time, my prince." She often sang to her son in the morning over breakfast and at bedtime when Jabez was passed out from a mixture of hard labor and drink.

He giggled. "I'm no prince."

"Ah, you are in my sight and in my heart."

"And Tatusiu? Am I his prince?"

Her breath seized. "Yes. You're Tatusiu's noble prince. Gather your toys and I'll help you with your coat. Hurry."

"The song, Mamusiu. First sing your bird song." He lifted the horse to join his companion, the hippo. "For us."

Zofia loved to sing. It was her voice, spotlighted in a solo at one of her parents' infamous get-togethers, that first attracted Jabez's attention. Later that evening when they'd both stepped outdoors to escape the din of boisterous talk and the heavy cigarette smoke, he confided his attraction to her cheerful lilt, her beautiful blue eyes, and her warm smile. She was the promise of an oasis in the midst of a horrible storm, he said. With his dark hair and autumn-brown eyes he was a feast for her to enjoy. When she asked if he had his share of trudging through storms he slanted his head and boyishly grinned. A few, he said, but if she'd been at the other end he'd have come out more triumphantly. *Boom.* Fireworks and royal cannons exploded in the evening's darkness. Trumpets blared. At least in her imagination. He not only listened with sincere interest to what she said that night, but he also looked at her with intense desire and kindness. Those two traits alone made her heart race. He stood close, and she let him.

Their time together stretched from moments to an hour or longer of conversation. Time ceased to matter, unlike in later years. There were a lot of laters. Like her parents dying within months of each other from a horrid flu that was reluctant to leave that winter. Like Jabez and Zofia marrying and settling in her parents' house and then having his parents and aunt move in with them. Like their beautiful, healthy son born barely a year later.

The song Eban wanted her to sing was one from her own childhood days. In it the fabled pure white stork circled over the forests full of birch trees clattering its exciting news of the imminent delivery of a baby. The unfortunate bird couldn't visit anyone until the Brzeziny villagers attached wagon wheels to their rooftops, providing a place to perch. The boy marveled over how the name of Brzeziny originated from the birch tree.

"Mamusiu?"

She crouched before him and planted a kiss on his head. "No more questions." *Do as I say* were her unspoken words.

She stood, rubbed the small of her back, and watched as Eban scrambled from the kitchen to retrieve his coat from a low hook by the front door. Within minutes they were hurrying toward Aanya's. Several times she had to slow her pace so her little boy could keep up with her. The temperature had fallen steadily throughout the afternoon, and from the outskirts of town where they lived they had a little walk to Aanya's. They had no other choice. She needed to talk with Lena and Inga away from her son; he wouldn't understand the news and its implications and needn't become alarmed. At the very least Zofia could count on Aanya helping to soothe Eban's concern—he was smitten with her.

An unexpected blast of wind gusted and jabbed Zofia's smarting back. In her hurry to leave the house she'd left without a kerchief to fight off the piercing cold. To shield herself from the wind's full force she stooped forward like the old woman bagel peddler she'd seen a few days ago at the town market. More and more street vendors combed the Brzeziny streets trying to earn enough coins for their needs, and the woman, with her barking spiel, had stood out to Zofia.

She put an arm around Eban and pulled him to her side. "Are you warm enough?"

He nodded, so robust and sturdy for his age that he often made her think of Jabez.

"Would you like my coat to keep you extra warm?" she asked.

"No. You need it. I'm not like the old lady we saw at the market."

Ah, he too remembered the threadbare woman. On one hand, she wished to shield her son from life's sorrows, yet on the other hand, she knew she couldn't. Not entirely. That was why she took Eban to the weekly town market where there were more beggars than she ever remembered seeing and murmurs of Nazis and doom spread, along with hostile attitudes toward Jews. The woman from last week's market had come up to them from behind. With a long bony finger she poked between Zofia's shoulder blades, catching her off guard. Wearing gray from head to toe, she had pleaded for the basics. Food. Warmth. A smile. Zofia could only offer the last. She too longed for a life without the fight for survival, a life she and most Brzeziners could only dream about in their fitful sleep. Hard times were no stranger to this town.

For years, Brzeziner men, women, and children toiled from as early as three in the morning until late in the evening. Lena and Inga worked in what had been Oskar's dry goods store, currently operated by one of the town men with no family members to help. Until a few years ago, Jabez had run a watch repair business in a corner of his father's store. As the venomous Nazi movement grew in Germany as well as in Poland, and the economy pinched more and more, Jabez was forced to close his repair shop-within-a-shop. Although he might have found work in Poland, his connections had him crossing the border in 1936 and securing a job at the Junkers Aircraft and Motor Works headquartered in Dessau, Germany, an approximately five-and-a-half-hour train ride from Brzeziny. He never complained about the manual labor, and the job paid livable wages. Housing was provided. Fortunately, he was able to leave periodically to visit home. While others were fleeing Brzeziny to bigger cities such as Warsaw or leaving the country, like the massive emigration before the Great War, Zofia and Jabez maintained their home in the town where they'd been born and raised, and where Zofia and Aanya had first met by the Mrozyca River.

Zofia felt a tug at her skirt and lifted her face despite the wind. "Yes, sweetheart?"

"Mama, is Papa well? Did the person at the door bring bad news?"

For better or worse, Eban at times was keenly aware of his surroundings. Too keenly aware, perhaps.

They had reached the cobblestones of Traugutta Street. With her hand cupped to the back of his head she steered him into an alleyway to escape the stinging cold. She'd be as honest as she could without laying needless burdens upon his little shoulders.

"Darling, yes, Papa is well. His friend was the one at the door earlier. He brought news that Papa had to stay at work for a few extra days because of a big project." She knelt in the snow to look directly into his honey brown eyes, the color of his father's. "There are a few adult things that Babcia, Aunt Inga, and I need to talk about. Things to help make matters easier for us."

"Can I help?"

"Yes. I would like for you to keep Aanya company."

He patted his coat pocket. "Me and my hippo and horse will keep Aanya company."

"That's my big boy."

She grew more anxious as they walked on and passed the row of three-storey brick blockhouses, modern compared to her old turn-of-the-century farmhouse. At the corner they turned right and walked through the stone arch that led to the courtyard of the older-style apartment where Aanya and her mama lived alone since Pan Gerszon's passing five years ago. It was a sad day when Chaim Gerszon died suddenly, without a goodbye on his lips, likely from either a heart attack or a stroke. He'd shocked them, passing before his ill wife. With Zofia's own father gone, Chaim always had a ready smile for her. *You, Zofia, a blessed friend to my daughter, are a true daughter to me as well*, he'd often said.

Aanya's mother, Frymet, was more frequently ill than not. She often kept to her bedroom. Zofia and Eban stepped into the small parlor without knocking. Zofia studied the *makatka* hanging over the sofa. Unlike the decorative handwoven heirloom that hung over her own sofa depicting the blessed Christ carrying the cross over His holy shoulder and surrounded by two angels, the wool and silk one over the Gerszon's sofa, once a rug, featured a gold menorah against a black and brown background. If one looked carefully, the background had woven into it tiny gold menorahs that sparkled like evening stars. When Zofia had asked Aanya if this beautiful wall hanging was meant to show hope, Aanya had shrugged. Zofia then asked if it had been in her family for a long time. Aanya responded that when she asked her parents the same question they had brushed her away. Either they could not say with certainty or would not.

The parlor opened to a kitchen area and to a hallway that led to two bedrooms, Aanya's and her mother's, and finally a bath. Not wanting to disturb the sickly woman, Zofia tiptoed to her friend's room. She peered through the open door, but the room was unoccupied.

"Zofia, is that you?" Pani Gerszon called out.

"Yes, and Eban."

"She's gathering the chickens."

Zofia managed a cheery tone. "Thank you, Pani Gerszon. May I get you tea before I go to Aanya?"

"No, thanks, dear. Rest is what I need."

Ever since Zofia could recall, the poor woman had suffered in health, but over the past few months she'd lost an alarming amount of weight. Both Zofia and Aanya were worried. Aanya, not deterred by what others saw as a *deaf problem*, studied nursing under the tutelage of a doctor friend since the Polish government had limited university-level education for Jews. She had her theories about the causes of her mother's ills, but it wouldn't make any difference. The woman refused to see a doctor.

"Sorry to disturb you," Zofia called out.

When no reply came, she figured the older woman had drifted off to sleep. Good. Needing to share the dreadful news with her friend and ask if she could watch Eban, she told her son to remain seated quietly on the sofa while she searched for Aanya.

Once outdoors, Zofia glanced about the courtyard at the chicken coop, at trash scattered on the ground, and at rickety stairs leading up to the rear entrances of other apartment buildings. No Aanya. Believing her friend wouldn't opt for a stroll by herself at this time of day meant the only other likely possibility was she had gone into the barn at the other end of the alley. The place gave Zofia the creeps, but not enough to cut off her search. She just hoped her friend's reason for entering the old building wasn't as troubling as the news she had to share with her.

She made her way carefully toward the old barn, lifting her skirt so as not to slip on the icy path.

2

Vibrations from the barn floor shot a warning through Aanya's shoes. A large, rough, grimy hand covered her mouth. Had this trespasser thought she'd shout? Fool. She pivoted and caught a blur of dark hair, longish and dirty, and broad shoulders. She lifted a foot to stomp his but he shoved her away. She stumbled. He grabbed her tight. Was he a captor or a rescuer? She couldn't tell if he'd wanted to restrain her or if he'd meant to catch her, preventing her from falling and hurting herself. Her blouse ripped from the right shoulder to nearly her elbow. She stared hard at this high-cheekboned man in hope that she'd unnerve him with her disgust and imagined he would look rugged if he had a bit of meat on his scrawny bones. She knew it would make sense for her to be frightened, but what she saw in his eyes seemed to be kindness, not violent intent. She waited for an explanation.

He pointed at the wayward chicken she'd chased into a corner so she could catch it and return it to its coop, then pointed at her torn top. His brow slanted upwards. He gaped at her as if she were the intruder.

"*Sprichst du Deutsch?*" he asked.

Quite skilled in reading lips, she waited for him to ask if she preferred him to speak in Polish, but when that question didn't come, she concluded he was German—obviously from outside of town. Yet, it was pretty safe to assume he knew at least a few Polish words. What was he doing in this barn? Her stomach tensed. Although on Polish soil, did he speak in German to intimidate her? Was he a Nazi? The little German she understood wouldn't help her a bit. She shook her head hoping to propel him away from her and ultimately, from her ailing mama. With Papa, may he rest in peace, having left her and Mama for the afterlife, she had become her mother's companion, nurse, helper and often cook and general caretaker of their apartment, in addition to her loving daughter. She loved her mother, though, and wouldn't consider devoting a minute less to caring for her. She needed to leave the barn as soon as possible, and needed him to leave as well.

"I can speak Polish, though not as fluently," the stranger said in Polish. "Was it because I spoke in German that you didn't answer me?"

His Polish was sufficient. Could she trust him and tell him that she was deaf? As long as he spoke Polish, and she could see his mouth, she could understand him. She nodded.

"I mean no harm," he said, continuing in her native language. He glanced over his shoulder, then back. "A woman is calling. Can you help me to hide? It's a matter of life or death."

He'd frightened her, yet wanted her assistance?

"Please." He released his grip. A shadow of what seemed like worry deepened his hazel irises. If eyes could speak, his would be begging. "You can trust me. I'll explain later."

Trust had become an unfamiliar word, the concept an oddity. German men were sneaking across the border and after spying on homes often barged indoors once the man of the household had left, forcing themselves upon the left-behind woman or grabbing items and food. Children were randomly disappearing. If this stranger before Aanya posed a danger similar to those who committed the atrocities becoming more prevalent by the day, she didn't stand a chance, especially if he belonged to Hitler's band of Jew-haters, and all the more so because she was deaf. He could whip out a gun or knife and press it against the side of her head or throat while he hissed commands.

Yet, there was a certain glint in his eyes that she hadn't seen in a long time. He roused her curiosity with a look of gentleness and concern. A touch of a gentle soul, was he?

Ack. *Me and my foolish daydreams.*

She locked her fingers around his wrist and led him to a stall in the opposite corner where a heap of hay remained. Without apology, she gave him a push toward the pile. He understood and slid under the old dried grass. Hopefully her feathered friend wouldn't find him and cluck, revealing his hiding place. As she turned her back to the hidden man to face Zofia—for no other woman would be searching for her here—it occurred to her that she'd never concealed information from her friend, let alone covered up an unusual situation. Not until now.

Footsteps vibrated from behind her and she hurried back to where she'd found the chicken. She stopped short of grabbing the bird when Zofia appeared.

"There you are," Zofia signed in the Polish one-handed sign language. Some years ago, on a one-year scholarship, Aanya had attended a special school for the deaf in Warsaw. Upon returning to Brzeziny, she quickly taught Zofia the proper Polish way to sign, replacing the long-ago childhood sign language they'd created between themselves.

Zofia regarded her friend from head to toes. "Are you well? You look a fright."

"I'm fine." About to sign more, she stopped when she saw Zofia startle, cover her heart, and shake her head at the chicken Aanya suspected had let loose a loud cluck. She glanced discreetly over her shoulder hoping the boisterous hen hadn't frightened the mysterious man from his hiding place. She pointed at Zofia. "I'm more worried about you, my friend. What's wrong?"

Zofia patted her chest. "Your troublemaking feathered friend nearly scared me to death." She plucked a strand of straw from Aanya's hair and shook it like a schoolteacher's pointer at Aanya's ruined blouse. "That's your nicest embroidered *bluzka* and look, the lovely purple and green stitchery is pulled and torn, the material soiled. Something's wrong."

"I assure you, no concerns. I tripped trying to catch that awful chicken. I should show her the pot for dinner." That was the second lie; the first by omission about hiding the stranger was bad enough. And all this in a matter of minutes? Already it was as if a weight pressed down on her shoulders and she couldn't stand tall.

"I remember your papa, as kind as he was, how he took an ax to those chickens without a blink. You, on the other hand, would never hurt a living soul."

Aanya was always touched and surprised by her friend and how she made her bubble inside with gaiety from finding humor in the day's events, discovering at least one new thing to be thankful for, or reminiscing, especially about their beloved parents. Suddenly, the barn's interior swayed. Or was it she who tilted back and forth?

"Aanya?"

The realization of the enormity of lying to Zofia, her dearest friend, her only friend, by her silence about the hidden stranger who might be a ruthless footman for Hitler, or a criminal on the run, riddled Aanya with anxiety. Her instincts bumped further into red alert—in addition to sending the man away from her mama, she also had to protect Zofia.

"Don't mind me. I need to eat." She forced a happy face, another charade she'd never needed or wanted to do before. "Of course I miss Papa, but now I'm the one who lifts the ax when necessary." Aanya rubbed her arms and was glad to see the movement had distracted Zofia. She'd try to gain control of the conversation. "I must check on Mama. What can I do for you?"

"Herszel just stopped by. Jabez is missing."

This news changed everything. She momentarily forgot about the man under the hay. She swung an arm around her friend's shoulders and led her to a small bench against the wall. Although they were both slim, the wooden seat wobbled as they sat.

"How can a grown man go missing?" As soon as the question flew from Aanya's fingers, she dropped her head. What a fool she was. Left and right, people were disappearing, as if in a perverse magic trick.

Pole. German. Catholic. Jew. Adult. Child. One by one. And the man under the hay? Evidently on the run, had he too gone missing from someone or some group? How she wished that this spreading horror in Europe was indeed a sleight of hand that would disappear with a poof, easing the constant tension, causing the missing to reappear suddenly and all to be well. This was a time for encouragement and support, not one for questioning. "I'm confident Jabez is fine. Watch him surprise you, walking into the house tonight."

No smile came to Zofia's lips. "I can only hope."

Her friend's pain was her own. "In the meantime, how can I help?"

"The two of us need to talk—not that I have more details to share. At least, not yet. First, I must tell the little I know to Lena and Inga and gauge their reaction. This is terribly confusing. Distressing, really."

"Do you want me to watch Eban while the three of you talk?" Aanya watched Zofia's mouth open to reply, but she knew what her sister in spirit was about to say and jumped in before she could continue. "Eban's already upstairs in the apartment, right? Probably playing with the toys you had him bring."

"Yes. Your mama woke, but fell back to sleep."

Aanya gasped. Her poor mother. As Zofia had done since entering the barn, she usually spoke and signed simultaneously. If this stranger she'd hidden under the straw was listening, and if he were of the criminal persuasion, she shuddered to think about what he might do with this knowledge. Aanya should never have taken the risk of talking with Zofia here, centimeters away from a man she shouldn't have aided. Already she'd committed too many shouldn'ts.

"What's wrong?" Zofia asked.

"Just a thought I had of Mama. It's of no matter. I'll happily watch Eban."

A small smile spread across Zofia's lips. "You're the best. We both love you. I'm glad I can count on you." She placed her hands on her lap but then lifted her right hand to sign. "This may not be as bad as our fears can imagine. For all we know, there's a perfectly fine explanation to this mystery. As for Jabez's disappearance, he likely fell asleep and woke only to get off at the wrong stop and then had to board another train." She covered her mouth, as if embarrassed the explanation was too naive for anyone to consider seriously.

"Yes, I'm sure a simple occurrence happened to delay him. Jabez is a good, smart, and resourceful man. He'll be home soon." Standing, Aanya extended a hand to Zofia. "You look tired. Let me help you up."

"Believe me, with this news, I'm filled with plenty of energy—nervous energy, I suppose." She stood on her own and smoothed her skirt. "I doubt I'll sleep a wink tonight."

Aanya rubbed her fingers. They were cold, unlike when she held the German stranger's warm wrist as she led him to the pile of hay. "Well then, you be safe walking home at this time of night."

Zofia gave a tentative nod and then a firmer one. "I'll be fine. At least it's not like the old days when our mamas had to worry about roaming Russian police officers and their villainous ways." She rushed toward the door of the barn.

Aanya turned away and was about to do her own hurrying to the hidden man. She stopped short when she sensed Zofia watching her. She faced her friend, who smiled warmly and waved. What would she ever do without sweet Zofia?

Precious seconds ticked by before Aanya reached the haypile. She unburied the stranger, her hand accidentally brushing his cheek. The warmth of his face sent an odd tingle down her arms. Whether from surprise or precaution, she stepped back.

"Is it safe? Is she gone, this friend of yours?"

Ah, she'd been correct. He'd heard Zofia speak. Was it safe to admit that it was again just the two of them in the barn? Aanya gave a tentative nod. She wanted to tell the man her name, wanted to know his name and see how else she might be able to help him. Her mama's warnings through the years of not trusting strangers blared through her mind. She had no idea who he was, where he came from, or why he was suddenly in the barn and terrified of being discovered. Just what or who was he hiding from? But she had no time now to ask him these things, not with her mother needing her and Eban requiring her attention while Zofia ran home to tell her husband's family that he'd gone missing.

She turned her back toward him and stepped closer to the entrance.

He pressed his hand on her shoulder and gently spun her around, one brow lifted higher than the other. "Why are you ignoring me? I told you my name—Artur. I asked for your name, but you won't tell me. Why won't you answer my questions?"

Questions, as in plural? And he'd told her his name. What had she missed? She rolled her bottom lip. There were both pluses and minuses of further helping him, complexity lacing both options. She'd be right and compassionate to aid him, but had to take precautions since she could be helping a person who might turn against her. He could hurt not only her but also her mama. She knew that people in desperate situations did not always make the best, most humane decisions.

Blood seeped through the side of his shirt. She pointed at the area.

"It's nothing," he said, his gaze never leaving her. "It's an old nick that broke open when I moved the wrong way under the hay."

Artur was just like her father had been. Like every man she knew, he was fueled by false bravado. They would rather bleed to death than admit they were hurt. She needed to act fast. She lifted her hands and placed one over each of her ears and shook her head. She then covered her mouth and also gestured with a shake of her head that she could not speak either.

"You're unable to hear?"

She nodded.

"And you can't speak?"

She shook her hand from side to side to indicate a little. It was by choice she hadn't articulated words more. With her parents using their special signing method ever since Aanya could recall, then Zofia and she developing their own secret sign language, it wasn't until she attended the school in Warsaw that she learned the official Polish sign language. By then, she was keenly aware—and impatient, she admitted—of the awkward reaction of the hearing world to her attempts at speech. At the school, the other students had a mix of preferences between signing, speaking, and lip reading. There she realized that she was exceptionally fluent in the latter, though she took care since several words due to structure could mislead. What her teachers stressed was the importance of permitting each deaf person to choose his or her best means of communication. Whether it was signing, or reading lips and articulating words, or a combination, the decision should be respected; every person was unique.

She saw understanding dawn on his face—he had realized that she'd been reading his lips. She thrust her hand into a skirt pocket and withdrew the small writing pad and pencil she always kept at the ready. She scribbled and shoved the paper at him, watching his eyes move as he read.

Artur set the paper aside. "Your name is Aanya, you are deaf and can speak only a minimum number of words but understand a full vocabulary like anyone else can."

Assuming he sought verification, she nodded.

"No wonder I heard only one voice, not two, speaking a few minutes ago." He glanced again at the paper she'd handed him. "You are studying to become a nurse." A slight twinge of red crept from his throat toward his face.

Her statement shouldn't have caused amazement, but since it was popular belief that the deaf were unable to function as well as *normal* people, news of her acquiring a profession contradicted quite a few preconceived notions. She'd also received official discouragement since the Polish government had placed limits on Jewish enrollment in certain educational institutions; her inability to hear acted against her as well. The fact that a revered Brzeziner physician oversaw Aanya's studies elicited laughter rather than admiration.

She nodded. More concerned about his bleeding wound, painfully aware of her limited time due to her mama's weak health and Zofia's eventual return for her son, she steered him toward the bench where she and her friend sat mere minutes ago.

She began to unbutton his shirt, but he brushed her hand away. "I'll do it."

When he began to slowly undo the shirt, ignoring the ticking of time, she stamped her foot to grab his attention then narrowed her eyes. *Hurry.*

Finally, with his shirt completely off and his torso exposed, Aanya fanned her fingers across his shoulders and chest to assess the scope of damage. No broken bones. No other wounds.

He smiled. "Ah, that feels good."

To check for internal bleeding, she poked him in the belly.

He winced. "Are you purposely trying to injure me?"

A lock of hair fell across her eyes. Intent on further examining his wound, she inspected the affected area a bit more tenderly. The blood flow had lessened to nearly nonexistent, likely because he held still. Without a doubt he'd need stitches.

He fingered the wisp of hair away from her eyes.

Holding back a reaction to his gesture, though acutely aware that his touch was light and gentle, she lifted her pencil. "Are you in pain? This is a nasty wound. When did it happen?"

"No pain. Just grazed my side a week ago. Took a little skin off. I have lots more."

What had he done to rip his side open? She was curious, but there were more important matters to discuss with him. "Your wound is open and needs stitches," she wrote. "You have a little swelling. I can help, but—"

Movement blurred her peripheral vision. She looked up from her pad to see that he'd crossed his arms against his chest.

"Are you writing a book?"

She itched to wipe that boyish grin from his face, but continued writing. When she was done, she fished out a clean handkerchief from a pocket, pushed it into his hand and guided it to his injury to apply pressure against his flesh. She pressed her written words into his free hand.

"I will tend to you in a while," Artur read aloud.

By the way he moved his mouth, she could tell that he spoke slowly. Out of a need for her to understand him better? Most likely. As an expression that he trusted her? She hoped so. That unexpected realization sent both warmth and chills through her body.

"Stay here," he continued to read. "You're safe, as long as you keep quiet and a watchful eye out. Rest. I will try to hurry back, but don't be alarmed if I'm delayed." He set the paper aside and looked directly at her. "Don't worry. I've looked out for myself these past months and plan on doing more than merely existing."

The man had mettle. She liked that. And if he were on the run, which he apparently was, it was good he had gumption. His tenacity, a rare quality these days, would serve him well. She stepped away, then stopped and faced him. Running her fingers up and down her arms and shaking to intimate the dead of winter, she then pointed at him.

"Am I cold?" he said.

She nodded.

"I'll be fine."

Without further delay she dodged the chicken that was making its way toward her and hurried home. Animal and man could keep each other plenty of company in that old barn until she returned. Not only would she suture his wound, but she'd also find out who he was on the run from, and why. That is, if he didn't skip out on her while she was away in the comfort of her own home.

3

More than halfway home from Aanya's, the wind played games with Zofia and carried a voice she shouldn't have heard. She halted mid-step, the wind whistling around her, and strained to listen. When no human sound summoned her, she scolded her foolish imagination and continued walking.

"Zofia, stop. Are you going to face me?"

She whirled around, expecting to see anyone but Jabez, and gasped. He narrowed the distance between them, covered her mouth with his cold bare hand and led her into the dark corner of a nearby building.

"Jabez!" she said, his name a muffled squeal between his fingers.

"Hush. Understand?"

She didn't understand anything at that moment, but nodded. He slid his hand from her mouth and lessened his grip on her shoulder. She threw herself back at him, squirmed into his embrace and kissed him fiercely.

He leaned back. Painfully away from her. Winter cold snaked between them. "I have things to tell you."

"Jabez," she murmured, his name never sounding so miraculous and beautiful as it did at that moment. "Thank God you're alive. Herszel came this evening with horrible news—"

"Quiet. Yes, I instructed him to."

Her belly tightened as irritation chased away joy. "You told him to scare me half to death? I'm on the way home to tell your mama and aunt, likely frightening them as well."

He leaned closer, his breath puffing in her face. "You're going to tell them exactly that—that I've disappeared. And no one has a clue to my whereabouts."

"What's happening? I don't like this at all." She shivered. "How did you find me here?"

"I have my resources."

What was he doing—spying on her? That was bad enough, if true. The next question was why. She silently swore at his cryptic ways, then at herself as it dawned upon her that by living in her protective fantasy of rosiness she'd been blind to a whole different side of her husband.

"And I have my reasons," he continued before she could say a word more. "There are countless developments all around us, none of them good. I can't rest easy unless I do my part and help prevent trouble."

What exactly was his part to prevent trouble? While she'd viewed him as a miraculous sight seconds ago, her husband was a mere human being, not trained in secret missions or government undertakings, nor possessing the competence to combat the Germans, as evil as the Nazis were. In front of her own two eyes, they'd lived together in her parents' house that became their own after her papa and mama passed away. They'd had a son, they'd laughed and cried together. Only since Jabez took the job in Dessau three years ago at Junkers had he remained absent from her for long periods.

Unless...

Unless he never worked there to begin with. Wouldn't Hitler have turned the factory into a military aircraft factory? She groaned, imagining her husband a spy. But Jabez had brought money home. Could he have procured the payment from another source? Her heart —and head—hammered, but not like when Herschel had pounded at the door. This going back and forth hashing out the possibilities was a waste of emotions and time. It was obvious that whatever Jabez was up to had to be of significance, with extreme and dangerous consequences, if it warranted her and their son's departure.

"What else are you hiding from me?" Curiosity got the best of her. She'd begun the last question intending to ask about this apparent work mystery, but ended in dreadful uncertainty that he might have hidden countless things. A mistress or two? Children fathered with another woman? Thieving? The trouble with deception was that one lie, by nature, became a cesspool that spawned other fabrications.

Hazy amber light from the corner lamppost illuminated his face and showed his narrowed eyes, which she ignored. "It's freezing. Let's go home and talk more. We shouldn't have secrets between us, and I want to know what you're involved in."

"I can't go home—can't chance it. You know plenty about me. That I'm one of the good ones. Don't start doubting me." He paused, then continued in a softer tone. "I wanted to see you again. To tell you to carry out our plans, that you and Eban leave for America. Do not worry about me. And please, no matter what happens, do not tell Eban or my mother or aunt—or Aanya—that you saw me tonight."

"Tell me where you're off to. What are the bad things happening that I, and the rest of Polska, aren't aware of? What trouble are you trying to prevent? Hitler is a fool with a big mouth. You'll see. He won't carry out the threats that we fear."

"You're too innocent, my love." Jabez brushed her cheek with his hand, his calloused fingertips landing at her lips. "We both know this horrible German ruler has already stripped away human rights from the deaf and other people with disabilities, and he's acting on his promise to rid the world of Jews. What's to stop this beast from wiping away another group of people he sees as substandard to his beloved Aryan race?" Jabez clutched both of her hands and tugged her against his chest. "It's time you open your eyes to reality. This madman and his troops will cross the border into Poland—it's only a matter of days. Or months, if we're lucky. That is, if luck comes into play on our side, rather than running away from us in the opposite direction."

She rubbed at the base of her throat, wishing she could push away the fact that her husband defined luck as a few extra months before Hitler's attack on Poland, as opposed to his not invading at all. Jabez made an invasion sound inevitable.

Months. Days? Hardly any time. She couldn't fathom what situations they might face in the near future.

He slipped an envelope into her hands. "This is also why I came back this once, to give you this directly. I didn't want to trust another person with it."

Not even his friend, Herszel?

"Or endanger anyone else," he added.

She glanced at the envelope in her hands and gulped in new understanding.

"Yes, it's what you're thinking it is. It's an amount that will help you to leave, to flee Brzeziny and all of Polska before you cannot. But without delay, Zofia. You and Eban must leave right away." He kissed her hard, his lips burning hers. "Now," he urged, as if she'd failed to understand the first time. "Contact my cousin immediately for help."

"But, your mama? She won't believe a word I say because she's unable to think of her son involved in danger of any kind. And what about Aunt Inga? Shouldn't I stay put and watch over them?"

"My father worked hard in his store, saving whenever he could, spending little. Believe me, my mother and aunt will be fine as far as finances go."

With truth upended, reality distorted, what should she believe? Accept? She waited for him to say more. Money could only go so far, and wouldn't save those dear older women if the Nazis took over Brzeziny and decided they, like their Jewish neighbors, weren't worthy of living. She was about to voice this concern when Jabez did what she never would have imagined.

He shoved her back onto the cobblestone street, a good distance from him. And he did not step beside her. She knew not to turn around to look at his face, nor to expect one more word from him. She also knew that he'd already slipped into the inky black of night and disappeared.

Placing one foot in front of the other, she pushed herself home. Alone.

Lena met Zofia at the door with a brown dish towel in one hand, a wooden spoon in the other, and a frown turning her pale lips downward. "We've been worried ever since we arrived home to an empty house." She craned her neck and looked past Zofia's shoulder. "Is Eban not with you? Is he hurt?"

Zofia shut the door behind her and stomped snow from her shoes onto the doormat. "Eban's fine. He's at Aanya's." Before Lena questioned her further, she continued. "I took him there because the three of us adults must talk."

"Is it about Jabez? Was he hurt at work?"

With Lena already agitated, Jabez's warning not to tell anyone about his unexpected appearance this evening rang noisily in her mind. Zofia set her gaze on her mother-in-law, hoping Lena didn't notice she'd swiped her skirt pocket to check on the envelope from Jabez. Good. The cash was there, not lost in a snowbank as she'd trudged home. "Let me begin from the beginning—Herszel visited earlier." She paused as Inga entered the room, stopping beside Lena.

"This cannot be good news," Lena muttered.

Inga stepped beside Zofia and helped her slip off her coat. "Did he have news about Jabez? Good or bad, do tell."

Zofia glanced at the two women. "If dinner isn't already made, let's warm up with tea and I'll explain."

Five minutes later they sat at the small kitchen table, teacups patterned with red poppies set before them. The oven with its roasting pork and potatoes radiated heat, but the chill wouldn't leave Zofia's arms. The aroma of the tangy tea mingled with the sweet and sour meaty smell of the cooking dinner jumbled her senses. When she made herself take a second sip of the tea, she noticed the other two were ignoring theirs. Not wanting another drop, she set the cup on its matching saucer.

"Yes?" Inga smiled playfully. "I'm sure Herszel didn't visit because he wanted your cooking secrets, though I wouldn't blame him if he desired your recipes."

Zofia wrapped a strand of hair around a finger and spoke fast, as if yanking off a bandage quickly before the mind registered discomfort. "Jabez has gone missing. His whereabouts are unknown. Whether he's in Germany or in Poland is anyone's guess." This untruth to her loved ones twisted her gut. "He's probably delayed at work in Dessau, safe and sound."

Lena, the proverbial pillar of strength in the family, reached for Zofia's hands. "Sweetheart, do you think there's a chance my son will arrive home in two days as expected?"

Zofia shrugged, her words unable to surface.

Inga patted Zofia's shoulder. "How are you taking this news? You must be anxious."

Zofia loved these two women but wanted to wiggle free of their touch. Wanted to wish she'd never seen Herszel, and more horrifyingly, to wish she hadn't seen Jabez this evening and heard what he'd instructed her to do and say—and not say. She had her son, Lena, and Inga. And Aanya, always Aanya. She needed to be brave for her loved ones' sakes. She looked directly into Lena and Inga's eyes. "When Jabez first took the job at the motor company, he and I spoke about our concerns regarding the changes taking place in Germany." Zofia remembered how Jabez had instructed her to frame their conversation around his wishes so that his mother and aunt wouldn't cast blame on her. "Since Jabez is a Pole, and may be suspect in the eyes of the Nazis despite his Catholic faith, he wanted to have a plan in place in case something unexpected occurred at work."

"This makes no sense. Why would the Nazis be concerned over Jabez's religious views?" Lena leaned over the table. "I don't mean to sound as if I don't believe you, but if you're covering up Herszel's bad news of an awful work injury to Jabez with a story of his disappearance due to political reasons, please just tell me the truth." She glanced at Inga. "Tell us both."

Would Lena accept the truth if she told her? Jabez's words replayed in Zofia's mind: *The less my mother and aunt know, the better.*

Zofia pushed aside intimidation from the crazy reality and the requests she faced. She tried not to flinch, a telltale giveaway of her rotten deceit of these two darling women. "The only information I have is that he has not suffered a work injury but has disappeared.

And before he took this job in Germany, he emphasized that there might come a time I should consider taking Eban and relocating to New York with his cousin."

"New York?" Lena said. "Isn't that a bit extreme of Jabez, to expect you to leave your home, to leave us? If he were hurt, you'd think he'd appreciate your company. And then there's Eban to think about. An upheaval of this nature, on top of separation from his papa, will surely cause anxiety for the child."

Oh, she'd thought of this, time and time again. And though she agreed, she couldn't convey a word of it.

Lena remained collected. She studied Zofia with that wise-woman look of hers. "Then again, there comes a time when a mama of adult children must trust their judgment and decisions. Yet if you're seeking my opinion, it might be best to wait, dear, and learn more about the situation. Let's not jump to the worst conclusions and see whether we will hear from him, or better yet, see him when he arrives home. My son's working at a factory that makes aircraft machinery. He's not working for the German government. I'm sure things will be fine."

Zofia lifted her fingernails toward her mouth, but stopped. She hadn't chewed her nails since childhood and the time Aanya reassured her that because she'd always have her shoulder to lean on when life became scary, she need never be afraid. But this scheme of getting away that Jabez had planned for her and their son, which would alter life also for Lena, Inga and Aanya, served not to soothe, but to kindle anguish. "Jabez took this job in Germany only when I promised to keep our vow to each other: that if there came a time when he failed to arrive home and no one could determine why, Eban and I must leave the country for New York to stay with Jabez's cousin there."

Lena's forehead furrowed. "You said that Jabez had cautioned you to *consider* leaving, but now you're saying you and he had already made an agreement for you to do so? And neither of you thought to tell us?"

"We didn't want to worry you. Didn't think the time would ever come for this to be necessary." Even to Zofia this excuse sounded weak.

"But why such a drastic reaction to events we're just now learning about? And please, let's consider that we don't yet know what has happened to Jabez. It may be insignificant."

The way Lena's gaze riveted hers, Zofia understood her mother-in-law suspected the truth: a bigger risk for Jabez, his wife and child was at play and Zofia had purposely failed to cough up the whole truth of the matter. Lena was a smart person, able to take the past, calculate the future, and call the truth the truth and a lie a lie. "This is what I know. If, when, I learn more, of course, I'll tell you."

"All right, my dear. We'll accept it for what it is, an as-yet unexplained disappearance, which is bad enough." Lena leaned back against her chair. "However, you just found out about Jabez's absence today. Isn't it rash to react to an extreme and make hasty plans?"

If she hadn't seen Jabez with her own eyes, and heard his demands with her own ears, she would have agreed. She and Jabez should have rehearsed the possibilities back when they had first discussed this, back when she first raised her misgivings over leaving Brzeziny and traveling to a foreign country with a young child in tow and no husband to help or to stand by her side.

"Jabez expressed pretty firm expectations of me, ones I shouldn't question."

Lena again leaned over the table, her jaw set. The gentle mother-in-law and doting grandmother had never looked so severe. This was her son they were talking about. Besides, the radical step of Zofia and Eban leaving would affect her and Inga too.

"Wait one month. That isn't a long time to wait to see if he comes home. Imagine Jabez arriving home with a silly excuse on his lips only to learn that you left him and took his son, and to a different country!"

Zofia wouldn't be the one responsible for leaving—it was Jabez. And by making her agree to his plans, he'd stripped away her ability to change course or alter this journey she would take. She was his wife, and as little as she dared speak up to Jabez, wives didn't contest their husbands. At least not here, not in Poland. However, she knew better than to argue with an upset Lena. This *was* her son they were talking about; her whole family structure would change at the snap of the fingers.

"You're right." She willed the tension away that was knotting up the back of her neck. "A month will go by fast enough."

"Let's remain positive," Inga said. "You'll see. We'll hear good news."

Zofia could only hope for truly good news. That would mean that Jabez was terribly mistaken, and the life they'd carved out for themselves in this corner of the world, in Brzeziny, would continue. She'd have her family at home where they all belonged. She'd have Aanya, and life wouldn't be so frightening. She gave a quick nod to Inga. "If you don't mind, why don't you finish up with the evening meal and I'll go to Aanya's and bring Eban home."

Lena smiled. "That's a grand plan."

4

While her mama played with Eban in the parlor, Aanya emptied the pot of boiled potatoes into a tin colander set in the sink. Mama may have dragged her feet when she came out of her bedroom, but she'd told Aanya not to fret, that nothing would keep her from playing with Eban, her little sweetie. They'd both chuckled when he reminded them that he'd soon turn a big seven and was no longer a little boy. Aanya had to smile. If it took a child's presence to foster enough energy for her mother to leave her sick bed, may her own little one grace their home one day and make his or her *babcia* beam.

Aanya rubbed her belly with its empty womb. Unmarried, with not one Brzeziner man interested in marrying her—*that deaf Gerszon woman*, she was called—she'd never bring a child into this world. And if she was wrong, if there was a smidgen of a chance that she'd marry one day, she feared her mother wouldn't live long enough to see a grandchild's birth.

A few drops of hot water splattered from the pot and she swore to herself. She picked up the dish cloth and wiped the mess around the sink. She didn't have time to ponder the rest of her life, children or no children. Zofia would be back soon, and on top of that, it was probable that a Nazi hid in the barn.

She placed the empty pot on the table, turned, and wiped the sweat from her brow. From the corner of her eye she saw movement and rocked back then realized it was Zofia standing by the kitchen door, though she shouldn't have been surprised. Her friend was welcome to stroll into their apartment at any time.

"Hello again. I didn't mean to startle you."

"That's what I get for daydreaming," Aanya signed. "I'm glad you're back."

"Has Eban behaved? I saw your mama—did Eban wake her?"

Aanya smoothed her skirt outwardly; internally, she tried to quiet her racing thoughts.

"You have a few things on your mind?" Zofia asked.

Aanya nodded and offered a little smile. Her friend always understood her. She couldn't imagine what she'd do without Zofia. But here she was, wanting to talk about this agreement between her and Jabez, she supposed. A plan that would take Zofia and her son permanently out of her life. As much as she would love to accompany Zofia and Eban to America, she had her mama to watch over, and wouldn't consider leaving her.

"Yes. Several things are keeping my thoughts occupied." She glanced toward the parlor. "No worries about Mama. You can't keep her away from Eban." Similar to words sticking in the throat of a speaking person when choked up, her fingers had frozen momentarily when it came to Eban as if she'd forgotten how to sign his name. She'd miss him incredibly if he left with Zofia, and of course he'd have to go. She glanced up at Zofia and continued to sign. "Your sweet darling behaved well. I think Mama was a handful for him rather than the other way around."

Zofia slid the opposite chair from under the table and sat. "Let's resume our conversation. I will only sign. Yes?"

Aanya nodded, understanding Zofia's need for keeping the others from hearing. She shoved the pot aside and sat, interlocking her fingers on her lap to prevent her from wringing her hands.

"Both Lena and Inga were home. They took the news of Jabez's disappearance better than I thought they would. Of course they were concerned, but not excessively so, as I'd feared. Actually, what bothered them most was the promise I'd made to Jabez about leaving."

"Did they think you were carrying on unnecessarily?"

"Yes. Lena, especially, thought I was overreacting. Who knows how I would have reacted if she and Inga had both broken out in sobs?" Zofia dropped her gaze to her lap. After a long moment she lifted her head. "It doesn't help matters any that I had no further explanations about Jabez. How foolish I feel. Lena suggested I wait a month to see if Jabez comes back, or at least if word comes to us of his whereabouts."

Aanya noted a sudden shift of Zofia's attention as her gaze strayed toward the window, remaining there a few seconds too long. It was as if Zofia avoided looking into her eyes, as if guilty of something, or lying. But probably her friend was simply busy getting her own runaway thoughts under control.

Aanya reached across the table to pat Zofia's hand. When Zofia faced her, Aanya lifted her hand to sign. "Lena is right. A month isn't a long time. Remember last winter when Jabez's train was caught in a blizzard and detained him for a few hours?"

"That was different. A few hours to wait for his arrival home, considering the weather conditions, was bearable. Understandable, even. Herszel hadn't come knocking on the door then with news of Jabez's disappearance."

"Well, people simply don't go missing without a trace." Aanya paused when she thought she saw Zofia give a short nod. She never suspected Zofia of concealing important matters from her, yet during these changing times, there were no limits to unpredictability. But keeping news from her? Aanya pushed away these discouraging thoughts and resumed. "Jabez must have been seen by now. I'm trusting word will get to you. Better yet, it will be Jabez himself who will speak directly with you and make you smile."

Aanya had imagined that the corners of Zofia's lips would have nudged up, at least a bit, with that scenario. The opposite happened: Zofia covered her face with both hands. Zofia wouldn't see Aanya sign, wouldn't see what she needed to express. Communication was cut off.

Aanya stood and did the only thing she knew to do for her friend. With three strides she reached Zofia, helped her onto her feet, and embraced her. She didn't let go until Zofia's shoulders and arms relaxed.

"Will you be strong enough to wait a month?" Aanya asked.

"I have a child to take care of, and you to watch out for me. I'll be fine." Zofia glanced over her shoulder toward the parlor. "It's getting close to Eban's bedtime and we must leave. I'll bring him back here for a good-night kiss."

Although she wobbled between the opposites of a sudden pang of loneliness and a feeling of relief, Aanya smiled. "I hate to see you go, but I need to tend to Mama."

As Zofia gathered Eban from the other room, Aanya flopped back onto her chair. She hoped she'd have longer—forever—to spend with her friend, and not have to watch her leave Brzeziny.

Artur was curled on top of the hay pile, his mouth open. Did he snore? At least, from what Aanya could see, he hadn't bled to death. He looked like a man enjoying a peaceful, deep sleep. She suspected that he'd missed hours or whole nights of sleep in the past few months. Despite lacking knowledge of the tragedy that had brought him to Brzeziny—and it had to be bad to propel him away from his family, let alone his homeland—she couldn't help but feel concern for him. Not wanting to rob him of the simple comfort the hay provided, she sat carefully on the bare spot of floor beside him.

A few minutes passed before he stirred and batted his eyes open. He smiled brightly.

She took out her notepad, wrote, and handed him the slip of paper.

"What am I thinking about?" Artur read aloud, moving his lips slowly. She nodded.

"I'm glad you're a real person and not only the woman I was dreaming about."

She grasped her brown and black-striped shawl tighter and pursed her lips.

"That's a funny face. I probably deserve that."

Suddenly self-conscious, then flummoxed over this self-awareness she almost never bothered with, she scrawled another message.

He looked at the paper and read her words aloud: "I didn't mean to make a face. I'm just surprised that you would think twice about me." He set the note down and looked at her. "Why wouldn't I think about you?"

Heat flushed her face and she wrote another message.

"You say you aren't accustomed to hiding fugitives. Well, just because I'm in your barn, doesn't mean I'm a wanted man. I might be running from religious persecution."

She understood. This wasn't her concern and he was brushing her off like crumbs stuck on his shirt. She'd stick to the basics of what she could offer and then ask him to leave.

He took the next note from her. "How am I? Am I bleeding anywhere?" He peered into her eyes. "No bleeding, and if you're curious, my full name is Artur Lang. I am a deserter from the German army."

She jumped to her feet. He was a Nazi. An on-the-run Nazi with the possibility of a whole slew of German soldiers on the hunt for him. And once they discovered that not only was she Jewish, but also that her sick mama lived in the apartment across from the barn, there was no guessing what the sorry lot of them would do in the name of having a little fun. She flew toward the door.

He grabbed her by the elbow within her first few steps, whirled her around and locked gazes with her—his seeking, hers wanting to hide. "I don't blame you for bolting from me," he said, pronouncing his words carefully despite time ticking and putting both of their lives in peril. He brushed the tender curve of her neck. "But I won't hurt you. Or your mother. And I believe they've stopped chasing me."

Artur had heard too much of what Zofia had said to her when she visited earlier. All of it, most likely. But he was a stranger. Why should she believe a word he said? Who exactly was he referring to? She wasn't about to ask this question or express her doubts. Given his lean and unkempt appearance, he'd likely been on the run for months or even a year. Yet that wound didn't seem so old. Unable to take a step forward or backward, she stared hard into his eyes.

"I know what you're thinking. Why should you believe me?"

She nodded, suddenly aware he'd released his grip on her, and she'd failed to notice the exact moment he let go. Free to leave, she found she didn't want to.

"Let me tell you a few things about myself. I'm 33 years old. I was born in Leipzig, in the state of Saxony, not far from Berlin."

He made her head swim with these geographical details, as if this was the right place and time to tell her useless facts—if indeed this was the truth. While she wanted to believe him, how could she? A man on the run would say anything if it were advantageous, wouldn't he?

"Ah, I can tell that you're concerned more about urgent matters. Let me summarize more succinctly." He paused, shifted his gaze away from her, then looked again into her eyes.

The realization that he understood what she was thinking by a mere observation—and that he was curious about her—was a new experience for her. If this was another time, situation, or man, she could spend an eternity looking into his spellbinding, greenish-brown eyes.

"Conscripted into the German army, I had no other choice but to obey. Assigned as an auxiliary serviceman—a lorry driver, to be exact—I thought I'd have an easier go than the men in action, but when I arrived at Buchenwald I learned differently. Have you heard about this camp for prisoners?"

She shook her head.

"I was assigned there when it opened in July of 1937. It's the largest camp in Germany at the moment. Political prisoners, homosexuals, Jehovah's Witnesses, and anyone else who doesn't fit into the Führer's beliefs and plans are sent there." He turned his head and spat. "They're rounded up and dumped in this camp without a chance of release. Many are tortured or executed, or both. Starvation is a significant killer. This I've seen with my own eyes."

Oscillating between her curiosity to learn more about Artur personally and the need to learn more about this awful situation, she scribbled: "Are there more camps like this?"

"They've built a few more, with plans to expand throughout Germany."

"And your desertion?"

"Instead of the supplies I expected to bring into the camp, I drove dead bodies into the surrounding woods for mass unmarked burial. I knew without a doubt it was time for me to leave the dictator and his followers and the country of my birth."

They sat hip to hip on the floor; he looked directly at her. Wanting to see her? Or just to accommodate her need to watch his mouth as he spoke?

"Aanya, there are things I could tell you that would cause you great distress. About what has already occurred, and about plans I have overheard about the near future. Things I can't explain easily because I fail to understand how one person can do these things to another... like the torturous experimentation done in the name of medical advancement that nobody would ever volunteer for. You must believe me. Working in Buchenwald made me question which was worse—the insanity and cruelty of the actions of a few, or the blind loyalty of many more who choose to follow the leader who commanded the insanity and cruelty in the first place."

She nodded. Then, as if it weren't enough to convey that she agreed passionately with him, she wrote a message that she'd never thought she would share with a stranger, let alone one who had served Hitler.

Artur read the note to himself and looked up at her. The paper fell from his hand. His gaze narrowed on the gun she aimed at his chest.

She jutted her chin at the note, keeping the gun barrel trained on him.

He read aloud. "I am a Jew, and believe passionately what you just said about those who follow a leader of madness. But don't dare try to kill me or my mama, because as much as I want to help you, I'll personally finish you off if I suspect that you're misleading me, because I am not, and will never be, a follower of evil or permit it to be perpetuated under my watch."

When he looked into her eyes again, she nodded.

"I understand. And I agree. I escaped from the Nazis because I cannot work on their behalf. I've put my life at risk for my convictions. I am not armed, and if I were, would not use it against you." With total composure he added, "If you do not believe me, then shoot me without delay."

Shooting Artur—killing him, or anyone—was the furthest thing from her mind.

Artur grabbed the gun from her with such force that she fell backwards.

Aanya's mind registered two things: Artur held the gun so that the barrel faced upwards, and then Zofia appeared from behind him, yanked the gun from his hand and pistol-whipped the back of his head.

He tottered and fell forward. His head rested on Aanya's lap.

"The gun was empty of bullets."

"How was I supposed to know that?" Zofia said as well as signed. She squatted beside Aanya. "I heard him say the word Nazi. Saw him —whoever he is—with a gun in his hand. And you're stroking his forehead?"

Thankfully, though Artur was stirring, Aanya doubted he would comprehend Zofia's words. Aanya stared at her fingers that seconds ago had touched Artur instinctively in a way that she'd never touched a man before. As she lifted these same fingers to reply to Zofia, absent from Artur's warmth, they became cool and achy.

"No lover. While I barely know Artur, I know enough to say comfortably that he wouldn't have harmed me. I was using my papa's old gun to make a point—it was I who aimed the weapon at him first, not the other way around."

Zofia rocked back onto her heels. "And what is the point, exactly, that you needed to make with a gun?"

"That I won't be fooled, that no one will harm me or the ones I love."

"What's going on here? Who is this man? What's this Nazi doing in the barn? How long have you been hiding him?"

"Sorry. I don't keep secrets from you. Artur and I met just this late afternoon. Then you wanted me to watch Eban and time hurried by. I would have told you eventually. And Zofia, he's not a Nazi."

Artur sat and drew his knees to his chest. He rubbed his head and eyed Zofia. "There are better ways to introduce oneself."

"I'd do anything I could to help my friend."

"Evidently." Artur turned his attention to Aanya. "What do you say, doctor? Will I live?"

To save time, instead of penning messages, Aanya asked Zofia to translate for her as she signed. "Oh, I'm no doctor, not yet, but I see no injury. By the way you're conversing, my estimation is you're more shaken than hurt."

Without a wince, Artur nodded, keeping his gaze fixed on her. She didn't want him to look away. "I didn't pass out. I just liked resting my head on your lap."

"Silly man," Aanya signed, and waited for Zofia to interpret, aware that her friend, her mouth agape, wore the oddest expression of bewilderment. She could read Zofia's thoughts: *What's going on between the two of you? Is there something more powerful working than I can see with my own eyes?* If Aanya was honest with herself, she'd shrug her reply to her friend, conveying her own befuddlement over what was happening between her and Artur.

"Why the gun, Aanya?" Artur asked her directly.

Aanya glanced at her medical bag where she'd asked Zofia to place the gun. She then looked at Zofia and asked if she was ready to interpret her signing for Artur. Zofia nodded.

"My papa's gun hasn't been loaded in years. But I must protect myself and my mother, and I wanted you to understand that I'm not one to cross, or to take advantage of."

Artur rubbed his head—a bit excessively, Aanya thought. Likely more for emphasis than from pain. "I don't doubt your abilities one bit. I also don't blame you, Aanya." Artur studied Zofia. "And I admire you, Aanya's friend, for wanting to protect her. She's a lovely woman, a lovely person."

Aanya's heart skipped a beat when she saw the words flow from Artur's lips. Whereas she occasionally misinterpreted spoken words, or failed to understand every single one, which was expected, she had no problem understanding his choice of the word *lovely,* nor perceiving he tied the word to her as if lacing it with a red ribbon. Yet, she struggled not to fall for his charm. This wasn't the place or the time. She opted for an attempt at humor.

"Looks like I might be mistaken about you not sustaining a head injury. Surely otherwise you would not describe a woman who seconds ago pointed a gun at you as lovely."

After Zofia interpreted, Artur's smile deepened. "I believe you were right the first time in your diagnosis—I have no grave injury. And I haven't misused the word lovely." He appeared more serious as he glanced at Zofia. "At most, I face an impending headache. At the very least, I've gained a healthy wariness of your friend."

Zofia's hard look softened. "Do call me Zofia."

"Zofia it is," Artur said as he stood, balancing steadily on his feet. "I'm thinking that a friend of Aanya's is a friend of mine, but I do hope her other friends leave my poor head alone or I won't make it through the introductions."

Aanya smiled at both Artur and Zofia. "Zofia is my only true, best, and beautiful friend," she signed and waited for Zofia to translate.

Artur curved his fingers toward his chest and riveted his gaze on Aanya. "And me? Aanya, I hope you'll give me a chance as well. I'd like to be your friend."

For the next two days Aanya visited Artur daily in the barn. She tended to his wound, brought him food, and returned under the pretense of any handy excuse she could think of. The most startling impact of Artur living a few steps away was discovering that his presence was a welcome change. She'd awake each morning, and slip under her blanket at night, aware that he'd brought a ray of sunshine to her darkening world.

On the fourth day of Artur's stay, while her mother rested in bed listening to the Polish Radio National Symphony Orchestra, Aanya hurried off to the barn earlier than her usual time.

Artur sat beside the haystack, his back against the splintery wooden wall, hugging his knees with skinny arms lacking muscles and staring at the opposite stall partition. With Aanya's papa's coat hanging over his bony frame, her guest appeared warm. Although light on her feet, her steps over the old, dry floor planks must have shaken the floor. When he failed to stir from his dazed state, her concern jumped to alarm. Either he had died or was in medical distress. She gripped the handle of her bag and stepped faster toward him when he began to thrash; his expression was anguished, and his lips moved in such a way that she understood he must have been screaming.

"*No. How could you? Removed eye... sewn... another body? Ice vats. No. Boiling water...*"

Aanya dropped to her knees and tried shaking him awake, tried saying his name for the first time.

"Aanya? Are you hurt?"

She shook her head and pointed at him.

He straightened his back. "Me? I'm fine, but you're the one who groaned."

Groaned? How embarrassing. She sighed and scrawled a note: "It looks like you were having a nightmare. I tried to wake you by saying your name. Before I leave for the day, tell me about your bad dream —if you want to share it with me, that is. And tomorrow I want you to teach me how to say your name so it doesn't sound like a groan."

He grinned. His hazel eyes were more luscious in color than the last glimpse of the Baltic Sea she'd enjoyed over two years ago. More pleasing, as well. "If you want to hear about the torture I witnessed in the camp, fine. Later I'll tell you. Be prepared. It will give you nightmares." He grasped her hand. "I will also teach you to say my name. I look forward to hearing my name sail from your mouth. I hope to teach you more things."

Was he talking only about articulation? She hoped not. He eyed the two buckets and medical bag she'd set down and offered a weak smile. She rushed over to the things she brought and started to sign, then stopped herself. She only signed with her mama and Zofia and Eban. How could she attempt this act of intimacy with him? With paper and pencil plucked from her skirt pocket, she scrawled another note.

"Am I all right?" he read aloud.

She nodded.

He smiled. "Now that you're with me, yes. I'm fine."

Judging by the way he was hunched over, his head slack as if too heavy to support, she wanted to argue the opposite but knew it wouldn't achieve a thing but to waste precious time. She wrote a more explicit question: "Are you bleeding? Do you have pain or a headache?"

He shook his head. His mouth fell open when she grabbed his hand and helped him to his feet. "Where are we going?"

Believing that he trusted her, she squeezed his hand, alarmingly icy, and tugged him toward the buckets.

"Water? Soap?"

Aanya couldn't tell whether he was surprised, delighted, touched, or all three. She rummaged through the black bag, withdrew two cloths, and handed him both.

"You want me to wash? I guess I shouldn't take that personally."

She pointed to him and then at the bucket, motioning for him to get busy. He unbuttoned his shirt in an odd way. With dread, she hoped it wasn't another wound he'd tried to conceal. She'd brought suture supplies, but if he needed more medical attention than she could offer, she was at a loss as far as what action to take. The shameful truth was she'd be hard pressed to find a single man or woman, including her doctor friend, who might be willing to risk the consequences of aiding a German soldier on the run. When he hesitated at shrugging off his shirt, she reached for the garment's shoulders and helped to shimmy the ragged top down his arms.

With only his trousers on, he covered her hand with his, the touch firm yet gentle. "Don't faint on me." He turned around.

When she took in Artur's back, she cupped both sides of her face in amazement.

"Well, that's a good sign. At least you're not backing away."

As she feared, he'd been shot, just to the right of his spine. It was a wonder that he'd escaped paralysis—or worse. She ran her fingers gingerly over the scar tissue that had hardened over the wound, tissue that would continue to traumatize the pocked area and cause him pain.

He grasped her fingers. "When I took off from the camp, I had the unfortunate experience of capturing the commanding officer's attention. He fired nonstop at me, but I kept my sight on freedom and ran like a wild animal. I made it to a barn... figured I'd either hide or die there. But I'd be damned if I surrendered to the Nazis to be put to death at their sadistic hands. A startled cow alerted its owner, an old scrap of a woman living by herself. Her chiseled face was the last thing I remember before I passed out."

Aanya decided to give him time; he didn't need to pause over her scribbling questions. Fortunately, he was in a talkative mood. She wanted to learn all about this intriguing man.

"A hot burning pain awoke me." He glanced at the buckets Aanya had lugged over then looked back at her. "I opened my eyes to see this white-haired woman sitting next to a pail of bloodied water, watching my every movement. She weaved the single bullet she'd removed from my back between her fingers, and then showed me the needle and thread she used to stitch me up. It took a good month, but Berta got me back on my feet, at least strong enough to continue my journey."

Aanya rubbed his shoulder. She stopped for mere seconds when she caught him looking at her, both delight and awe swimming in his eyes.

He flashed that beguiling look of his. "Believe me, you look different from old Berta."

This time, she couldn't resist writing a reply: "And you believe me, Artur Lang. You can't imagine the fright I truly look like after a night's sleep, with my hair flying every which way."

She gasped. And flushed. She hadn't meant to insert into his head the image of her appearance in bed first thing in the morning. Abruptly, she busied herself with immersing the smaller of the two cloths into the warmish water and wringing it out. He reached for the cloth but she moved his hand away and began to wash his bruised and battered body, as gently as if handling a baby. This man needed a loving touch of kindness.

Artur didn't say a peep until she finished and with the second cloth patted him dry. "You are most caring, Aanya. Thank you."

"You're welcome," she signed without thinking. When she realized what she'd done, she dropped her gaze.

With a fingertip, he lifted her chin. "I'm guessing you told me I'm welcome."

She nodded.

He grasped her hand, his touch warm for the first time since they'd met. "Teach me how to sign what you just said."

Without hesitation, she lifted his right hand to mirror hers. It took him two attempts to sign the words to express appreciation, but he succeeded. She rewarded him with a big smile.

"Teach me how to say I'm hungry—do you have more food to spare?"

She began to show him how to sign the words, but stopped mid-sentence. "Follow me," she signed then backed it with a motion of her hand. At the other bucket she removed the cloth covering. About to scrawl an apology that the cold pieces of chicken, cooked cabbage and carrots were more meager than she'd have liked, she stood back instead and watched him shovel the food into his mouth with his hand. Poor Artur. She withdrew a fork from her pocket and handed it to him.

He ceased eating. Although he had eaten the food she'd given him the past few days, was his stomach suddenly rebelling? She searched his face for signs of discomfort. His smile greeted her before he gently pressed his lips over hers, as hungry for her as she was for him.

5

Zofia watched Eban awaken the morning of his *imieniny*, the first of February. This special day marked his name day. He'd turned seven years old on January 17th, that date not carrying the significance as today as far as customs went, though her heart would forever keep the date of his birth special.

"Good-morning, Mamusiu." Eban stretched his arms, flexed his feet, and gave her a big smile. The sun shining through the window, just beginning to make its appearance on this frosty morning, splotched his right cheek.

"You make me proud, my little man. I should say my big man since you're growing faster than I can blink my eyes. What a fine day we shall have. Babcia and Aunt Inga will celebrate with us before they leave for work. Afterwards, Aanya will arrive and we'll have a feast. The weather is also cooperating. It's not clobbering us with more snow."

"But I like snow."

"Oh, yes, you do." Good thing, especially if they ended up in New York with Jabez's cousin, as Jabez had planned for them. From what Jabez had told her, based upon letters from his cousin, New York and Brzeziny shared similar climates, especially their long, frosty winters. "At times, darling, for us grownups, not having a great amount of snow makes for easier living. Shoveling paths to the coal bin or walking into town during the winter is often difficult."

"Like I fell on the ice last week. But that was fun. I skidded a big distance."

"It's a good thing you didn't break your arm, or worse."

"Mamusiu, you worry a lot." Eban grinned.

"My, look at you. When did you lose your upper tooth?"

He slipped a hand under his pillow and plopped a tooth into her palm. "Last night before I fell asleep. It was loose and I wiggled it out. I think it's my last baby tooth. Is that proof that I'm a big man, like you say?"

"Yes indeed, darling. That's why we're celebrating your name day." Eban had sulked the past few days. If she filled the air with light, fun talk, would it take away her son's sadness—or worse, was it resentment?—that his papa wasn't around for the festivities? Would it delay the badly needed conversation awaiting them about how his papa wanted them to leave the only home they'd ever lived in? Predictably, her son, with his healthy curiosity, would ask why they needed to travel to a faraway country to live when they were happy here. His name day may have arrived, marking another year of growth and maturing, but her son was still a young child and wouldn't fully understand the changing world around him, nor his parents' reactions to it. For that matter, she didn't understand the changes very well herself.

"For your special day I've prepared several kinds of meats and eggs in your favorite sauces. Aanya will bring relishes and pickles. We will have ourselves a feast at lunchtime in your honor."

"Sweets too?"

"Hmm. I did bake *drożdżówki* last night after you went to sleep, but you don't like those buns, do you?"

"I love them. Not the fruit ones, but the other ones."

"The poppyseed-filled buns or the pudding?"

"Poppyseed. Please."

"That's exactly what I baked for you, my prince."

She waited for her son to smile, or say something cute. His frown surprised her. She sat down on his bed. "What's wrong, darling?"

He sighed. She reached out to him, but he leaned away. His growing independence was normal behavior, yet it made her off-balance, as if the world had slanted one more degree toward disarray. "Talk to me, Eban. Use words to tell me what you're thinking."

"Mamusiu, I'm seven years old. You say I'm a big man, not a little boy."

Oh dear, she hadn't thought he'd take that literally. "You're certainly growing fast."

"But I'm angry."

Zofia worried her lip. Her son never verbally expressed this emotion. "Sweetheart, no matter how old you are, whether you're seven like today or 77, you will have emotions and reactions that are strong, and at times scary. That's part of life."

He scrunched his face. "Seventy-seven? That's old. Older than Babcia."

"I'm older than you, and at times I become angry. Other times I'm sad and afraid, but I'm also eager to see what each new day will greet me with." She paused a moment to allow that to sink into his thoughts, as well as to find the words to address what she suspected troubled him.

"Why do you get angry? Are you angry with me?"

"Oh, no, darling." She leaned over to kiss the top of his head. "You're part of my heart. At times when you disobey, like when you don't do your chores or speak rudely to your grandmother and aunt, I might become disappointed and then I tell you. But I'm your mama and mothers do those things to help children become good people. You can understand this?"

"But Tatusiu is away. He's not home to celebrate my special day."

"Oh, my precious one." She held him tight, hoping he wouldn't wriggle away again. "Papa loves you."

"Mamusiu, what does that mean? He's not here with me. It's not the same."

She slipped a hand into her pocket and withdrew a folded piece of paper, one that Jabez had given her during his last official break away from his job—if indeed he was working back then at the German plant. A just-in-case message to his son. Had he already known that he wouldn't be home in February? Regardless of his nebulous work, that man of hers had thought well ahead. He was a good father, though, and must have had mixed feelings about possibly not celebrating this special day with his son.

Zofia fixed a smile on her face. "Look what I have."

"A letter from Tatusiu?"

"Yes, and it's addressed to you. Would you like me to read it?"

Eban shrugged. Zofia's heart clenched at his indifference. She asked herself whether she too struggled with ambivalence toward Jabez. She wanted to love him. Forever. He was her husband. They had promised to love each other for better or worse, and like the strong parental love for a child, this love was meant to be unconditional. Yet she didn't understand this growing doubt perplexing her mind and heart. When she allowed herself to think about him, her already shaky thoughts would launch her further into nervousness over the approaching journey to America. Would she ever see him again? She hoped that their love was sturdy enough to survive until they reunited.

The approaching journey to America. That was another thing—a big thing. When and how would she break the news to Eban? How could she fill him in with the details she herself lacked? How to explain Jabez's secretive work that warranted such an upheaval in their lives as fleeing Polska?

"Mamusiu?"

Zofia shook away her thoughts and focused again on her son. "Aren't you a little curious about what your father has to say? He timed this letter well to arrive for your name day." Her last words were a bit of a stretch, but it was the best she could come up with to encourage her son.

Eban poked his finger in the empty tooth socket. "Read it, Mamusiu. Please."

She tugged his hand away from his mouth and suggested it might be healthier to leave the gap alone. "Good boy." She smoothed out the crinkled pages but glanced away, wishing she could slip away only to come back to this same place, at this exact spot on Eban's bed, but in a safer world: one that wasn't tense and on the brink of war. A world whose occupants got along with each other. Several months ago she'd expressed that desire to Jabez. Although she could tell that he held back a laugh, he had called her a dreamer. *Zofia, sweetheart, a place like that doesn't exist on this planet.* Then he glanced toward the ceiling. *That place is where the angels live.*

Eban touched her lips. "Where did your smile go?"

The curtain between the dining area and the kitchen snapped open. Lena faced them, wiping her hands repeatedly on the apron she wore over her work clothes.

"Come quick. There is trouble."

Zofia went to her mother-in-law, vaguely aware that Eban followed. "What's wrong?"

"Come see. Aanya's here. She's hurt." Lena placed firm hands on Eban's shoulders. "Eban, you stay with me."

Despite her son's protests, Zofia rushed into the other room. As if stuck in tar and unable to budge at the sight of a bloody-faced Aanya sitting on a chair in the parlor, she stopped moving and gasped. Inga knelt before Aanya, pressing a dinner napkin against what looked like the worst of her cuts. The wound above her left eye gushed blood down her cheek, and the white cloth napkin had already turned a dark red.

Zofia snapped out of her momentary inability to act and dropped to her knees beside Inga. She began to sign, briskly. "Tell me what happened. Who did this to you?"

Aanya shook her head and winced. Zofia glanced at Inga.

Inga patted another of Aanya's wounds with the cloth. "When I stepped outside to check the weather, Aanya was hobbling toward the door."

Zofia focused on her friend, whose gaze was fixed on her lap, and lightly tapped Aanya's knee to get her attention. When Aanya peered at her, she continued to sign as well as speak.

"Please talk to me. You're hurt. We want to help, but need more information." A horrid thought crossed Zofia's mind. "Did Artur do this to you?"

"Artur?" Inga said. "Who's Artur?"

Aanya jumped to her feet, shaking her head. She winced, paled, and groped the air around her as if dizzy.

"Easy," Zofia said as she helped Aanya sit again. "I didn't mean to upset you, but thought—"

Aanya snatched her hand from Zofia's and began to sign. "You thought wrong. Artur would never, ever hurt me."

"I'm sorry," Zofia replied verbally, patting Aanya's shoulder. "I can see you hold him in high esteem, and I'm wrong to misjudge him."

"Believe me, we're familiar enough with each other to the point that I can say Artur has never hurt me and never would."

How could those two know each other so well, and in such a short time, that Aanya could be sure of that... unless...

"Aanya, are the two of—"

Aanya's gaze, darting back and forth between Zofia and Inga, interrupted.

"Fine, then," Zofia said. "Again, my apologies."

Inga stood. "I'll give you two more privacy to talk."

Zofia thanked her. Aanya smiled, winced, and rubbed her mouth. When Jabez's aunt left the room Zofia returned her full attention to Aanya. "I'm switching fully to signing to keep this between the two of us. That is, if you want to share with me what happened."

Slowly, Aanya moved her fingers to reply. "I guess you won't accept from me that I fell."

Aanya's bruises weren't caused by an unfortunate fall, but by someone's hand. It took all of Zofia's will power to remain strong for her friend when all she wanted to do was find the person or group of people who did this to her and wring their necks. "Do we need to send for the doctor?"

"No. Please don't. No one must know about this. It may be worse if I report the incident."

Incident? Zofia didn't like the implications of that word, nor how this *incident* could worsen if Aanya spoke to the authorities. Eager to find out more, she stopped short when footsteps rattled over the dry wooden floor.

"Aanya," Eban shouted, as if he'd forgotten she couldn't hear. He ran to her, his grandmother rushing after him.

"I tried to hold him back," Lena said. "He's getting too strong for me."

"Aanya, Aanya," Eban said and signed at the same time. "What happened to you? Are you hurt? Will you die?"

"Calm down," Lena said and with a grunt, hoisting the child to her hip. "Aanya will be all right. My, you're getting heavier and bigger each day." She carried Eban to the other side of the parlor, a distance away but close enough to see and hear what was going on.

Zofia helped Aanya to her feet. "Let's talk in the other room, just the two of us." Without waiting for a reply, she guided Aanya into the kitchen-bedroom where moments ago she and her son had chatted leisurely about name day foods and missing baby teeth. After she eased Aanya onto Eban's unmade bed, she took the blood-soaked napkin from her, tossed it into the sink, and fetched a clean cloth from the shelf where she kept the glasses.

"Use this fresh one," she said in full view of Aanya so that she wouldn't miss a word. She gingerly pressed the fabric against the wound and placed Aanya's fingers on top. "The blood is lessening, but lie back on Eban's pillow to stop the flow. You might need stitches. Please let me send for the doctor."

Aanya groaned, which Zofia interpreted as a definite *no*. She knew her friend well.

"I'm sorry," Aanya signed as she stretched across the bed.

"You're sorry? For what?"

"Because I ruined Eban's celebration."

"Don't fret." As Zofia took in the sight of the grown woman lying across a child's bed, bruised and bloodied, she felt her faint smile fade, her jaw tighten. The last of her patience disappeared. "Put Eban's name day aside and tell me what happened."

Aanya began to sign but faltered. She shook her head and tried again. "With the sack of the promised treats for Eban—which got left behind—I began the stroll over here. As I left the apartment my thoughts were occupied with Artur."

"You two are in love, aren't you?"

Aanya's eyes flooded with tears; she bit her lower lip.

"Now, now," Zofia signed. "This isn't quite the reaction I was expecting."

"Believe me, my friend, neither was I." Aanya took the second cloth Zofia offered and blotted her tears. She leaned back on the pillow. "With my mind on Artur, I suspect that's why I didn't notice the handful of young men—barely out of their teens. They moved toward me with an odd swagger."

"Were they drunk?"

"Nie." Aanya spoke the word. She rubbed the side of her mouth.

Zofia thought of her son's missing tooth. "Did they hit you? Is a tooth loose?"

Aanya switched back to signing. "That would have been easier to take. They knew who I am. Knew I'm Jewish. Knew I could read lips."

What these ruffians knew about Aanya made Zofia surmise that they were likely from Brzeziny or the surrounding area. Knowing that these people weren't strangers but were of their own townspeople rippled her arms with goosebumps.

"They weren't drunk on alcohol, but on hatred," Aanya added.

"What do you mean? Why would they hate you? You've never hurt anybody."

"There was no stench of drink, Zofia; their actions and words were controlled. They called me vulgar names, accused me falsely of horrible things. They told me what Hitler said two days ago." Disgust darkened Aanya's eyes. "Are you familiar with the Nazi leader's speech to the supportive Reichstag, the German parliament? These youths I encountered—these idiots— took it upon themselves to tell me about it since a deaf Jewish woman *'couldn't possibly have a clue about Hitler.'* As though being deaf meant being uninformed! They had no idea that I knew all about the two-hour-long hateful speech. Artur and Mama listened to it on the radio, and told me all of the details."

As if Zofia's mind split in two, her imagination fought with her reason. She wanted to try to comprehend the mental image of Artur sitting beside Pani Gerszon on the sofa, before the radio, listening to each word of the German leader. Had a dish of cookies, baked by Aanya, sat before them on the table, its contents untouched, their bellies soured by the dictator's words that were easily translated by Artur? Before Hitler's growling, commanding voice traveled via radio transmission from Germany to Poland, were the three of them enjoying an afternoon of delightful conversation? Artur telling of his boyhood days, the tales steeped in a traditional German lifestyle? Was this the first time Pani Gerszon had met Artur, or had he been invited to supper several times already? Just how cozy was Aanya with Artur that he, a former Nazi—at least on paper—had been invited to spend time in the privacy of the Gerszon's apartment? What did he think of the *mezuzah* fastened to the doorpost leading into their Jewish home? It was more palatable for Zofia to ponder these scenarios than to brace herself mentally for the vitriol that had spewed from Hitler's mouth, news she hadn't yet heard herself.

She wanted to block out the world, because inevitably the news would also impact Jabez and the secret mission he'd taken upon himself. It would also influence her and Eban and the direction they needed to take. Instead, she sat up straight and pushed aside her own fears and concerns. She had to be the solid rock her friend needed. "Tell me what Hitler said."

Aanya blew her nose into the cloth and apologized again. Zofia waved off her worries.

"Hitler gave this speech, regarding what he called the Jewish Problem, as if he was a prophet. He said that if Jews continue to behave like parasites and feed off of the German nation—turning Germans into '*beggars in their own* country,' his exact words—then what would stop the Jews from moving onto the next country and stripping them bare, like Germany? Hitler went on to say that if Jews control international finances like they did leading up to the last world war and succeed in plunging the nations again into another world war, the result won't be a victory for the Jews, but their annihilation."

Zofia gasped, then signed furiously. "Wait. I'm not sure I understand. He implied that Jews will start a world war and cause their own destruction? He's saying that Jews deserve to be wiped off the face of the earth?"

Aanya propped herself up on her elbows. "His speech was his

justification on why Jews need to be hated and why—on behalf of the rest of Europe—they must be stopped."

"I can't believe people are following this monster and are choosing to hate fellow human beings."

"I have trouble accepting this as well. Whether they are obeying this leader because of their personal convictions or from fear of what consequences they face if they don't follow—or both—doesn't matter. What counts is that they are choosing to perpetuate hatred and prejudice."

"And these boys on the street? What did they do to you?"

"They surrounded me like a pack of wild animals. They praised and saluted Hitler, reminding me that he has big and awful plans for people like me because we deserve punishment."

Zofia's chest ached with heaviness, as if a sandbag weighted down her spirit. Her poor friend! Aanya didn't deserve ridicule or blame. Like anywhere else, strife had flared up in Brzeziny in the past, and at times grew out of hand into feuds, but this kind of hostility? This went way beyond anything they'd known there. Aanya had done no harm to anyone. What could Zofia say to her friend? How can anyone explain such hateful behavior? Would these arbitrary acts one day become more frequent? Would more people demonstrate agression?

"What happened then?"

"After hurling insults at me, one of the delinquents grabbed my elbow and shoved me to another of his pals and down the chain I went, from one louse to another. Each time I was passed they did worse things to me. Spat in my face. Yanked my hair." She closed her eyes. "A grope. A punch. A knife cut. Finally, the last one tossed me to the ground. My face hit the icy cobblestone. By that time, we were in front of the butcher shop. Pan Waldman ran out, waving his sharp knife at them like a soldier. He would have given chase, but the wild pack was fast, and already a block away."

Zofia grabbed a towel from the sink and wiped Aanya's eyes. "Could the butcher identify them?"

"I doubt it. As I said, they ran away so fast, and I ran here as quickly as I could manage."

"We should go to the police."

"No." Aanya covered her face.

Zofia gently removed Aanya's hands from her eyes. "Please, look at me and tell me why they shouldn't be reported."

"Because they threatened to go after Mama, as well as attack more Brzeziny Jews, if I dared open my mouth to alert the police."

"I'm so sorry," she signed, aware of the inability of those three words to right a horrible wrong. "Those overgrown boys are not men, but beasts. How can—"

Aanya palmed both sides of her head and lurched forward, sobbing with an intensity Zofia had never seen in her.

Intuition guided Zofia. She placed her hand on Aanya's shoulder and gently eased her back so her friend could see her mouth. "It's a horrible thing these bullies did to you, and have threatened to do, in the name of Hitler." She nudged a few locks of hair from Aanya's forehead. "Darling, you're rightly upset, but I sense there's more than those thugs' vicious behavior that is troubling you."

Aanya held so motionless that Zofia was afraid to breathe in case she missed a reply or a reaction. Finally, she lifted her hand to sign. "Artur left early this morning. He'd warned me that he needed to keep moving to dodge the patrols that could still be searching for him. I didn't think he'd leave, but he did." She sniffled. "He left a note saying he'd be back, if he could manage it."

"I'm so sorry. What can I—"

Aanya seized Zofia's moving fingers. "I'm upset because I might have just made love to Artur for the last time. And—" She peered over Zofia's shoulder as if to see if anyone was there, though Eban was the only one besides Zofia who knew how to sign, and he only knew the basics. "... and if he doesn't come back, I won't be able to tell him." She placed her left hand over her belly. "My cycle may just be late, but I suspect I'm pregnant with Artur's child."

6

Six days after the attack on Aanya, Zofia arrived home from church with Eban to find Lena and Inga, sick with nasty colds, sitting beside the radio in the parlor. They didn't look up when the door banged against the wall from the strong February wind, nor when the floorboards squeaked as Zofia slid her coat off and helped Eban with his. The older women's uncharacteristically focused concentration, the paleness of their faces, and their scrunched brows drew Zofia's attention to the broadcast. She sent Eban to his room to change out of his good clothes and then sat quietly on the sofa and listened.

The group of men was last seen running into the surrounding woods. A team of local police and German military guards, accompanied by dogs, gave chase. These dangerous men, believed to be from Poland, have yet to be apprehended. We will add new information as we receive it.

Lena glanced at Zofia. "Are you aware that an undercover operation successfully blew up a bridge on the German side of the border? Those involved are wanted, dead or alive, by the German authorities. Can you imagine men and women taking it upon themselves to fight the Nazis when their own country isn't engaged in combat?"

"Nie," Zofia murmured, and it was the truth. She definitely couldn't imagine… was too afraid to imagine. As difficult as it was, she tamped down worries that Jabez had participated in this stunning event. She didn't know which was worse to ponder: the fate of those men if caught, or that of herself and Eban. Was it wrong to worry about herself and her young son more than to be concerned about who had destroyed the bridge, despite the possibility of Jabez's involvement? Was this the sin of survival of the fittest?

Eban entered the room with a storybook in hand. He looked from one adult's face to the other's in turn. "What's wrong?"

Zofia, wanting to jump to her feet and pace, ordered herself to calmly stand. "Nothing's wrong. Babcia and Aunt Lena were listening to a radio broadcast and asked if I've heard about it." She glanced covertly at the other two women. *There, see? I'm collected and haven't lied to my son. I'm not falling to pieces and would appreciate it if you don't upset my little one.* Woman to woman, Zofia knew that Lena and Inga understood her silent message. "Darling, let's bring your storybook over to Aanya's. We haven't seen her for a few days, and I'd like to check on her. Besides, despite the frosty temperature, I could use a breath of fresh air." Eban asked if his babcia and aunt could come along, but Inga said that with their colds, it was best they stay put. Five minutes later, with boots once again laced up, winter coats fastened to the neck, and hats covering their ears, Zofia and Eban set off at a good clip toward town.

Halfway there, the wind cracked like a whip against their backs. Zofia opened her arms wide to snuggle with Eban.

He declined with a firm shake of his head. "I'm fine, Mama. Remember, I'm not scared by the wind like you are." He flexed his red-mittened hands. "Want me to hold your hand? I'll help keep you safe like Papa used to."

Her son's father had been absent—unaccounted for, not that Eban knew that part—for five weeks. On one hand, too long, but on the other, a blink of an eye. And here their son was no longer asking about his papa but instead volunteering to assume his role. The bittersweet realization caught Zofia off guard; suddenly she noticed that she was cold and breathing too fast. She stopped alongside the road, stamping the snow from her boots in an attempt to hide her anxiety from her son.

"Are you tired, Mamusiu? We can rest, if you like."

"Darling," she said as she stooped to peck his forehead. She smiled when he wiped the kiss from his face. "You're a good, thoughtful boy. Thank you for your consideration, for watching out for me."

"So, we'll rest?" When she nodded, he slipped off his mittens and packed a snowball, pitching it toward the road.

In the distance, she heard a dog bark and thought instantly of the possibility of Jabez being involved with the bridge explosion. She wondered whether he was running from snarling dogs energized by his scent. Night after night she prayed for her husband, begging God to bring him home safe and sound. But Jabez hadn't come home.

"Mamusiu, did you hear that?"

Zofia glanced up from a lump of snow on the road she'd been staring at absently. Winter, with its expertise in silencing the world, made no exception in that moment; even the noisy dog had grown silent. "No, I'm afraid not."

"A man yelled. At us, I think."

Then, a sound rode on the wind as a gust blasted by them. She tugged Eban to her side, relieved he didn't resist this time.

Eban pointed at the field before them. At the far end stood a rambling house, one that had become so commonplace in her life that she no longer paid attention to it. Its two chimneys poked through one of the last thatched roofs in Brzeziny. She shielded her eyes from the sharp sunshine with her palm and swallowed hard when she saw Wincenty Nowak standing before the front door, his hand clamped on the ruff of a medium-sized dog.

"Go away, you Jude-lover," he bellowed.

"Mama, why is Pan Nowak yelling at us? What's a Jude?"

Zofia didn't know many German words, but did recognize the one word he used—Jude. Why would Wincenty, a Brzeziner who lived here ever since she could remember, suddenly yell at them and use a

German word in a damnable manner? "Eban, put your mittens on and let's hurry on to Aanya's."

"He sounded angry. What did he mean?"

"He spoke nonsense."

Zofia grabbed Eban's hand and started to half march, half pull him down the road. When he griped, she let go of his hand, but kept a firm hold on his shoulder to keep their pace up. How would she ever again go to and from town, passing this house with its foolish, arrogant occupant? He knew who she was, and that she and Aanya were friends. Evidently, he'd taken it upon himself to harass Zofia, her family, and Aanya.

Once past the decrepit house, as pathetic as its resident, she let out a long breath, and a curse word rode on the tail end of it. That captured Eban's attention. He lifted a brow.

"Pardon me, Eban. That man upset me. Pay him, and my choice of words, no mind."

"Mamusiu, are you afraid of him? Should I be too?"

Zofia wanted to laugh in denial at the absurdity of this situation —being intimidated by a man who had never once spoken to her in all the years she'd walked by his house. She wanted to shake in fear of a changing world, a world where so many people, even her own countrymen, sided with the mad ruler next door in Germany. Most of all, she wanted to yell in anger: her young son's life was spiraling out of control. He should be playing with toys, learning to read more, growing in confidence, and daydreaming of one day marrying a good woman—of which faith or heritage did not matter to Zofia, only that she was a good, moral person and loved her son—and helping to do good in their community. He shouldn't have to be concerned about a man shouting slurs against people who believed differently from him. Jabez was right, after all, to take action against this spreading Nazi evil before it worsened and spread further.

As she guided Eban into the courtyard that led to Aanya's door, she stopped. "Darling," she said, as she stroked his cheek. "Do not be afraid of anyone. Fear isn't your friend. Instead, be the bravest you can be. Will you do this for me?"

"Yes, Mamusiu."

"Thank you, my good boy. One thing more, sweetheart." She waited until her son looked up at her. "Aanya has a lot on her mind these days. I don't want to trouble her unnecessarily. Let's not tell her about that man and what he just shouted at us. Yes?"

Eban nodded, though his clouded eyes and wrinkled brow showed confusion.

"You're a dear. Let's go greet Aanya and Pani Gerszon with a big smile."

Her brave boy shined his sunny smile. He raced to the door and pushed it open, calling Aanya's name because in his heart, he saw her as his equal, tossing aside her deafness and, bless his kind heart, not thinking twice about her religious beliefs.

Zofia followed her son into the Gerszons' apartment. She did a double take at Aanya's mama seated on the sofa. Absent was her daughter. Eban sat on the floor beside his second grandma, already showing her his toys and telling her about how cold it was outside. "Eban, darling. You're soiling Pani Gerszon's carpet with your boots. Take them off, and your coat as well." She slipped from her own boots and set them beside the door.

"Oh, it's no bother," Pani Gerszon said, her tone happy. Her beloved Eban could never do wrong in her eyes. "Zofia, go to Aanya. She's in her room."

Zofia didn't inquire aloud, in front of her son, about what she suspected was behind Aanya retiring to her room so early. She kept her gaze fixed on the woman.

Pani Gerszon shook her head slightly, enough for Zofia to understand that her friend wasn't well. She reminded Eban about his boots and coat and then without delay padded stocking-footed down the hallway toward Aanya's bedroom.

Zofia pushed open the bedroom door and saw her friend tucked under the covers, facing the wall. Zofia sat on the bed and gently touched Aanya's shoulder. She'd expected her to jump, but her poor friend lay as motionless as a one-dimensional portrait. After a few moments she turned enough to watch Zofia sign.

"Are you ill?"

Aanya shook her head, which made her wince.

Zofia touched her forehead. "No fever. Do you have pain?"

Aanya rubbed her belly.

"You're nauseous? Any vomiting?"

Aanya covered her mouth and gagged.

"I take that as a yes. Have you had these symptoms since you told me you might be pregnant?"

"The way I feel, believe me, I'm expecting." Aanya rubbed at her throat then signed for water.

Zofia reached for the glass on the nightstand and pressed it to Aanya's lips, relieved she sipped the drink. She held Aanya's left hand, freeing her right to reply. "What other symptoms do you have besides queasiness?"

"My breasts are achy and I'm bloated, but Mama's like that." Aanya frowned. "If I didn't know my medicine, and the workings of my own body, I'd worry that I was ill like Mama." Aanya pushed the covers off of her and propped herself against the headboard. "Please don't say a word to Mama. I don't want to upset or worry her."

Poor Pani Gerszon. At the age of 55, Frymet was in the throes of a horrid illness. Her distended stomach likely signaled a cancer, yet she refused to see a doctor. Aanya didn't want to burden her mother with her own complaints. However, if she was carrying a child, she certainly couldn't ignore it or her changing body. Soon enough, others wouldn't be able to look the other way as she changed from a slim young woman to an obviously maternal figure. As a single woman, she would be on the receiving end of judgmental opinions.

"And I'm moody, so beware," Aanya added. "The big mystery of the day is whether I should cry or laugh."

"You sound like me in my early months of pregnancy with Eban." No response came.

"Aanya? A baby is a joy, a promise that life goes on."

Aanya dropped her gaze toward her belly, but continued to sign slowly, as if a weight on her tiny shoulders made her arms heavy too. "Although I have high hopes that Artur will come back to me, as he promised, the sad truth is that I have no husband. And because of Artur's precarious circumstances—with the risk of Nazis searching for him—I can't dare name the father and risk danger to Mama, let alone me and the baby. What should be joyous news will instead bring shame not only to me, but to Mama. What will she think of me?"

"Likely she will be a bit shocked. You watch, though. Your mama loves you. You're her beautiful daughter and she'll continue to love you when you become a beautiful mother and bless her with a grandchild. I'm certain she'll love you both without reservation. Life will continue—you, your mama, the baby and hopefully Artur, will settle down and enjoy life to the fullest. This isn't the first time since the beginning of society as we know it that a pregnancy without the benefit of marriage has occurred."

"We aren't living in the best of times, not that I need to tell you about the sadness and danger around us." Aanya wrapped her arms around her middle then suddenly undid them to continue to sign. "You say a new baby means life continues, but it won't for a woman in my circumstances." She stared hard at Zofia. "Brzeziners will shun me. Ah, Zofia, I envy you and your son. You have a husband who is trying to make a better life for his family. You'll go to America one day soon, and fall back into Jabez's arms, and have more children. You'll be a blessing to your husband and sons and daughters and they will adore you. Not like me."

Jabez's face, with his high forehead, charming eyes, and rugged chin, distracted Zofia's attention away from Aanya. In her memory she saw him as clearly as if he was standing in front of her, asking her to dance and whirling her around in a waltz that only the two of them could hear. Echoes of his opinions, sophisticated but not stuffy, his clever insight to happenings around him and in the larger world, and especially his sensitivity to others, reminded her of what drew her to him in the first place. He was a good man, her husband. The next time she saw him, she'd tell him that. Years of marriage had a way of pushing aside kind remarks and praise of one's spouse, but she would try to make up for her silence.

If Jabez came back to her.

"Aanya, please don't envy me. Bitterness will destroy our friendship. I don't want that, and I can't imagine you do, either."

Aanya sniffled, then signed, "You're right. I never want us to part."

"Want to tell me a little more about Artur?"

"Sure, I will tell you because I know you'll keep this in confidence."

"Yes, of course."

"Artur was a soldier in the German army. He told me about unimaginable atrocities he witnessed, acts that he couldn't accept or tolerate. That's why he deserted, fully aware that there would be a price on his head, as well as horrid consequences if caught." She paused. When she glanced again at Zofia, tears swam in her eyes. "The trouble is, he never expected to fall in love during his time as a fugitive."

Zofia grasped Aanya's hands. "He loves you. He'll come back. You'll see, I'm sure he will."

Aanya shrugged.

Zofia was about to squeeze Aanya's hand, but stopped when she realized that her words were practically identical to Aanya's when her friend had tried to comfort her regarding Jabez. This wasn't the time to offer a one-size-fits-all emotional blanket of solicitude. Her friend, worried about very real dangers to Artur, would benefit more if Zofia learned and dealt with facts. "Is he concerned the Nazis will find him? And Brzeziners will rat him out?"

Aanya signed yes. "As I already told you, he disappeared when I fell asleep after our last passionate lovemaking—forgive me for being so blunt."

Zofia waved a hand to signal it didn't bother her. Aanya continued.

"He said in his note that he planned to go to a place he hadn't, for my sake, told me about." She patted her belly. "And here I am, pregnant with his baby. There are no other men in my life, nor do I want anyone else."

"What does your mother think of Artur?"

"She likes him, trusts him. But, Artur and I... We've chosen to keep from Mama certain details."

A horrid picture sliced through Zofia's mind. As if she heard a clap of thunder, she covered her mouth to stifle a gasp.

"What is it, Zofia?"

"You wouldn't do away... get rid—"

"No! I never could do that to an unborn baby."

Zofia sighed in relief. "I'm very glad to hear it."

"What should I do, then?"

Zofia smiled. "My friend, you do what other women do. You see a doctor for a confirmation on the joyous news and then you tell your mother. You take care of yourself so the baby growing within you stands a chance of being born healthy and strong. Once your daughter or son is born, you love the child, no matter what, throughout her or his lifetime."

"You're wrong."

"Oh?"

Aanya smiled and stroked her tummy as if already touching her baby. Her eyes gleamed with devotion, love, and awe. "I already love this child."

Zofia went to hug her friend, but Aanya stopped her with a lift of her hand and began to sign.

"Will you help me, Zofia? I'm scared."

"You can always count on me." With her free hand, Zofia placed a fingertip on each corner of Aanya's mouth and lifted the corners into a little smile. "You're going to have a child, one who will call you Mamusiu. How exciting. What a blessing."

Beneath Zofia's fingers, Aanya frowned.

"Oh, Aanya, you're afraid. That's understandable. All expectant mothers experience uncertainty. I did."

Aanya glanced at her belly and sighed.

Zofia nodded. "Tell me your fears."

"I've told you my concerns about the illegitimacy—well, as others would see it—of this child and what may happen, but I'm also frightened about the baby's health."

"Every mother-to-be wishes and prays for a healthy child."

"Yes, of course. But what happens if the baby is deaf? Like me?"

"There's nothing wrong with you. You are a beautiful, intelligent, loving woman who cares about people. You don't allow your lack of hearing to control your life."

"And if the baby is born with the gift of hearing, but I cannot hear him laugh or hear her cry out in the middle of the night because she's scared of the dark?"

After a stretch of silence Zofia kissed her fingertips and touched Aanya's cheek. "Darling, what would happen if you could hear and gave birth to a child who couldn't? Or birthed a healthy child who would later lose her hearing because of an illness or accident?"

"I would love my precious one and teach him or her how to enjoy and make the most of life. I would teach my child to communicate with me like I taught you years ago when we were little girls."

"That's exactly what I expected you to say, and the reason why you and the baby will be fine."

Aanya began to swing her feet off the bed, but Zofia stopped her. "One more thing. Of utmost importance."

Aanya looked at her and waited.

"Never keep news—good or bad—from me again, understand? We are friends. Forever."

"You're right. Forever. Will you forgive me for keeping truths from you?"

Zofia nodded. "Of course. True friends always forgive each other."

"I want you to tell me about Jabez, if you heard from him yet. Then if you will go with me, I'll dress and see the doctor today."

"Of course I'll go with you. Wise decision, Mama."

"Oh, stop." This time, Aanya smiled widely.

The bedroom door crashed open. Eban, with brows pointed inward and eyes full of alarm, motioned for them to exit the room. "Hurry! Aanya, your mama fell to the floor."

Zofia grasped Aanya's hand. For her friend's sake, she willed herself to remain strong as they raced into the parlor where only minutes ago, Pani Gerszon smiled as she enjoyed her little guest.

7

Beloved wife. Beloved mother.

Aanya couldn't get the words out of her mind. She'd chosen those four words, simple yet deep and loving, for her dearest mamusiu's gravestone. She didn't want to banish them from her thoughts, either. Her only relief—if that was how she dared to think of it—was that Mama no longer suffered.

Alone in the apartment, the walls closed in upon her. She pushed her untouched breakfast away and stared at nothing. The past two months had drained her. Not even the longer days and warmer temperatures of an early April day soothed her. The shock and disappointment of Artur's departure, followed by discovering she was carrying his baby, and then losing her mother had left her numb. Paralyzed, almost. Yet staying idle was a foreign concept. She knew that if she didn't actively attempt to shake loose from this slump of inactivity she'd fallen into, she'd remain that way indefinitely, a state that even her grieving heart realized would only make things worse. She sprang to her feet.

A sunny morning made for an excellent walk, and visiting Zofia, a perfect destination. She knew from her medical studies with Dr. Paweł that exercise was beneficial to both her and her developing baby, and her burgeoning maternal intuition confirmed it. She hastened her steps toward the door. She slipped a tan jacket over a simple white blouse and blue skirt, tied her trusty walking shoes, and opened the apartment door to step out.

Then she screamed.

You filthy Jew.

Her mind refused to make sense of the angry, atrocious message painted in blood red letters across her door. Outrage and fear mingled and exploded within her lungs. Hurt boiled and twisted itself upward toward her throat, and despite her inability to hear the piercing sound, a second scream erupted from her mouth.

When she stilled, she looked about. What was wrong here? It was eight in the morning. The immediate neighbors, who worked later shifts, were usually home at this time of day, and must have heard her scream. They were not deaf. Yet no one had opened their doors to see what had was happening. She ran as best as she could away from Brzeziny proper and straight to Zofia's. Her friend would know what to do.

Alarm and shock might have propelled Aanya forward, but as soon as her friend's house came into view, a fresh indignity set her heart hammering.

Don't buy in Jewish shops. They'll steal our economy.

Nie! The message was painted on the front of Zofia's house in the same blood red paint as on her own apartment door. What was happening to their town? What would happen to them?

Just as she was about to pound on the front door, it swung open and Zofia nearly collided with her. Aanya, wide-eyed, pointed at the words. They grasped each other's forearms and stared.

"This is outrageous," Zofia said. "Eban had discovered this savagery. I'm on my way to town to buy paint to cover this disgusting untruth."

Untruth? Was Zofia upset that the attacker had painted the message in error, since she didn't own a shop and wasn't Jewish? Or was she upset on behalf of every Jew that a person or a group of people would spread a hateful ideology of intolerance and paint propaganda on her house? Aanya reeled back and shook her head. What was wrong with her? Why would she ever imagine that Zofia would be troubled over the mistake that she'd been considered a Jew and had her house disturbed, rather than aggrieved over the vile slander leveled at Jews? That wasn't like her friend at all. More disturbingly, it wasn't like herself to take a defensive attitude toward Zofia because she wasn't Jewish.

"What is it, Aanya?"

"Disturbed, scary thoughts," she signed. Wrong thoughts. "I also found awful words this morning." She frowned. Zofia needed her comfort and assistance too. "I came here because I needed your support." She eyed the written warning. "I'm horrified and confused that you've also been targeted."

Zofia's forehead wrinkled. "What smears did you find? When do you think it was done?"

"*You filthy Jew* was painted on my apartment door, with the same red paint." Aanya shuddered. "It wasn't there when I took the trash out before I went to bed, so it happened overnight or early this morning. If my neighbors saw, they didn't tell me, nor stop the wrongdoers."

"What do you think these messages mean? Are they warnings, threats, scare tactics? You aren't even Jewish. And this is Brzeziny, a loving, good town, where for years Jews who have mingled well with non-Jews. I don't understand."

"Things are changing fast in other countries, and I'm afraid it's reached our once treasured town where minds and opinions are also susceptible to persuasion." Zofia glanced back at her house. "The only thing I can think of—as far as not buying in Jewish shops goes—is that Lena and Inga work in Oskar's old store, which is now owned by Pan Kern, who of course you know is Jewish, not that it should make an *uncja* of difference."

"Evidently, it does, sadly, make a difference now. What about Eban? How's he reacting to this?"

"He's upset, but insists he's up to watching out for his babcia and aunt. I've told everyone to stay put indoors while I go to town for the paint. Aanya?" Zofia reached for her arm. "You're pale as a sheet. What's wrong?"

She patted her tummy, then began to sign. "No worries. Indigestion. As of late, nothing new. I'm going with you to town—no arguments."

As they left Zofia's and passed the surrounding houses, the fresh air boosted their energy and they strode at a good pace down the section of road where farm fields lined both sides. A jalopy from the early '30s rattled by, its windows opaque from either inner steam or filth or both. Zofia motioned for them to rest, and waited for the car to make it over the crest of a hill, out of view.

"Darling," Zofia signed. "I want to be totally honest with you."

"Aren't you always?"

Zofia tilted her head. "A while back…"

"Before Mama passed? It's fine, continue."

"It was the last time when Eban and I visited with you and your mother, may she rest in peace. She entertained Eban, adoring him as if he was her own grandchild."

"Yes, I remember."

"Well, that house we're approaching, the one with the thatched roof? Wincenty Nowak stood before his door and called Eban and me Jude-lovers."

"That's awful. Like you said earlier, this Nazi hatred has spread to Brzeziny. A place I'd never dreamed it would contaminate."

"Based upon what we've both encountered today at our homes, it sadly has." Zofia reached for her hand. "I'm sorry I didn't tell you then, but I didn't want to disturb you, especially since you were fighting morning sickness. You certainly had enough on your mind." Zofia dropped her gaze to Aanya's middle. "You're rubbing your tummy again—do you want to continue into town? I can go ahead if you'd like to head back to the house."

Aanya stared at her hand, frozen in mid-stroke. Absent-mindedly, she'd been rubbing her stomach. "I'm fine. Fit for a walk, but never for this growing, menacing evil."

"You should rest. I've changed my mind. Let's both turn around. I'll get the paint tomorrow."

Zofia dropped hold of Aanya's hand; her eyes widened as she peered over Aanya's shoulder.

"What's wrong?" Anya was about to turn to see for herself what troubled her friend, but

Zofia hooked her elbow and hurried her off the road. Four men ran toward them. Boyish looking, though likely in their mid-to-late twenties, they were only a few years younger than Aanya and Zofia. One clutched a fistful of rope; another wielded a hammer. Were they from the car that had passed a few minutes ago?

The one with oily blond hair draped over his eyes like a mask spoke first. "By chance, you two weren't after paint for your lovely homes? No need to coverup such masterpieces."

They knew.

"Did you paint our houses with those nasty words?" Zofia said, her words pronounced within Aanya's sight so she would understand.

The blond grinned. "Nasty words? Try *warnings*, you bitch."

Aanya pressed against Zofia's side, unsure whether she was offering comfort, or taking it.

The shortest of the four, a dark-haired man in farmer jeans and a ragged dress shirt, leaned toward Aanya's face, so close that his stale breath would have sent her back a couple of steps if he hadn't grabbed her upper arm and squeezed tight. "What's wrong, Jew? Holding onto your Jude-loving friend. He sneered. "You're a deaf and dumb Jew—you can't defend yourself, and you sure can't justify your sorry life."

One at a time, she stomped on his feet.

A thin-mustached man shoved his pal aside and gripped Aanya's arms. "We'll make you a deal, Jew. Say you'll follow Hitler and we'll let you go."

Aanya shoved both of her captors hard. The first stumbled, but regained balance. The second one, with the mustache, landed on the ground, his head striking a rock. Blood gushed.

Hands grabbed her. Feet kicked her ankles. The grass she landed on was a momentary comfort until she saw one of the thugs reaching for a hammer.

She watched helplessly as Zofia was knocked to the ground and two of the men shoved each other while another flung himself on top of her, squirming to unbuckle his trousers. She couldn't bear witnessing the attack on her friend without being able to stop it. She shut her eyes and welcomed a black abyss. After an unknown amount of time, Aanya opened her eyes—and saw Artur.

8

The first person Zofia saw when she stepped from her bedroom into the hallway was Artur.

She grasped his hands and looked softly into his eyes. "Aanya's resting as comfortably as possible. Dr. Paweł is finishing up with her and then he'll talk to us."

Artur leaned against the wall. "Is she in pain?"

"It's eased, thank God." If her friend was experiencing discomfort, she wouldn't admit it, though it was a good sign she hadn't grimaced or groaned in quite some time. "Of course, she's black and blue from the beating by those—"

A fierce growl flew from Artur's mouth and he tightened his fists around Zofia's hands. She flinched. Artur released his hold. "I didn't mean to hurt you. I just want to kill those bastards."

"Well, you nearly did before they fled for their lives."

Artur squeezed his eyes shut then opened them. "And Aanya's bleeding?"

"She said the cramping she's had—that she admitted she'd experienced before that wretched encounter with those animals—is mostly gone. She probably would have lost the baby even if she hadn't met up with those savages." Zofia glanced at her dear friend's lover who had returned, and hopefully would stay. She tugged Artur into a hug. "She's miscarried, Artur. I'm so sorry." Her tone was gentle.

"I didn't know she was…" He lowered his head. "… that Aanya was pregnant until she told me as I carried her here. If I had known, I never would have left."

Zofia heard his guilt in his unspoken words: *But I took off on her.* "You and Aanya will have to talk. I believe she's concentrating on you coming back to her. I mean, of course she's upset about the baby. She'll mourn this loss for a while, probably always. That's normal." She rubbed his arm. "She said several times that she's relieved—overjoyed, in fact—that you're here with her again. She hopes you'll stay. And I hope you and Aanya accept my invitation to live with us."

"I want to see her. Want to tell this woman, who I want to marry —if she forgives me for leaving her—that I came back because I'm willing to take my chances on whether or not there's a Nazi price tag on my head, because she means the world to me." He went to open the bedroom door but Zofia placed a hand on his arm to stop him.

"Wait until the doctor comes out—a matter of minutes, I expect. The good man is a friend of Aanya's. He's the one who has been instructing her in her medical studies. There's more I'd like to say to you, as well."

"I hope it's good because I can't tolerate a drop more grief."

She willed him to lift his head and to make eye contact with her. He did, and she was glad. "I don't believe it was random luck that you appeared when you did, just when those men, those—"

"Beasts?" he suggested.

"Yes, beasts." She paused to compose herself. "Thank you for scaring them off before they had a chance to—" She wanted to thank him for saving her from those lowlifes who had been about to rape her, but she couldn't bring herself to say the ugly word. She hadn't realized she'd squeezed her eyes tightly shut until Artur patted her on the shoulder. She looked into his warm hazel eyes; kindness glinted there.

"They'll leave you alone from now on," he said gently.

"Yes." A little grin played on her lips. "The way you clobbered them and had them running like little dogs with tails drooping between their legs, I doubt they'll show their ugly faces to us again. Thank you, Artur. I'm happy you and Aanya have found each other." A thought popped into her mind. "How did you know where she'd be today?"

"I went to the barn, then to Aanya's apartment. When I saw the horrid door with its painted message, I knocked, but of course there was no answer. I knocked on a neighbor's door, learned about her poor mama's passing and that Aanya must have gone to visit a friend. I immediately thought of you and asked where I might find you. I moved quickly, but not quickly enough."

"Oh, Artur. You arrived just in time. That's all that counts. Again, thank you."

"And I thank you, Zofia, on behalf of Aanya and myself. It's most generous and gracious of you to welcome us into your home to live."

"Sincerely, I say this—my home is also yours and Aanya's."

The doctor stepped into the hallway. "Aanya is tired, physically stressed and emotionally strained, as can be expected, but she will be fine. She's young, healthy, and strong." He faced Artur. "She's asking for you." Without waiting for Artur's response, the doctor opened the bedroom door, patted Artur on his shoulder, and indicated with a firm jut of his chin that he expected Artur to go to her. Artur needed no prodding; he zipped inside the room.

"Zofia?"

Lena stood at the top of the stairs gripping the handrail. "Let's see the good doctor to the door. Afterwards, I'd like to talk with you."

While Eban and Inga listened to the radio, thankfully turned up to accommodate Inga's diminishing hearing range, Zofia and Lena sat at the kitchen table. Zofia had offered to make tea, but Lena declined, admitting that between the pressing conversation and the day's occurrences, not even tea would sit well in her stomach.

"We have lots to catch up on," Lena said as she slid her chair closer to Zofia's. She spread her hands out. "Our safety may be a good place to begin."

"Yes. Learning that those Nazi-lovers also targeted Aanya makes it unsafe for her to be alone. While the message they painted on the front of our house isn't good, I suspect it's more of a scare attempt than a direct threat and—"

"Sweetheart," Lena said, then abruptly paused. Never good at concealing her thoughts, her sad eyes radiated concern. "A threat is a threat. It's widely known that Aanya is Jewish and that the two of you are friends. They tried to hurt you today, too."

Zofia jumped to her feet. Usually patient, especially with her mother-in-law, she began to pace. "What? Are you telling me to distance myself from my dearest friend?"

Lena's face paled. "Of course not. I would no more utter such nonsense than believe you'd accept it." She gestured to the chair Zofia had vacated. "Come sit again with me."

Zofia dropped into her abandoned seat, plopped her elbows onto the table, and leaned into her palms to message the knots at her temples. "I'm sorry. I shouldn't be snappy with you. Of all people, you have my best interests at heart."

"I understand. We need to take action. Without our husbands here, I admit I'm nervous."

"I am too." Before Jabez left to supposedly return to his job more than three months ago, he'd told her that he was leaving behind his rifle, kept locked in his half of the bedroom armoire. Years ago, before Eban was born, having taught Zofia how to use the gun, he told her that if she ever needed to defend herself she shouldn't think twice about fishing out the weapon. Although she would defend her loved ones, she doubted she could actually kill another person. But, a Nazi? She moaned as she straightened and slid her hands from her face. This was technically, legally, her house and she didn't need anyone's permission to do what she wanted, but family was family and her love and consideration for Jabez's mother and aunt equaled the love she had for her own blood relations.

She squared her shoulders and looked at Lena. "Although you've just met Artur today and have yet to learn all about him, Artur and Aanya love each other. Baby or no baby, he's come back to Aanya because he's willing to sacrifice his freedom to be with her and watch out for her. So although those two aren't married—yet—I suspect they soon will be, and I've invited them to move in with us. I hope you don't mind terribly." She paused; her next words would require a delicate balance. "This house is mine. However, I say this to you because I love and respect you dearly. So, although I'm not asking for your permission regarding Aanya and Artur living here, I truly don't want to upset you or Inga."

"I appreciate your consideration of us, but honestly, it would be nice, and wise, to have a man around. Oh, I'd like to believe the three of us women are perfectly capable of handling an intrusion, but..." Lena smiled. "Well, I have trouble opening a canning jar. Artur, with his male muscle and strength, might be a nice addition. And of course, we already know and love Aanya."

Zofia again leaped to her feet and extended her arms to hug Lena, but the older woman lifted a hand to stop her. "I want to discuss a subject I believe won't be to your liking."

9

Aanya walked into the kitchen and stepped up to Zofia. She removed the pot from Zofia's hands, placed it on the table, and began to sign. "Can we talk?"

"What are you doing out of bed?"

Zofia scrutinized Aanya's red blouse and black skirt. Aanya glanced at her clothes for a rip or a stain that she might have missed.

"Your outfit is fine," Zofia signed. "I'm worried about your condition. You don't need to over-work yourself so soon after the…"

Aanya swallowed hard but kept her head up. "Miscarriage. There, I said—signed—that awful word. It's out between us, so let's not tiptoe around it. It's been a week. I'm physically fine, all things considered. A little weak from the shock of it all, to be truthful, which I always am around you."

Zofia's eyes widened. "I'm unclear what you're implying."

Aanya gestured for them to sit. The pot of golumpki, with its tangy aroma of beef and rice-stuffed cabbage rolls, teased her appetite despite having lost the desire for food the morning she saw the message on her apartment door, when she and Zofia were attacked, when she miscarried… when Artur came back into her life, for good. And she hadn't been eating much at all before that, either.

She held back a sigh. "First, let me again thank you for letting me and Artur live here with you."

"We're thrilled that you both accepted the invitation. Just sorry that Artur is stuck sleeping in the cellar."

"Don't worry. We think it's for the best, especially with curious eyes watching our every move." Aanya was confident that Zofia caught her reference to Lena, Inga, and Eban, in light of her current single status. "Besides, with you and I sharing your bedroom, it's like we're girls again and can chat as freely as we wish." Although that was sadly not the case. There were several things she kept close to her chest; there were several topics that she could tell Zofia kept mum about too. Certainly that was an oddity between the two of them. But now she needed to extract from Zofia the one elephant of a subject wedged between them, the one making it awfully uncomfortable these past few days.

"Out with it, then," Zofia signed. With those eagerly listening pairs of ears around the house, she'd used more signing lately rather than her usual combination of signing and speaking, except when she needed to translate Aanya's signed words to the others. That would soon change, though. Since Aanya moved in with Zofia and her family, she'd begun to teach them to sign. Artur was an especially apt pupil.

"Something's weighing you down—I can tell. Please, tell me about it." She paused for the briefest of seconds. Although Zofia had reassured her several times that she was fine with her and Artur moving in, she wanted to know whether her friend had any misgivings. "If it's Artur and me suddenly living with you—and endangering you—say the word and we'll leave immediately."

"Nie, and nie." Zofia's lips lifted in a little smile. "Aanya, I could never ask you to leave. Nor Artur. He's a good man. I love how he adores you and desires to make your world full of goodness."

"Yes," she signed, but couldn't bring herself to smile, not without learning what was on Zofia's mind. "I sense you're still holding back news from me."

"Lena had me face a truth I didn't want to. But I have to, especially after what happened to you and me a week ago."

Ah. Aanya suddenly understood. "Your promise to Jabez, right? To leave with Eban for America?"

"Yes. I couldn't dodge around matters when Lena pointed out that several months have passed since I agreed with her to wait one month before leaving for New York." Zofia began to twist a napkin. "It's mid-April and Jabez still hasn't come home, hasn't sent word that he's alive and well, nor a hint of his whereabouts. It's as if I'm an unmarried woman again, but with a son that I must be both mama and papa to."

"Yes, I understand. And Lena? What does she say?"

"Lena accepts that though she doesn't understand her son's plans for us to depart to a faraway country, we must trust him. That if he wanted us to leave, there must be a good reason and we must go. I braved telling her the truth—that I didn't know whether Jabez's disappearance meant he went mysteriously missing from his job in Germany or my suspicion that he's joined a Polish resistance group against the Nazis. Between you and me, this is a group that Jabez has barely informed me about, so I emphasized to Lena that though I suspect the latter to be the case, I may or may not be right. It's all uncertain, which is the frightening part."

"What did Lena reply?"

"With touches of both pride and alarm, she said she could see her son joining a resistance movement. But then she said words that shook me with cold reality—she said it doesn't matter. If Jabez ordered me and Eban to leave for New York, he knew what he was saying. It's time for us to leave." She winced.

"What is it?"

"Between signing and wringing this poor napkin, my hands are cramping."

Aanya seized Zofia's hand and began to massage her fingers, using her left hand. With her right hand she continued to sign. "Lena's right. You must leave."

Zofia blinked. She stammered a word or two Aanya couldn't make out. She asked Zofia to sign.

"Sorry. I can't leave you. Can't leave Brzeziny."

"You must, Zofia."

"But how can you say this? Don't you want me with you? I can't bear to leave you, my friend. You've been a sister to me in many more ways than if blood had made us so."

Aanya pointed at her own eyes and then her mouth, a long-established signal between the two of them that Zofia should look carefully into Aanya's eyes to see the genuineness of her feelings and at her mouth, to catch the sincerity of her words.

Zofia obliged.

"You must go. You have a young son to think of, first and foremost. And, your husband, who, knowing him, probably is involved with an undercover group, long ago arranged for you and Eban to depart, when and if he should go missing. Trust Jabez and honor his wishes. He knows particulars you don't. Details that are important, and may pose peril specifically to you and your son. The fact that you're overdue to leave increases your risk by the minute."

"Do you think those four miserable Nazi supporters who attacked us are behind what Jabez fears?"

"It's a possibility, but I don't think so." Aanya frowned. "I think they're more a sign of the growing problem of the Nazis and their hatred against Jews. I think it's an indication that trouble is heading to Brzeziny—if it's not already here. Hatred and prejudice have taken root and multiplied so rapidly that it's more a question of when rather than whether the scourge of suffering will occur."

"How can you expect me to accept that you, of all people, want me to leave? Shouldn't I remain by your side? That's what friends do."

"Zofia," Aanya said aloud. It was one of the few words she could easily and perfectly say, a word that came as naturally to her tongue as drinking water. When the furrows on Zofia's forehead eased, Aanya switched back to signing. "It's because I love you, my dearest friend, that I'm willing to bear the loss of you." She leaned closer. "I want you safe. If your husband is convinced that you must leave for another country on the other side of the ocean, then that's what I want for you and Eban."

Zofia's bottom lip quivered. "But—"

"No buts. I will be fine. Artur and I have talked, and he has come back to me for the same reason I want you to leave."

Zofia picked up the napkin she'd set down and patted her eyes, watery from fresh tears. "And that reason?"

"Because I love and cherish you. I want you to go so you will be safe just like Artur is willing to risk his freedom because of his love for me and his desire to protect me."

It was a toss-up whether Zofia was touched or shaken. "Zofia?" Aanya again said aloud.

"I'm sorry. I'm lost in my thoughts." She looked long into Aanya's eyes. "My dear

friend, how can I leave you here, especially now with antisemitism exploding and war looming?"

Aanya placed a hand on Zofia's arm, then lifted it to sign. "I will be fine here in Brzeziny. We'll be fine. Artur has asked me to marry him and I've accepted. He's already spoken to the rabbi regarding his conversion to Judaism. Dr. Paweł will perform the circumcision at the end of this week."

"Oh, my," Zofia mouthed. "That's fast."

"We're in love. We want to marry. And we want you to be at our wedding before you leave."

Zofia remained quiet so long that Aanya was certain she had nothing more to say. Then her stiff posture relaxed and she leaned back into her seat. "Do you have a date set?"

Aanya smiled. "We do. Now that Pesach—Passover—has ended, we will marry on the first Tuesday of May."

"On a Tuesday? That's an odd day, isn't it?"

"It's the third day of the week. The rabbi says that since God saw the third day of creation was good, it's an especially good day for a wedding." She felt her spirits lifting. "We want you to witness our wedding and are hoping that the approaching date will also enable you and Eban to get onto a ship."

"Have no fears, my friend." Zofia set her gaze firmly on Aanya and held it there, as if she had no intention of looking away. Slowly, she smiled a long, leisurely smile. "I won't go anywhere until I see you and Artur wed."

Aanya breathed easy.

10

Zofia stepped into the Brzeziny poczta the day after Aanya, with her blessing and a wedding date in place, told her it would be best for her to leave for America. She'd collect the mail and send a telegram to Jabez's cousin Isaac. It was time, as Aanya and Lena had pressed, for her and Eban to leave.

Maybe.

She dialed the combination of the brass postbox and withdrew the mail. No letters from Isaac. If she tiptoed out, neglecting to send a telegram to ask Isaac to proceed with final travel arrangements, she could forge ahead, putting aside world developments, and concentrate on daily life in Brzeziny. Her place was at home with her loved ones. Not only did she want to see Aanya and Artur marry, but she wanted to see them settle down, to see a smile return permanently to both of their beautiful faces.

"One moment, Pani Badower," called the postmaster. "There's a letter addressed to you that requires your signature."

She couldn't imagine what this was about or who would have sent it. Without delay she signed for the letter, strode to the corner of the lobby, and ripped open the envelope, which was posted from Florida. The first thing she noted was the date. The letter had taken more than a month to reach her.

. . .

March 15, 1939

Dear Zofia,

I'm writing to you while on a vacation that Louise and I are enjoying
    in sunny and delightfully warm Miami. I hope you are well. I'm concerned
    about you, especially after not hearing from you when expected. I also haven't
    heard from your charming aunt and miss her insightful words. Fortunately, I'm
    aware of her desires and will fulfill them.

Louise and I will arrive home next week. We do eagerly look forward to your
    planned visit—our home is your home. We know you will enjoy your time
    with us.

I'm looking forward to receiving a telegram from you. At this point,
    arrangements for your visit are complete and cannot be changed.

Yours truly,

Maxwell

. . .

Zofia pressed against the wall, crumbling the letter. When she realized what she'd done, she smoothed the thick off-white stationery, folded it into her coat pocket, and tried to breathe evenly. Maxwell was Isaac's code name. A bachelor, he was not married to a Louise. And devoted to his work—obsessively, according to Jabez—he wouldn't consider taking a vacation anywhere. He must have asked a colleague to send it from Florida for him. More importantly was Isaac's secret message to her: he hadn't heard from Jabez—whose identity he concealed as *your charming aunt*. The fact that Isaac had stated that he missed her aunt's *insightful words* spoke of likely misfortune to Jabez, a delay they must work around. The big news was that Isaac's travel plans for her were complete and he waited for her response. She could only pray that the ship's departure would come after her friends' wedding.

She waited in line at the postmaster's window. A painfully long amount of time later, she stepped up to the young man.

"Yes, Pani Badower? How may I help you?"

"I'd like to send a telegram, please."

Eban greeted Zofia upon her arrival home from the poczta. Prepared to break the news to him of their upcoming departure, his frown stopped her short. He sat on the top step of the porch, his chin resting on his hands propped on his knees. If it weren't for Lena standing on the other side of the screen door with her index finger pressed against her lips to signal for Zofia to keep her presence unknown to Eban, Zofia might have panicked.

"Hello, my favorite son."

Eban's brows lifted and his nose scrunched. "Mamusiu, how can I be your favorite son when I'm your only son?" He dropped his gaze to her middle. "Are you having a baby, like Aanya was supposed to?"

Oh, my. How could this conversation turn serious and sad within seconds?

"May I sit beside you, Eban?"

He patted the empty place beside him. She sat and reached for his hand. "Darling, no, I'm not expecting a baby. I was simply trying to make a joke."

"Oh." Although he didn't wiggle free of her hold, he stared straight ahead. "I did two bad things while you were away."

"Two? That's a surprise, but I'm glad you're truthful. Want to tell me the first one?"

"I went on a walk without asking permission from Babcia or Aunt Inga."

Numerous bad things—awful things—could have happened to her little darling, especially in light of the horrific attack on her and Aanya just a few weeks ago. Yet, she sensed a more pressing issue at hand, one that might require immediate action. "And the second bad thing, my son?"

"I found a girl."

She couldn't imagine what this was about. Or, for that matter, why he'd see it as bad.

"Eban, darling, what's this about a girl?"

He faced the door and pointed. When Zofia turned, she noticed that Lena had stepped away. "It's bad because I brought her home without asking permission. She's inside, with Aanya and Artur. She's littler than me, and like Aanya, can't hear."

Zofia stood. "Let's go indoors. I want to meet this girl, and then we'll talk more." She held back that she too had news to share.

"They're in the kitchen," Lena said by way of greeting. She had stood about three meters from the front door, but if Eban had noticed, his blank expression didn't show curiosity.

"Her name is Laja," Eban said as he led the way. "She's only four years old. I already told her that she can have my bed. I can sleep on the sofa."

Zofia gave a slight nod, though she was confused about Laja. Did the girl not have a home of her own?

In the kitchen, Artur, with his back against the wall, sat opposite Aanya at the table. A slip of a girl wearing a faded burgundy dress with a heavily soiled white collar sat between the two adults. She resembled a child of three, not four as Eban had said, though Zofia didn't doubt her son.

"Hello, Laja," Zofia said. She watched three pairs of eyes fix on her. "And welcome to our home."

Aanya signed Zofia's words to the girl. She also added a simple explanation of who Zofia was. The child looked up at Zofia and signed hello.

Zofia sat on the last available chair and suggested Eban sit and wait for her on his nearby bed. Lena was probably keeping Inga company in the parlor, their ears attentive.

"Is Laja hurt?" Zofia asked. "Abandoned... parentless? How well can she sign?"

"I'll go first, but Aanya will tell you the majority of the story." Artur faced Aanya to include her in the discussion. "Sorry to say it, but Eban sneaked out from our attention for a stroll, heading north away from town. He found Laja sitting in the middle of a field, crying."

"Eban asked her to come home to us," Aanya signed.

Zofia nodded. She was pleased Aanya said *come home to us*. Home. The words family, friends, and love were wonderful, but to Zofia, home was the most powerful word of all. And now, she and Eban had to leave this house, the only home they had ever known.

"For her age, she has a good signing vocabulary." Aanya, with sparkling eyes, beamed at the girl and looked back at Zofia, continuing to sign. "She's also able to read a few basic words from our lips."

"And she's upset, why?" Zofia asked aloud, and simultaneously signed.

"Remember how we drew diagrams of our families in the dirt, and where we lived, when we first met?" Aanya asked.

"Most definitely. It's one of my fondest memories."

A faint smile crossed Aanya's lips. She pointed at the pile of papers stacked on the foot of Eban's bed. "Through drawings, Laja shared with us that her mother died recently. As for her father, she says she doesn't have one. Nor any other family. She's wandered the countryside for days now." Tears trickled down Aanya's cheeks.

Artur reached for Aanya's hands. "Laja sat down in the field because she couldn't walk a step further, and didn't want to. She told us she wanted to sleep beside her mama in heaven." He blinked back tears; no shame reddened his face. "We fed her lunch." He smiled at the girl like a proud papa. "Laja ate every morsel of food on her plate like a good, hungry girl."

"One, evidently, who wants to continue living," Zofia reflected softly.

Both Aanya and Artur nodded.

Aanya wiped her eyes then resumed signing. "Right before Laja came to us, Artur and I were talking about wedding plans. With Laja coming into our lives, we also need to talk about adoption plans—if that is attainable. We'll look into matters right away."

"Already you know you want to take this major step?"

"Yes," both Aanya and Artur said together, aloud.

"Beautiful. I hope it works out smoothly and quickly." Zofia smiled at Laja, who had just yawned. "Your sleepyhead will be a true blessing. You'll make wonderful parents for this sweet child."

Artur jumped in his seat and waited for Aanya to look at him. "I just realized that Laja might be a wedding present from God."

Aanya wiped her eyes again and signed, "Now I'm crying happy tears."

Zofia told Eban to fetch his jacket, that they would take a walk and share a much needed talk. After her son darted from the kitchen, Zofia stood. "Pardon me," she signed and spoke. "I received news today that couldn't be put off a minute longer."

Aanya's shoulders sagged. "About your departure?"

Eban called from the other room that he was ready.

"Pardon me, once again. I must leave."

Halfway to the front door she realized she'd failed to utter those words of promise: *I'll be back.*

11

With poor Artur at home without one regret, despite holding a pack of ice to his privates as he recuperated from surgery, and Lena and Inga fussing over Laja, Zofia, Aanya, and Eban enjoyed a post-supper stroll. Eban kicked an old soccer ball down the road ahead of Zofia and Aanya. Ever since Ernest Wilimowski scored four goals for Poland against Brazil in the World Cup, her son had idolized the athlete. Like the other boys in his school, Eban wanted to be the next Ernest.

"This is the best I've seen you in a long time," Aanya signed. "You look splendid—are you that way inside as well? Be honest. Has that inner turmoil of yours calmed down?"

"Enough." Zofia grimaced. "That's not quite right. I don't want to leave. But I understand and have accepted that we must. I have you to thank, Aanya. If it weren't for your encouragement and support, I don't believe I could walk beside you today without retreating from you, diving into bed, and threatening to never step out from under the bedcovers again."

"Stinky sheets, stinky you."

Aware Aanya aimed for levity to keep her spirits up, Zofia tamped down a snippety
    reply. "Well, I mean it. Thanks."

"You're welcome, but that's bunk."

Zofia narrowed her eyes.

"No look like that," Aanya said aloud, testing a few words that Artur had committed to teaching her to say. She lifted her hand to sign more. "I don't think I said that correctly—I meant to say you shouldn't look at me that way. I've told you several times, but I'll say it again. Zofia, you're a strong woman. That's why Jabez respects and cherishes you—he married you and can't wait to be by your side again one day, and soon. Formidable. Yes, that's the word. You're his worthy partner. You inspire respect."

Zofia chuckled. "Or a headache. Truth be told, that's what Jabez would say about me. I mean, the headache part."

Aanya halted her steps. By this time, they had reached the cobblestone street leading into the town proper of Brzeziny. "Did I ever tell you what your husband said about you the last time I saw him?"

Out of the corner of her eye Zofia watched a robin fly from one tree to another. It was nice to have the howling winter winds fading from memory. "You've piqued my curiosity. Tell me."

"It was the second time he'd come home from Germany after beginning his new job."

If he'd indeed ever had a job in Germany. "The night when you returned a book you'd borrowed from him, right?"

"Yes. And Lena tempted me with cheesecake, and Jabez shared a joke... then Inga wanted my opinion about a tear in one of her blouses."

"And Eban asked you to read him a bedtime story." Zofia smiled as if her whole family stood before her, making her world cozy and comfortable like an extra blanket beside the coal stove. "The time raced by, and Jabez volunteered to walk you home. My husband, the gentleman. Or was it because he wanted to sneak a cigarette?"

"Well, he is a fine gentleman."

Aanya's omission of the cigarette part left Zofia longing to wrap her arms around Jabez and inhale the spearmint leaves he'd chew to disguise the tobacco he favored. Eager to learn more, Zofia waited for Aanya to continue.

"We walked back to my apartment. Once we arrived, Jabez asked for paper scraps and a pen to ensure we could communicate. He told me that he was thrilled you and I are friends, that a woman needs another woman in her life to talk to, to confide in, to share dreams... and secrets."

"Secrets?"

Aanya winked, then resumed signing. "Don't worry. Jabez didn't pull confidences from my sealed lips."

"That's good."

"He also told me that he was the luckiest man in Poland—and then he corrected himself and said, no, in all of the world—because he's so fortunate to have you as his wife."

"Truly?" she asked aloud, the whisper barely reaching her ears. She hoped Aanya had understood her pronunciation.

"Yes. He said he cannot imagine what his life would have been like if you weren't part of it. Zofia, he truly loves you."

As if a dense fog shrouded the rest of the world, the only person Zofia could see at that moment was her husband.

One winter morning before Jabez had started working in Germany, they enjoyed an unusual time alone at home. The others were occupied elsewhere, a rarity.

The sun had awoken them, but neither of them had to rush off. He'd swung an arm around her and pulled her closer to him, the bedsheets wrinkling between them. She asked him if he wanted his eggs scrambled and if he preferred leftover potatoes from last night's meal or if he'd enjoy a cheese biscuit she could bake in a jiffy. Instead of replying he helped her out of her nightclothes, covered her body with his—his fire instantly igniting hers—held her arms over her head and made her forget about everything but the two of them.

Afterwards, when they lay hip to hip, hand in hand, she turned toward him with a smile. "What would either one of us do, if we didn't have the other to help us navigate through this thing called life?" she murmured into his ear.

Jabez kissed her, one second gently, the next with devouring passion. Zofia knew that was the best answer he could offer for the unknown she'd posed.

Zofia understood that her place was at Jabez's side. He truly was her partner in life. This husband of hers, a watch aficionado, had taught her that in the delicate dance of life, it was essential to have good timing.

She looked at Aanya. "I've gone back and forth on this decision of leaving for America. Though Jabez's cousin has looked into securing passage on a ship for Eban and me, sailing from Germany on the 13th of May, I've decided to wait. Just a little longer. The time to leave will announce itself."

Aanya stepped back as if Zofia had grown an extra head. "And how exactly will you know it's the perfect time?"

"It will be obvious," she said, without hesitation.

12

Two nights later, unable to sleep from frustration, Zofia raised her hand to punch her pillow. She stopped short when her foggy brain remembered Aanya sleeping beside her. Instead, she slipped gingerly from the bed. She'd go downstairs to the parlor, to her favorite chair, and read. No. She wouldn't be able to concentrate. She'd only irritate herself if she tried. Whereas taking a walk might prove to be a better path toward relaxation, as of yesterday she had decided walking alone would not be in her best interest. With guilt and fear whirling in her mind, however, she'd be lucky if she remained in place for a handful of minutes.

When she was halfway down the stairs, the light coming from the lamp beside the sofa stopped her short. Artur's head slumped to the right; a single snore escaped from his mouth. Laja slept, stretched across her new papa's lap. Thanks to the swelling numbers of orphans since the Great War, complicated by the Great Depression, adoptions were expedited. In some situations, that meant children were adopted into homes that were a bad match. In others, like Laja's case, with no one contesting, the authorities gave Aanya and Artur provisional permission with the assurance of full legal adoption as soon as they were married. Zofia was happy for the three of them.

Since she didn't want to disturb Artur or the child, she stood on the stairway thinking about where to go and what to do. Not wanting to wake Aanya by going back to bed, she glanced toward the front door. Then she remembered Eban had fallen asleep tucked in bed beside his babcia. The kitchen was gloriously hers to enjoy a solitary cup of tea. She could sit alone and ponder her immediate circumstances without the scrutiny of others for a change.

She shifted. The oak step squeaked under her feet.

Artur stirred and looked about. "Zofia? Come keep me company."

Zofia tightened the sash on her robe and accepted his invitation. "I didn't mean to wake you," she whispered as she sat to Artur's right, forgetting momentarily that the child was deaf. She smiled at Laja. The darling girl, still asleep, had changed her position and rested her head against his arm. Warmth filled her heart. That was the funny thing about love: rather than staying stagnant and limiting its capacity, the human heart knew no bounds. "She's flourishing with your and Aanya's love."

"Aanya and I are also flourishing with Laja's love." Artur stroked the child's cheek. "I'm concerned about her health. The doctor says she's fine, but I look at her slight body, and all I can think about are the hardships she must have encountered. I worry how that might affect her overall health."

"I understand your concerns. But I wouldn't worry. Aanya—with her medical knowledge and loving heart—is the perfect new mama for Laja. You watch. In this loving family and home, she'll bloom and thrive."

"Children and I... how can I say this? We haven't exactly had opportunities to keep each other company." Artur squeezed his eyes shut. His forehead was deeply furrowed for a 33-year-old man, only one year older than both Aanya and her.

She suspected his anguish wasn't over his lack of knowledge about babies, or four-year-olds like Laja. "Most new parents learn the practicalities of childcare after their little ones are born, not before. Believe me, based upon my own experiences, that learning process is ongoing."

"Lena and Inga have said as much."

She patted his arm. "We're friends. You can talk to me, if you like."

He glanced at Laja. "Curse this world we live in."

"It's not an easy time, in Polska or anywhere."

He again looked at the sleeping child. "Why people turn against each other and cause unnecessary chaos, I'll never understand. It takes more effort to hate than it does to love." Artur turned from the girl and looked at Zofia. "Aanya and I have no choice, but to trust fate to work things out for us."

His word, *trust,* wrapped around Zofia as if a life preserver had been flung to her—and she caught it. And that was why, after telling Aanya that she was going to delay her travel plans, she again changed her mind about leaving Brzeziny. She hadn't mentioned this to anyone, yet, especially Aanya, who carried enough weight on her shoulders.

She reached for Artur's hand. "I tend to believe that leaving matters to fate is to surrender taking charge of one's life, though I do understand that often what happens in life is out of our control." She sighed, looking at Laja. "Sorry I sound contradictory. You and Aanya have chosen marriage—swimming against the tide of history and your different faith backgrounds and nationalities, and especially during escalating tensions across the border. You and Aanya have chosen to adopt this sweet child beside you—against the odds of no guarantees of a perfect future, or even a safe one."

"So what do you suggest?"

"Go after what is most important for you, and don't let fear stop you. Do everything in your power to make Aanya's, your daughter's, and your life brighter."

"I'm sorry I wasn't there for Aanya the past few months. At times I think I acted like a coward, and other times like a man whose only instinct was to survive, like a wild animal."

"I assure you, Artur, neither Aanya nor I—nor the others who live in this house—see you as a coward." She shook her head. "These are difficult times. You did what you had to do—you did what a good-hearted and compassionate person in your situation should have done. Aanya loves you; she holds no resentment against you. This she's told me."

"I've seen the hand of evil at work, both before I came back and sadly, several times since. The truth about current world developments is becoming less accessible—it's a camouflage, I tell you. There's a reason—one I fear is beyond terrible—why day-to-day events aren't transmitted to us common people. Aanya is Jewish, not that she is an observant one, as she admits. But that doesn't matter to Hitler, or the ones who follow and obey him as if he was a god. In their eyes, born a Jew, always a Jew, like the rabbi has taught me in studying *halakhah*, Jewish religious law. They see Jews and other non-Aryans as a race of subhumans who will infect Aryans with poison." Artur smoothed back Laja's hair from her forehead. "My Laja, who will have a Jewish mother and father, will be a Jew in Nazi eyes, if she isn't one already by birth. For that reason alone, she isn't safe here a day more in Brzeziny, or anywhere else in Poland."

"Artur, let me tell you something about my precious friend. The two of us have seldom been at odds with one another. I do recollect, though, one time as girls we sparred. Don't ask over what because that part is foggy—probably it was a silly matter. She called me Pani Stubborn." Zofia grinned. "Do you know what I called her in return?"

Artur shook his head.

"Pani Determined. Artur, your fiancée is an amazing, strong woman. Because she's deaf, she has to be in order to accomplish much that even a hearing person struggles to achieve, though I believe she's naturally tenacious anyway. She doesn't have patience for the frivolous, nor tolerance for the ugly. She's most determined to plow ahead. Once she has a notion in her mind there's no stopping her." Zofia reached for his hand and gave it a gentle squeeze. "She and I disagree somewhat regarding this trouble looming over Europe and how Poland may be impacted—though Polska has certainly made it through years and years of other troubles. But that's not my point." She dropped her gaze to her lap. "Things have slipped out of my control: Jabez wants me to leave for America and Aanya agrees that it's the right thing to do. Relocating to America may turn my world upside down while yours, here, may continue on blissfully happy. It's hard to know. Decisions don't exactly come with guarantees."

They both settled back against the sofa and watched the sleeping

Laja as if she was a bright candle. A few minutes ticked by in silence. Zofia glanced at Artur, convinced she'd see him asleep again. Instead, he was staring at her.

"Yes?"

"So, Pani Stubborn, what is it that has you so rattled?"

This man understood her incredibly well considering he barely knew her.

"I have several options to choose from. None are easy."

"No guarantees, then?" he asked.

There was that word again—*guarantee*. Was it back to haunt her, or to motivate her to face unknown challenges in the hope of a kinder world?

Laja turned onto her back. The child didn't crack open an eye to check her surroundings, nor cry in her sleep from a nightmare, nor wake to run from Artur. She rested soundly in her new home, trusting she belonged right where she slept. Zofia needed to do the same thing: make a good home for her family, whichever town or country life directed her to live in, with the kind of confidence shown by this tiny girl.

An explosive crack snapped through the air. They sprang to their feet, the sleeping child in Artur's arms. One by one, lights were turned on throughout the first floor of the house. Lena and Inga ran into the parlor. When Inga took Laja from Artur, he and Zofia bolted outdoors, not knowing if it was their lives that depended on it, or another's.

13

A glimmering light coaxed Aanya from the dreamworld where she, Artur, and Laja were walking up a steep path. To where, she hadn't a clue. Honeysuckle bushes adorned both sides of the path; their heady, sweet aroma tempted Aanya to hold still and inhale deeply, but aware that Artur and Laja wouldn't keep climbing without her, she led her family forward. At the end of the path a light flickered several times, as if winking a message. *Come on. Come on. Open your eyes.*

She obeyed the dream-light and when she did she found herself in the darkened bedroom that she shared with Zofia. A distinct flutter of light drew her gaze toward the window. She scrambled from the bed. The second quilt she'd added last night puddled around her feet. She righted herself in time to prevent a fall and bounded to the window overlooking the barn, a structure left over from Zofia's father's farming days.

Before the barn door, Artur held a kerosene light with one hand and with the other, he rotated Zofia so she faced the house. He pointed to her and then gestured toward the house, but Zofia shook her head. They both entered the old building.

Aanya had seen enough. She ran from the room, but stopped at the base of the stairs when she saw Inga with her arms wrapped around her waist.

"Stay here," Inga said, accustomed to pronouncing her words with precision and at a pace to accommodate Aanya.

Aanya swore to herself. Though she'd practiced saying Laja's name the past few days, the word continued to trick her mouth. But Inga only had a few words in her signing vocabulary, so Aanya tried saying the child's name.

Inga's forehead creased. "Laja? She and Lena are hiding in Lena's bedroom."

Hiding? Aanya stepped to the front door and reached for the doorknob.

Inga placed an unusually firm hand on her shoulder. "Wait here. We heard three gunshots," Inga said. "From the barn, we think."

Aanya wiggled free of Inga's grip, but the older woman reached for her again. "Stay here, where it's safer."

Artur was at the barn. Zofia too. She'd apologize later for not heeding Inga's plea. She sidestepped the older woman and ran outside. The fears and worries she'd pushed aside the past few weeks surfaced. Were the night visitors the same Nazi-loving jerks who had thrown her to the ground, ramming their fists at her as if she was a punching bag while their friends piled onto Zofia to rape her? Had they returned full of zeal to execute each of them in the name of the Führer? Would she lose Artur again? Or Laja, the innocent child that had just come into her life?

Or did another horror face them? Had Zofia's failure to heed Jabez's warning and leave the country months ago now resulted in peril, as Jabez had foreseen? What would happen to her newfound home and family?

Aanya flung open the barn door, blinking to correct the strange, almost incomprehensible sight: Artur, his foot planted on a shotgun lying on the wide-planked floor, stared at Eban, draped over his mother's knee. A deep red flush covered the boy's face. Zofia struck Eban's bottom with a single spank. He rolled off his mother's lap onto the floor and began to cry. Zofia, eyes wide, palmed the sides of her face and stepped back.

Without another thought, Aanya rushed to Eban's side and picked him up. He wrapped his legs tightly around her middle.

"Aanya," Artur said, stepping before her, face-to-face, to communicate. "Let me hold Eban—he's more than you should handle after..."

She shook her head. Medically, she'd recovered well enough from the miscarriage. Emotionally was a different story but it didn't matter right then. Like Zofia, she also stepped back, with Eban still in her embrace.

Zofia appeared before her; their gazes locked. "Give me my son. I'll deal with his bad behavior."

Aanya slipped her right hand from around Eban to sign. "Zofia, you're upset. Go inside the house and calm down. Then we'll talk."

"He's my son." Zofia stepped forward and reached for Eban.

"You're too troubled, too upset."

"What do you know about children?"

Heat flushed Aanya's face. She rubbed her cheek as if Zofia had slapped her. Then she moved her fingers in a flurry. "What I know is I love you and Eban."

"Well, you missed what happened before you came in here," Zofia said out loud. "My son found his grandfather's shotgun and fired practice shots so he could learn to protect me. Behavior that could have killed him. Could have killed both Artur and me if we'd made one false move."

Artur patted Zofia's arm. "No one was hurt. Aanya's right—you must calm down."

Zofia glared at Artur, but he didn't react visibly to her temper.

"Yes," Aanya signed. "A child with a gun could lead to unintentional death, so I can appreciate your concern and understand your worry. But no one was hurt, and anger won't resolve a thing. Please, let's go inside and discuss what happened."

"This isn't your concern," Zofia said.

Aanya handed Eban to Artur; the boy quieted. She took a large step toward Zofia and pulled her into a hug, relieved Zofia didn't struggle. After a few seconds slipped by, she leaned back so Zofia could see her sign. "Of course, this is my concern. Why? Because when you hurt, I do too. Never, ever, forget that." She jutted her chin at Artur then at the door to indicate that he should take Eban inside. "Let's go inside and talk." Holding onto Zofia's hand, she led her friend into the house, grateful she didn't have to pull her along.

With Laja and Eban having drifted off to sleep in Lena's bed, the adults gathered in the parlor. Glad that Artur sat beside her on the sofa, Aanya squeezed his hand. They faced Zofia who sat opposite them in a chair brought from the dining room table. Lena and Inga sat quietly in corner armchairs, observing. Like members of a jury?

"Please, you go first," Aanya signed. "Tell me your concerns."

"I'm not sure where to begin. "Actually, I do know. Eban has seen and heard things over the past few weeks." Zofia both spoke and signed. "Things too confusing and disturbing for a child to understand. Like the antisemitic shouts of the man in the thatch-roofed house that time we were walking to your apartment. Like the attack by those Nazi-worshippers."

"You're right," Lena interjected. "That's a lot for a child to comprehend. I'm an adult, and I don't understand it either."

"With his father gone," Zofia continued, "Eban took it upon himself to protect me. He remembered his Dziadek Oskar kept a shotgun in the barn and decided he needed to practice and become good enough to shoot the bad Nazis if they show up here." She bit her lower lip. "What upsets me is that I should be the one protecting him. I'm his mother. He should not have to worry about strangers, about Hitler's footmen breaking into his home and doing the unthinkable."

"You're right," Aanya signed. Then, she prepared herself to sign again, words in gesture that dated back to their childhood days that only she and Zofia understood, a language that neither had forgotten. And God forgive her, but she was going to risk coming off more forcefully than her friend had ever seen her. "There is something else I can tell you're holding back, and it's major and upsetting. I want to know what it is and I want to know right now."

Zofia bent over and sank her head into her hands. A few minutes passed. Aanya moved beside her friend and put an arm around her.

Zofia glanced up. "Where is everyone?"

"They thought it was best if you and I had the room to ourselves to continue this conversation."

"I didn't realize they'd left," Zofia signed in the current method.

That came as no surprise to Aanya—Zofia often became unaware of her surroundings when she meditated deeply on a particular subject. "They didn't want to bother you." Aanya, eyes trained on her friend, leaned forward and waited.

Zofia rubbed her temples. "Make no mistake about it; I'm greatly troubled that Eban found a gun and took it upon himself to practice in the name of defending me. He could have killed himself, or any one of us that stumbled into the barn. But I spanked him. I can't remember the last time I did that—if ever."

"You had a terrible fright, seeing your child in an alarming situation. Without knowing what might happen next, you certainly didn't have time to teach a little boy how dangerous it is to play with a gun and to explain your reaction."

"What happens if he hates me for the rest of his life? If he loses his respect for me or stays angry for a long time? What happens if..."

In an effort to help Zofia stop her runaway thoughts, Aanya placed a hand on her arm. "Your son loves you," she signed. "You and he will talk. Eban might not understand each point you make, and might challenge what you say, but what he'll hear is your love for him and how that love exerted itself because you were afraid of him getting hurt."

"Do you think Eban will forgive me, then?"

"Of course he will. He loves you and knows that you love him. That's why he's such a caring, confident boy." Aanya tried to recall what Zofia had mentioned about her parents through the years. "Confess, Zofia. Your mama must have disciplined you with a spanking—that's the way it is for us."

"Yes. I'd like to pride myself in thinking I was a lovely and well-behaved girl all the time, but the truth is, Mama occasionally took a wooden spoon to me. As I grew older, all she had to do was remind me that actions had consequences and I became the best child in Brzeziny, probably in all of Poland."

"And did you hate your mother for that reason?"

"Oh, no. I never hated her, nor Papa, despite his strict hand. It's not as if they were cruel to me. I always loved them both." She sniffled. "I still miss them terribly."

"So, see? You and Eban will resolve this matter without complications."

Zofia smoothed her wrinkle-free skirt.

"Out with it," Aanya signed, her hand motioning in such a rapid flutter that it caught Zofia's attention. "You can't hide a thing from me."

"Never could."

"Yes."

"Sorry," Zofia said, then resumed signing. "I mean it—I'm sorry. Sorry I just walked away. Sorry I snapped at you in the barn. I've never expressed anger toward you and have no right to because you are a true gem of a person and I can't afford to lose you in my life. I said a few awful things that I shouldn't have. And I'm sorry."

Aanya's lips quirked. "Well, no worries. I never heard you."

Zofia's laughed at Aanya's play on words. Before she could utter or sign another word, Aanya beat her to it.

"There's more. Tell me."

Tears cascaded down Zofia's cheeks and she began to rock forward and back. "I have no idea where my husband is, or even if he's alive. I've been both mama and papa to my son, and I'm not very good at it. Worse—this whole might-have-been-disaster with Eban is telling me, loudly and clearly, that for the sake of my son's welfare and future, I have to do what Jabez told me to. Eban and I really must leave Brzeziny. With no other choices, I… we're—"

"Out with it. What are you trying to tell me?"

Zofia withdrew a handkerchief from a skirt pocket, dabbed at her eyes, and wiped her nose. "I've changed my mind again, and this time, there's no changing plans. Eban and I leave Brzeziny four days after your wedding, to sail out of Hamburg for America."

"Good," Aanya said aloud as well as signed, holding back a

pained sigh. That date—when she would wed Artur—would mark a change full of joy and yet tinged deeply with sorrow. She would gain a life partner in the most beautiful man she could imagine. She would lose—at least in terms of proximity—her dearest and only true friend, one who was more sister than not.

Aanya laid hold of her fortitude, choosing courage and an optimistic spirit. Zofia needed her; Aanya needed her friend as well. With the threat of danger to Zofia and Eban, and war hovering over both their heads, this was no time to fall apart.

But it was so hard to do. Yet she had to try.

"Thank goodness you can attend the wedding," Aanya signed. "It wouldn't be the same without you and Eban there with us on our special day." This wasn't the time to talk wedding plans, plus she wanted to avoid stoking Zofia's anxiety; she had a hunch she'd just failed. "Leaving for a different country, one that's far away with a whole different way of life than you're accustomed to, would be jarring for anyone. I understand why you're nervous."

Aanya winced mentally at the words she'd chosen to use. She peered into Zofia's eyes and waited for her response.

Zofia paled. "Jarring? Nervous? Leaving Polska, leaving you, is a calamity in the making."

"Oh, Zofia. You'll get through this, you'll see. You're a strong woman."

This time, it was Zofia who grasped Aanya's non-signing hand. "You have me wrong," she said aloud. "I may be strong but I'm not particularly brave."

"At one time or another, we each face challenges that make us want to hide like a frightened child and wish trouble away. As adults, we cannot do this, and that's what makes you strong."

"But brave?" Zofia shook her head. "I don't think so."

"You have a son to take care of. Are you telling me you won't take him by the hand and board that boat and sail to America to make the most of life?"

"I didn't say that."

"You absolutely did not. And that shows your courage. You don't have to don armor, mount a horse and charge into the thick of war with a battle cry roaring from your lips just to prove you're brave."

Zofia's mouth toggled between a grin and a frown. The grin won.

"That's better." Aanya stood and extended a hand to Zofia to help her up. "Let's both go and check on the children. That is, if you want my company."

"I definitely want your company. Always."

14

This special day in May had finally arrived. Zofia looked forward to seeing Aanya and Artur marry, vowing lifelong love and companionship to each other. She wanted to lift a glass of vodka in a toast, showering the newlyweds with adoring words she'd set aside within her heart to encourage them to step forward as Pan and Pani Lang and face the world together. It was also Artur's 34th birthday and Zofia wanted to say that he couldn't be given a better gift than her precious friend Aanya.

Zofia sighed dreamily as she revisited Artur's words to Aanya that he had said during dinner last night.

This is the day, when I wed you, Aanya, that I'll become the man I want to be.

In the kitchen where Zofia had helped Lena and Inga with last-minute wedding feast preparations, she peered out the window, taking in the golden late morning sunlight that reminded her of that perfect spring day when she had first met Aanya. The only trouble they were aware of back then was that others didn't understand why they would want to be friends since they were of two different faiths, and more remarkably, Zofia could hear and Aanya could not. They couldn't have cared less. They saw in each other what others failed to see: they were both little girls, living in Brzeziny, who liked flowers and sunlight and cookies, and together, as friends, had nothing to be afraid of.

But, as adults? She stifled a sob. Turning away from the window, she felt a touch on her arm and when she looked up, Inga smiled.

"You're far away in your dreams, my dear. I hope they're good ones. It's too wondrous a day for gloom."

Zofia nodded, though she couldn't fully agree, not when she was about to separate herself from Aanya, from Brzeziny... from Polska. In four incredibly short days, she and Eban would step onto a train that would take them to Hamburg, Germany, where they would board a ship to sail across the Atlantic Ocean. She'd never seen Germany before, let alone the ocean. Quite content during her 32 years with the large-enough perimters of life in her native town, she hadn't yearned for elsewhere.

"Sweetheart," Lena said, laying a hand on her shoulder.

Zofia was flanked by her mother-in-law and Jabez's aunt, two women she was grateful for. Two women she'd also soon depart from. Too aware of what would happen in less than a handful of days, it was comparable to having received, in advance, the exact minute of her death, and all that was left to do was plod through the mornings, afternoons, and nights until that day when the train would whisk her son and her away. To her own mind her thoughts sounded melodramatic, yet the emotions swirling inside her were real and painful.

"Look out there," Lena said, and pointed to the open window with the gentle warm breeze flowing indoors, chasing away the earlier morning's dampness. "That's a lovely canopy the men set up, isn't it?"

Bless Lena. And Inga. They loved her as a daughter by blood and not marriage, and meant well by trying to occupy her thoughts with the festivities, directing her attention away from leaving.

"Yes," she murmured, appreciating the beauty of the outdoor wedding ceremony site, happy, at least, that the lovebirds had chosen to accept her invitation and marry on her property. The chuppah, adorned with white peonies, pink heather, and greenery, beckoned to the bride and bridegroom. Already guests mingled and cast anticipatory glances to see if the bride or groom was in sight. Eban, dressed in his Sunday best, chased after the rabbi's youngest son and Laja. One of Artur's unmarried friends, whom Artur had met while studying with the rabbi and subsequently converting to Judaism, eyed the long empty table where the food would be placed after the ceremony. Was he hungry? Daydreaming about how he wished it was himself about to marry, instead of Artur? And where was Jabez on this lovely day? He loved weddings, loved celebrations. Adoring Aanya as he did, he'd have enjoyed this wedding. Was he hurt? Off completing a secret mission in the name of making Poland a safer country?

Was he alive? The only thing Zofia knew was that he was not with her.

Lena shoved a kitchen towel at her. "You're weeping, and the wedding has yet to begin."

Zofia managed a tiny smile. "I can't help being joyful for my darling friend."

"With joy like that," Inga teased. "You'll scare the poor girl away."

Zofia dabbed at her eyes with the blue and yellow towel. "Sorry. I have a few hundred or so things on my mind."

"Yes," Lena said, tenderly. "We're aware of this."

How she would miss the way Lena and Inga spoke, including the other as if they were one rather than two different women.

Inga took the towel from Zofia. "Lena and I will finish up the last details of the wedding cake. Go check on the bride."

"Good idea." Zofia breathed deeply and strode into the other room, determined to offer her friend support. The past few days Aanya and she had enjoyed strolls, sat together on the porch, and visited the river spot where they'd first met. Zofia wanted to do these things with her friend to provide an opportunity for Aanya to ask any questions she wanted to concerning marriage, or just for general talk. In all honesty, it was Aanya who provided Zofia the needed one-on-one time to share her own worries. Today marked a difference, one that Zofia had come to accept: Even if life in Europe were simply divine, with no Hitler, Nazis, or threat of war, Aanya was getting married. Her friend would now center her whole life around the man she'd chosen to love for the rest of her days. It was time for Zofia to step aside.

In the parlor, a swirl of ivory chiffon caught Zofia's attention and snatched her breath away. "Aanya," she gasped. She circled Aanya twice before coming to a halt before her friend. "You are beauty itself."

Aanya smiled and verbally thanked her. She then patted her hair before reverting to signing. "Is my hair a fright?"

"You're a picture-perfect bride, Aanya." Zofia wiped her eyes. "I haven't stopped crying with joy for you since I awoke this morning."

"Stop your tears or I'll follow and scare my groom away."

Zofia shook her head. "You, wearing your beloved mamusiu's wedding gown, would scare not a single soul." She fingered the delicately beaded lace bodice. "You're an angel and I'm beyond happy I'm with you today." She choked on her last word and glanced away. Aanya could not have heard the thick way her last word had come out, but she was a very astute observer. She would have seen the mix of happiness and sadness on her friend's face, and feel it as well. This was Aanya's special day, and Zofia refused to ruin it.

A hand rested on her shoulder. She turned to see Aanya with brows lifted in concern. "Are you well?" Aanya said aloud, another phrase Artur had helped her learn to pronounce. She had especially wanted to learn those words because the doctor who was her mentor and tutor planned to step down from his practice, referring the majority of his patients to her care. These men, women, and children, who were once wary of her now trusted her simply because Dr. Paweł did, and were no longer concerned about her deafness nor her lack of a degree. Their fretting each morning whether this would be the day the Germans attacked had changed everything.

"I'm as well as can be. Don't mind me."

Aanya turned back to signing. "Weddings can be quite an emotional ride. And this one?" She glanced down at the stunning gown. "I'm afraid we aren't following enough traditions on this special day."

"You do have a rabbi willing to marry you two. That alone speaks volumes."

"Yes. I'm thankful for that. My parents—may they rest in peace—wouldn't want it otherwise. But I wanted you by my side under the chuppah, because as far as I'm concerned, you're truly my sister."

"And you're my sister, as well. But the rabbi says only Jewish people should be under the canopy." Zofia squeezed Aanya's hand. "We know what we mean to each other, and that is all that matters."

"We certainly do. As for the ceremony, Artur and I had to jiggle things around on his side as well. One of Artur's new friends is filling in for his father. Of course, Artur would have preferred his father, but that wasn't a possibility, because of both his faith and his politics."

A wave of grief for Aanya rolled within Zofia's chest. The day Artur ran off from the Buchenwald camp and deserted the Nazi party, he'd forfeited his chances of ever seeing his parents again. Not only were they fervent Hitler supporters, which meant they would issue a distinct dismissal to their son—if not worse—were Artur to be caught in their presence; it would also endanger his whole family. Furthermore, Artur's conversion to Judaism and marriage to a Jewish woman also meant he could not so much as step into Germany safely.

Zofia ran the back of her fingers tenderly across Aanya's cheek. "The important thing is that you and Artur are marrying today, and I'm able to witness this blessing with my own eyes."

Eban rushed through the front door, open to let the day's warmth indoors. "Mama, the rabbi sent me to tell you it's time for the wedding to happen."

"And a grand wedding it shall be." Zofia beamed at the bride. "Are you ready, darling?"

"Yes." Aanya had spoken aloud. It was the clearest and strongest *yes* Zofia had ever heard her say.

Artur had insisted on the tradition of veiling his bride by his own hand, declaring that no matter how beautiful Aanya was, what mattered most to him was her soul and character. This exchange between the two of them took place in the house while the guests sat before the chuppah. The men, who included a handful of Artur's new male Jewish friends, Dr. Paweł, the rabbi's two sons, and Eban, sat on the left side of the lawn. To the right, the women's side, sat Zofia with Laja on her lap, Lena and Inga, and the rabbi's wife and daughter. A small group, Zofia thought, but certainly they were there because they loved and supported the bride and groom. That was what counted.

From under the chuppah, its four corners representing the future home of the united bride and groom, the rabbi motioned for the guests to stand. They turned toward Artur, escorted by his friend, as he walked down the aisle. Aanya followed, holding the arm of the wife of one of Artur's friends. The smiles on the faces of the bride and groom made them shine. Once they stood before the rabbi, the guests sat.

Aanya's escort helped her to circle Artur seven times, the tradition stemming from building a wall to protect from evil spirits and temptations, as well as creating a new family circle. When they exchanged rings, slipping the plain silver bands on each other's fingers, Zofia cried, but she didn't wipe her eyes. What was the use when they were already brimming with the next wave of tears?

The rabbi recited the seven blessings over a cup of wine. Although Zofia didn't understand Hebrew, Artur had explained what she could expect. These blessings focused on joy, celebration, the power of love, and peace and companionship, what every couple should want in their lifetime together. The rabbi then placed a cloth bag containing a glass on the floor before Artur and invited the groom to smash it with his right foot.

"Mazel tov," shouted Zofia, on her feet with Laja. The others also stood and called out their congratulations. She cried through joyous laughter, and watched Eban, on the groom's side, cover his ears from the zealous cheering. Laja held Zofia's hands and jumped repeatedly, beaming for her new mama. Zofia was relieved when Lena ordered her to remain outdoors while she, Inga, and the bachelor friend of Artur's, enlisted earlier by Lena, brought out the festive dishes of chicken, pickled herring, sauerkraut, sweet noodle pudding, lots of sweets, and of course, the wedding cake. Before they feasted on the food, they'd enjoy the anticipated vodka toast.

Zofia was about to step beside Aanya and Artur to congratulate and hug them when Jabez's friend Herszel stepped into her view on the roadside. She'd come to think of him as the bearer of bad news, poor man. What startling revelations did he bring this time, on an otherwise splendid day? His sad, droopy eyes chased the joy from her heart and replaced it with bone-deep chills.

She bent down to Laja's eye-level to sign. "Go to Mama and give her a big hug." The curly-haired girl, whose fine locks were growing shiny and thick now that her belly was full of decent food, trotted off to Aanya. Zofia rushed to Herszel.

The man stood with his hat in his hand. He looked a decade older than his 50 years. "I have news concerning Jabez."

Zofia tried to smile, but couldn't. She simply nodded. Silently praying the news would be good, she said, "Tell me, Herszel."

"Have you made the arrangements that Jabez asked of you?"

"Yes. Within days, Eban and I will be leaving." She pulled at the collar of her dress, the material suddenly feeling tight around her throat and cutting off her air. She glanced over her shoulder, and when she caught sight of the newlyweds, she ordered herself to remain level-headed. "Herszel, please. I'm about to leave Brzeziny. I need to know whether my family and friends here are in danger. You must tell me the truth."

Herszel put on his hat and it landed lopsided, matching the way the world had come to tilt these past few years. "Truth?" He set his gaze hard on her. "We'd appreciate the truth too, good or bad. Unfortunately, it's not as easy as we would like."

She curbed her impulse to lash out at him. Would the man ever stop talking in riddles?

"As I said months ago, Jabez is missing," Herszel said. "We now believe the Nazis have him, though we don't know for certain—"

"Then he's alive?" she blurted, unable to hold back. But she remembered the time Herszel had pounded on her door with news of Jabez's disappearance, only for Jabez to track her down on the street later to say that he'd purposely misled Herszel. Perhaps her husband's friend was mistaken now, too. Then again, perhaps this time he was sadly correct. "That is what you told me last time. I thought you said there was news."

Herszel held up a hand to stop her. "We have our doubts that the Germans would cross the border to trouble themselves with retaliation to his family and friends at this point, but..." He seized her forearms, yet instead of holding her tenderly like a father, he gripped firmly, like a figure designated to give a severe warning. "... there's no logic to Hitler's armed forces. They are willing to die for the twisted cause of spreading the Aryan ideology. These days, what Hitler wants is what Hitler gets, and no one around him dares to challenge him."

Zofia tried to wiggle free of Herszel's grasp, but he tightened his hold. The faces of Aanya and Artur, of Laja, and of Lena and Inga flashed before her. Zofia straightened, squared her shoulders, and steadied her voice. Unwilling to concede a drop more authority to her husband's messenger, she demanded that he release his hold on her. When he complied, she stepped back. "Why then, should my son and I leave? Shouldn't we wait to learn more about what has happened to Jabez?"

"Jabez loves you and your son. Believe me, if he ordered you to leave, there would be a horrible price—on both his head and yours— to pay if you don't carry through with your plans to leave. You've waited too long as it is."

God forgive her. Her thoughts and worries had focused on the difficulties for her and Eban if they left Brzeziny. But, a price on Jabez's head? Would he be tortured, wishing he was dead instead of suffering the gruesome infliction of pain? If killed, would he be tossed into an unmarked grave? She would never know what had become of him.

"We have passage on the St. Louis departing on the 13th of May. Eban and I will be on the ship. Do not worry." She watched Herszel turn to leave and step away. She called out to him.

But her voice trembled, and he must not have heard her, for he walked away.

After he hurried off, Zofia faced the house where a bride and groom and wedding guests were about to celebrate life and love. She hadn't an idea about how to tell her dearest friend and her new husband what she had just learned. Then again, maybe she wouldn't have to explain. They knew what was happening across the border, knew why she and her son needed to leave, and understood the dangers lurking. And yet, they embraced the future. She wouldn't dare destroy their hopes and dreams. No one deserved that.

15

Zofia smiled as Eban and Laja placed two glass ornaments, one gold, the other red, onto the Christmas tree—a mangy little fir tree that would have to serve the purpose. It stood before the double parlor window, an invitation to celebrate and have a joyous spirit announced by its needles. Prior to decorating the tree, the children had helped Babcia set the holiday plates on the table, careful not to disturb the silver menorah with its gold candles in the center of the table. Out of respect to Jewish law they would not light the candles on the candelabrum until a half hour after they completed their meal, but that was about the extent of celebrating both holidays in a traditional way. After all, it was May. With Eban and Zofia leaving tomorrow to begin their journey to America, this was the closest they would come to observing Christmas and Hanukkah with their loved ones, at least here in Brzeziny. Inga had been the one to suggest this special, if unconventional, occasion and they seized upon the idea gratefully.

A floorboard creaking from behind her caused Zofia to spin around.

"It's Christmastime," Lena trilled. "I see the first star."

Eban, kneeling to hang an ornament on a lower branch, whipped his attention away from the tree decorating. "Babcia, it's daytime. Stars aren't out yet."

"Hmm," Lena said with a smile playing on her lips. "Since this is a pretend day, I guess you two don't want real presents."

Eban sprang to his feet. Bouncing on his toes, he signed to Laja their babcia's announcement of the first star, the Polska tradition of beginning Christmas, and that she had gifts for them.

"I like Hanukkah and Christmas," Laja signed, using the new words Aanya had taught her. "And presents." She beamed, and her smile was almost as large as her tiny self.

"Of course, you do, sweetheart." Zofia tousled the girl's hair. "In this household," she signed and gestured around the room, "we celebrate both Jewish and Christian holidays. Each is important and special, just like you." She bopped the tip of Laja's nose, then Eban's, delighting in their chorus of giggles.

With the two children on their feet peering expectantly at Lena, the woman swung her arms forward from behind her where she'd concealed two gifts.

"Oh, dear Lena," Zofia said. "You didn't have to."

"I certainly did. Actually, this is from all of us." She called Inga out from the kitchen, who appeared with Aanya, both of them wearing aprons. They'd spent the afternoon cooking and were rosy-cheeked from the heat. Zofia did her share of summoning by going to the stairs that led to the cellar and shouting Artur's name. They were all soon seated beside the tree waiting for Eban and Laja to open their gifts.

From the corner of her eye, she caught Aanya enveloping Artur's hand and smiling. So in love they were. Zofia sighed. If she must leave, it was a tiny bit easier knowing that her dear friend was married to a good, loving man and together, they were already building a family with the adoption of Laja. That Lena and Inga were part of their new family as well served to sweeten their lives.

Laja opened her gift first. Eban didn't object. He had a big-brotherly affection for Laja, and tolerance for her more childish ways. The string that fastened the wrapping paper of ice-skating couples was no match for the girl's agile little fingers. Within seconds she lifted the lid off a shoebox and withdrew a baby doll swaddled in a yellow blanket, its bright blue eyes opening and closing as she moved it. Laja hugged the doll to her chest and beamed pure joy. She stood, clutching the dolly, and starting with Eban, circled around the room and planted a kiss on everyone's cheek.

Next was Eban's turn. Zofia held her breath, hoping his gift was practical and compact enough to bring with them to New York.

"Wow," Eban said as he held up a book for all to see; its slim size made for easy packing into their baggage.

"Read the title, sweetheart," Inga said.

With his index finger trailing each word, Eban read aloud the title printed in Polish: "A Picture Book of Countries." He read more, then glanced at Zofia. "Mother, is English and American the same thing?"

"Yes," she replied. Her simple answer would suffice for now.

"Mamusiu?"

Eban's usage of the Polish word for mommy set Zofia's heart racing. Less and less he'd used that word, substituting the more universal *Mother*. She'd thought the change was a sign of maturing, but now she believed it was his way of accepting that they were relocating to America.

"Yes, Eban?"

"Will Papa be waiting for us in New York? Will he read me this story?"

She wanted to say yes, and yes. That his father would welcome his fast-growing son, that he'd teach him how to say a whole slew of English words, that the three of them would live happily ever after, just like in Eban's storybooks, because that was what happened to boys and girls: they grew into healthy adults, learned how to live peacefully with their neighbors and how to help one another, and grew old happily, welcoming hordes of grandchildren born to carry on when it came their turn to meet their maker.

How could she respond? Of all days, this one before they departed, the one when they celebrated the holidays one last time with family, she didn't want her son to break down in sobs.

A gentle hand came to her shoulder. There was no need to turn around to see; it would be Anya. Always Aanya. Tears stung Zofia's eyes; she willed herself to remain strong for Eban's sake. "Your Papa hopes to be there for you, darling. He can't wait to see you."

The hand on her shoulder began to pat it. Unable to move forward toward Eban or sideways to Aanya, or for that matter, backwards to the others without risking buckets of tears, Zofia remained in place.

Eban broke the thick silence in the room. "Do you want to see Papa too?"

"Oh, yes," she said, without hesitation. "Most definitely."

Artur stepped forward. "Children," he said aloud as well as signed. "Let's go for a walk and leave the wise women in this room to finish fussing with our dinners. I'm hungry."

"Me too," Eban said.

Laja pointed at her papa then at Eban. She began to sign. Zofia chuckled and translated.

"Laja says you two are always hungry."

A chorus of laughs filled the room. The children and Artur stepped outdoors; Inga took Aanya's dishcloth from her and accompanied Lena back to the kitchen.

Zofia faced Aanya. Her chest tightened. *Nie, sadness. Go away. No tears today, not on this special day of two holidays, not on this last full day with my loved ones.*

Aanya, in a maroon holiday dress that hugged her waist, with long waves of her strawberry hair cascading down in front of her shoulders, signed for them to sit on the sofa. She led the way and Zofia followed. With each step, Zofia slipped back into memories of her past.

There stood Aanya. They ran, hand in hand, through spring fields splashed with the oranges and reds of poppies and the purple of lavender, followed later in the summer with the gold of sunflowers. Beside the river they chatted; Zofia, wanting to get to know the girl and her dancing hand, quickly learned her friend's special language, which was eventually replaced by the formal Polish sign language when Aanya went to the school in Warsaw. As they grew older and were permitted by their mothers to attend market day on Thursdays unescorted, they made purchases and learned from others the art of bargaining. Then the special days came for Zofia with first her wedding to Jabez, followed by the birth of Eban, and Aanya's promotions at work, first in the tailoring shops then at the medical clinic when she apprenticed with her doctor friend. They'd wiped away each other's tears as well, with the passing of Zofia's parents and the more recent deaths of Jabez's father and Aanya's papa and mama. That was what made friendship special, nearly sacred, and worth nurturing—understanding the other and accompanying them through good times and bad. Well, as much as a crazy on-the-verge-of-war world permitted two friends to, never mind that they'd soon separate.

"You look lovely," Zofia murmured, the words barely audible. She lifted her hand to sign. "I imagine Artur can't stop telling you that."

"Yes, my husband, the romantic. He loves to heap adoration on me until I blush like a schoolgirl. That's fine, though. I don't think I'll ever tire of his praises." A smile tugged at Aanya's lips. "You also look beautiful in your Christmas skirt. I've always liked that shade of blue on you."

"This? It's as old as I am." Zofia patted her sides as she laughed. "Winter blue isn't too bad for a lovely, sunny spring day. I guess it's never untimely to celebrate Christmas or Hanukkah."

"Jabez would..." Aanya's signing trailed off. She slipped her low-heeled shoes off and rubbed her feet—likely, Zofia suspected, to change the subject—or to distract from her expressive face? "I hope in America women have a better selection of shoes to choose from than here in Polska."

Zofia nodded, yet tears again filled her eyes. Not trusting her voice, she began to sign. "Don't mind me, I'm a mess."

"I can imagine."

Zofia's gaze left her friend's face and traveled around the room. Blue glass stars twinkling on the mantel— family heirlooms placed every Christmas Eve by dear Mamusiu and now by Zofia—and by someone else next Christmastime. Her tatusiu's writing desk where often her father's pipe had sat in a ceramic ashtray, the tobacco aroma that reminded her of sweet cherries, leafy plants, and damp paper, still tickling her nose these years later, whether real or in her imagination. A hanging wooden cabinet, painted pale green, with glass doors—locked to prevent little ones' hands from roaming—showcasing Jabez's collection of pocket watches. A table cluttered with potted plants, the majority having seen better days. It was a simple room, a cozy one. It was home.

Her attention strayed to the small hallway lined with the oil portrait of her grandparents, both born in 1858, and the photograph of Zofia holding newborn Eban. At the end of this corridor was her parents' old bedroom where Zofia was born, the one that Lena now used.

The kitchen also held fond memories: Jabez sneaking up from behind her and nuzzling her neck before carrying her upstairs for heated lovemaking, which they both couldn't get enough of. Zofia and Lena baking cookies for the men of the household, untroubled by the fact that their hours of labor would crumble away in seconds as every last morsel was devoured. Every nook of this house held lovely memories. Despite some sad times, and a few plain awful ones, there were mostly good times to remember, and she was grateful to have lived in this house since childhood. She knew others who didn't have fond memories of home life, whether due to moving from house to house or country to country, or because of a tragic upbringing. Yet she had no other choice but to face tomorrow. She would leave this place behind, and the people and town that meant the world to her. Home.

Zofia glanced at Aanya, seated to her left. She lifted her hand to sign, pausing as her thoughts drifted to living in New York—without Aanya. Would she forget how to communicate this way? She made herself focus on the present. "This isn't easy." She sniffled. "This is my only home, the only one I want."

"I understand what you're feeling. I was troubled by gloomy thoughts when I left my parents' apartment and moved in with you, despite the golden ray of you also living under this roof." Aanya gave Zofia's hand a squeeze. "Our childhood days are behind us. At least we have kind memories, and are making room for more with our husbands and children, building new lives as grown women. Our lives aren't over." A little grin lifted Aanya's lips. "Considering what's happening in the world, not too far from us—and never did I think I'd say this—but I'm looking forward to growing old."

"And living happily ever after, like in Eban and Laja's storybooks."

"Right you are, my friend."

"The thing is, my friend, you are remaining in Brzeziny while I move to a whole different country far away."

"Zofia, it's 1939, not the time of our grandparents. We'll see each other again. I promise you we will. One day, Artur and I may be your new neighbors." Aanya offered her handkerchief. "Dry your eyes and be optimistic. We'll get through this mess. Hitler and his Nazis, the foolishness with prejudices against Jews, gypsies, and the deaf, blind, and mentally disturbed—you'll see. It will end, and soon. It must. We'll be witnesses, you in New York and me here, to the end of this craziness by New Year's Eve. It certainly can't get worse."

"I'm going to miss you, my friend." Zofia patted her chest. "Already my heart's aching. Already—"

The front door slammed open against the wall. "Mother!" Eban shouted. "Come quick."

Zofia sprang toward the door; Aanya followed. "What's wrong?" Zofia said. "Where's Laja? Artur?"

"Laja's right behind me—Artur made sure of that."

She didn't like the sound of that. She poked her head out the door just as Laja stumbled inside, apparently shoved by Artur. At least, Zofia assumed it was Artur. Laja fell but didn't cry. Alarms sounded in Zofia's mind, but there was no time for questions.

Artur entered, an obvious stagger in his gait. He stared at the wall. "Lock the damn door!"

"What happened?" Aanya signed as Zofia fastened the lock.

Zofia shrugged. She couldn't guess.

Aanya reached out to her husband, but he sidestepped away. She touched his back. He pushed away her hand and began to lumber down the hallway. "Artur," Aanya screeched, her agony unhidden.

Artur stopped. Slowly, he turned, showing his bloodied face and swollen right eye with black and red bruises.

Zofia watched her friend follow after her husband. While there were still some puzzling pieces she couldn't figure out about Jabez and his demand for Eban and her to leave, one thing had now been made clearer: Her friends were in as much danger as she was. Lena and Inga, too. Yet she was powerless to help them.

16

The house, full of scurrying occupants and emotions ranging from excitement to melancholy, seemed to smother Aanya. In ironic need of privacy, considering the imminent farewell thickening the air between Zofia and her, Aanya rushed to the far side of the barn. Yesterday, in anticipation of this moment, she'd placed a metal bucket there to sit on, to breathe and let her swirling thoughts calm before facing what she had never imagined would occur.

Oh, she admitted to herself, for the past four months it had become apparent that Zofia and Eban would leave Poland for the United States and one day become American citizens; this wasn't news. She'd also admit that she had counted on a miracle to change that plan and stop the developments convulsing the world—people hating each other and violent antisemitism as the calling card of a mad leader. She'd hoped against hope that Zofia's long-missing husband would arrive home, sweep his wife into his arms, and murmur into her ear that it was no longer necessary to leave.

And Artur? As his newly wedded wife, she wanted to stand by his side always, through the good and the bad, hopefully more of the former than latter. Yet, since he'd been attacked yesterday, her beloved husband had not wanted to tell her about it. From the little she and Zofia deduced from talking with Eban, while Artur and the children were enjoying their walk a scary-looking man had called Artur's name and lured him into a patch of field down the road. Artur had ordered Eban to take Laja's hand and hurry home, and although Eban obeyed, he'd walked with the girl slowly toward the house, keeping within listening range. Eban heard odd shouts. There was that *Jude* word again. Then, *Jude-loving husband. Worthless. You're a fake Jew. Leave town.* Eventually, Artur had caught up with Eban and Laja.

The one thing Aanya got Artur to tell her was that he'd been forcefully encouraged to leave Brzeziny: "According to the latest batch of soulless, demented beasts," Artur told her, "I'm to take with me on my exodus from town 'my deaf Jewish wife and deaf, moronic pretend daughter.'" After this admission, Artur had peered into Aanya's eyes, kissed her sweetly on the lips, and winced in pain from his wounds. "Aanya, I refuse to leave," he signed. "We are staying here in Brzeziny, the one place more home to me than any other town. No one will make us do otherwise."

"Is that a promise?" she asked.

"My solemn vow."

Tucked behind the barn now, Aanya squeezed her eyes shut and willed away tears. She had to be strong for her husband and her little one. They were her future, giving her reason to live.

But saying a final goodbye to Zofia... Inseparable friends for 27 years, they'd journeyed through both bright and stormy days. Together they had never feared what tomorrow would bring. Until recently. And now the moment had arrived from which there was no going back.

Nie. Nie. This can't be happening.

A breeze stroked the back of her neck. She turned and saw Artur. Ah, it was his touch that caressed her skin, and not a gentle wind.

She couldn't sign. Couldn't speak. Just stared at his bruised face.

"It's time." He offered a hand. She took it, aware her wobbly legs couldn't support her without him to lean on.

As they rounded the corner, Lena, wearing a somber gray dress, and Inga, in a navy blue one, stepped outdoors from the house. Dark colors. Funeral colors. In May.

Lena hurried to Aanya. "We will make it fine, you as well as us." She then grasped her by the arm that until seconds ago Artur had held.

Where had Artur gone? Instead of seeing her husband, she saw Inga approaching; her relaxed eyes, brows, and mouth showed her care and affection.

Aanya nodded at Lena, not even trying to produce a smile she couldn't muster anyway. Inga, who had fought exhaustion the past two days, flanked her other side, offering her supportive presence rather than words.

And there she was. Zofia. She stepped out of the house, carrying a tote bag and a leather suitcase. Eban followed, a cloth sack in his grip. The boy, who had turned seven in January and resembled Jabez more each day, wore a comfortable light blue shorts set, a gray and white-checkered cap, and a look of relief. His attitude had fluctuated between acceptance of this move that meant leaving his home, and wanting to stay put with his family and Aanya. But acceptance had won out since Artur's beating the day before. Remembering this, Aanya was swept back to yesterday. While the child couldn't easily understand the buildup of prejudice and its repercussions, he'd finally realized that if his father wanted them to leave his boyhood hometown, it was for their safety, but not before shedding tears on his last evening at home.

"Mamusiu," Eban had cried, tears flowing down rosy cheeks, his gaze locked on Aanya, not his mother. "If bad men attacked Artur because of Aanya, but Aanya didn't do anything wrong, then what will happen to her and Artur and Laja when we leave?" He'd wiped his hand across his eyes, refusing to be hushed, to hear the false comforting words of *things will get better* that little boys were often told. "Bad words were painted on our house and on Aanya's apartment door. Nasty words were shouted at us about filthy Jews. And Artur was beaten. When will it stop?"

When Zofia failed to come up with an explanation, resorting to blanket reassurances that things would be fine, Eban had turned around, stared at the wall, and fallen asleep. That was when Aanya grasped Zofia's hand and led her from the room. They doubted sleep would come to either of them, but turned in for the evening. Tomorrow would arrive soon enough.

Now, in front of the house a horse stirred and Lena started, pulling Aanya's attention back to the present. Jabez's friend, the same one who had given a ride to Jabez when he first left for the job in Germany—if indeed that was where he'd headed—helped Zofia with her bags. While others were swapping horses and carts for shiny automobiles, Aanya suspected this was the same tired old horse and tattered cart that had carried Jabez to the train station. On the verge of bawling like a baby, fearing she'd alarm Eban and Laja, as well as the adults, Aanya pivoted to face a pine tree. A pair of arms wrapped around her legs.

Eban. His mouth wiggled; a sweet smile took turns with a sad frown. "Aanya," he signed. "You are special to me."

Breathe in. Be still, my heart. Exhale. Focus on the child, not myself.

"And you're forever a big part of me." She patted her chest. "You're forever in my thoughts and heart. Don't ever forget that."

"Aanya, I can't forget you because I love you."

She squatted and wrapped her arms around this beloved boy whom she had loved since the second she learned Zofia was expecting. Then, she leaned back to speak the most powerful words she'd ever learned to say aloud: "I love you." After another exchange of hugs, she signed, "Will you watch out for your mama?"

"Yes." Eban bounced on his toes. "Aanya?"

She looked into his beautiful eyes. He may have resembled his papa, but he had his mama's lovely sky-blue eyes, the color forever inked in her mind.

"Are you afraid, or sad, or both?"

This question from a child? She felt humbled. She couldn't tell him the truth: that yes, she was indeed afraid and sad. She was the adult, and she had to help him leave on a positive note.

A sharp pain streaked through her chest; her sinuses stung with the holding back of a cry. "Here's the truth—I will miss you and your mama."

"And here's my truth—I'll love Mama so much that it will be like you're with us." Eban stroked her arm. "Will you take my hand and walk me to the cart? We must go."

What other choice did she have? About to grasp Eban's hand for the last time, she realized Artur had stepped to her side. He slipped his arm around her waist.

She dropped her gaze. Artur lifted her chin.

"We will make life good for us," he signed. Was he also beside himself emotionally, unable to speak?

Without a glance, she knew Zofia stood beside her. When wasn't she at her side? *When she leaves for a faraway country... and I'll never see her again.* When she turned to face her friend, Artur let go and walked Eban to the cart. Zofia tugged her into a fierce hug, then leaned back enough to clasp the sides of Aanya's face and began to speak.

"This is not a final goodbye, my darling Aanya. God will reunite us."

Aanya gave a little nod, wanting badly to believe it.

Zofia took a handkerchief to Aanya's eyes and wiped her tears. Aanya tugged the white cloth from Zofia's hand and blotted her friend's tears.

"We will always be the best of friends. Sisters. Yes?"

"Yes," Aanya managed to say, her breath a flutter like a butterfly.

"One day, you and I will find homes near each other and will visit each other often, if not every day. Do not worry. Our friendship shall not shatter by the hands of hatred like the glass at *Kristallnacht*."

Aanya nodded and signed, "Agreed. We shall not shatter. We'll hold strong and find each other again." She glanced toward the cart and saw Artur helping Eban settle onto the seat. Aanya looked away and again focused on Zofia. An odd grin tugged at Aanya's mouth and a tingling came to her fingers. "I can't promise the no worry part, but I have confidence that one way or another, we'll see each other again."

"Have you memorized the address I gave you of the house Jabez's cousin has purchased for us in Brooklyn? The one where I want to one day soon open my front door and find you and Artur there?"

Aanya swallowed past the lump in her throat. "Yes. On Kent Street."

Artur approached. "It's time," he said aloud. The words... *for them to leave* were unspoken, but Aanya had no trouble hearing them. Certain words always reached the ears even of the deaf.

Zofia rushed to the cart. Aanya knew her friend. Knew that a torrent of tears flowed from Zofia's eyes, down her cheeks, as Aanya's own tears coursed down hers. Knew Zofia, by the time she reached Eban, would will the tears away, shielding her son from them as she herself had to do for her daughter.

Artur wrapped an arm around her. When she looked into her soulmate's face, she saw for the first time tears streaming down his cheeks. She didn't wipe them away, but instead, watched as the horse-drawn cart clopped down the drive to take Zofia and Eban toward the beginning of their new lives.

When the horse and cart turned right, away from Brzeziny, a tingling sensation prickled the back of Aanya's neck. She turned around.

And locked eyes with Jabez.

Evidently, he hadn't been captured by the Nazis as feared. He leaned against a tree by the barn. Thinner, ragged in appearance, he'd watched his wife and child leave. About to alert Artur, Aanya stopped herself when Jabez stepped backwards, pivoted, and disappeared into the woods. Had she seen a mirage, or a man who had come out of hiding from the enemy just long enough to see for himself that his family had obeyed his wishes to depart for America and safety, and to capture a glimpse of his loved ones and pray it wouldn't be the last time?

17

Zofia and Eban boarded the Nord Express in Łódź. Compared to Jabez's cousin's description of his train ride when he'd left for New York 20 years ago, the year after the Great War ended, this train was modern in its clean and simple shape and its emphasis on straight lines. While they waited at the railway station, she'd heard other passengers speak about the train's impressive speed. Oohs and ahs crisscrossed through the air over the train's luxurious sleeper and dining cars, though with a modest budget, Eban and she would be riding coach.

With each clack of the wheels as the train headed west toward the border, Zofia was torn between gazing one last time on her homeland slipping from view and focusing straight ahead as they approached Germany. She wished there was a way to detour around the Nazi state, but a feasible alternative didn't exist, especially if they were to make it to the port in Hamburg on time to board the ship. So she chose a silent goodbye for her beloved Polska—the country, the life, that for her would be no more.

With a lift of her hand, she spread her fingers across the glass window. Partially open, it permitted the afternoon air, now moist compared to the cool morning, to flow in. The air circulation also helped to blow the stench from the unwashed bodies of the other travelers out through the opposite windows. She imagined she wasn't such a pretty sight herself, and was sure she didn't smell sweet from the sweat of anxiety and heartbreak. Thankfully, the strangers in the car managed to tolerate each other.

Farewell, my country and beloved Brzeziny. May God bless you with peace and keep you far from hardship.

A hand tugged on her left sleeve. She looked at Eban, who yawned without covering his mouth. He'd been so brave and sweet upon bidding goodbye to his grandmother, Inga, Laja, Artur, with a hearfelt hug for each one... and saying a special farewell to Aanya. She was proud of him.

"Mother, what's hardship?"

Oh, dear. Had she voiced those words and not simply thought them? Apparently so. She leaned over and whispered her appreciation of his usage of the English word *mother* rather than mamusiu, as they'd agreed upon. Little by little, if they learned and inserted English words into their conversation, soon enough they'd start speaking their new language better, she hoped. If they had to leave Poland, then it would be best to leave their old ways behind as well, including their native language. That would be hard, she thought, not because learning a new language was so difficult, but because her language was a part of who she was. But as this train voyage—followed by sailing across the ocean—symbolized, they'd entered into a passage of change and were about to begin a new way of living. She didn't have to view this necessarily as traumatic; rather, as a foruntate opportunity. How blessed they were to have this chance of a new beginning.

"Are you enjoying the train ride, my handsome boy?"

"Yes." He rewarded her with a smile. "Why were you talking to the window?"

"I just whispered goodbye to Poland." She kissed his cheek and hoped he'd forget his first question. "We've entered Germany." A drastic truth, she realized, as they slowed and passed a railroad station. Above its brick two-door entrance hung two large black, white, and red swastika banners framing an equally large poster of an unsmiling Hitler. The frippery adorned the front of the building like a tarnished medal.

"Are we almost to the ship? To... I forget where, Mother."

"Hamburg, darling. This *Eisenbahn* is big, full of numerous stops. We still have a distance to travel before we arrive at the dock where they keep the ships. We'll transfer trains in Berlin, about another hour. The new train will take us to Hamburg."

"And hardships? What are they?"

She shuddered and wrapped her sweater tighter around her middle, hoping Eban didn't notice. *May you never know the reality of hardship, my son.* "It means when things don't go right. Like when you use the last of the coal for the winter, and yet there is one more snowstorm and you must suffer the cold temperature. Like when I forget I'm making soup and overcook the meal and it tastes awful, but we have to eat it because there is nothing else available. Like—"

"Like Papa using his belt when I didn't put away my toys when he told me to?"

"Yes." That situation was more a punishment for bad behavior than an unfortunate hardship, but she could tell his young mind understood the gist of her examples. More troubling was his negative memory of Jabez. Then again, he was a child and certainly wouldn't understand or count as hardships the wickedness spreading across Europe, faltering economies, out-of-control antisemitism and other hatred between people fueled by fanatics.

Eban wedged his fingers into her balled-up fist. "It's good you asked God to bless Brzeziny and our country."

She strived to convey the truth, though she chose her words carefully to soften their impact. "Darling, Brzeziny will always be dear to us. It's a big part of who we are, isn't it?"

His brows pinched together. "Yes, Mother. We're going to America, but we'll always be Brzeziners, right? Is that what you mean?"

"You, my thoughtful, smart son, are correct." She batted her lashes against her watery eyes. Would the threat of tears ever cease to be so near? "We can be both Brzeziners and Americans. That way, we'll never forget our past while we enjoy the present and look forward to the future." That was a lot for a child to understand. But with his sharp insight, she had a hunch he'd grasp the idea. "How does that sound?"

"I like that. It's less scary that way."

She squeezed his hand. "What a brilliant way to think. Yes, it is less scary. I've begun to think this way too."

A boy who never acted as if compliments went to his head, Eban glanced at the window.

"Do you want me to change seats with you?" she asked.

He shook his head. "Nie. Can you hold me on your lap?"

Oh, her heart. Her growing child wanted to cuddle; she wanted to hold him and never let go—an unrealistic prospect to be sure. She was about to respond when the door between their car and the next slid open with a metallic clank.

"*Fahrkarte.*"

Zofia met the eyes of an unsmiling conductor who appeared to have seen beyond his share of people leaving the old country. He worked his way from seat to seat. Another man wearing a grayish-green tunic with matching trousers, a dark brown collar and cuffs stood by the door like a sentry. On his sleeve was a white eagle carrying a white swastika against a black background, his uniform a bleak reminder of the danger that lurked everywhere in this country they were traveling through. How long had this Nazi occupied the car? Were there others on board? Could one not walk a step in Germany without visual reminders of the dictator that controlled life here?

The conductor reached their row of seats and stretched his hand toward her. She handed the conductor the two tickets. He studied her and Eban long and hard. Was he wary of false identity documents? In spite of having followed Cousin Isaac's instructions to obtain new identities to conceal the Badower family name, and to have them forged by one of the best men he knew, she was thankful the conductor only asked for tickets and not her papers. She pasted a look of happiness and anticipationon on her face. *Relax*, she ordered herself. She also reminded herself the less said the better; volunteering unrequested information courted danger.

The train began to slow. What now? They were supposed to travel non-stop to Berlin.

A hiss and a squeal sounded. They were jerked forward, then back. Zofia put out an arm to prevent Eban from falling. Grunts and grumbles could be heard throughout the car. When she peered toward the front of the car she saw the Nazi was gone and breathed easier. The conductor barked a command in German as he pointed out the window toward the station. Using both hands, he swooshed the air to indicate they should rise from their seats and head toward the exit. Isaac hadn't mentioned a border stop. Had he lived in America so long he'd forgotten about such security checks, or had she been naive to think such an inconvenience wouldn't occur in Nazi Germany? She frowned. Despite her resolution of moments ago not to surrender her past as she embraced the present, uncertainty about the future was a reality. Yet, she was the one Eban looked to for guidance. She needed to be strong and brave. This was no time to ponder the possibilities of what might go wrong or what potential dangers they faced. She dug deep for the grit to move forward without showing fear, and pushed away the temptation to turn around and return to Brzeziny.

She reached for the purse she'd stored under her seat and was instructing Eban to gather his bag when the conductor shook his head. How she wished he spoke Polish. The little German she knew wasn't enough. Then again, who was to say that, because the man only spoke German to them, he couldn't speak—or at least understand—other languages? God help them. They needed to be careful in what they chose to say.

Eban tugged at her skirt and pointed at the other passengers scrambling off the train. Ah, they'd left their belongings behind. That's what the conductor was trying to convey. She withdrew their documentation from the purse and slipped the papers into her skirt pocket.

As Eban made his way down the aisle, past the watchful conductor and toward the front of the car to the exit, this precarious moment on the train when plans could backfire and they could be ordered back to Brzeziny due to uncovered truths made Zofia sway.

Their little town—a *shtetl* predominantly populated by Jews and a few Catholics—was no longer home. She had let go. In a few days, they'd board a ship and sail toward their new home.

The train shook once more and she stumbled. A firm grip to her upper left arm helped her to straighten. She planted her feet more firmly and smiled at the conductor, a man from whom she wouldn't have expected a helping hand. He waved her down the aisle.

"Thank you," she replied in Polish.

He nodded, apparently understanding.

Perfectly aware she wasn't in Berlin, but wanting to appear unruffled, she kept her smile in place and hoped her pronunciation of the German words wasn't laughable. "Schlesischer Bahnhof?"

"Nein." He lifted his chin toward the door. This time, she followed his orders.

"Eban?" She assumed he would be waiting for her by the door, but he was nowhere to be seen. Her breath tightened. She rushed off the trian and was about to shout his name when she saw him running toward her.

"Mother!"

"Are you all right?"

"Yes, but look." Eban pointed to a man and woman. Near the couple stood two men dressed in similar uniforms to the one worn by the man accompanying the conductor in their car, except these Nazi guards had black-trimmed collars and cuffs. She quickly told Eban to lower his hand.

"They're from Lublin," Eban continued. "We understood each other and talked."

"Did you talk to them away from the men in uniforms?" she asked in the most casual tone she could summon. When he nodded she asked if the people from Lublin had ideas as to what was happening.

"It's a surprise border check. They said it could happen again."

Zofia readied their identity documents and asked Eban to stay with her. Then they waited. And waited. By the time the uniformed men approached the neighboring people, Zofia's blouse was soaked with perspiration and her nerves jangled.

A cry erupted, followed by shouts. The crowd watched as four guards escorted a couple and four young children to the wooden station. Once inside, words in various languages funneled their way between the onlookers on the platform.

"False papers."

"Lies."

"They're being sent back."

"Juden."

The conductor from their train car blew a whistle and signaled for them to board.

Zofia stuffed the travel papers away. "Looks like they're satisfied with enough commotion for one afternoon." She told Eban to hold onto her skirt as they merged into the boarding crowd. "Let's get back onto the train, shall we?"

Several stops and documentation inspections later, the train hissed and slowed to a halt at Schlesischer Bahnhof in Berlin, their connection to the harbor in Hamburg. All but two passengers stood and began to gather their belongings.

"Mother," Eban signed. "Where are the big boats?"

She glanced about to see if anyone observed them before speaking in a low voice. "You must speak to me using words. Forget you sign. Understand?"

Eban rolled his lip in a pout. He nodded then shook his head. "Sorry, Mamusiu... I mean, Mother. I don't understand. I just wanted to talk to you, in our special way."

She understood that he'd wanted to talk privately with her so that no one else would understand them unless, of course, they knew how to communicate the way of the deaf. How could she begin to explain that they were traveling through a country infested with Nazis on the lookout for anyone who might weaken the Aryan race with differences of faith, cultural beliefs, and by what they declared to be physical *defects* like deafness? The last thing Zofia needed was to bring the wrong sort of attention their direction by her innocent son's signing. If the slightest suspicions were raised, they might be imprisoned and would never see Jabez, let alone freedom. There was the whole other concern about teaching a young child to be wary of others, to mistrust. She didn't want to raise her son to harbor suspicion and doubt, especially when they'd be the new ones in a country whose citizens might belittle them because they were viewed as different or as a threat to perceived exclusive privileges, just like when outsiders to Brzeziny first came to town. To say that the current times were strange and difficult was to understate a dismal situation.

There was no one for her to rely on. No Jabez. No Aanya. She had to do this herself.

"Eban, darling. You're behaving like a big boy. I'm proud of you."

He opened his mouth, but she put a finger to his lips. "Hush. Listen, my love. We're in a different country, about to sail to yet another country. Remember I told you before we left home that we'd meet people who have different ways of living than what we're used to? Until we learn their ways, it's best we keep certain things, like signing, to ourselves."

Eban slowly lifted his gaze to meet hers. "Are you angry at me? Did I make you more sad?"

She leaned over and kissed him on both cheeks. "I love you. You never make me sad. Can you do what I say and keep our old ways a secret, just between us?"

"Like signing?"

"Yes."

"I will, Mother."

Zofia dragged the suitcase out from under her seat, the traveling case likely weighing more than her son. "Darling, we're in Berlin. We're about to transfer trains and complete our journey to Hamburg, where the ship awaits us."

"I can't wait to go on the boat!" Eban rubbed his tummy. "I'm hungry."

To save cash, she had packed food that would remain fresh for the journey. The dwindling stash wouldn't last beyond a few more days. She would endure crumbs if necessary, but Eban was a different matter. He had no complaints about the buttered bread or the slices of cake, but made a face at the dried salted pork, though, good boy that he was, he ate it without complaint. The poor darling, she couldn't blame him for wanting tastier, more satisfying foods.

"Once we board the next train, I'll look into purchasing us a small treat. Good?"

Eban nodded and, without prodding, moved out into the aisle at the same time a woman stepped into the narrow corridor. A few years older than Zofia, the stranger appeared to be traveling without anyone's company and had avoided contact with other passengers. In coach passage, this woman, traveling solo, needed to keep on guard against others who might take advantage of her position and confusion in traveling. At least Zofia had her son for companionship. Then again, each person's journey was unique. She'd heard of poor peasants, before the outbreak of the Great War, who walked three weeks from various Polish towns to Hamburg because they couldn't afford the price of rail passage. They risked imprisonment or death while sneaking past border guards. Zofia took one last look about the train. Coach had several luxuries, indeed.

The Berlin station was the largest they'd yet encountered. Between the familiar overtones of Russian and Polish conversation, the different nuances of German body language, and shouts in unrecognizable languages, Zofia, overwhelmed by being in a foreign country and soon another country, swayed to her right as if already on a ship cutting through choppy waves. She wondered if these travelers were also going to America. Did that new country truly have room for them all?

After asking for directions, Zofia and Eban walked past yet another poster of Hitler and boarded the train to Hamburg. They plopped into their seats where they'd order a meal to share, sleep and hopefully dream sweet dreams, and awaken pre-dawn to set foot in the city of Hamburg and begin the second half of their journey. From this point on, she chose to believe that the rest of the trip would go smoothly for them.

18

Aanya glanced at Lena as she slipped into the room carrying a tray of chicken soup. The comforting aroma, with its sprinkle of anise-like fennel mixed with the sweetness of basil and the salt of its broth, failed to stir Inga from her sleep. Lena crossed the room and set the tray down on the chestnut bureau, and looked lovingly at her sister-in-law, who had come down with pneumonia.

Aanya had tried to steel herself for the task of telling this woman, who had become almost like a mother to her since her own had passed away, that the news of Inga's health was grim. Oddly, it was a good thing that Zofia and Eban had left Brzeziny yesterday. If her friend was here now, seeing Inga's rapid decline, Aanya doubted she would have left.

Lena grasped Inga's hand, but looked at Aanya. "She's not going to survive the pneumonia, is she?"

"Patients often surprise me," Aanya signed. Life amazed her. For the better: meeting Artur under the oddest of circumstances and falling rapidly in love with him; moving into Zofia's home, a bad situation turned bright; for Artur, Lena, and Inga's diligence in learning how to sign, at least enough to converse; and Laja coming into Artur's and her lives as their daughter. Life's sorrows competed, it was true, but she wouldn't inventory those. She returned her focus to

Lena's question. "I'm encouraged by how Inga has kept up her strength these past few days." She smiled at the sleeping woman. "I believe there's a good chance for her recovery."

"I can hear her raspy breathing," Lena signed. "She's not eating. Why did I fuss with the soup?"

"She's a good, sweet dear." What kind of reply was this, coming from one who studied medicine? She couldn't fool Lena. She attempted another response. "She's resting comfortably, considering the circumstances." Oh, goodness. Another lukewarm evasion. She stood from her perch at Inga's bedside. "You sit, Lena. I'm going to stretch my legs."

"Wait."

Aanya stopped. She wanted to fly into Artur's arms, wanted to check on Laja, wanted to run upstairs into the bedroom where she'd slept beside Zofia when she first moved into this house because there was no other space for her—the room which, as of last night, became her and Artur's bedroom. Instead, she peered into Lena's eyes. Fighting not to become overwhelmed by sadness, she forced a gentle smile for both of these women's sakes.

"You've suffered quite a few unfortunate circumstances in a short time," Lena said aloud slowly for Aanya to read her lips. "Yet you've managed to persevere with your head high and strong. I admire you for that, Aanya." Lena paused, rubbing between her eyes. "I'm aware there's a chance that Inga—who is like a sister to me as Zofia is to you—may leave this world. Leave me. You've done everything to the best of your ability to help her medically, as well as loving and caring for her like a daughter would care for her beloved aunt. Thank you, Aanya. From both Inga and me."

Words cramped Aanya's fingers and clogged her throat. She hugged Lena and gestured for her to sit. She hurried from the bedroom before tears betrayed her.

Artur stood at the end of the hallway and greeted her with a tender smile. "I love you, Aanya," he said aloud.

"Say it again," she signed, not because she didn't understand him the first time, but because she needed to see him say it a second time, or however many times it took for the power of love to overcome the specter of death.

Instead of repeating himself, Artur pressed a kiss onto her lips. Not a gentle kiss, but a hungry and desperate one, a loneliness longing to brush aside heartache. They both knew it was impossible.

She felt a tug at the hem of her dress.

Laja. Like an angel, she smiled, and then as if in reinforcement, she waved.

Artur scooped her into his arms. "My sweet princess," he signed.

Laja giggled. "I'm me, Papa. No princess," she signed back.

For the first time in hours, lightness touched Aanya's soul. Just a tiny bit, but considering the moment, it seemed abundant. She toggled her gaze between her husband and daughter. "Let's tiptoe out and get a breath of air." She led the way outdoors.

Later, after tucking Laja into Eban's old bed in the kitchen that the girl had claimed as her own, Aanya looked in on Inga. Her labored breathing had eased. A miracle. If Inga's improving health was an indication of more miracles to come, Aanya couldn't wait to see what would greet them in the future. She left the room and climbed the stairs to her bedroom.

Earlier, she had imagined slipping into her nightgown and staggering into bed, fighting sleep but then eventually falling into a deep, dreamless black void. As soon as she shut the door, she saw Artur sitting on the edge of the bed and staring out the bare window into the dark. Out of her clothes within seconds, she padded across the room to the man she loved with her whole being, and tugged off his shirt and trousers.

"Make love to me," she said aloud.

"I may not stop."

For the first time in hours, or was it a matter of days—she no longer knew—she was set ablaze with the fervor of passion, carnal and yearning. There had to be a tomorrow, a better one for all.

19

Seated in the passenger waiting area prior to boarding the ship, Zofia twisted her purse strap as Eban kicked the legs of the wooden bench. Although she feared her restless son grew more irritable as each second marched by, she couldn't rightly complain, considering how well behaved he'd been since they departed Brzeziny. She'd asked a lot from a seven-year-old boy. At this stage, though, if he were to become more fidgety and act up, it could draw unwanted, and perhaps dangerous, public scrutiny. Already weary from their travels to the Hamburg port, even her fellow passengers waiting in the boarding queue wouldn't look kindly on a disturbance—not to mention the ever-present officials.

"Eban, darling, while we're waiting, let's have a little fun." She glanced about. A rabbi sat to her right; a couple and their two girls to Eban's left. "We can take turns telling a story about pirates who sailed the seas a long time ago."

"I don't want to tell stories. I want to read them." Eban stopped swinging his legs. "I forgot to pack my Christmas present, the book about countries. My other storybooks are home, in Brzeziny."

"Yes, I know where we used to live." Just the name of Brzeziny escaping his lips stirred a pang of homesickness and longing. She flinched. Regret that she capitulated to her emotions rather than rein them in, her shoulders straightened. Who was acting like a child now? How in heaven's name would she be strong enough to make it on the next part of their trip?

"Pirates," Eban said dully. "Not pirates, Mamusiu... Mother. Pirates are pretend. They only live in my storybooks." Tears welled in his eyes.

She rubbed Eban's back. "What is it, darling?"

"My books. They're back home, with Babcia and Aunt Inga. And Aanya and Artur and Laja. I won't ever see them again."

Was he referring to his left-behind books, or to his beloved family, also left behind? A quick, soothing reply eluded her, as so many answers had in her own attempts to make sense out of both their personal turmoil and the world's.

One of the girls beside Eban stepped in front of him. She looked about ten years old, and her long brunette hair was as lush and sweet as her gentle smile. "Take this," she said in German-accented Polish. She glanced at her parents, then back at Eban. "My name is Edith. My sister is Krista. We want you to have this storybook. It's not about pirates, though. It's about a boy who travels to a new country."

"Like me?" Eban pointed at his chest. "I'm from Poland."

The girl nodded. "We're from Germany. The book's in German, but once we get on the ship, I can teach you what it says, if you want."

In reverent silence, Eban opened the book carefully. He traced the first illustration with the tip of his index finger then lifted the book to Zofia. She nodded and Eban returned his attention to the girl. "It's a very nice book, but it's yours. Don't you want it?"

"Mutter and Vater say we can have new books once we're in America. It's your turn to enjoy the story." She sat on the floor, looked from her sister to Eban, patted the floor on either side of her, and motioned for the two to join her. "While we wait, I'll explain a few things."

Zofia leaned toward the girls' parents. "Do you also speak Polish?"

The man nodded. "We both do."

"Thank you." Zofia introduced herself and then explained that she could only speak Polish, though she hoped to expand her English soon. "My son has behaved like a big boy since leaving home, but I'm not sure I could have handled this moment well without your daughter's lovely offer."

"My name is Herta Weber, and this is my husband Karl. Our girls—Edith, the elder, and Krista, the younger one—as well as both of us, have struggled in leaving our home in Berlin. With a promise from our relatives in New York that there will be books and toys to look forward to, our traveling with the girls has become a little easier. Not that we have a choice."

About to say that after transferring ships in Cuba and sailing to New York, they might be living near each other and could visit, Herta's last few words had given Zofia pause. "If I may ask, what do you mean that you had no choice but to leave home?"

Kurt whispered in Herta's ear. He glanced for a moment at the rabbi sitting next to Zofia. "Since this is upsetting for my wife, I'll answer. It's no secret about the antisemitism spreading in Germany." He paused, looked about. "And elsewhere."

He spoke low and Zofia had to lean closer to hear him.

"After the November pogrom, *Kristallnacht*... In Poland, you heard about what happened?"

"Yes." She glanced at the children playing nicely together. "My son Eban and I are not Jewish, but come from a mostly Jewish town and have dear friends who are. We've been quite upset and troubled by events."

"We lost a cousin that evening. He was beaten to death after being dragged from his store, which he was defending. Friends also lost their businesses and homes. When we learned about available passage on the St. Louis, we believed our prayers to leave were finally answered." He clasped his wife's hand and looked at his daughters. "It is their future we think of. They have no future in Germany at all. Once our home, our *fatherland*, Germany, has become a country that doesn't want us and we don't want it. And you?"

She longed to share her own story of leaving her childhood home and loved ones behind, but didn't dare whisper a word and chance breaking down in sobs. "We're traveling to New York, where my husband's cousin will meet us and help us settle as we wait for my husband to join us. New beginnings are both scary and exciting, don't you think?"

"We must talk more as we sail to Havana. I'm glad we've met."

Indeed, it was nice to have a sailing companion. Zofia had heard that there were 937 passengers and over 200 crew, which was nothing compared to the Vaterland ship Jabez's cousin's grandparents sailed on in 1914, on one of that grand ship's last voyages before the Great War. The size of the St. Louis, of the same Hamburg-Amerika Linie as the Vaterland, would suffice nicely.

An announcement in German blared through the waiting area. Chatter quieted. Kurt translated for Zofia: it was time to board the ship. Parents gathered children and clusters of passengers formed.

"Eban," Zofia said, reaching for his hand to help him from the floor. "It's time to board the ship and sail the ocean. With new friends, this promises to be a fun trip."

20

Aanya stood to clear the dinner dishes from the table, but Lena jumped up to take over the task. Ever since Zofia and Eban's departure two weeks ago, as well as Lena's recent job loss, she insisted on keeping busy to the extreme. The cooking was suddenly her full responsibility, though there were fewer mouths to feed. And the laundry and cleaning? She claimed they were also hers alone to accomplish. Aunt Inga, who grew sturdier in health each day, also couldn't keep busy enough. Like Lena, with more Brzeziny shops eliminating positions in the name of profit, she too had lost her job. The small house had grown tinier with frenzied occupants. If Aanya didn't have Artur and Laja to look after, she would have tripped over these two anxious and irritable women.

Lena picked up Artur's untouched dinner dish. "Should I leave his food?"

Not certain where Artur was, Aanya didn't have a hunch on how to answer Lena. Since his arrival back in Brzeziny and his conversion to Judaism, he'd made a few solid friendships with neighboring men and others who lived in the town proper. He was well liked by customers at the pharmacy where he'd begun work as an apprentice to the apothecary. He still needed to be careful of his whereabouts and activities. With speculation rife about Hitler's next move, and the increasing popularity and growing ranks of Nazism throughout Europe, folks in Brzeziny looked over their shoulders constantly. The threat of harm to Artur, as well as to other Brzeziners, was real and unrelenting. It was like navigating a road with buried mines.

Aanya took the dish full of smoked sausage, sauerkraut, and dumplings. "You relax, Lena," she said aloud, surprising herself by both the vocalization and the authoritative role she had assumed. She switched to signing. "Laja, please help me clear the dishes."

Without delay, Laja took Inga's empty dish and Lena's half-eaten dinner. She followed Aanya into the kitchen. "Where is Tatusiu?" Laja adored Artur and had called him Tatusiu long before he became her official father. She scraped the leftover bits of food from the dishes into the compost bucket, set the dinnerware into the sink, and waited for Aanya to sign her reply.

"I'm not sure," Aanya replied honestly, shoving away the fear that threatened to invade her mind over whether Artur's delay might portend a disappearance similar to Jabez's. "He'll be home soon. Maybe he'll bring a surprise for you. Would you like that?"

Laja clapped her hands. "Yes."

Just when they'd finished washing and drying the plates, Artur entered the kitchen. Aanya's gaze roamed over him from head to toe. No injuries from what she could see, nor signs, such as a knotted brow, that might indicate a headache. There was, however, something about his solemn face and the unusual unexpressiveness of his eyes that told her what she needed to do.

"How's my sweet Laja?" Artur signed and hugged the child before she could reply. This made her giggle.

Was it Aanya's imagination or did Artur hold onto Laja a few extra seconds, like a papa who didn't ever want to let go of his daughter? When Aanya caught him glancing over Laja's shoulder at her, he bent down to the child's level.

"I have a treat for you. Guess which pocket it's in."

Laja's eyes widened. She smiled. "I like this game."

Artur tousled her hair. "Guess we won't play tea party with your dolls anymore."

She stamped her foot and a playful pout teased her lips. "That's not fair, Tatusiu."

"Fine. I'll surrender this one time." He slipped a hand into the pocket of his brown suede vest and withdrew a red and white swirled lollipop. "Here you are, a sweet for my sweetheart."

"Laja," Aanya jumped in. "Please keep your babcia and aunt company in the dining room while I speak to Tatusiu." She waited until Laja left the kitchen, then wrapped her arms around Artur's neck. "I love how you love our daughter."

He nodded and lifted her signing hand and kissed her fingers. "I love her. I love you," he said aloud.

She sighed and dropped her gaze.

He lifted her chin and their eyes met. "And that's why I'm late, and why I need to speak with you privately. Let's step outside." He led her to the far side of the house.

"What's wrong, Artur? Tell me."

"Germany and Italy signed a military and political alliance today."

She didn't understand. Lena and Inga listened to the radio every day and would have conveyed any alarming news. "This wasn't broadcasted on today's news."

"That's correct, making it more troubling. I learned from my sources."

By his *sources*, Artur meant a similar, though new, network such as Jabez had joined, fellow Brzeziners formed to watch for German military action or political activity. Artur, from Germany and a former German soldier, had no trust whatsoever in the country of his birth. He, and this group of trusted men, suspected an attack—outright war—was imminent.

"What do you know about this new alliance?"

"This pact—the Pact of Steel—continues the trust and cooperation between Germany and Italy, but also cements their policy of military and economic collaboration."

"Two enemies now instead of one?"

"Essentially."

"And?" she asked, aware that learning of international developments wasn't simply a new hobby for her husband.

"We have two choices, neither easy. First, as Brzeziny residents, we can watch and wait and do what we can, when we can. Or we can plan for the worst to happen and explore possible responses. Of course, there aren't any guarantees, either way. And on a personal matter, I have a big question for Lena. But I'd like to see what you think about it first."

They were both aware of the danger hovering over their heads, and how little time could be left before they might lose each other again, this time permanently. He kissed her hard. Her heart pounded.

Fear fueled her to lean away. "Artur?" She'd spoken his name in hope that it sounded like how she heard his name in her mind: a fragment from a heavenly song she didn't want to let go of.

"With everything around us so unpredictable, having more money on hand will be important. Ever since I heard this news about the new pact between the madman Hitler and his pal, Mussolini, I kept thinking about what we might sell for cash. You know, just in case."

She didn't need to ask for what. Bribes. Permissions. Clearances. Forgeries. Food. Water. Immediately she understood why Artur wanted to talk with Lena.

"I know what you want to do—and it's what Jabez and Zofia would want us to do. Would you like me to accompany you?"

"Yes." He grabbed her hand and they hurried indoors.

Seeing Jabez's watch collection, including several rare timepieces, displayed on a special lint-free cloth momentarily transported Aanya away from Brzeziny, away from the border between Germany and Poland, away from harm. For a few moments she was a wife in a specialty shop considering a gift for her husband. Would he appreciate a gold or a silver case? One with a perpetual calendar and moon phases? Or would he care if the white porcelain case included a signature? She dreaded having to face reality again, but knew better than to lapse into a passive role; if she were to do so, it would be the equivalent of wearing a sign identifying her religious beliefs and her deafness and walking into a parade of Nazis.

While Inga and Laja weeded the garden, Lena, Artur, and Aanya had the parlor to themselves. Artur hadn't wanted to frighten Lena, but he had informed her—as much as he dared—about what might happen if Poland were to be attacked.

Lena glanced away from Artur and examined her son's watch collection. Aanya intuited that if Lena didn't know the proper way to care for these time pieces she'd handle them one by one with her bare hands, caressing them as if she were seeing her son for the first time since his venture into Germany for work, touching each watch with a sweep of her fingertips as if it was proof he was alive and well. But she didn't do any of those things. She faced Artur and Aanya.

"I want to tell you what my son said to me the day before he last left," she said aloud, careful to articulate with precision. "We were alone in the house. It was after breakfast—the others had either gone off to work or were busy. Jabez led me to this special cabinet, a treasure he never openly or willingly shared." She smiled, her eyes beaming trust and fondness. "I didn't want to share this with Zofia because she'd take this information as a warning sign and insist on remaining here with us—the action Jabez feared—rather than travel to New York. You see, Jabez had told me he'd made arrangements for his wife and son. So this is my confession to you two. I didn't want to deceive Zofia by my pretense of not knowing about the possibility of Jabez's disappearance, but my son made me promise to encourage her to begin her journey. And I did the best I could without appearing that I wanted her out of my life."

Aanya felt lightheaded. Lena had known about Jabez's plans to send Zofia and Eban to America before he informed Zofia? Then Lena must also know of Jabez's involvement with a resistance group, or whatever he was engaged in. Evidently, his wife and son could be harmed or even killed as retaliation against Jabez if the wrong people discovered his activities. That was probably why Jabez had come back the day Zofia and Eban left Brzeziny, to see with his own eyes that they would have a chance to live, whether or not he did.

Lena dropped her gaze, and when she lifted it to face Artur and Aanya again, her furrowed brows and thinly stretched lips expressed her anguish over deceiving Zofia.

Aanya inched to the edge of her seat and started to sign. "Lena, considering the circumstances, you did the reasonable thing, but may I ask—"

"Please, I'm not looking for affirmation of my actions. I made a decision to help my son because I believed—and still do—that Jabez cares deeply for his family and would do whatever was necessary to help them." She wiped tears from her eyes. "Or, at least would die trying to help them, to help all of us. Now, it's time for me to move beyond deceiving my daughter-in-law, whom I've loved like a daughter, and do what I can to help the two of you, Laja, and Inga. So please, no questions. It's too much for me to think about. Understand?"

"Thank you for this trust, Lena," Artur said. "In tough situations like these present times, we all do what's necessary to survive while trying our best to be kind and good."

"I agree," Aanya signed. "Jabez is doing what is good for us all, and you're doing what's good for your family."

"Mothers do what they have to do to protect their children," Lena said. "Let's return to the subject of Jabez's watches, shall we? He told me three things concerning the watches: the value of the best ones, that he'd be shocked if another Great War didn't break out, in which case we might need them, and lastly, he made me promise to sell them for as much cash as possible. He told me to hide the money in a place where no one would likely search. This idea of yours, Artur, to trade them now for needed cash, is a wise one. My son would be relieved that they'll help to protect us. When I look into your honest eyes, I see that the time is approaching sooner, not later. A shame, but it's the way things are."

Artur enfolded his hands around Lena's, but remained facing Aanya so she could watch his mouth as he spoke. "With what I told you a few minutes ago, you're current on the latest developments. Dear Lena, it's not looking good. I don't have a specific date. None of us do. I hope I'm wrong. And that you may laugh at me and my friends if the day comes when Hitler calls off his advances against our country, but—"

"That day will not happen," Lena said, and wiggled her hands free from Artur's grasp to fold them tightly on her lap. "Hitler will move forward with his plans. But we know that Poland has suffered many times throughout the years and each time, has managed to rise with pride and strength. We will get through this."

Artur studied the pocket watches and compared them with a list of names he'd slipped from his trouser pocket. "I can fetch a good amount for both of the George and Edward Prior watches, the Patek Philippe, and the Rolex. I'll see what I can do with the others. As I said, and want to emphasize, this cash will not be used for luxuries, but will be saved and used if and when the time arrives. A good bribe can go far."

Lena reached for Artur and Aanya's hands and squeezed them. "Take the watches, with my blessing. I'll pray that a time like you're talking about won't find us, but it's best to be prepared."

Artur kissed both women's cheeks, packed the watches carefully, and left to strike a deal with the man he'd already lined up.

21

With eyes wide and hands pressed against the large window in the passenger waiting area, Eban pointed at the ship's two funnels. "That is the biggest boat I've ever seen."

"The St. Louis is certainly large," Zofia said, relieved to hear excitement is her son's tone. "This ship has nice cabins for us to sleep in, a dining room where our meals will be served, a swimming pool—and we'll even get to see movies for the first time. Imagine the fun we'll have." She peeked again at the ship, this large steel transport that would soon take her away from Europe, bring her to Cuba, an interim stop for them before they would board another ship to sail to Manhattan where they'd meet Isaac and go on to Brooklyn and their new home. It was easier for her to imagine the fun Eban and she would enjoy on the ship, than to envision settling in a country incredibly far away from her beloved Polska.

"Mother, why are we waiting to go onto the ship?" Eban pointed at other passengers gathering their carry-on possessions and forming lines to board. "If they're going on, can't we?"

The major distinction between other ships and the St Louis was how the third-class passengers were treated. They'd enjoy what once was considered second-class status, an improvement in amenities and privileges. Despite the more pleasant accommodations, Zofia's heart remained splintered over how people weren't treated equally, depending on their finances. If the world functioned on love rather than on monetary value, all would benefit. This social difference, assigned to people by the hand of other people, certainly fueled Hitler and his band of Nazis. Why else would they want to overrun country after country, to the extreme of claiming the majority of the population inferior and undeserving of the basic needs and dignities in life?

Her personal, unembellished reality boiled down to her son, and any additional children if they were to come along. She wasn't pondering a mere example from a philosophy textbook. The whole basis of Jabez wanting to establish a home in America was for Eban's welfare, for their child to have a future. She glanced at Eban. She didn't want her son to suffer because of the social definition of success hinging on wealth. Nor would she want him to let the wrong attitude about money tarnish his outlook and influence him to become one who lorded it over the less fortunate. Well, as a mother, she had a say in this matter. She'd raise her son to be fair-minded and to show respect for others. At least, that was what she could aim for. Once he became an adult, she'd have to step back.

About to reply to Eban, joyful tears stung her eyes. Possibilities flooded her mind. Energy flowed through her veins more intensely than it had in months. Had she found a new purpose in life? Could she determine her future, instead of leaving it to fate? Although she longed to settle down with Jabez and Eban in their new home, she wouldn't remain within its walls for long, with an apron tied around her waist, baking cookies or fretting over an overcooked roast. Instead, she'd rally for economic and social rights for each man, woman, and child, putting action behind her thoughts. Once settled, she'd find a group of like-minded women. If no group existed, she'd start one. America symbolized opportunity—for all, she hoped. About to partake of this new experience, she'd embrace it to the fullest. If Jabez truly wanted the best for his family, which included her, he'd have to see it her way.

She gulped. She'd tell her husband of her new views, something the Polska Zofia was always reluctant to do. The American Zofia was a new woman, at least one in the making. The world teetered on the edge of a new decade. Mentally, she lifted a glass of wine and made a toast to the 1940s. *Here's to the exciting possibilities ahead. May they be splendid times for all.*

Zofia glanced out the large picture window at the port full of ships and smaller boats, passengers and uniformed crew hurrying about, ground transports moving to or unloading from the ship goods like food, luggage, and packages. She hugged Eban fiercely. "Darling, the cabin passengers go onto the ship first and then we will have our turn. It's thrilling, my son. Yes?"

Eban nodded, his mouth hanging open. He turned back to the window.

Herta Weber and her family walked toward them from the washroom. Her two daughters encircled Eban; Kurt waved, sat on a nearby bench, and rummaged through his suitcase.

"And once again," Herta said, with a smile in her tone, "we're about to make major changes to our lives. This time, for the better. I'm glad you and I have met and can make this voyage together."

"Yes."

Herta took her sweater off and Zofia noticed a pin she wore on the collar of her blouse.

"Ah, you like my butterfly. The butterfly flaps around in the air, freely, just like we are—free." Herta glanced at the children then looked into Zofia's eyes. "It is a miracle to have the freedom to wear this simple pin of a butterfly that enjoys its freedom, and to renew our own hope to live such a life."

Sensing this conversation was about something larger than the nature of butterflies, Zofia said nothing and waited for Herta to continue.

"When *Kristallnacht* shattered life back in November, Jews were forced to march behind a big yellow Star of David to signify our faith and show that we were supposedly useless and sub-human. While some Berliners were sympathetic to us, there were not enough to sway Nazi policy. Did you know that during the Middle Ages Jews were forced to wear identification badges? I wouldn't be surprised if Hitler mandates German Jews wear one on their clothing." She fiddled with the pin. "To say that we're about to board a ship to take us far away from Germany is to not say enough. Finally, at least several of us now have the opportunity to go to *Die Goldene Medina*."

"Pardon?"

"The Golden Land, the United States of America." She rolled her bottom lip. "There have been a few *goldene medinas* in the past. I pray this new country will be the kindest and favor us immigrants."

"I've been praying the same. You mentioned *Kristallnacht*. That's what my dearest friend and I promised each other—that we will hold strong in the hope of seeing each other again and not shatter like the glass of shops and homes during that fatefull night."

"Many of us have promised that to our loved ones. We can only hope and pray we'll see each other again."

Zofia thought she heard Herta sniffle, but couldn't tell whether the woman teared up for she turned to look out the window. On the dock, two Hasidic men in traditional long black suits and black hats climbed the ramp onto the ship. "I'm beyond pleased that you have this opportunity. I hope there are many more Jews making this trip."

Herta faced her. "You don't know about this particular ship's passengers?"

Zofia shook her head.

"With the exception of a handful or two, like yourself, the passengers of this ship are all Jewish. We see this as our last chance to survive."

"Last chance? Survive?" And here she was, minutes ago, thinking of fair distribution of finances when the people onboard this ship simply wanted to live. The confluence of events necessitating these passengers' journey was grossly unfair and unjust. It was insanity. No, those were weak words. It was evil. Incomprehensible, unadulterated evil.

"This is a ship of hope," Herta continued. "It's not one of doom. Our relatives and friends back home face persecution, the stripping away of their right to practice their religion and to have dignity... their humanity. We look forward to a future."

Dear God, Zofia murmured under her breath. What she'd heard under her own Brzeziny roof was unerring truth. And this evil was what Jabez and the watchers were on the lookout for? With no doubt, she wanted him beside her, but after hearing Herta's firsthand account of the atrocities happening in Germany made her hope that Jabez was indeed doing something more aggressive than simply watching for Nazi activity. As soon as she set her eyes on Jabez again, she'd throw herself into his arms and after telling him to never let go of her, she'd apologize for the little she believed him regarding the disastrous direction Poland—and the whole of Europe—was headed in. Would he say he couldn't blame her for her naive but understandable desire to believe goodness would right the bad? That he'd learned the hard way that she too was right in wanting to cling to hope and a future?

Zofia nodded at Herta. "We are all human beings. We each, regardless of religious beliefs, deserve to live and to be treated justly. This Hitler dictator has no right to say or act differently. Nor does anyone else."

"Zofia, it's better if we talk of this privately, on the ship. But we're of like minds. I can see that you and I will become good friends."

"I'd like that."

Zofia assumed the ship attendant below the deck was giving directions to their assigned cabin, but he spoke in German and she couldn't understand. If it weren't for Herta's husband, Kurt, explaining how the tickets were marked with the assigned cabin, Zofia would have been lost. Eban had enjoyed the novelty of riding the elevator down to the third-class level, but she knew he'd quickly lose enthusiasm if she didn't hurry him to the room that would become their little refuge for the next 14 days, a temporary home of steel, aluminum, and countless parts transporting them to the new home awaiting them made of wood, brick, and lots of love. They—and Jabez, when he arrived—would supply the love.

They rounded a corner and there was the cabin number that matched the one on their tickets. "Ah, here we are." She unlocked the door, and Eban pushed it wide open and sprang over the doorsill.

"Mother—look at the carpeting. Our feet won't get cold."

She'd expected a cramped, unpleasant cabin, not this cozy, clean chamber. The room contained two berths, one above the other, each with privacy curtains. The beds had plump pillows, fresh sheets, and comfy blankets. A net—for storage, she imagined—hung over each bed. To the left of the beds were two side-by-side sinks complete with shelves containing folded towels. A mounted electric fan positioned to the right of the mirror hanging over the sinks appeared dust-free and ready for use.

"There aren't any windows."

"No worries, darling. We'll only be sleeping in this room and will spend our time above, on the decks. We'll see magnificent sights you'll never forget."

"Where do we eat?"

Zofia held back a smile as a memory of Jabez asking about supper visited... *Men and children always thought about their bellies.* "There's a big dining room. Once we're permitted to leave the cabin, we'll explore this ship from top to bottom. Won't that be fun?"

Instead of responding, Eban climbed onto the top berth. "I want this one."

A rap came at the door. A steward greeted them in German. When Zofia didn't respond, he tried again in stilted Polish. He handed her a piece of paper. "This map, of where third-class passengers are to stay." He pointed out a large room. "Here is dining room where you eat, social hall to enjoy piano and movies." He pointed over his shoulder. "Lavatories in corridor."

"Thank you," Zofia said. "Where do we go for fresh air?"

The man pointed to a stairwell on the map. "To promenade deck." He pointed to the other side of the ship and traced an X with his finger. "No go here. No third-class allowed."

A gasp drew her attention to her son, his protest not only audible but visible in his wrinkled brow. Although she was his mama, she couldn't change the rules for her darling. *Yes, Eban. Life isn't fair.*

Zofia managed a polite smile. She then thought of her farewell handkerchief—the one frivolity she'd brought along—stuffed in her pocket and ready to wave goodbye to Europe. "May we go to the deck when the ship sails?"

The steward again pointed at the location of the staircase on the map leading to the third-class deck. "Yes, but here." He exited, likely assigned to inform the neighboring passengers of the same instructions.

Eban climbed down from the upper bunk and rocked from side to side. "I've got to pee."

Zofia, map in hand, opened the door and motioned for him to follow. That simple act of signaling made her think of Aanya.

What was her friend doing now back in Brzeziny? Helping Lena prepare dinner? Taking a walk with her husband? Reading one of Eban's storybooks to Laja, teaching her how to sign new words? Zofia prayed they were happy and healthy. Safe. *Free.*

Freedom. That word had taken a different shape since she'd met the Weber family and learned of the plight of this ship's passengers.

They passed a framed painting of Hitler.

"Who is that man?" Eban asked. "I keep seeing his picture."

"Let's not spoil our trip." She pointed at a door. "Finally, the bathroom." This time she beat Eban to opening the door, anxious to sidetrack her son's curiosity. "Look at the bathtub, Eban." About to comment on the porthole to steer her son's attention away from Hitler, she sighed in relief when Eban stepped up to the toilet. When they left the bathroom, Herta and the girls stood in line for their turn. Quick smiles were exchanged.

"Would you like to meet us on the deck when we sail?" Herta asked.

"Yes," Eban replied.

The two women winked at each other and laughed, excitement trilling in their light-hearted tones.

"Will we arrive at our new home soon?"

Zofia wanted to say that yes, they were almost home. But of course, the fact was that first they had a long journey. They'd cruise by Belgium and France, cross the Atlantic, disembark at Cuba, and then board another ship to sail to Florida before completing their journey to New York.

Her breath caught. Since Jabez first revealed his plan for her and Eban to go to America, she'd resisted. Yet, here she was, looking forward to a new beginning in a new land. Not only had the way she used to define home changed, but something else had changed as well: how she saw herself. She'd been reshaped and revamped, like an old neglected piece of art lovingly restored, looking better than the original. She was no longer *only* Jabez's wife, or her child's caretaker. She was an individual, with her own mind and the freedom to use it, with a good heart to use her intelligence carefully and wisely, and soon would become an American. It would be her responsibility to treasure this freedom as a gift and not to abuse her privileges. This would become her new vow to live by daily.

She fanned her fingers alongside Eban's face. "Soon enough, darling. We'll be home soon enough." As the last word left her mouth, her eyes misted. What about those on the ship fleeing from their homeland because of a darkening Germany? And those left behind, trapped in a country that caged them as if they were ferocious animals?

"Mamusiu? What's wrong? Your happy face is gone again."

"Don't mind me. I'm just thankful we're making this journey to our new home."

22

With a day off from the health center, Aanya planned to finish the laundry and complete the chores she'd ignored the past week in hopes the housework would go away by itself. With Inga again growing unusually fatigued and short of breath, she was relieved to stay around the house and keep an eye on the older woman who had become as devoted an aunt to her as she was to Jabez. This time she suspected Inga's illness wasn't a relapse of pneumonia but a condition that would worsen or prove fatal.

Hoisting a basked of wet laundry against her hip, she crossed the parlor from the washroom and headed toward the kitchen to go out through the side door. Thoughts of Zofia and Eban filled her mind. It was the 26th of May, the day before the St. Louis was set to arrive in Havana. Would the passengers on board have a special dinner followed by festivities? She pictured Zofia wearing her lovely spring-green dress, the one that highlighted her hair and made her as beautiful as a princess out of the childhood storybooks they once enjoyed sharing. Would men gawk at her friend, forgetting sensibility and manners? And Eban? Would he fuss over wearing his best church outfit? She imagined that if she were a passenger, full of anticipation of what the next day would bring in a different country, she definitely wouldn't get a restful night's sleep.

Laja met her outside by the clothesline, wiggling the wicker basket full of wet clothes free from Aanya's arms; the basket was almost heavier than her sprite-like frame, yet the child kept a tight grip on the handles. "Mama. Are you lost in your silly dreams again?"

Aanya reached for one of Artur's good shirts she couldn't bear allowing to wrinkle more and pinned it to the clothesline. "They're sweet dreams, but nothing like you."

"Me? I don't understand, Mama."

Aanya knelt to Laja's eye level and continued to sign. "Sweetheart, you're the real thing. You're before my eyes when I awake each new day and you're also in my dreams. I just can't get enough of you." She kissed the top of Laja's head. Little-girl giggles erupted against Aanya's chest.

Abruptly, Laja went rigid. Aanya followed her gaze to see Artur approaching. Why was he home early from work? No smile lit his face. She stood quickly; a wave of dizziness surprised her. She placed her hands on Laja's shoulders, not from a need to lean, but from the instinct to protect her little bird from somber news her husband seemed to be bringing. "What's wrong?"

Artur took the time to kiss her, as well as Laja. Aanya relaxed a tiny bit, and her fear of a Nazi attack receded a little.

Facing away from Laja and peering directly at Aanya, he said aloud, "There's a man who needs your help."

"Is he at the health center?"

"No."

This conversation had already become odd. Aanya asked Laja to check on Aunt Inga, and if she were awake, to keep her company. Both she and Artur waited until the girl went indoors.

"Is the man a Brzeziner?" she said, returning to signing.

"Does it make a difference?"

"I treat all hurting people. But I'm curious about the way you're presenting this situation to me—a bit on the vague side, which is not like you. Please tell me it's not one of Hitler's men on the hunt for you and that he's about to arrest you."

With one long step, Artur stood before her, eye-to-eye, shaking his head. "No, but he is a German, and a Nazi."

"Is he by himself?"

"From what we can tell, yes. It appears he got into drunken mischief, and his fellow comrades dumped him alongside the road as they exited town."

"Where is he?"

"I'll show you." She was about to question him more, but he continued before she could ask. "Aanya, we don't want you going there by yourself."

She understood that by *we,* Artur referred to the growing band of his own friends who had stepped into the watchers' place when the group that Jabez had belonged to went missing. More alarming, though, was the thought that while they slept in their own beds in their own homes, safe and sound, Nazi soldiers were traipsing through their town during the inky black of night, as if scoping out their beloved streets, where Brzeziners had lived for centuries.

Without further delay, she started for the house. Artur's firm hand upon her shoulder stopped her short. She spun around.

"Is that a yes or a no about coming with me?"

"Of course it's a yes. I'm fetching my medical bag. Then I'll follow you."

The man was different than Aanya had imagined. He barely appeared to be out of his early teens. The rugged tightness etched across his face while asleep, however, showed that he either didn't have an easy childhood or had hardened since entering young adulthood, or both.

The first thing she did after checking the stranger's vital signs was to shake him awake. It concerned her that he hadn't stirred from his unconscious state with her touching, poking, and probing. Although there was a chance his sleep was a ruse in an attempt to monitor any discussion, she had doubts.

The German attempted to move his arms and hands but with his hands bound and secured to the bed, he could only flutter his eyes open. He started to speak, but Aanya didn't understand. She looked to Artur for interpretation.

"He's doing more groaning than talking. The few words that were coherent were in German, but gibberish in nature."

Aanya glanced about the small bedroom in Abe Jacobson's house. Abe, one of the men in the new group Artur had recently joined to guard Brzeziners, had helped him carry the German soldier into his grown son's former bedroom. Two other men stood guard at the closed bedroom door.

"His pupils are dilated and he's having trouble rousing from his sleep. Ask him his name."

Artur turned the man's face toward him. The wounded soldier blinked until his eyes were wide open. After attempting several times to get him to say his name, the man muttered "Rolf," but no last name. He closed his eyes.

"Tell Rolf it's imperative for him to stay awake. I'm concerned about a concussion. Find out the details leading to his injury." On top of a concussion, she also suspected Rolf battled a hangover.

Artur nodded and shook Rolf awake. Aanya watched the two men's lips. Artur did most of the talking; Rolf mostly nodded and winced. Unable to interpret what was said, she concluded the two spoke in German, as they had earlier.

Artur led Aanya to a far corner. With his back toward the German, shielding Aanya, he began to sign. "From what I gather, he and his comrades were riding through Brzeziny overnight, heading toward the German border. Apparently, they'd gotten lost, but not before they broke into the innkeeper's stash of liquor and helped themselves to the booze. He has no recollection of what happened when he gulped the last of his vodka and fell out of the vehicle. The first time he woke he realized his fellow soldiers had deserted him. The second time he awoke, in this bed, he realized he hadn't a clue to his whereabouts, asking if he was back at the camp in Munich." Artur jutted his chin at Rolf then glanced back at her. "I told him you're a doctor—a good enough explanation for you to treat him."

Despite not having earned doctor status yet, she nodded.

"I think it's wise that we sign between us, away from Rolf's eyes. At least, for now."

She agreed and walked to the bed, and realized she needn't worry about his reaction to her actions: he'd fallen asleep again. Artur asked her if he should shake him awake and she told him to wait a few minutes, that she'd continue her examination free from concern about Rolf's possible objections.

After encountering a steady heartbeat, and not seeing broken bones or signs of internal bleeding, Aanya asked Artur, after stirring Rolf awake, if the two of them could step out of the room to speak further. Aware that Artur's friends were unfamiliar with sign language, she ignored their raised brows as she led the way into the hallway. Uncertain times brought out the best and the worst in people. This was not the first time she'd behaved boldly. That was a positive aspect of being a deaf person in a hearing world—you had to have confidence, or at least, act in a fashion that led others to believe you were courageous. And she'd perfected her acting abilities a long time ago for the sake of survival.

They stepped to the far end of the corridor by an open window. The late afternoon sun beamed its warmth into the house.

"Do you trust him?" she asked.

"I don't trust anyone fighting on behalf of Hitler. As an ex-citizen of Germany, I'd spit in the dictator's face if I could."

"Yes, I'm aware of that. How do we know Rolf's pals won't come back for him?"

"We don't, but we can make it work for us, don't you think?"

One character trait Aanya had admired in her husband was what she'd seen upon first meeting him: He never wasted words. This special man in her life, fully committed to her as she was to him, always crafted his sentences to mean more than what was on the surface. It was up to the listener to take the time to understand Artur, and to learn that he saw things that others didn't.

"For the sake of Laja and the future of Brzeziny, for the future of Poland, I'm willing to give it a try. Tell me what you're planning, my smart husband. I want to be part of your scheme."

23

On the last full day of travel aboard the St. Louis, the third-class passengers were treated to an afternoon surprise of a buffet of delicious cakes and confections, with coffee for the adults and milk for the children. A movie followed, shown in the cinema for all of the ship's passengers. This time, it was an American movie, *The Adventures of Robin Hood*. Despite the actors speaking English, the passengers were on the edge of their seats during the exciting parts, booing for the bad guys and cheering for the good ones. The best part for Zofia, though, was sitting beside Herta. They'd become friends and had already planned to visit once they settled down in their new country.

As the day crawled by, with Cuba almost in reach, the tropical heat came as a surprise. The cabin's single fan couldn't manage enough air circulation. Moisture clung to Zofia's and Eban's bodies; their discomfort made them short of patience and downright cranky. Zofia had to constantly check herself not to snap at her darling. It was an effort and a half, but with gentle prompting and a tender hand, she managed to get Eban dressed in his good outfit, and herself in her green dress, and they left the cabin to attend the last night's festivities.

The grand celebration was held in the larger cabin class's more formal dining room, opened to both classes to accommodate the large number of passengers. As arranged, Zofia and Eban met the Webers at the main door to the dining room so they could sit with each other.

"Look at you sweethearts," Herta cooed. She blew kisses at Zofia and Eban, making them smile wide.

"Zofia, you look lovely," Kurt said. "And Eban, you're quite the handsome boy. Do you resemble your father?"

When Eban looked at Zofia for her opinion, she smiled at the couple. "Thank you. Eban's a good mix between Jabez and me, in both looks and personality. You two look quite dashing tonight, and your daughters very pretty." She faltered on what else to say and what not to. She chose to leave well enough alone.

While Kurt conversed with his girls and Eban, Herta leaned conspiratorially toward Zofia. "The word *dashing* was an excellent choice. In this heat and humidity, I admit it was quite a feat to get my daughters, let alone my husband, to put on their good clothes. For the girls, it took the promise of a scrumptious dinner, with special desserts, to shoo them out of the cabin looking halfway respectable."

"How did you manage with Kurt?"

Herta glanced at her husband. "I confess that it was a chore to get Kurt shaved, dressed, and away from the fan. He was content to stay glued to that itty bitty cooling device."

"What did you bribe him with?" As soon as the question was out of Zofia's mouth, heat spread over her from head to toe. She imagined she appeared redder than the apple she'd eaten earlier at lunchtime. She pressed her fingers against her lips and murmured an apology around them.

Herta winked. "I have my ways."

Kurt strode across the corridor, leaving Edith and Krista with Eban. He hooked elbows with Herta and Zofia. "How nice it is to see you two charming ladies getting along." He peered into Zofia's eyes. "My wife thought she'd be lonely on this voyage, but I'm glad she's made a friend in you."

"It works both ways." Thoughts of Aanya competed for space in her mind. What would her childhood friend think about her making a new companion? Aanya had expressed relief when Zofia had finalized travel plans to America—she couldn't imagine Aanya jealous over Herta. Yet, Zofia fought a distinct sense of betrayal. How she wished that Aanya would one day make her way to New York and that they could see each other whenever they wanted to. And who knew about the future—wouldn't it be grand if the three of them became friends? Anything was possible, with hope.

Herta asked Kurt to gather the children and find their assigned table for the special dinner. "Zofia, I'd like to speak with you if you don't mind."

"Yes? I'm sorry—"

"No, no. There's no need to apologize about what you said earlier. We women can freely talk like this to each other. I'm more concerned about you. You appear to have lots on your mind, which I can understand. Would you like to talk about it?"

"I'm fine," Zofia said. "A little nervous, I confess. This trip isn't easy for me. Not only have I left the country I never wanted to leave, but I have no idea what to expect in my new country. I haven't seen my husband for a while. At times, nervousness creeps up on me in the oddest of ways. I'm not even sure that when my husband and I see each other again, we won't be so changed that..." She sighed. "Why am I telling you this? You're also leaving your native country for a new place to call home—you must have enough on your mind without listening to my worries."

"Oh, please. You're more than welcome to share with me, as friends should. And though we haven't known each other for long, I do hope you consider me a friend." Herta patted her arm. "My dear, as for your husband, people do change and grow, and for a couple it's hard when that happens during a time apart. But I can tell you love him, and that you know he loves you. Love can overcome any difficulty. One time Kurt had to travel to Switzerland to see his dying grandmother. He was away for a whole month. I have a hunch that you and your husband have been separated longer than that, but still, we were apart. We were a bit awkward with each other when he arrived home, sort of like getting to know each other again, seeing if things were all right between us. That feeling passed, though. True love will never abandon a couple in love, and certainly not two who are devoted to each other."

"I believe you're right."

Herta's eyes sparkled. "I have an idea. After dinner tonight, we'll take care of Eban while you enjoy a breath of air and a little time alone on the deck to collect your thoughts. I imagine it won't be crowded, since most of the passengers will be attending the gala. Would you like that?"

"What a lovely idea. Thank you." Zofia glanced at the dining hall doors. "Let's go in and indulge in this special dinner. All anyone could talk about today was how they looked forward to plates stacked high with roast beef, creamed potatoes, carrots, and cheesecake for dessert. Honestly, I've heard so much about this meal I think I'm full already. Thanks to you, I'm looking forward to enjoying the night's fresh air more than dinner." She laughed comfortably, and, as if they've enjoyed each other's friendship for years, appreciated Herta's companionable chuckle.

The gala dinner progressed as perfectly as Zofia had hoped, if not better. The ship's band serenaded the guests with a mixture of tangos, waltzes, and popular American tunes like "Jeepers Creepers" and "Tea for Two." Silence fell on the room when the band played "God Bless America."

Just as the seated travelers stood, believing the festivities were over, Captain Gustav Schröder, a middle-aged man with a mustache, a polished look, and impressive bearing, stepped to the microphone and asked for a few additional minutes of their time. His shoulders sagged, as if carrying the weight of the world's burdens on his shoulders. During their voyage, he'd gone out of his way to comfort his Jewish passengers by covering up several of the paintings and photographs of Hitler that were strewn throughout the ship like stubborn weeds. For each activity that occurred in both the cabin and the third-class social halls, the busts of Hitler were removed. He'd also instructed his crew to behave extra courteously and respectfully.

The biggest surprise was his allowance of religious services, an act that contradicted firm Nazi decrees. Tonight, though, Zofia saw worry lines furrow the captain's face. Right away she felt that he knew of grave matters that his passengers weren't aware of. If that was the case, why would the kind captain keep the news from them?

"Ladies and gentlemen," he said in German, while Kurt whispered the Polish interpretation into Zofia's ear. "I began my career at sea at the age of 16 and advanced to captain after 24 years of service." He tried to continue but the audience stood to applaud him. He smiled hesitantly, nodded his head in appreciation, and continued. "During the Great War I was interned in India as an enemy alien. I say this because I understand what you're going through in your struggles to claim a new home. I'm rooting for each of you as you make this new beginning. May God bless each one of you." He took a step away from the microphone, but another thundering ovation stopped him. He bowed and saluted them, then exited the room.

Zofia turned to check on Eban. Although apparently amused at the applause, he rubbed his eyes. A big yawn took up half his face. "Let's get you tucked into bed, sleepyhead. Tomorrow promises to be busy enough."

Herta reached for Zofia's shoulder. "Uh-uh. Remember my promise? Give me your cabin key and I'll look after your son while you snatch a breath of air." Before Zofia could interject one word of disagreement, Herta knelt before Eban. "Your mama has to see to an important matter. Would you like me to tell you a special bedtime story, one that Edith and Krystal adore?"

Eban nodded, his eyes brightening with expectation.

Herta took the key from Zofia. "Go and enjoy your alone time. I'll take good care of Eban."

After Zofia kissed Eban goodnight and promised she'd return to the cabin soon, she watched him leave with the Webers, thankful she could trust her new friends.

On the third-class deck two couples peered over the railing at the evening sky. Their hushed conversations made it apparent they wanted to be left alone. Good. If Zofia couldn't have the place to herself, this was the next best thing. She crossed the deck to an unattended corner. With arms on the railing, she looked with awe at the orange and red sunset and tried to imagine how the sunrise would appear over the Manhattan skyline. Earlier she'd experienced a tingle of enthusiasm as she thought about her old Brzeziny self and the woman she might become as she embraced a different way of life in a new land. But with the promise of a new beginning upon her, shouldn't she be feeling more excitement? Instead, familiar pangs of fear and uncertainty crept back, dimming the prospect of eager anticipation.

"It's a splendid evening, isn't it?"

Unsure of what was said since it sounded like German, Zofia turned to find a lone man; he must have just stepped onto the deck. Similar to her in age, she could detect a few striking details illuminated by a nearby electric light. His moustache framed full, smiling lips, and his unruly dark hair poked out from a straw hat appropriate for the muggy air.

She looked at him quizzically.

"Deutsche?" he asked.

"Polskie."

"Ah, good," he replied in fluent Polish. "Then we can understand each other with ease."

Indoors, the stifling humidity had Zofia dreaming of slipping into a bathtub filled with ice. Here, on the deck, the breeze was surprisingly cool; her arms were pocked with goosebumps. He must have noticed her discomfort and shrugged off his jacket and presented it to her. On the verge of shivering, she accepted his kind offer. When he settled the jacket around her shoulders, she sighed happily from its warmth.

"Thank you."

"It's nothing. Though I find this southern climate warm, others are chilled at sea."

She couldn't quite pin down his accent. "I hope you don't mind me asking, but your accent makes me curious about where you're from."

"Oh, that. I've become accustomed to that question and don't mind it at all."

She waited, but he remained quiet, more reverent than simply silent, as if he was treasuring the night and the scenic beauty of the quickly setting sun. Curious and a bit amused by his charm, she asked, "Will you tell me?" She realized a teasing tone laced her question. She hoped he didn't think she was flirting. "Or must I guess?"

"I was raised in Germany. Though my parents are from Poland, they now live in Brooklyn. A quick study of languages, I speak a mix of Polish-German with a Brooklyn edge, or put another way, Brooklynese with an edge of Polish-German. I can no longer tell."

She laughed, loud and clear. Wrapping her arms around her middle, she calmed herself down. "Thank you for that overdue chuckle. Are you visiting or immigrating to Brooklyn?"

He patted his vest pocket. "I carry my landing certificate with me, counting the seconds until I see my parents once again. This time I will become an American citizen."

Landing certificate? She and Eban had valid US visas, but who was she to make a correction, or to question? "You sound quite excited."

"From what my parents have told me in letters, America is a land of opportunities that we from Germany—and I'd think Poland—have never experienced. I come to America to search for a job and place to live before bringing my family on this journey."

An odd flutter stirred within her, and she rubbed her side.

"Do you need to sit?" he asked, indicating with his chin a bench.

"No, thank you. I'm fine."

"Yes, you are fine." The corners of his lips lifted at the end of his last word.

She turned away and glanced again at the sun, barely visible in the blackening night sky. Aware that she should return to her cabin and turn in for the night in preparation for the big day tomorrow, her feet anchored her there. "Your wife will be happy when you summon her to join you."

"No wife. My brother's children, whom I've adopted as my own, are back in Frankfurt. When my brother died in an accident at work, I became the legal guardian of his two boys. We've lived with my uncle and aunt. It's my plan to bring the rest of my family over before things get worse, to get them away from the filthy hands of the Nazis who hate our people."

"I have a son—I can certainly appreciate your concern."

"Is he on the ship with you?"

She nodded and smiled as the image of Eban's adorable face appeared before her.

"Is your husband meeting you tomorrow?"

She could lie about Jabez. Like Eve in the Garden, the temptation to live an independent life in a new country tantalized her like the offer of the apple. But ironically, it was this ocean trip away from her past that made her aware of how desirous she was of Jabez. A powerful longing for her husband filled her with an ache as if she lacked the air she needed to breathe. "No, he's been detained. His cousin will meet us when we arrive in New York. I'm looking forward to my husband joining us in a short while."

"How nice."

She gave a little nod and thought about seeing Jabez for the first time when they were reunited. How would she appear to her husband? Older, more ragged looking? Would he see her as set in her ways and unwilling to bow down to his demands and whims? Would he also be perplexed by jitters about her reaction to him, whether she saw in him the same attractiveness that had helped hold them together before this odd separation came between them?

The stranger cupped the back of his ear. "Listen carefully. I believe the cabin class is enjoying a band from their deck, and its music is reaching us from the other side of the ship. Ah, the night air can prove resourceful."

"Magical"

"Care to dance?"

She glanced about to discover that the two couples had left the deck. She was alone with this stranger, this charming and amusing man.

"Yes. That would be nice." It had been a while since she danced.

Could she manage to avoid stepping on his feet? Would she turn too soon or too late?

He gripped her hand firmly and led her to the center of the deck and into a waltz. With each turn she noticed a new star decorating the night sky. A delicious peace she hadn't experienced in weeks, months, or admittedly, in years, filled her heart.

At the conclusion of their dance, he kissed her hand. "It's been a pleasure to meet you. Enjoy the rest of your life in the United States."

She wished him the same, and watched him descend the stairs. When she went to do the same, she realized three things: his jacket remained around her shoulders, its warmth a tonic of sorts; they had not exchanged names; and for the barest of moments, she'd forgotten her own name and past.

She and Jabez would soon be reunited. Her husband had taken a huge risk to usher his family to this new country because he loved them and wanted the best for them.

Then why, as a married woman, one who was truly committed to her husband, had she accepted the stranger's jacket for warmth, let alone his invitation to dance under the twinkling stars? Would she falter and grab the next stranger who stood before her?

With her back against the railing, she rested her eyes. She remembered Aanya's gentle teasing that when she and Jabez were together again, they'd compensate for the lost time between a man and his wife and soon enough their lovemaking would bring forth another baby. Jabez was the one she wanted to dance under the night sky with, the one she wanted to make small talk or big talk with—or both—as they lay side by side in their shared bed, with nothing between them and the music of the earth spinning around them. This, she was certain of.

She didn't want another man. She wanted her husband, and looked forward to the day when he would show up at their new home. He'd wrap her in his arms and say how he'd missed her. He would promise to never again let her go. And she would tell him the same. They'd affirm that they were each other's life partner and vow to forever remain side by side, enjoying life until death separated them, at least here on earth.

She'd accept nothing less.

Zofia arrived at her cabin and knocked softly.

Herta opened the door at the third rap. "Ah, you have color to your cheeks again. Looks like the night air agreed with you."

"Yes, I have no regrets." And Zofia didn't, nor did she feel shame. If Herta was curious about the man's jacket draped over her shoulders, she didn't pry. "I had a perfectly nice time." She glanced at the upper berth. Eban slept spooned against his pillow, reminding her of how he'd slept with his teddy bear a few short years ago.

"He is quite the precious child." Herta blew the sleeping boy a kiss. "He reminds me of my oldest when she was his age — a sweet little dumpling."

"Was Eban well behaved?"

"Yes, though he'd managed to recharge his energy by the time I got to the end of the story."

"Oh, no. Eban can be a handful at times. What did you do to quiet him down?"

"What my mama used to do for me. I took him to the hall bath and let him relax in the warm water. Made him sleepy right away."

Zofia gave in to her sixth sense. "Did Eban say anything of interest?"

"A bit. About his papa's disappearance, and how bad people hated your friend and called her *Jude* and beat up her husband who used to be a Nazi, and you had no choice but to leave Brzeziny and you have no clue whether you'll ever see your husband again."

Eban had revealed nearly all their agreed-upon secrets to Herta; he too must have needed a kind, caring listener to share what he'd clutched close to his heart in secrecy. Zofia's belly tightened. She dropped her chin toward her chest. Of course, her bright, intuitive son understood more about what was happening than he'd let on. She should have cautioned him more firmly to be careful what he revealed to others, although Herta seemed nice and trustworthy. Yet, each person was complex. An adult had already lived through many decades of both good and bad situations, right and wrong decisions, shaping him or her. Herta was not an exception.

"I won't breathe a word of this to a soul," Herta whispered. With the tip of a finger, she gently prodded Zofia's chin upward, reminding her what she'd often done with Aanya. "Your past is not my concern, my friend. What matters between us is only from this day on. That's the magnificence of starting over again in a new country."

Trust, not an easy task these days, but a necessity. Eban wasn't the only one with a confession. Zofia gave a little nod then pointed at the door. "Let's step out into the corridor." She was relieved when Herta didn't counter by excusing herself to her cabin.

They both leaned against the wall, side by side.

Zofia glanced up and down the corridor, but no one approached. To be safe, she talked softly. "I want to tell you what finally pushed me to leave home in Brzeziny. I haven't told anyone, including my dearest friend back home." She squeezed her eyes shut for mere seconds, wishing she could push the rest of the world out for hours. She looked straight into Herta's soft blue eyes. "I'm just coming to terms with this. I've denied it and fought to block it for the longest of times and I believe that was why I foolishly delayed leaving during a time that would have been more advantageous for traveling."

The corners of Herta's mouth lifted, but not quite in a smile. "You're not about to break the news to me that you're a spy on a secret mission?"

"No. That would have been quite the dramatic tale, though."

Herta nodded and remained silent, waiting.

Zofia inhaled deeply. "I've put my son first before the others who are also significant in my life—my friend who is like a sister, my mother-in-law who is like a mama, and then there's Aunt Inga and Artur, my friend's husband."

"That's understandable. You're a mama and we mothers must put our children's needs and welfare first, always."

"Well, yes, but there's more." Zofia slowly released a sigh. When she realized that Herta was waiting for her to continue, she plowed into her admission as if she was before the priest back in the small Brzeziny Catholic church. "It wasn't seeing Artur come back for

Aanya—my friend—that taught me the strength of a husband's love. It wasn't Aanya losing her mother that retaught me the sacred value of having a mama; after losing my own mother, I had come to admire and love my husband's mother dearly. It wasn't coming close to, but thankfully not, being raped by beasts who treated me like dirt because my best friend Anaya is Jewish." *Calm down. Steady your breathing.*

Herta squeezed her hand. "You don't have to say more if it's too difficult."

Zofia shook her head exaggeratedly, as if a child wanting to leave no doubt in anyone's mind what exactly she thought. "Two nights before I caught my son practicing with a shotgun because of his desire to protect me—all of us—against the Nazis, I couldn't sleep. So I wandered outdoors and headed in the opposite direction from town." The images of what had happened next paraded before her and she fought to take control, concentrating on telling this woman as they sailed to Havana, far, far from Brzeziny. "Footsteps suddenly came to my ear—so deep in thought was I that I hadn't heard them sooner—followed by a hand over my mouth and the cold blade of a knife pressed against my throat."

"I'm so sorry."

"This person threatened me that if I breathed a single word of this to anyone, my whole family—including my friend *the Jew*, her husband, and their child who lived with me, would burn in a mysterious house fire. He then informed me that he knew what my husband was up to—part of a resistance group against the Nazi Party—and that he'd also see a quick end to his life."

"What did he want, or demand of you, then?"

"That I must take my *stinking son* and leave Brzeziny, leave Poland, immediately. That was when I contacted my husband's cousin and made the final arrangements to sail to America."

"And, you're obviously feeling guilty." With her fingertips, Herta wiped away the tears cascading down Zofia's cheeks. "I don't understand why, though."

"Because I waited to the next-to-last second to leave, jeopardizing my loved ones' lives. It hurts here." She patted her heart. "I waited because I didn't want to admit how horrible life was becoming. All I did was make things worse."

"Oh, my dear." Herta grasped Zofia's arms. "You cannot hold yourself responsible for the changes happening in Europe. What you did was not selfish, not at all. You honestly tried to make life bearable for those you loved while the ugliness and terror spreading is turning men, women, and children against each other." She pointed at the cabin door. "Your little boy, who needs his mother more than ever, is sound asleep in there. He's resting comfortably because he has you for his mama and trusts you."

"What am I going to do? How can I go on, starting a new life in a new country while I've left behind the people I love, and they are in danger?" Zofia's breath hitched. She was talking to a woman, who although she was traveling with her husband and two daughters, also had left behind family, friends, their town, and their native country to travel to the unfamiliar.

"You're going to go into your cabin, continue loving your son, and tomorrow leave this ship to begin the last part of your trip to make a new home. You're almost home, Zofia. Neither one of us knows why we have this privilege to go forward in life while others do not, but we must simply take one step at a time. We have no other choice, do we?"

"No."

"What we can do is pray for the best. Hopefully, Brzeziny won't fall victim to the harm that Hitler is wreaking in Germany. Let's go back to our cabins. Tomorrow we shall begin anew. It will be good, for each one of us."

24

The second day of June started on a crisp note. Gradually, the cool morning turned warm but pleasant. Home life for Aanya was peaceful, routine. There was comfort in that.

Aanya set off to Abe's house to check on Rolf. The German who had been left behind by his Nazi pals was just beginning to get back on his feet. He'd suffered several seizures that had kept him confined to Aanya's care and led her to re-diagnose him as having some sort of head injury beyond a concussion as she'd initially believed. Still absent were his fellow soldiers. Hopefully, it would stay that way. Artur and his own pals, who took turns guarding the door to Rolf's room, made use of this time to scheme in detail, making plans for Brzeziny to escape suffering from the hand of evil. But Artur wasn't at Abe's today.

When Aanya arrived home, the day ceased to be uneventful. Lena, Inga, and Artur gathered around the radio. Their eyes and lips sagged downward. She rushed to her husband, who stood beside the tabletop radio with the flower-print tablecloth underneath it. These days, not even flowers, whether designed on cloth or real, could make the news pretty.

"Tell me," she said aloud to Artur. Two simple, but powerful words.

He would not sugarcoat the truth. "The St. Louis—the ship Zofia and Eban sailed on—was forced to leave Cuba today. Most passengers were told that they didn't have valid visas and weren't permitted to leave the ship and enter Havana. Twenty-eight passengers were admitted into the country by the Cuban government. No names have been released yet."

A stab of worry twisted Aanya's insides. She lifted her hand to sign. "Zofia and Eban? Were they allowed off the boat? Where is the ship sailing to now?"

Artur took her hand and led her to the sofa. Inga scooted over to let them sit.

This couldn't be good.

Artur repeated that the identities of the passengers permitted into Cuba were yet not made public. "Reports are calling this a Death Ship, Aanya." He spoke slowly, taking care that she wouldn't misunderstand. "It's been revealed that before the ship reached Cuba the authorities knew that the majority of what the passengers thought they'd purchased as visas were actually landing certificates. Fake ones, at that. Nearly 937 passengers were swindled out of their money. Making the agony worse, like other countries that have said no to Jewish immigrants, the United States has issued a firm no to these passengers without a home."

"America said no? To all of them?"

"Let's think positively. Zofia and Eban might be two of the 28 passengers granted entry into Cuba." Artur switched to sigining. "Zofia and Eban have good documentation, actual visas. They should be fine, but I can't tell you more. We must wait until she contacts us. Meanwhile, the ship is sailing back."

"To Germany? To the country that hates Jews?"

Like a man turning to a friend in anticipation of good news, Artur looked long and hard at the radio. He faced Aanya again. "They didn't say where," he signed, struggling to move his fingers, to relay the words, to admit uncertainty. "I'm sure we'll learn over the next few days."

Artur sprang to his feet. He signed that a caller had just pounded on the front door. He hurried over, stepped outside to speak to the visitor, and then summoned Aanya. "It's Abe. He says Rolf is complaining that ringing in his ears is making it difficult to hear."

Minutes later when Aanya entered Rolf's room she saw two different sides of him. The first was a striking young man, tall and lanky, blond and fair, fearful and hurting. He was a long way from home, in a country that didn't want him. Ultimately, he was her patient, one whose recovery she held in her hands. But the other side was that, despite the absence—so far—of a declaration of war, this stranger was an enemy and wore the look of an unfriendly and uncooperative opponent.

She strode to the desk to read the notes she'd entered from her last visit. Approaching the bed, she stood by his side and observed him. Rolf squinted and started to speak.

Artur, who had followed her into the room, interpreted. "He asks why you never speak, especially to him. Wants to know how long he'll be forced to stay in this room, in this town."

Aanya lifted a brow.

"Yes, he's chatty today," Artur said, reading her thoughts. "Says the ringing in his ears is bad. He can barely hear himself speak. Says if you're a doctor, prove your worth by healing him."

Aanya laughed.

Artur glanced over his shoulder at Rolf and then faced Aanya again with a smirk on his face. "The arrogant fool says you have no right to laugh at him."

"Well, he certainly heard my laughter without a problem," she signed. She slipped a pad and pencil from her white clinical jacket pocket. She scrawled a message to Rolf, which Artur reworded in German and handed to him. He then listened to Rolf's reply.

"He's incredulous that you won't talk to him—as if he were a flea on a dog—but fails to understand why you treat him as kindly as you do."

She smiled as she wrote her next response. This time she sat beside Rolf while Artur translated the note into German before he shoved the paper at him.

I don't communicate directly with you because, like you, I cannot hear. See, my friend, the two of us—you a German, and I a Pole, we who cannot hear—are no different. And that's why I treat you with kindness. We are both human beings, both fragile, both deserving to live.

Rolf spoke to Artur, who again translated for Aanya.

"He doubts you because there are guards armed with rifles at his door." The corners of Artur's mouth turned down; his brows pinched together. "He says that one day soon, our guns will be no more and that Poland's time will come to an end."

"What is he implying, Artur? What can Hitler be scheming?"

"Nothing good." Artur pressed down on his lip, likely suppressing the urge to swear. After a few moments of silence, he lifted his hand to sign. "Germany's madman does whatever he wants to do whenever he wants to do it. That's the definition of a dictator." He pointed to Rolf then faced her again. "Since Hitler keeps a tight lip until he deems action is necessary, I don't think our friend knows squat."

Aanya's peripheral vision registered movement from the bed. She turned as Rolf's pupils rolled back and chest muscles tightened. She darted to the supply chest she'd set up in the hallway. Thanks to her dear friend Dr. Paweł's teaching and sharing his knowledge of medicine, including his pioneer usage in the Brzeziny area of intravenous injection, Aanya assembled the vacuum-sealed glass bottle of phenytoin she'd stored for emergencies, rushed to her patient's side, and administered the drug. She watched as Rolf relaxed.

"He'll complain of dizziness or headache, perhaps drowsiness. The phenytoin may slow his speech or weaken his memory, but I'll add the drug to his treatment to prevent more seizures." She covered Rolf's hand with hers. "He's suffered enough."

Artur opened his mouth as if to speak, but closed it abruptly. Deep grooves furrowed his forehead.

"What?" she asked aloud.

He stroked her cheek with the back of his hands. "When he awakes, we'll put a bit more pressure on him to reveal what he can."

Artur's sentence both chilled and comforted her. She trusted him. He was a good man. No further questions were necessary. She kissed Artur and hurried out of the room, past the two guards. She may have sensed her husband's gaze riveted to her back, but she didn't turn around. Not when her eyes brimmed with tears over Zofia. At the end of the hallway she flung the door open and stepped outside.

The earlier mild and sunny June day had clouded up. With a headache developing, she knew rain was heading their way within the next two days. Her thoughts again drifted to Zofia, and how she also suffered from weather-induced headaches. Aanya hoped her friend, unlike the other ill-fated St Louis passengers, was experiencing sunshine and warmth and ease on her travels to her new home. And she hoped the other passengers would find a country that would welcome them.

25

The first successful phone connection from Cuba to New York that Zofia was able to make occurred three days after the St. Louis sailed away from Puerto de La Habana, the port in Havana. It was the longest three days Zofia had ever experienced. Yet, not long enough to stop seeing, like a reel of film playing over and over in her mind, the tearful faces of Herta and Kurt and their daughters. Or the man who slit his wrist and jumped overboard only to be rescued by a sailor. Not long enough to block the whispered planning she'd heard before she and Eban disembarked to scuttle the ship, the plotters preferring to sink and perish in the ocean rather than face the evil grip of those who worked the labor and prison camps and ordered Jews and other non-Aryans tortured, starved, and other inhumane punishments she imagined she and many did not know about.

Zofia's dreams were no better. In these haunting states of mind, she danced an endless waltz with her nameless deck companion; he was one of the hundreds of passengers who was not allowed to leave the ship and begin a new life. The cries, the shrieks, and the angry shouts from the left-behind passengers not granted permission to leave the ship and live a life of freedom stirred her awake, leaving her unable to fall back asleep.

"Isaac?" she said into the phone receiver when the connection went through to New York.

"Yes, it's me." Jabez's cousin's deep voice sailed over the long-wave radio circuit transmitted from the northeastern part of the United States, across the water, and into Cuba. "Tell me what I should do and I'll do it. If it gets you and Eban here to New York, it will be well worth it. That's what Jabez would want, and that's what I'll do."

Her mind froze as if the thick, moist air hanging over Havana had suddenly turned to the bitter cold of Polish winters. Should she tell him she had no clue as to her husband's whereabouts? Would he stop caring about their fate if she did? No, she couldn't imagine this close relative of Jabez's would turn indifferent toward her and her son.

"Zofia, are you and your son well? Have those Cubans mistreated you?"

"Eban and I are fine, Isaac. No worries. I'm both nervous and excited that we'll soon see you." She told him how the Cuban government had approved their visas, but how he needed to wire a 500-dollar bond plus their shipping cost to New York. Worrying that government officials may be listening in on their conversation, she held back her agitation that this bond was likely a bogus charge and that the shipping cost made her feel more like merchandise than a person. Once again, reality hit her and brought her close to hysteric sobs. She and Eban were two of the only 28 people permitted off the ship, and now it was sailing back to Germany because not one other country would open their borders to them to keep them out of harm's way. The president of the United States had failed to respond to the captain's plea to save at least the children. She hoped for a miracle for the St Louis's passengers, that the ship would be permitted to dock somewhere else other than Nazi Germany.

"Can you manage, Isaac? This is a lot to ask, and I'm sorry to do so."

"Of course. I've worked hard these years and will provide. Zofia, you and your son are family. That I haven't seen you since your wedding, let alone ever set eyes on your little boy, doesn't change our relationship at all."

"Thank you. I don't understand why the American government won't help the other passengers."

"Several countries have met their quotas of immigrants, refugees included. But back to you, Zofia. I'm more than eager to help. At this point, despite Jabez not contacting me recently, he made clear a while back that he wants you and your son here because he's determined to keep you safe and when he meets up with you again, he will be the one to watch over you and Eban. I'll take care of the financial transfer right away, and will see you in five days."

Five long, excruciating days, she thought, and then chastised herself for complaining about such a small inconvenience. What about Herta and her family and everyone else on the ship?

"And there's one more item," Isaac added. "I promise, once you and Eban arrive safely and we settle you down in your new home, we'll find Jabez and get him to you."

She didn't know who the *we* he referred to were, but he sounded as firm as her husband. She trusted this man, the only family member she and Eban had in their new country.

26

Regardless of the hard work Aanya put into building trust with Rolf, she made it a point of always having Artur, or one of his male friends, accompany her when she visited the young man in his guarded private room at Abe's house. Fortunately, on this particular June day, the 25th, emotionally stretched to the maximum with concerns about Zofia and Eban, Artur stood beside her as she checked on her German patient.

"Good news," she said aloud, rather than her customary hello.

When it came to communication, Rolf didn't interact with her, at least not directly, but instead fielded his questions or concerns through Artur. She noted, though, that ever since she'd started to treat and control his seizures, Rolf had stopped making disrespectful faces at her attempts to speak. She suspected that his own clogged hearing gained her a little empathy, though she wouldn't wait around for him to admit it. Today, he looked into her eyes. She'd spoken in Polish and whether or not he'd understood was a question that she didn't have the time or patience to consider. She faced Artur to sign and for him to communicate the rest to Rolf.

"The good news is that I believe your body is healing to the point that you will not need to continue on the antiseizure medication."

Judging by the way Artur moved his shoulders and chest, Aanya suspected that he was talking louder than normal so Rolf could hear him. Artur paid attention to Rolf's response and passed it on to Aanya, who couldn't help but marvel at how her husband was fluent in three languages: German, Polish, and PJM, the Polish sign language. With his ease in communication, it was no surprise Artur had already established firm friendships in the Brzeziny community.

"So what?" Artur said, repeating each of Rolf's words directly. "If you keep me prisoner for the rest of my miserable life, what difference does it make if I twitch and jerk like an imbecile or can walk around these four walls without falling down?" As Rolf had done, Artur pointed toward the window. "I need to be out there, free. I need to be in Germany, with my own people."

Up to this point, Artur and his men had extracted from Rolf that he and the other Nazis—Rolf proclaimed the title with a smug grin—had been traveling back to the German-Polish border having completed a reconnaissance mission to assess strong and weak defense points between Brzeziny and Łódź. Why, he wouldn't cough up. Ordered by whom, he wouldn't drop a hint. But this knowledge alone was ominous. Would his pals come back? He shrugged.

"It is not our fault you've been ill," Aanya signed. She fixed a casual smile on her face. "Count as good fortune that of all the places despised by the Nazi Party, you fell off the jeep in Brzeziny, a town full of good and kind people. And that I've been overseeing your recovery, because I doubt anyone else would have."

She watched Artur speak to Rolf, surprised that the two of them went at it a couple of rounds before Artur faced her fully to convey what they'd talked about.

"Rolf thanks you."

"Pardon?" Aanya said aloud, then covered her mouth, though not fast enough to hide her shock.

"Well, indirectly, he thanks you."

She lifted a brow.

"Says that although he appreciates your efforts, he doesn't trust us. I told him that we don't trust him either. He again demanded his release, but I told him that wasn't doable, not now, at least."

Aanya glanced at the wrist and foot restraints that fastened Rolf to the bed that the guards had placed on him before she and Artur entered the room. The control devices were meant to help ensure their own safety. But today was different. She studied Rolf's chart as she thought back to how she and Artur had talked with Abe about what she would like to see happen with the German, pleased that after careful consideration and discussion Abe saw merit in her idea. She approached the bed again and unfastened the restraints on his feet. "I've shown you how Artur and I can be trusted. Now it is your turn to show to us that you're willing to reciprocate. If you cooperate, I'll be happy to unfasten your wrists."

"I told him," Artur signed to her, "that this trust is only within this room. That there will still be guards stationed at the door around the clock. He says he understands."

Good. Their plan was going smoothly. They'd work on building more trust, continue to treat him medically, and hope that Rolf had a sense of honor. But eventually, like releasing a wild animal back into the wilderness, they'd have to let their captive go, or chance having a slew of Nazis returning to claim him, if not a far worse development. Although several in town would have no qualms about locking him up behind bars, Artur, his men, and Aanya didn't want to provoke Nazi patrols to pay a visit. Troubling to Aanya was the mystery behind why Rolf was dropped on the road and forgotten about. If it weren't for his head injury, she might have surmised that it was an act, that he was planted in Brzeziny to spy on them. Artur, a deserter from the Nazi Party, knew a thing or two about how the Nazi mind worked. He believed Rolf was bound to cause trouble. On the other hand, she knew people could have a change of heart. Artur certainly had. He chose to risk his life by defecting from the Nazi Party rather than spend one more day—one more minute—continuing to carry out Hitler's commands. But she didn't see any signs in Rolf of any such crisis of conscience. He was a Nazi and proud of it. Artur was probably right in his estimate of Rolf.

She needed to find a bit of privacy or she'd lose her composure, or worse, her objectivity. With no intention of divulging these intimate thoughts to a Nazi, no matter how much she and the others desired to have him show that he was trustworthy, she pardoned herself and left the room.

27

Aanya could only tend to a wounded enemy with expertise and kindness for a limited time before releasing him into the world. After nursing Rolf back to health, and showing him ways to compensate for his partial loss of hearing, it was time to say goodbye.

The starless midnight August sky may have failed to brighten the inside room where Rolf had convalesced, and for that matter, the paths that he would soon travel on, but her former patient appeared buoyed in spirit. She stood beside Artur; Rolf stood opposite them, his balance steady on two firm feet. The three of them had come a long way in nearly the full month of June and into half of August since Rolf had come to Brzeziny, building a trust that they had once believed impossible.

Aanya pointed at Rolf's chest. "You look well."

After Artur translated this into German, Rolf nodded, a clipped movement that seemed to belie the slight smile curling his lips. Or maybe it was vice versa. A handsome man, he was bound to make a woman a happy wife—if he survived possible further behavior like his fellow soldiers abandoning him alongside the road—or, if Germany did declare war, he survived combat. *Survive.* What an odd word. Hitler might have been trying to dictate who had the right to live, but in Aanya's eyes and heart, everyone deserved to thrive rather than merely survive, like a stray animal.

"Danke, Frau Lang."

Aanya glanced at Artur. When had he revealed their last name to Rolf? This surprised her, and struck her as risky. She'd have to ask him later. She lifted her hand to sign instructions for Rolf, via translation through Artur, but Rolf grasped her hand to shake it. Then he did the last thing she'd ever expected from the Nazi who had practically growled at her at their first meeting. With her hand still clutched in his, he stepped forward and kissed her on the cheek.

"Danke," he repeated. Rolf then addressed Artur and she waited for a translation.

Artur faced Aanya fully. She didn't see suspicion or doubt in her husband's blank expression, but she sensed his uncertainty.

"Our friend," Artur began, "vows that he will do everything in his capacity to steer the Nazi forces away from Brzeziny. One way or the other, he will help us."

A tall task and probably impossible pledge, Aanya concluded, but she smiled back with a tinge of hope fluttering within her chest. "You take care of yourself," she signed and patted his arm. She watched from the window as Artur and Abe drove Rolf toward the Polish-German border where they'd let him out a few kilometers from the heavily patrolled area. Exhausted, she dragged herself back to the house and slumped into bed.

Yet she couldn't sleep. All the *shoulds* rushed into her mind. She should have checked on Laja, Lena, and especially Inga. Lately, the sweet woman was more ill than not. Heart failure, Aanya had diagnosed several weeks ago, and a fast and relentless decline. Only in her early sixties, she spent her days in bed, hardly able to eat a morsel of food. Aanya had tried to prepare Lena and Artur, and the three of them waited, on guard for death's visit. And there was Zofia. She should have received a letter from her by now. She had to push back building anxiety and concern over her childhood friend and her son, trusting that any day now she'd receive a note saying, in her Zofia-way, that *things were grand*.

She felt the mattress dip, opened her eyes, and smiled at Artur under the covers. The early morning sun sneaking around the bedroom curtains gave them just enough light to see. She stretched and began to sign. "I must have fallen asleep, after all. Did you get Rolf off and running?"

"Yes, and thankfully, no problems." He inched closer to her; he wasn't wearing a stitch of clothing.

She propped herself on an elbow. The light summer blanket slipped down from her neck. "How did my most notorious patient learn our last name?"

"Oh, that?"

She nodded.

"A week ago, one of the men guarding Rolf's door called me by my last name. And, like a fool, I looked up."

"That's unfortunate." She fanned her fingers against the stubble growing on his cheeks.

"I don't expect trouble will come of it, but of course, I'll watch for indications." He seized her hand and rolled on top of her. "Enough about your former German patient. He's past tense. I'd rather focus on you."

She grinned as she freed her hand from his hold to sign. With her other hand, she whipped the bedcovers off and glanced downward. "I can tell you're doing an excellent job at focusing on... us." She wiggled them around and positioned herself over him. "I'm glad you're home, safe and sound."

"And I can tell how glad you are, my one and only Aanya." He covered her mouth with his. No further words were necessary.

Inga's passing was not the next tragedy. It was the morning of the first day of September that shook not only Aanya's life, but Poland's— and the world's.

In bed, dreaming of dancing with Artur under a sky full of glimmering stars, Aanya batted her lashes when a shove came to her arm. A Friday, she was due at the health center early that afternoon, and all she wanted was to slumber lazily on this late summer morning. When another strong shake came, to both arms this time, her eyes shot open.

"Wake up. Quickly!" Artur said.

He'd never said that combination of words to her before. "Inga?" she signed.

"No. Worse."

Worse than a dying woman? She then remembered the German-staged skirmishes at the border; information leaked to Artur and his men revealed them to be fake fights to justify German action. Had Rolf made it back to Germany and hidden his partial hearing loss, only to be sent to participate in these? It was just last evening they learned that supposed SS troops wearing Polish army uniforms staged yet another attack on several minor German installations on the German side of the border. Several casualties were left behind. Aanya and Artur had remained awake late into the night, unable to figure out which would be worse: were those dead Germans or Poles, or prisoners from the Nazi camps, like the one Artur had been stationed at? Were these victims forced to put on Polish uniforms and sacrifice their lives to make Poland look as if it was starting a war with Germany?

"Get dressed. Meet me by the window."

In no time, Aanya followed his pointed finger and saw masses of people running, and others staggering but managing to keep moving forward. They'd come from the west and were headed east toward Warsaw. Already dressed, and fully awake as if she'd never slept, she kissed him and turned to leave. His hand on her shoulder turned her around to face him.

"Where are you going?" he signed.

"To grab my medical bag, then outdoors to help. There must be many who are injured and in need of attention."

"I'm going with you—on the way we'll tell Lena to watch Laja and Inga—"

Aanya clutched Artur's shoulder. "Tell them that under no circumstances are they to step outside of this house."

Once outdoors, Artur managed to stop a woman and her three sons as they made their way down the road. They were Jews, she said, from a town west of Łódź. The Germans had crossed the border and were attacking Poland—her husband had been killed by a tank that rolled over him when he refused to move from in front of their house.

Aanya assessed them quickly for injury. Concluding they were fine—as fine as someone could be when running for their lives, let alone newly widowed and fatherless—she rushed indoors, grabbed the half loaf of bread left over from last night's meal, and in a flash gave it to the woman and her boys. They stashed the food in their pockets for later and resumed running—there was no time yet to indulge in eating.

When the woman and children were out of view, Aanya clutched her stomach. Artur's eyes widened.

"I'm fine," she signed. "I just realized this poor woman and her sons have been on the run for at least 27 to 30 kilometers, if not more. It's all so awful." She glanced at the crowd passing before her eyes; she could not see an end to the multitude. Their collective agonies were absorbed into her as if they were her own. She swore aloud sadly, a word she'd asked Artur to teach her the day Zofia left.

"Do you want to wait inside?"

She glared at him. "If people need help, there's no way I'm shying away from offering my two hands."

Artur eyed her medical bag and studied her face. She hoped he saw unmitigated determination because that was what she was prepared to give.

While Lena cared for Laja and Inga, Aanya and Artur, like their other fellow Brzeziners, gave food, medical help, and sleeping accommodations to those fleeing from German attack. During the summer months the Polish government hadn't mounted an opposing force because it assumed Great Britain and France would help. Although those two countries demanded Germany withdraw by the end of September second, on the third of September, British Prime Minister Chamberlain announced Britain was at war with Germany. Australia, New Zealand, India, and France followed. The Polish government had mobilized its forces and those on reserve, though they'd been sent to eastern Poland due to false German propaganda. No one was prepared for the German panzer divisions plowing through Poland, destroying everything in their path, whether an inanimate object, an animal, or a human being. The Polish troops that had reached the western front were trapped in the chaos. The blood shed by Germany's hand grew even worse. Planes provided the means of shooting people en masse, obliterating individual lives as if they were ants. On land, the enemy murdered both Gentile and Jew.

On September sixth, a Wednesday, the Germans came to Brzeziny.

Since the day the Germans had crossed the border into Poland, Aanya and her family, like the others in town, had prepared the cellar for living with blankets, clothing, and food, and had started to spend their days and nights there instead of in the main house. They slept in their day clothes and shoes, prepared to flee if necessary. The cellar had no windows, but it wasn't necessary to see what happened during the night when all five of them were shaken and rattled as the first bomb was dropped on Brzeziny. Artur, Inga, and Lena shuddered —an unintentional warning to Aanya and Laja—as they heard the high pitch of the whistle affixed to the bomb to further shake the morale of those on the ground; Aanya and Laja trembled from the vibrations when the bomb fell. Filled with sheer terror, they clung to each other as bombs went off, one after another.

Then, silence. Time stood ghostly, unflinching. The bombing had ended—at least for now.

Artur shot to his feet. "Stay here." Aanya scrambled upright from her bedding. Artur took one look at her and insisted she remain with the others.

"I cannot, will not, stay put. I'm going with you."

Artur grabbed her hand and turned away from her, but not before she could see a curse leave his lips, likely murmured under his breath to keep it from the women. But their daughter could read lips as well as Aanya.

Daughter.

Aanya slipped back to the floor and took her trembling daughter into her arms, but left enough distance so they could sign. "I must go with Papa. Be brave and stay with Babcia and Aunt Inga. Yes?"

Laja nodded. "Hurry back, Mama."

"For you, yes, I will. Love you." Aanya met Artur by the stairs. He'd waited for her; she knew he would because he understood her, accepted her, loved her for her better or worse, and knew that when she said that she was going with him, she wouldn't back down.

"You're not going to like what you see," Artur said.

"War is never pretty, nor is death," she signed, and followed him up the stairs and outdoors.

They expected horror, but what they saw was worse. Fire and smoke covered the streets. What the bombs didn't destroy, the German army had tackled, removing almost every trace of what life had been like in the quiet Polska town that had existed since the 13th century.

As if they had both felt a blast, Aanya and Artur leaned against the front of the house, shocked. He squeezed her hand; she kissed him fully on the mouth. She wanted minutes of this love shared between them—hours, days. Wanted to erase the destruction and replace it with love. In the face of war, love shined brighter, especially compared to the alternative. It would have to, wouldn't it?

"I'm going to search for my friends and see what we can do to help," Artur said.

Aanya lifted the medical bag that she'd brought out with them. She glanced at the road, both ways, and then back at Artur. No words. No signing. They stepped into action.

Quick on his feet, within seconds Artur vanished from her sight. She made her way around fallen pieces of wood, brick, downed trees and assorted debris from the bomb explosions that covered the ground. It was a miracle their house had remained standing.

Once across the road, her mind couldn't grasp what she saw. Their neighbor, an old woman who lived alone, lay in a heap on the road like a pile of trash. Jonas Meyer, a neighbor from up the road, ground his foot into the woman's chest as if he posed for a photograph with a big game animal he'd just killed.

"Pani Lang," he said, aware Aanya could understand his spoken words. He removed his foot from the woman.

Aanya couldn't assimilate his casual air. Jonas was one of the few Germans living in Brzeziny. His family had lived here long enough that no one thought of them as outsiders. Why would he act as if he were reveling in this invasion? For years, he'd always offered a smile to his fellow Brzeziners, talking about the weather and a bargain found at the weekly market. And now, he was suddenly on the German side, as if denying he'd enjoyed life in this little town that had been good to him. Was it by his hand this poor woman had suffered?

She knelt to check the woman's vital signs, though it was a waste of precious time. The woman was dead.

Jonas crouched before Aanya. "She died on her doorstep—I suspect her heart gave out when she saw what was happening. I dragged her to the road. That way, the house doesn't get contaminated."

He dragged a dead woman? Didn't carry her? Contaminated. Who was expecting to live there next? A takeover, a war was happening before their eyes. This wasn't the time to plan on obtaining a new house to live in. Unless... Confused by events and in shock like the rest of them, Jonas might be misspeaking.

She pointed at his chest. "Need medical help?"

He spat, the landing point of the trajectory not far from the deceased woman's head. He slipped a pistol from his waistband, which Aanya hadn't noticed earlier. "You go back to your home. I'll spare you since you can help my German friends medically if we need you."

Again, she pointed at him. "You're Brzeziner." She looked about at the disaster around them. "Brzeziny—atttacked. Invaded."

"Yes, by the Germans. And I'm German and will help them and they'll be grateful." He aimed the pistol at her, then pointed it toward her house. "Go on. Get away from me, you worthless Jew. I don't want you near me."

Never argue with a man holding a gun. With her fists clenched, she realized that every cell in her body rebelled in silent anger against this man, against all who claimed they were of the human race but gave themselves the right to kill anyone they wanted to. She turned away from the dead woman and made herself put one foot in front of the other. She then did the thing she'd been ordered to do, and wanted to do: She hurried back to the cellar, to her family.

Lena put down the storybook that she and Laja were looking at and glanced up. No smile curved her lips; her eyes didn't sparkle with her customary hope. To think this was only a beginning to what surely would be an ongoing tragedy.

"Come sit with us," Lena said.

Aanya checked on Inga, sound asleep, and then wedged herself between Lena and Laja. She stared at the book Laja fingered, and grew numb, almost empty. It was safer that way. Aanya ignored Lena's motioning hand as she read Laja storybook after storybook, and slipped into her own version of storyland.

A story of wading ducks on the river uniting her with Zofia when they were five years old.

Of bouquets of wildflowers plucked from the fields for their mamas.

Of girlish dreams of the men they'd one day marry, shared with giggles; of children they would have and what they would name them.

Of the time when she broke the news that she and Zofia would have to separate—but only for a year—as she attended a special school for the deaf. While there, the lessons learned would prove beneficial, yet, the memory of the kilometers that had separated her from the only friend she had, the only one who easily understood her, was painful.

Flashes of Zofia marrying Jabez waltzed in her mind. Her friend was so in love with her husband. And soon enough, Eban came along and made their lives grander. Instead of excluding Aanya as her family grew, Zofia had done the opposite. They saw each other nearly every day, and Aanya was declared an auntie to Zofia's beautiful little boy.

Of Artur coming back into her life, forever and ever. It was this thought that carried her into a deep sleep, away from Brzeziny and its bombs, into a delicious respite of nothingness.

When she awoke, Artur stood before her. Lena scrambled to her feet and let him slip beside Aanya. He put his arm around their sleeping daughter, keeping a hand free to sign.

"Where should I begin? It's all bad."

"I expected it to be." Aanya glanced at the cellar stairs he'd trodden down in order to rejoin his family and then faced him and continued to sign. "Our once nice neighbor, Jonas, ordered me home at gunpoint, away from him because I'm Jewish. But oh, he wouldn't shoot me since I can help him and his German pals, medically speaking. It's as if he's never enjoyed living in Brzeziny, as if he's forgotten how kindly his German family has been treated by Brzeziner Jews."

Artur scrubbed his face with dirt-stained fingers. "There's looting going on in town—the shops have been broken into. Food and necessities taken."

"By Brzeziners?"

"Actually, by the local Germans," he said, rubbing his mouth as if a vile taste had just stung his tongue. He glanced at Lena, who was watching the interchange between them with a careful eye. "Like Jonas, suddenly, the few Germans who live in Brzeziny seem to have forgotten that Germany once kicked them out and Poland took them in with welcoming arms."

"What else have you learned and seen?"

"The German army is advancing toward Warsaw, capturing or annihilating anyone they come across, no questions asked."

Lena sank to her knees on the dirt floor before them. "And we here in Brzeziny?"

Artur's chest expanded as he inhaled deeply. He cast his gaze, beaming affection, at Aanya, Laja, and Inga, stopping last at Lena, the woman who had become more of a mama to him than his own mother. "We pray. We remain brave and hope. We wait."

28

Zofia did one more check around the dining room. The bright September sun had slipped around the white curtains, adding splendor to the already welcoming room. Although the house was smaller than she'd imagined—what Isaac had described as a stepping-stone house, one they could live in until they were able to afford a grander place—it was the perfect home for Eban and her; they couldn't wish for a better one. With a roof over their heads, the luxuries of electricity, two bedrooms that Isaac had furnished, a large bathroom equipped with a new shower and bathtub, and its convenient location to easy-to-walk-to shopping, this humble house Isaac was apologetic about was a palace in Zofia's opinion. The neighborhood, Brooklyn's Little Poland in Greenpoint, stood clean, quiet, and respectable with maple-lined streets and little through traffic.

She wiped a tear trickling from her left eye. She had more to be grateful for than not: she and her son had safely left Poland, were permitted to disembark the ship in Cuba, and arrived in a country that promised a new beginning for her family—one with more opportunities than if she had remained in Brzeziny. But she couldn't help but miss Jabez. Today marked their eighth wedding anniversary, and the loneliness, the emptiness of the occasion, served to accent not only her heartache, but also her guilt.

She should have listened to Jabez when he'd first told her to leave for America.

A whoop cut across the room and jarred her thoughts. She looked away from the dining room window in time to see Eban, wearing a child's feathered American Indian headdress, run through the room. Isaac had given Eban the headdress as a gift, along with a large toy chest packed with games and a bookcase full of new storybooks. What a good, kindhearted man. It was surprising that he wasn't married yet, but he did admit his love of business and income were his first priorities. Zofia imagined that if Jabez didn't arrive soon she, like Isaac, would have to pursue hard work to support her son and herself in this new country of theirs.

Eban placed a hand on her arm. "Mother?"

"Yes, Eban? Are you okay?" She liked this new American word *okay*. She'd begun to use it instead of *fine*.

"Yes." Eban's eyes drooped. "But you aren't. I can tell."

Her perceptive son knew her well. Smart beyond his years, and taking after her side of the family in physique, he was growing like summer grass, reaching in height midway between her elbow and shoulder.

"I'm busy thinking."

He rolled his eyes. "You think a lot. About Papa?"

"Not necessarily." Aware of how silly her reply must have sounded, she frowned.

"If Papa were here, he'd say you have no faith in him."

Eban was correct. Those were the words Jabez had often flung at her when they had argued. To think their son had overheard them; to think their careless exchanges were etched in his memory. If Jabez ever came back to her—she corrected herself, *when* Jabez comes—she'd strive for gentleness to reign between them. A new country, a new beginning.

"With Papa away temporarily, he's left me in charge. Eban, darling, I'm okay." She smiled. "Together, you and I will continue to be okay."

"Mamusiu," Eban said softly. He understood how that singular word could both capture her attention and squeeze her heart, and how he could use it affectionately—or sometimes disingenuously, to try and get his way. But she was no inexperienced mother.

"Yes?"

"I miss him too. But you'll see, he'll come home. He must miss us, too." He ran from the room as suddenly as he had whooped into it.

Eban's words washed over her like the lapping of a wave coming to shore. She leaned against the windowsill, but those seconds of quiet were interrupted by the buzzing of the doorbell.

When they had first moved in she and Eban met the immediate neighbors on both sides of their house. The Tanchems, to the right, had greeted them with a freshly baked loaf of honey-molasses bread and a heaping tray of oatmeal raisin cookies. The Liddon family showered them with macaroni and cheese and a casserole with chicken smothered in a thick white sauce and a crispy Ritz cracker topping. Yet, since the day they moved in two months ago, she and Eban rarely saw their neighbors other than occasionally in passing. Unlike folks in Brzeziny, New Yorkers were always in a hurry, going places with a sense of urgency and keeping to themselves. Zofia and her son followed their example. When she opened her door and saw Gladys Liddon waving a copy of the *New York Times* with motions too jerky for Zofia to read the headline, she swallowed hard.

"Mrs. Liddon, what's wrong?"

"Have you heard the news?"

Zofia reached out and steadied the woman's hands, long enough to read the headline: "German Army Attacks Poland; Cities Bombed, Port Blockaded; Danzig Is Accepted Into Reich."

She couldn't grasp the words, not because of the English but rather, the horror. "Poland's been attacked?"

Her neighbor narrowed her eyes at Zofia as if she was daft. "Yes! That's what it says, does it not? And this is no squabble that will end by tomorrow." She jutted her chin toward the sidewalk. "Why, this is world news. It may be breaking just now here in the States, but with the time already late afternoon in Poland, those Nazis are terrorizing

—if not killing—helpless multitudes." The young woman's face paled. "Do you have loved ones there?"

Her husband, family, and friends—everyone she loved, with the exception of her son— were all in Poland, if they were still alive. That word again, *if*, set Zofia to shaking as if she'd just walked out into a blizzard. Barely able to breathe, she murmured a thank you and quietly shut the door. And locked it, something she normally did only at night before going to bed.

She sank to her knees, her back pinned flat against the door, and prayed from the depths of her heart. For Jabez. Aanya and Artur. Sweet little Laja. Lena and Inga. For her fellow Brzeziners.

For Polska... whatever was left of it.

29

A horrid nightmare tormented Aanya. Smoke filled the air, but rather than billowing outward, it sucked pieces of life into its gray grip like a monstrous tornado. Furniture. Food. Animals. Breath. Words. Human life. She couldn't sign, couldn't talk, couldn't scream. All she could do was watch in silence as her world burned and disappeared.

When she awoke her heart pounded as her vision adjusted to the nightmare of her new reality, too similar to her dream. Her family had managed to fall asleep in the dusty cellar full of filmy cobwebs. Laja had an arm draped over a crate of jarred smoked kielbasa, sauerkraut, pickles, and potatoes as if she held a teddy bear. Artur, his head resting on Lena's shoulder, snored away. And Inga? She was gone. About to shake Artur awake, Aanya stopped when she saw a note lying in the place where Inga should have lain.

I am an old woman who will die soon. It's best if I leave in a way that will not bring attention to you. I love each one of you and will meet you in heaven.

Nie... nie... nie! This couldn't be. Inga was in a state of declining physical and cognitive health, unable to fully grasp her surroundings, let alone understand about the bombings, and most certainly not lucid enough to write a note with a clear message. Aanya shook Artur and Lena. Though her tongue was heavy and clumsy with dread, she spoke their names hoping they'd hear and tell her to relax, that Inga was fine, that in fact she'd miraculously recovered and had stepped outdoors to use the privy.

Artur woke first. He clamped his hand around a pistol before opening his eyes. When and where had he gotten the weapon Aanya would ask him later, but she was relieved he had it.

Lena stirred. "What is it?"

"Inga," she said, as they scrambled to their feet.

Artur told Lena and Laja to stay put, and he and Aanya hurried outside. Artur squinted to his right; Aanya peered left toward town. They faced each other.

"What do you think?" Artur asked.

If Aanya were Inga, an older woman on the fringe of death, in a weakened state of mind, and had stepped outdoors from the cellar only to discover her ordinary world of blues, greens, oranges, pinks, and a rainbow of other colors plunged into the grays and blacks of war, her instincts would draw her to the familiar. Aanya pointed in the direction of Brzeziny—what was left of it. Without a further word between them, she and Artur ran as fast as they could maneuver through the tank-rutted road, around dead animals, in a ghostly landscape they failed to recognize.

When they reached the point where the dirt road turned to cobblestone before entering the town, Artur seized her by the elbow. "Stay here."

Aanya could not understand what he had said, but she saw his eyes register terror and alarm and she knew he'd shouted. She followed him and sprinted the remaining meters to the slumped body on the road. Inga lay prostrate, her face smashed against the hard stone. Aanya dropped to her knees. Artur crouched next to her.

Death had claimed sweet, loving Inga, but rather than die from natural causes, she had been killed by a single bullet to the back of the head, her blood puddled around her like a shroud for burial. No gun was found, nor its owner.

Artur broke into sobs. Aanya prayed her parents' prayer for eternal rest, and signed a cross in respect for her adopted Aunt Inga's faith.

"What to do?" she asked aloud.

Artur weaved his fingers through the bloody tangle of Inga's silvery hair. He stood, extending a hand to help Aanya up. "It won't be easy. May be dangerous, but let's bring her home."

"We'll bury her ourselves?" Aanya signed.

"This is war. We can't count on anyone else to help us."

"You take her shoulders and I her feet?"

Artur stooped and put his arms under the slight woman; the blood from her head wound seeped onto his shoulder but he didn't pause. "I'll carry her home."

"But—"

He'd taken a step but stopped to face Aanya. "It's enough—it's everything—that you're beside me. That's the only thing that counts." He glanced over his shoulder then back at her. "Let's go, before we can't."

Barely a half hour after Aanya and Artur had deposited the last shovelful of earth covering the mound behind the house that sheltered Inga's body, a German military vehicle stopped in front of the house. Artur ducked indoors. When he stepped outside moments later, a jacket covered his bloody, dirt-stained shirt. Two uniformed men approached the porch where Aanya and Artur sat on the steps to rest.

Aanya stared at their double-breasted black uniforms. She faced Artur and lifted a brow, though she knew Artur wouldn't dare sign his reply, thus revealing her deafness. She watched his mouth carefully.

"Waffen—SS. Armed."

She got his gist. Let them do the talking. Obey. No other choice.

The taller soldier, a fresh scar over his left brow that Aanya had to resist offering to tend to, pointed to the house. Without showing one scrap of documentation, he commandeered the house for German military purposes and ordered their immediate evacuation. The second German withdrew a paper from his pocket, scanned what was evidently a list of structures that had survived the bombings, then stated the house in town where they were to relocate. Artur nodded. The men left, probably to drive off to the next household to confiscate another family's home. The few houses up the road, heading east toward Warsaw, were old ones; a few dated back to the last century. Men and women raised children in these houses, made memories as they celebrated holidays and special occasions, decorated the walls with paintings and photographs of loved ones, placed heirloom mementos on tables, and visited family graves in their backyards. A sense of history, of family, of the continuity of life no longer counted. At least, not for the Poles, as determined by the Germans.

It was only day two of the invasion of Brzeziny. Aanya couldn't bring herself to contemplate what else awaited them.

Fate appeared to intervene on their behalf, if one could think of a small measure of protection during war as good luck. While others were left to live on the streets or at best, move into cramped quarters with four or more families sharing one house that barely fit one family comfortably, Aanya, Artur, Lena, and Laja moved into a sizable town house with only two other families. They soon learned they'd been favored because of Aanya's medical expertise. With her ability to read lips, and speaking a minimum of necessary words—the Germans didn't expect or want her to get chatty anyway—she was able to keep her deafness hidden. Thankfully, it appeared that the other Brzeziners wanted to preserve her medical skills as well and didn't squeal about her condition. This was a drastic change from the months leading up to the invasion when she maintained her guard against those neighbors who were in opposition to their acquaintances. Apparently, for the sake of survival, men and women were willing to use whatever others had to offer to enhance their own lives.

The Nazis searched and looted each house, stripped away ownership of personal goods and businesses, and burned the town's beloved synagogue. The Brzeziners were allowed no right to protest. Town intellectuals and leaders were rounded up and removed from Brzeziny, never to be seen again; there were many other sudden disappearances as well, of the healthy, the ill, the old and the young. Some townspeople were ordered to perform work assignments while others were herded, like cattle, and taken outside of town. Not afforded the consideration and respect even cattle would have received, the people were buried alive.

Aanya treated patients at the health center, often downplaying the severity of their conditions to spare them from sudden *disappearances*. Artur dug on-the-spot graves and hauled water and dead bodies. The Nazis forged ahead in their takeover, commandeering the tailoring organization that had been synonymous with Brzeziny. They put most of the people to work, day and night, making new uniforms and other items for the Nazi Party and its military. This helped to stave off further abuse; for how long was anyone's guess.

In addition, the occupiers created a hierarchy among Jews by tapping into the Jewish criminal underground and other assorted lowlifes. These men bossed and harassed their fellow Jews. This was incomprehensible to Aanya and the other residents. No one trusted the next person; no one could take the chance.

Life changed once again when the Soviet Union attacked Poland on the 17th of September, 16 days after the German invasion. Poland had not one oppressor now, but two. News first reached Artur and his thinning team of men. He shared the tragic statistics with Aanya and the others who lived in the house. Between the German Western front and the Soviet Eastern front, over 67,000 Poles were killed, and more were taken prisoner or injured. Although Poland put up a good fight, after the Polish Army was defeated at the Battle of Kock, Germany and the Soviet Union gained full control of Poland on the sixth of October.

As the news, stark and horrifying, spread throughout Brzeziny, huddles were formed post-work, whispers exchanged. Aanya and Artur claimed the closet under the stairwell in their assigned residence. Aided by cracking the door open to allow just enough light inside to see each other, they had the temporary seclusion to sign.

After Artur told her the news, they stared in silence for a painful minute until Aanya showered him with kisses she didn't want to end.

"I don't want to talk more about what's happening presently," she signed when they stood apart. "I can't."

Artur squeezed her hand. "What would you like to talk about, then?"

"How about our new home when this madness is over? Where it will be, what it will be like?"

"Far from here," he responded without delay. "How does France appeal to you?"

She wiggled her hand to indicate her uncertainty.

"Palestine?" Artur arched a brow. "My friends tell me they're heading there when this is over."

Sorrow wrapped around Aanya's shoulders; it felt heavy, like wearing a winter coat on a summer day. This little town in the middle of Poland was the only place she'd ever called home. "No one wants to stay in Brzeziny?"

"We don't believe Brzeziny—or Poland—will exist much longer. At least, not as we know and love it."

Aanya shoved the knuckle of her index finger into her mouth to stop a cry from escaping. She didn't want to imagine life without the relative peace she'd enjoyed in Brzeziny until Nazism and its tenets of hatred stormed into town. As in many other countries, there were several rough spots in Poland's past that its people had soldiered through and come out for the better. Her own history had its share of joy along with heartbreak; the worst were losing her parents, and when she miscarried. Poles were hearty, hopeful, and like her friend Zofia, resilient.

Oh, dear God. Zofia.

"Aanya? What is it?"

"Not France. Not Palestine. I want to live in America. I want to see Zofia."

"I want—"

"Don't say no. I'll have it no other way. I can't."

Artur enveloped both her hands in his and then pressed his lips onto hers. She forgot where they were, what horrors were obliterating their world, and how bleak their future looked. All she could comprehend was the beauty and strength of the noble-souled man she married.

He leaned back. "Do you have the address Zofia gave you?"

She pointed to her left temple then signed with her other hand. "I will never forget it."

Brzeziners held their breath and hoped the systematic spread of Nazi-enforced ghettos would skip over their town. Widespread tales of wretched living conditions in those segregated and monitored areas filled the minds of the old and young with dread. But April 1940 brought the ghetto to Brzeziny. It was located on several streets in the Apothecary, Court, Synagogue, and Butcher Street district. Within the ghetto, Jews were prevented from strolls on the streets. If one dared to visit family or friends they had to sneak through courtyards, and that was taking a large risk.

The day after the establishment of the Brzeziny ghetto, Aanya was stitching a wounded man's hand at the health center when Artur walked into the examination room. Though he wore his customary post-invasion countenance—a blank face—she couldn't help but notice a slight narrowing of his eyes when his gaze fell upon the patient's Nazi uniform draped over a chair near the examination table where he was perched. Since he knew she hadn't any say in whether or not she treated Nazis, she didn't explain herself and was thankful Artur didn't ask for an explanation. It would have been foolhardy to have done so.

"Oh, pardon," Artur said aloud, looking squarely at her. "I'll wait outside."

"Thank you," Aanya said, trusting she enunciated the oft-practiced phrase well enough. She then returned her attention to the German, who, after she was done with the sutures, returned to his assignment of conquering and pillaging without a word to Aanya or the expectation of an utterance from her. Artur didn't bound back in. Worried, she looked in the waiting area to see if he was there, breathing easier when he stared up from his chair.

"I thought it would be best if you called my name, like I was a patient waiting my turn."

She nodded and motioned for him to follow. Alone in the examination room she began to examine him, but Artur waved her off.

"I'm fine. No injuries. I have news, though."

She pointed to her mouth and waved her hand to remind him that if he was careful in his pronunciation, she'd understand him using mouth movements, without speaking, and they both wouldn't have to worry about others hearing him. As it was, they didn't dare risk signing in public, not with legions of Nazis eager to snatch Jewish Aanya with her 'deaf problem.' It might even win them a commendation.

"The Nazis, with their penchant for meticulous registration, lists, and inventories, have included me as part of the *Judenrat*."

The Jewish Council? Aanya shook her head furiously. Her mouth dropped open; her throat tightened. As much as she wanted to scream *Nie!* she swallowed the three letters. They clawed and scratched their way down to her gut.

"I have no other choice—they're not giving me an option." Artur palmed both sides of her head tenderly until their gazes connected. "The Nazis may not have human souls, but their minds are crafty—they've created the Judenrat so Jews can blame them, their fellow Jews, and not the Nazis. This can be used to our advantage."

She blinked. Had she understood him correctly? How could Jews turning against other Jews and holding each other accountable—and not the Nazis—for any trouble ranging from a slight mishap to a horror like death utlitmately be beneficial? She shook her head, unable to comprehend how this could be a good thing.

He kissed her sweetly. "This way, I can at least watch out for you, Laja, and Lena. With my connections, it will be the best means for me to prevent harm from coming your way."

If the Nazis ever discovered that Artur was one of their own—German-born and German-raised, serving in their army, then defecting—what would they do to him and his loved ones? On the other hand, they didn't have the luxury of choice when it was man against man, woman against woman, or horrifically, child against child, trying to cling to life in this time of unprecedented horror.

"I must go," Artur said. "We'll speak more tonight."

He stepped toward the door but Aanya grabbed him by the shoulder. She palmed his face and kissed him as if tomorrow didn't exist. Never before had she wanted to be so wrong about her worries for the next day.

30

On a cold early January morning, Artur barreled through the door of the house they lived in. He barely made it to bathroom, where he vomited several times.

Aanya, who was cleaning their bedroom opposite the bathroom, rushed to him. Without the luxury of towels, she used the cuff of her sleeve to wipe his mouth. Typhoid? Dysentery? A flu? Like the spreading evil, illness had overtaken Brzeziny the past few months. 1941 seemed to be starting out without a promise of hope. She checked his eyes, his stomach, touched his forehead and ignored his push of her hand away from him. "Let me examine you."

He shook his head, squinted, and vomited again into the toilet. He blinked a few times and winced.

"Tell me," she said, aloud.

"I'm not sick, but wish I was."

She couldn't guess what this was about and looked at him quizzically.

"There's been a gruesome order. To be carried out tomorrow."

She didn't ask for details, didn't have to. When Artur was stationed at the Buchenwald camp in Germany, he had seen torture and execution, had driven dead bodies into the woods and dumped them into unmarked mass graves, and had told her this without becoming sick to his stomach. She'd seen him angry, flustered, but never unnerved to the point of being ill like this.

"We'll get through this," she signed.

"What if it's the beginning of—"

Of more horrible things? Of the unimaginable worst? Of the end of their lives?

He narrowed his eyes. She knew that he wanted this evil to end immediately, to wake from this hellish nightmare and have nothing more serious to complain about than the weather for the remainder of their days on this planet. She had to be brave for this special man, for the love of her life. She weaved her fingers through his hair, then signed the same words from seconds ago: "We'll get through this."

He glanced over his shoulder to check if they had privacy. "Aanya," he signed, "one way or another, I vow on what is left of goodness in this world that I'll look after you. We'll escape from this madness. I have my connections, remember; that's one good part of being in the Judenrat."

"Will you tell me what is upsetting you?"

Artur leaned against the wall and raised his knees. "A new decree. New orders for me, specifically. I don't want to talk about it further. No more questions."

The decree was worse than Aanya imagined: Ten Jews were ordered hanged. Artur, as part of the Judenrat, had been instructed to sort through the pages of lists they'd made over the past months and choose the unfortunate victims. Women were also included on the list and must not be overlooked. No wonder his stomach rebelled.

At noon, with hands bound behind their backs, these chosen Brzeziners, two women, one of them mentally ill, Mundzia, the other a water carrier, Fajga, and eight men, were marched to the gallows erected beside the river where a field of ashes and debris marked the spot where the old synagogue had stood before the Nazis burned the historic building. Every resident was ordered to watch, including the children. A person who turned away from the executions could expect to be shot. A few days later, they swallowed tears and angry shouts as the Nazis removed the tombstones from the Jewish cemetery, to be used as paving blocks. No record of ancestors was permitted for documentation purposes, including of Aanya's parents' graves.

Although relative quiet, as far as events, followed the executions and the destruction of the cemetery, Aanya couldn't relax. Nor could the rest of her family or the other families living with them. No one dared let their guard down, or their hope bloom. Yet Aanya sometimes thought she couldn't dare not to hope. Then Artur informed her of another order: the Jewish elderly and infirm must gather into a hall for a branding demonstration by the SS. The Judenrat had to attend this event. Afterwards, he told her how the corralled people, trembling with fear and the winter cold, obeyed the order to strip off their clothing. They cried and moaned as they followed the orders to dance and do untoward acts to each other. They were rewarded with kicks by the SS, especially to their private parts. The healthy ones were branded with a "B" after the building where the incident was held; the infirm were sent elsewhere to die. Shocked, dumbfounded, and in pain, no one asked where the badly wounded and weak were sent.

That night, as Aanya, her family, and the others who lived with them crowded around the dinner table, she could not lift her fork to her mouth.

"Aanya, sweetheart," Lena said when Aanya looked her way. "Have I cooked the food poorly? Are you well?"

Aanya stood. "Pardon me," she said aloud then headed toward the bedroom. She didn't make it past the hallway. She leaned heavily against the wall and her head, too heavy for her to hold upright, slumped. She closed her eyes.

A warm, tender touch came to her shoulder. Lena. Aanya opened her eyes, and after her habitual glance to see if anyone else stood in the hallway, she began to sign. "Your cooking, as always, is fine. Physically, I'm also good... as fine as one can be these days."

"Ah, I understand."

Needing to touch Lena, as if to verify she was a real and good person, and they were both indeed alive, Aanya brought her cold fingertips to the face of the woman who had slipped lovingly and almost fully into Aanya's mother's place. "For the first time, I am happy you're not Jewish."

"Jewish or Christian, we're human beings and need to respect each other."

"Lena, that's most compassionate to say, but this is a time of war. You're Catholic—you could have told that to the Nazis who took our home. You and Inga didn't have to suffer. You didn't have to come live in this Godforsaken ghetto."

"That's where you're wrong, sweetheart. You are part of my family, and I am part of yours. I wouldn't have it any other way, and certainly wouldn't suddenly disclaim you, Artur, or Laja in order to save my own neck." Her eyes narrowed. "And the ugly truth is, it wouldn't have mattered. The Nazis see me living with Jews, so in their eyes, I'm not worth their time to listen to even if I did want to explain anything."

"But—"

Lena wrapped her arms around Aanya. The commiserative embrace was all that was necessary to exchange between them, for no words could erase the heartache that had overtaken the Jews of Brzeziny.

31

Zofia and Eban smiled as they left Radio City Music Hall after enjoying *The Night Before Christmas* with Tom and Jerry. Although Eban would turn nine next month, and was behind only one grade in public school due to first having to learn English, he and Zofia often went to the movie theater to see cartoons in particular because they found it an easy way to learn their new language. She hoped to improve her English before enrolling in business courses at Brooklyn College. Fortunately, with Isaac seeing to her mortgage payments, she managed to take a couple of quarters from her weekly pay check as a receptionist in Isaac's real estate and property management firm and treat her son to a movie on Sunday afternoons.

They'd barely taken a few strides outdoors in the cold Manhattan air when Eban pointed at the men streaming past them and running around the corner. "What's happening, Mother?"

Zofia lifted the collar of her red wool coat to fight off the dampness, a sign that snow must be on the way. Since war broke out in Europe when Germany invaded Poland in 1939, Americans held their collective breath and wondered how much longer the US could avoid entering the combat. She gripped Eban's hand tightly.

"I'm not a little boy!" His whine told Zofia's ears the opposite of what he protested. He still needed her protection.

"Darling," she began, trying to keep her focus on the conversation and her son rather than on the men running before her. But how do you explain danger to a child without scaring him? "With this nervous crowd, I think it's best if we head directly home."

Eban wiggled loose from her tight grasp on his hand. "We should look around the corner and see what the others see. It might be good, not bad."

She adored Eban's optimism and hoped as he grew into a man, his positive attitude wouldn't become tarnished from the challenges he'd certainly face. About to reiterate her objection, a shove spun her sideways. Her skirt caught on a metal garbage can and part of the hem came undone. She steadied herself in time to call out to the man, but if he heard her, he chose to ignore her shout of annoyance and forged ahead through the thickening crowd without a glance over his shoulder.

"Eban, let's go." She whipped her head around in either direction; her neck smarted with a burning pain. Her son was out of sight. She looked in the direction the people were running. There he was. That had to be him—had to be Eban's blue and gray striped cap. He ducked left, around the corner. She took off running, shouting his name.

"Watch it, lady," a stranger yelled as they collided a couple of feet short of Fiftieth Street.

Why didn't people apologize in this city?

"Pardon me," she said. "Can you tell me what's happening?"

He looked at her as if she had two heads. "Pearl Harbor, ma'am. It's been bombed."

She knew little about the major naval base in Hawaii, but understood that it meant the country had been attacked. "And these men running all over the place?"

"Jeepers. Don't you get it? The Japs bombed us. You watch—the president will declare war on them. Germany and the Soviet Union, too, if he has half a brain." He yanked her off the curb and onto the road to avoid a collision with another man ducking around the corner. "These men are lining up to enlist in the military."

Japs? Bombs or no bombs, if he was referring to the Japanese, her mind couldn't wrap around his loathing, not when all people from a particular country or race or faith were tossed into the same heap for judgement. Wasn't it similar to the hostile usage of *Jude* by those who had turned against all people of Jewish heritage? She'd been deemed a Juden-lover; Aanya had been called a Jude. Or maybe it wasn't the same. Japan was now an enemy, having attacked the country that had given her and her son refuge. And hadn't she heard that Japan was an official ally of Germany? Did enemies by association deserve respect or contempt? For the life of her, she had no answers, but another question: Would this mad hatred ever end?

"Lady, are you listening to me?"

"Enlist?"

"Where you from, lady?"

From Polska, a country torn apart by hatred.

He stepped backwards from her, as if she suddenly wore a Nazi uniform. "Join up—call it what you like. We want to volunteer to save our country. We're gonna go to war. Finally." He reentered the flow of men eager to engage in what appeared to be turning into a war that would rival the Great War.

Jabez. Aanya and Artur. Laja. Lena and Inga. Where were they that very second? Were they alive?

She tugged her hat over her ears and pushed forward in the crowd to find Eban. Once around the corner, she adjusted not only her eyesight but her frame of mind when she took in the sea of men. This wasn't a time for panic. The men were smoking their cigarettes, the tobacco puffs spiraling into the air. While several formed huddles, others craned their necks at the handful of police officers arriving on the spot. Were they expecting guidance from the officers? Updates on this Pearl Harbor attack?

She stood on her toes and looked for Eban. A few boys mingled in the crowd; a young child could easily be concealed, especially against the backdrop of the gray and black winter garments the men wore. She caught a shimmer of blue in her peripheral vision. Eban! She twisted, jostled, and bulldozed her way toward the one person no one would ever be able to keep her away from.

"Eban," she said, her tone ringing in her ears as firm but not angry. During this crisis—or any calamity—she was the mother, the adult, and needed to stay in control of her emotions. A change from when she was back in Brzeziny, with Jabez under the family roof, and she'd let the man of the house take charge. Coming to America alone with her child had changed her. For better? For worse? Jabez would definitely have an opinion—if he ever came back into their lives. Zofia glanced about the crowd. She stood on a street in New York City, in a country that had just been attacked by another country, during a time when the world was turning against itself. She couldn't worry about what her husband would think of her.

"Mother, the men say we're going to fight a war."

Zofia blinked when she realized Eban had said *we*. After a year and a half living in Brooklyn, he was thinking of himself as an American.

"I want to help."

"Darling, take my hand. Let's go home and talk there. No arguments, please."

"Okay. But I'm not holding your hand."

She placed her hands squarely on his shoulders and guided him through the maze of men, their faces etched with lines of worry and anger. Two blocks farther on, Zofia and Eban ducked into the entrance of the subway—a most amazing luxury of transportation that had been privately owned until the city took it over in 1940—and caught the first train back to Brooklyn.

A sense of sanity and peace enveloped Zofia when they arrived home. On the voyage across the Atlantic, followed by the tragedy of the St. Louis in Havana, she'd never imagined she could feel comfortable in a new home outside of Brzeziny—let alone anywhere away from Poland. But this new home of hers had become a sanctuary. She understood well the fervor of the men she and Eban witnessed earlier. They wanted to protect this country that had opened its doors—at least at one time—to the massive numbers of immigrants who had come to embrace the US as their homeland and were ready to defend it. Yet the underlying prejudice against newcomers like her son and her was unsettling. As long as she lived, she'd never comprehend this inconsistent behavior.

She warmed milk on the stove and fixed Eban and herself a mug of hot chocolate, their favorite on a cold, wintry day. At the round oak kitchen table, she smiled at her son, or at least tried to.

"Mother, are you upset? At me?"

"Not at you. I'm troubled by what is happening between countries, between people." She spooned a dollop of whipped cream from her cocoa and held it before her, concentrating on her English, the only language they spoke with each other now. "Eban, you're a sensitive boy. This is good. This world would be a better place if people cared more about others." She lifted her brows. "Do you understand what I mean?"

"I think so." He shrugged. "But those men lining up to fight. They were good men, not bad ones. Bad is dropping bombs on our boats. Bad is killing men in the navy."

The irony of stopping war by fighting, killing, destroying... this was a complex discussion to have with a child. She shoved aside her mug and leaned over the table. "Darling, I don't know what will happen over the next few days and weeks. I want you to stay close to home—do not wander off. Will you do that for me?"

He nodded and gulped down his drink. She held back a chuckle at his chocolate mustache.

"Will I go to school? And you to work?"

"Yes, of course. Both are important." That is, she hoped the schools would remain open and that there weren't drastic changes to come if the United States were to enter the war. As far as her own work, she was fortunate to have the security of employment at Jabez's cousin's realty firm. This new development at Pearl Harbor had her thinking more seriously regarding work, about changes she wanted to make in response to a changing world. Tomorrow, she'd talk at length with Isaac. She couldn't indefinitely answer a ringing phone at work or bake apple pie in her kitchen. For now, on this late Sunday afternoon, she and her son would enjoy their home.

"Help me set the table for supper."

"Why do I set three places instead of two? It's just the two of us living here."

Zofia had explained her reasoning often. She summoned her

patience once again. "It's out of respect for your papa. Darling, one day your father will walk through that door. I know he will. And in the meantime, we will always hold a place for him." She touched her heart, then her temple. "In our hearts, and in our minds."

32

Brzeziners were not prepared for the 14th of May in 1942. While rain soaked the ground, hell on earth opened its doors wider. SS Chief Hans Biebow arrived in town. He ordered Jewish mothers to bring their children, up to the age of ten, to the town square.

Aanya had no choice but to follow the command and walk Laja to the appointed site. This time, Artur could not intervene, nor did he have information on what was about to happen.

Tears ran rivers down the cheeks of the women. Children, seeing their mamas upset, cried as well. They were made to stand in the square until three in the morning, when another command was shouted: "Turn over your children!" The SS men began ripping the children from their mothers' arms.

"Mamusiu!" Laja cried as she was yanked by an SS officer from Aanya's tight embrace.

Aanya dropped to the ground and kissed the SS soldier's boots. "Mercy, please. Have mercy!"

He kicked her in the chest and ribs; she rolled to her side, the pain real, but not as intense as the grief. There were no words for that.

Lena broke through the barricade of the SS that separated the crowd of wailing onlookers from the chaos. She ran toward Aanya and Laja. "I'm the child's grandmother. I'll go with her to keep her calm."

Aanya saw Artur in the crowd. She sat up. He struggled to pass through the SS, but they wouldn't let him. Lena's name was on his lips. Aanya knew what he was doing—yelling to anyone who cared to listen that Lena was a Christian, not a Jew. Yelling to Lena that the children were ordered to leave, not the adults, and then yelling that she was a beautiful woman.

Those words. They would always haunt Aanya.

Artur, apparently realizing that he wasn't going to change Lena's mind, quieted. Aanya couldn't blame him—Lena would not give up her desperate gambit, though Aanya wasn't sure what it was she intended. When the officer holding Laja, his talons digging into her neck and arms, glanced at Aanya, then at Lena, Aanya understood that she had lost her precious daughter. The yellow patch Aanya was made to wear on her chest and back proclaimed she was Jewish. The yellow star Laja wore identified her as a Jewish child. She had to be removed. The soldier looked at Lena, who did not wear a star. With a flick of his fingers, as if swatting away a fly, he motioned for Lena to go with the departing crowd of children. "If that's what you want, woman."

Black dots exploded before Aanya's eyes; her head felt as heavy as a sack of bricks, and she sank to the ground. A firm hand gripped her. Artur. She could see her name on his lips. He helped her up and put his arm around her shoulders. He gingerly rotated her face for their gazes to meet and pulled her back into life—but it was a life she didn't want to live a second longer.

With images of Laja and Lena playing over and over before her, she was thankful that Artur kept tight to her side as she leaned against him. She couldn't think, couldn't make sense of what had happened, and couldn't speculate what might be about to occur.

He helped her hobble back to the house, settled her in their bed, and then explained that he had to attend an urgent meeting of the Judenrat. He didn't mention that they expected a crowd of mothers demanding to know where their children were taken. It was unnecessary. Not only did his sad eyes convey this news, but it was a given that if children were snatched from their mothers by a bunch of men in Nazi uniforms, the purpose had to be heartbreaking. Mothers and fathers would surely storm the meeting and insist on an explanation. But how could anyone understand the incomprehensible—that their beloved children were on the way to a camp to be slaughtered?

"What will you tell the mamas and papas?"

"The chairman has it figured out. That the children were relocated to Łódź, to a children's home, and the parents will soon see them."

They both knew that was a lie. Aanya lifted her hand to sign, heedless of the tears flowing down her cheeks. These were tears that would never end. "Lena sacrificed herself."

Artur nodded. "She wouldn't have sent Laja away on her own."

"It should have been me. I should have been the one by my daughter's side, not Lena. I sent them both to their deaths. They'll never see another flower bloom... never absorb the warmth of sunlight on their faces. Never—"

Artur silenced her words with a gentle kiss. "You were kicked to the ground—I saw it with my own eyes. The SS bastard kicked you hard. I doubt you could have moved. No one could have saved her."

Sobs rocked Aanya.

Artur grasped her arms and steadied her. "I too loved Laja. I always will. The only thing I'm grateful for is that they didn't take you away from me. I'm also full of guilt."

She lifted a brow.

"I have to live with the undeniable truth that I was relieved they left you behind, with me. I love you, Aanya, like I've never loved another person." He cradled her cheek in his hand. "Here's the undeniable truth you must remember: You loved Laja as much or more than her birth mother, the poor troubled woman. You gave her the most beautiful days on earth she ever had."

Fresh, stinging tears flooded Aanya's eyes.

He held her tight. She didn't want him to let go, ever. But he leaned back to sign. "I promise I will get us both out of this hell we're in. One way or another, you will live and be happy again."

"And I promise you, if I live through the next few days and weeks and years, if I ever see that monster who took Laja and Lena from us, I will kill him with my own hands, so help me God. Believe me, I'll be on the lookout for him."

For those who hadn't already perished from another round of tuberculosis, Hans Biebow's visit was the beginning of the liquidation of the Brzeziny ghetto. The adults were soon carted off to the Łódź ghetto. Hitler got what he wanted: Brzeziny was entirely free of its 6,000 Jews. No longer did it bear the name Brzeziny, but rather its new German name, Loewenstadt.

And the iron hand that had crushed Aanya's heart strengthened its grip on them all.

33

As the cramped wagon full of Brzeziners and enough armed Nazis to snuff out each life if even one dared an escape approached Litzmannstadt, the new name for Łódź, Aanya could tell by the wrinkled brows, the hands clamped over mouths and noses, and the arms wrapped over bellies, that the smell in the air nauseated the others as it did her. When they left the wagon and entered the ghetto, situated in the impoverished, dilapidated Jewish quarter in the northern area of this, the second largest city in Poland, she saw the source of the stench. A cart heaped with raw sewage was drawn past by three women and two men. Even more startling than the state of the buildings, their gutters studded with large holes and their shabby roofs in disrepair, was the condition of its human occupants: battered, beaten down, and hopeless.

Aanya expected to live, if one could call it that, in a Nazi-created hell in Łódź, and for housing to be cramped, disease rampant, and food sparse. What she didn't expect was to step over dead bodies in the streets of those who died from starvation or those who simply gave up, sat down, and surrendered their lives. She saw people carrying empty pots and suspected it was in hope of finding an unexpected morsel of food. What she also didn't expect, especially having been trained in medicine, was fighting off the shame she felt of what she did in the name of survival: numbing her mind to the death around her.

She and Artur were assigned to a three-family dwelling on Jakuba Street that housed, not including them, five other families. They were given ten minutes to settle into their new residence before they had to meet a guard outside the house who would escort them to the office where they'd be assigned jobs.

"What?" Artur said aloud in their communal bedroom, close enough to her face that she smelled his decaying breath. It was very difficult to maintain basic hygiene in the conditions of the ghetto, even in their own town before coming here; she knew that she was no exception. "You too are giving up, just waiting for death? Aanya, don't you dare do this to me."

Crumpled to the floor, they were tucked in the corner of a bedroom they would share with a family of three—a mother, her aunt, and a 13-year-old daughter. The room was bare except for one mattress. As newcomers, Aanya doubted the others would share this small comfort. Fortunately, the two women and girl were absent, probably at work, and they had the room to themselves for the moment. Despite their immediate circumstances of privacy, Artur and she agreed to not invite trouble and chose to speak rather than use sign language.

"Why live?" she muttered, not caring if he understood her or not.

"Because we must. There will be life after this is over. One day this horror will end. Evil always gets defeated by good."

"No Laja. No hope."

Artur grabbed her arms and shook her. "You must live. For me. And in memory of those we lost and love. Because I love you. If that's not enough, here are two more reasons." He then reminded her of her own vow: to kill the Nazi who had taken Laja from her.

Foolish, she thought. What good would killing that beast accomplish other than her own execution if discovered, which was likely, considering the confined area and observant eyes of those willing to squeal in the hope of a reward of food. This was how Brzeziners had acted in their own ghetto. The only difference was the larger size of this ghetto and the sheer number of people living here, amidst starvation and disease and the threat of extermination, on borrowed time.

"The second reason is because you want to see your friend Zofia one day. You won't see her again on this side of the grave if you're dead. Right?"

Slowly, Aanya nodded.

"Then, sweetheart, stand up." He stood from his crouched position and offered a hand to help her onto her feet. She appreciated his physical strength since she had grown quite weak. "That's my girl. We must show up in front of the council and see what work assignment Rumkowski has given us."

"Yes." Unlike in the Brzeziny ghetto, Artur wouldn't participate in this Judenrat council, actually named the Ältestenrat, Council of the Elders. The chairman, Mordechai Chaim Rumkowski, had his own selected men. Artur had no interest in working with Rumkowski, but rather desired to stay close to Aanya, and she was glad of this. For that matter, they'd both agreed that she wouldn't reveal her medical expertise; hopefully her skills would remain undetected. Their reasoning was simple: the less visible they were to the Nazis and the Ältestenrat, the better.

As they exited the Jakuba Street house they squinted, not from the glare of the hazy sky, but rather from the guard assigned to them: Rolf, their long-lost Nazi patient from the summer of 1939 when he was tossed off the vehicle while he and his buddies drove through Brzeziny in a drunken stupor.

Artur was the first to react. He wisely kept his surprise silent. With a mere squaring of his shoulders and a slight lift of his chin toward Rolf, he acknowledged the young man. For his part, Rolf's wide-eyed expression revealed he recognized them despite their weight loss and stooped posture that they, like every ghetto occupant, wore like a uniform.

"This way," Rolf said in German, which Artur translated for her.

Aanya believed his facing her, so that she could watch his lips, was no coincidence.

"Where are we going?" Artur asked, though he knew well their destination.

Aanya, walking beside Artur, watched the two men carefully. Was this a coded conversation her husband attempted with this Nazi who had vowed to keep the Nazi forces away from Brzeziny? She had doubted back when they had exchanged farewells, and he'd made that pledge, that he would have any power to prevent the German army from invading Brzeziny. Yet here he was, three years later, evidently as healthy and well-fed as all Nazis who helped carry out their beloved Führer's objectives. Gauging by the way he interacted in conversation, his hearing had improved as well. Perhaps he would be willing to make a few concessions for them. Food? Better job positions? Keeping them away from deportation to a death camp?

Rolf replied directly to Artur. Artur waited a few seconds before he translated for Aanya. "We'll visit the office of the Council of the Elders first, then report right away to work."

Her hope of an easier work detail was dashed when Rolf exited without a further look their way after leading them indoors. Artur received the assignment of working in a paper factory; Aanya in the Glazer Factory at 14 Dworska Street. At least Artur wouldn't be hauling dead bodies to an unmarked grave outside of the ghetto, similarly as he had done when he was stationed in Buchenwald. As for her work detail, she helped manufacture undergarments, bedsheets, and doll clothing for German stores for German citizens who had no idea what it was like to live in a ghetto stripped of comforts. At least she didn't have to tend to the aches of Nazis in a clinic that refused to treat the thousands of malnourished Jewish ghetto prisoners.

That first night, as they settled down on the bare floor of the bedroom, the last of the summer light trickled in through the uncovered window. With their heads on the one pillow they shared—left from a previous occupant about whose fate they didn't want to speculate—Artur kissed her good night, and held her face in his palms. She understood. He was going to mouth words to her.

"He said he'll get us out."

She mouthed Rolf's name.

Artur nodded. She didn't ask when or how. When the time came —if death didn't call their names first—they'd find out exactly what Rolf had in mind.

34

The last thing Zofia expected that lovely crisp autumn morning, during a season of spectacular color that had followed a dry and dingy August marked by the Harlem Race Riot, was a phone call from Eban's principal. With her passion for wanting to help poorer Americans still trying to recover from the Great Depression, Zofia, single mother and struggling immigrant, attended night school en route to earning a college degree. With Isaac's help and influence she'd stepped higher on the realty ladder. In early 1943 she was appointed to a federal position at OPA, the Office of Price Administration. Her position with the OPA was to teach women—since they were the principal shoppers of the household, especially with a war occurring and so many men overseas in combat—about price stabilization and how to watch out for stores that took unfair advantage of the fragile economic situation. After the Harlem incident, in which a white police officer tried to arrest a black woman for supposed disorderly conduct and a black soldier attempted to intervene, Mayor La Guardia, in response to the rioting that broke out, imposed a curfew enforced by US Army troops. The OPA office where Zofia worked was then established in Harlem on 135th Street to look into complaints about price gouging.

"Yes, I see. I'll leave immediately," Zofia replied to her son's principal. After she instructed her receptionist, she hailed a taxicab and went directly to Eban's school in Brooklyn.

Mr. Goodman, the principal of the elementary school where Eban attended fifth grade, was a tall, rotund man who reminded Zofia of the potbelly wood stoves of her childhood in Brzeziny. She'd met him several times since the day she enrolled Eban in the public school and insisted her son didn't need to be held back a grade due to his poor English skills. She'd learned that day that the principal was a no-nonsense person with a polite forcefulness and little imagination. Furthermore, he didn't tolerate complaints from mothers who set their children on a throne. This was *his* school, *his* rules.

"Do I make myself clear on why Eban is suspended for one week, Mrs. Badower?"

"Not quite. My son is not one to lash out at anyone."

With awful timing, Eban kicked the principal's desk. "I have to defend my mother. My father's not around to do it."

"Quiet," Zofia murmured from the side of her mouth.

Eban frowned. "But Mother, you didn't hear what Billy and Richard said about you."

"Please behave."

The principal lifted a tiny gavel from the corner of his desk, and like a judge, banged it to demand their attention. He stared first at Zofia, then at Eban. "That's enough commotion. I will be speaking to both of those boys, but understand they fought with words, whereas you fought with your fist."

"Eban, is this true?" Zofia asked. When he dropped his gaze to his lap, she had her answer. She thanked the principal, grabbed her son's hand, and led him out of the office for a rapid walk home, heels or no heels. The sooner they arrived home, and she could close and lock their front door, the happier—or at least, the more relieved —she'd be.

The first sign of Eban's lack of cooperation came at the corner when she started to cross the road and he veered right, toward

McGoldrick Park. The traffic light had changed and it took her a few minutes to catch up to him. One block short of the park she managed to seize him by the crook of his arm and swing him around before he crossed the busy intersection. She was surprised to see the little-boy tears her son hadn't shed since leaving Brzeziny. Thinking Eban's troubles wouldn't sit idle until they arrived home, she told him they'd find a bench in a quiet section of the park, sit together, and have themselves a chat. When he agreed with a nod, she released a breath of relief.

With children in school and parents at work, finding a quiet area wasn't hard. If it hadn't been for a dog walker, the occasional young mother pushing a stroller, and a pair of old men seated nearby, hunkered over a stone table with its top made for playing chess, she could have assumed the park was cleared out that day just for their convenience. After watching a squirrel leap from one tree to another, Zofia was about to start the conversation when Eban burst out with words she wouldn't have imagined could come from his mouth.

"I hate Papa!"

Hate? Yet, he called Jabez the affectionate Papa rather than the more formal Father, which he had begun to use the past few months. "Hate's a strong word, darling. What has happened today to make you conclude that you hate your papa?"

"I've been angry at Papa for a long time."

"Yes, I see. I'm sorry I didn't notice earlier." She relaxed her attention for a brief moment as she eyed a grandmotherly woman and a young toddler walking hand-in-hand across the lawn. It would be lovely, she thought, to enjoy a simple stroll with a grandchild.

"You're always sorry. Sorry that Papa isn't here with us. Sorry you have to work because Papa isn't here. Sorry you have to make plans without asking Papa first because he used to tell you whether something was a good or bad idea. Aren't you tired of being sorry, and all having to do with Papa?"

About to respond to this string of sentiments he'd bottled up within himself, she snapped her mouth shut when he narrowed his eyes.

"Mother, you've made a lot of decisions without Papa. Not because you had to, but because you knew what was good and right. Because you can."

She ran her tongue over her dry bottom lip. She came close to blurting that she was sorry she'd expressed these concerns aloud, but she caught herself in time.

"Darling, I've had to make decisions that other adults don't necessarily face, but I have no regrets. Do you know why? Because each decision I've made has improved our lives. The trip across the Atlantic Ocean was certainly full of surprises—both pleasant and not so good—but it brought us to a new, safer home. One that your father trusted would be better for us, and sweetie, he was right. I've also made decisions to have a career, one that helps other women—"

"That's where that idiot Billy and do-nothing Richard come in. They called me names. They called you uglier names."

"Sticks and stones, Eban."

"That's a silly expression. Yeah, sticks and stones hurt, but so do awful names and insults."

"Were they making fun of our Polish accents? Our religious beliefs? We've talked about this before."

"Yeah. You said to ignore them, that they're misspoken words not needing a reply. This time, it was different."

Why was it that at times, talking to her son was like trying to extract a tooth with deep roots? "I can't imagine what those two boys said to make you so upset that you felt you had to hit them."

"That's because you're a nice person. Nice people don't think in bad ways."

She would have taken that as a sweet compliment, if it weren't for the unfortunate fact that while one could act nicely, one could also indeed think in bad ways. Also, considering that his actions had resulted in suspension, this wasn't the time to fall for flattery. "Eban, it's time to tell me what happened that was so awful you got suspended for a week. That's a big and serious punishment. I expect this will be your last suspension, which young man, we'll talk further about later at home."

"It was during recess. I hung out by the monkey bars. Richard came along, followed by Billy. Billy asked me why you have to work your behind off when—if you were woman enough to have a man—you'd be married like his mother. I told him to shut up 'cause I do have a father. He said that it doesn't count since Papa isn't around, and because he didn't like how I said what I did, he shoved me."

"Did you shove him back?"

"Nope. But I wanted to."

"Good. And?"

"Richard asked me where my *pretend daddy* was—that's how he said it. I told him back in Poland. That's when they started to make fun of Poland, and of the way I talked. That's when they told me I should go back there, back to… back where—"

She put her arm around her son. "Yes? Eban, tell me."

"He told me I should go back to Poland where the Nazis are killing Jews and other idiots, like me and you. I cursed at them and told them to shut their nasty mouths… that they don't know what it's like to worry about if your Jewish friends are even still alive." Eban snorted. "Mama? Is Aanya alive? What about Artur and Laja? And Babcia and Aunt Inga? They don't answer your letters—does that mean they're dead? Is Papa dead too?"

For reasons she didn't understand, if these beloved people—her family and dearest friends—weren't alive, Zofia wasn't sure she wanted to find out. Not every truth was meant to be revealed; not all truth sets one free. At least that's what she thought right then.

"Darling," she said softly. "I believe we will find out soon, and that there is good news awaiting us." What else could she say to her young son? She'd written dozens of letters addressed to Aanya at her old Brzeziny home. They'd failed to be returned, unopened, so she concluded that the letters had arrived safely, though Aanya hadn't responded. Or, if she had posted a letter, it never made it overseas to New York. Just when Zofia was going to investigate on a more extensive level, the war broke out and she'd assumed that communication attempts were futile. Since then, her worry had grown horribly and nearly out of control, like a monster poised to break down its restraints. Her concerns over Jabez had taken the same route. Yet she refused to burden her son with the negative. If she could barely cling to the positive, Eban, with a young, developing mind, needed her help to throw himself onto the raft of pure hope and to continue forward in life with optimism.

"So about those boys? Billy spat in my face. Then Richard did the same thing. I punched Billy first, then Richard. That's when Principal Goodman pulled us apart."

"What those kids said to you wasn't right, but without doubt, how you responded wasn't good either. I need to think about this for a while, and will further discuss it with you later." She stood. "Let's go home."

Eban got to his feet, but shoved his hands into his pants pockets and stared at the ground. "Are you going to our old house again? You've done that since we moved here."

Zofia had worked hard in her new country. Without Jabez by her side, not only did she have to be both a mother and a father to her son, but had to ensure, especially in a new country that cast a questioning glance at its immigrants, that the two of them would never become destitute and live on welfare, or worse, on the streets, homeless. Although she was confident that Isaac would never let that happen, she didn't want to always have to rely on this man who had already given them so much. One of the benefits of her industrious work habits in the real estate business was the ability to sell the house on Kent Street profitably and move into another lovely but bigger brownstone on Huron Street. Though it was an easy walk between the two houses, if one didn't know the layout of the neighborhood it could be confusing. When it came to Jabez finding his way home to them—one day soon, she hoped—if he wound up scratching his head in confusion when a stranger opened the door to the Kent Street house, he'd simply contact his cousin Isaac. But that wouldn't work for anyone else, like Aanya.

"The people who bought our old house don't mind me sitting on their steps for a little while."

Eban set his gaze, full of love and gentleness, on her. "Mamusiu, you wait for Aanya, but you can't always sit outside. Winter snow and ice will come. She'll find us."

Her son was right. Aanya—if she ever made it to Brooklyn—wouldn't give up searching for her until they met again. Yet, Zofia wasn't ready to stop sitting on the steps of her former house, in the hope of smiling at Aanya upon her arrival, nor was she willing to surrender her memories of those days when she'd picked wild flowers with her childhood friend.

35

After 13-year-old Naomi, weak and ill from starvation, was selected, along with thousands of other children and sick and elderly sufferers, for deportation from the ghetto to the Chelmno death camp, the girl's mother and aunt began to alternate nights sleeping on the mattress with Aanya and Artur. Since that awful day of the *Gehsperre* back in September of 1942, when each ghetto resident had to line up in front of their assigned housing or face getting shot if found indoors, a ghoulish silence had shrouded the ghetto during the day. But at night cries were heard. Whimpers from bad dreams. The last gasps of breath from the dying. The mad shrieks from either the hysteria that visited in the middle of the dark night, or the torment of the bugs that crawled out of the old plastered walls in droves to bite, leaving red welts all over one's flesh.

One cool 1944 April night, Aanya rolled onto her side on the lumpy mattress in an attempt to shake off an odd dream. It was one of those dreams that bordered on a nightmare and kept repeating itself over and over. Mama and she were walking over a bridge, but instead of taking them to the other side, the bridge ended, never reaching the ground on the other side. Yet they didn't fall, but rather floated in the air. Then, suddenly, pinching, stinging bugs crawled over her arms, neck, and feet. She glanced at Mama, but instead of seeing her covered with insects, she was gone, as if she hadn't been there at all.

Artur shook her until the last of the dream dissipated and she opened her eyes. For the briefest of seconds, she couldn't decide which was worse—the dream or the ghetto. Artur knew what to do, though. He helped her up and swept his hand over her body from head to toes, in an effort to swat the bugs off. After the last of the biting insects dropped to the floor, she joined him in stomping them into flattened dead former menaces.

She led Artur to the window where the full moon provided enough light to communicate. "I can't live like this," she mouthed. "No more."

He kissed her softly on the forehead. "You must. For me."

"Why? We're walking dead." She gestured toward the two sleeping women. "All of us."

"This will end."

She pointed at his chest. "Too positive."

"You're too negative." He grasped her hands. "I can understand why, though. But pessimism and defeatism aren't your natural state."

He definitely got that right. But there was nothing natural about their situation, either. She mouthed a name and knew he'd understand the implication. "Rolf."

He shrugged, and shook his head.

She squeezed her eyes shut. If their Nazi *pal* failed to help, tomorrow would be the day when she'd stop fantazing about searching for and killing the degenerate who yanked Laja away from her and permitted dear Lena to accompany them, and become the day when she'd put action behind her thoughts. The other Brzeziner women she worked with in the Glazer Factory talked often about that horrible day they lost their children when SS Chief Hans Biebow demanded those sweet innocent boys and girls be taken from their parents. Maybe they'd want to help her find this awful excuse for a human being. Aanya recognized their descriptions of that particular Nazi. A few claimed they'd sighted the tall, dark-haired man whose face was studded with pock marks. She was bound to find him.

She knew all about medicines, herbs, and toxins. If she located him and tracked his daily activities, a little bribe with the cash Artur had exchanged for Jabez's pocket watches might prove helpful. If she couldn't obtain the drugs, she'd secure a knife, a sharp utensil... make a lethal weapon. She had nothing left to lose; she'd lost her life already, hadn't she? Was it a crazy scheme? This was an absurd time they were suffering through, and called for drastic measures to combat the extreme evil raging down on them like a relentless deluge with no end in sight.

Artur shook her arm. She looked at him, his face the only beam of light in this fenced-in, guarded hell. Seconds ago, her dark thoughts screamed that her life was over. But when she looked at this man before her? She'd never experienced love like his. Sure, her parents loved her, but a husband's love was different, came from a different place. What if she lost him too? She couldn't imagine. Yet, left and right these cursed Nazis in this ghetto separated spouses, parents and children, multi-generations of family members, if not by death then by reassigning and isolating them in different living quarters. She had to guard against her plans of retribution backfiring. If she were caught, they'd have no mercy on Artur either.

"Aanya," Artur mouthed. "You look as if panic is taking you far away from here. Stay with me. Stay in this moment."

About to respond, she noticed a bead of sweat trickle from his forehead and meander down his cheek. She touched his brow. He was burning with fever. Why hadn't he told her? Worse, why had she failed to notice?

"You're sick," she mouthed, thankful that they could have this private conversation and keep it from the ears of the two women who slept in the room. He waved her off—as if that would work. So as not to stir the other occupants, she walked gingerly to the pile of work clothes strewn over a crate they'd found in the street next to a dead elderly man. At least, he appeared old; starvation and illness aged a person. They'd used the crate as a storage bin for their clothing—the assigned skirt and blouse she wore daily, the one pair of trousers and shirt of Artur's. They slept in their only undergarments in warm weather, their clothes when it was cold. She retrieved her skirt and returned to Artur.

She insisted he sit, helped him to the bare, filthy floor, and knelt beside him. While others had sewed coins and jewels in the hems of their clothing, she'd stashed aspirin. She hoped to God it wasn't too late to help her beloved husband. "Take these," she mouthed and shoved two pills into his palm.

His eyes widened. She nodded, and he swallowed the aspirin dry. She asked if he'd had the various symptoms of typhoid, dysentery, or tuberculosis. He wasn't scratching frantically, a good indication he wasn't infested with scabies. From the absence of more serious symptoms, she suspected influenza, not that the lesser illness, if noticed by others, would keep Artur from being sent to the *Durchgangszimmer*. There, if a doctor determined his case terminal—though in actuality it might not be—he'd be killed by the SS soldiers. Thankfully he wasn't coughing. A bad cough was almost impossible to hide.

"You have the flu. Keep hydrated." She patted her skirt and continued mouthing her words. "More aspirin. You'll improve. Must go undetected." Little had she guessed when she'd learned how to pronounce *undetected* that she'd ever use the word, albeit unspoken, in this awful situation.

"Yes," he replied, staring at her. "I must go to work, regardless."

She got to her feet and reached out a hand. He shook his head firmly. With a set jaw, he stood on his own. She glanced at the mattress then back at Artur. "Sleep."

"I doubt I can, but let's try."

Morning came soon enough.

The aspirin and some sleep had helped restore a tinge of color to his cheeks. Good. They might have caught the illness early. The fever was a good thing to help his body shake off the infection. She hoped that their two roommates, who had already left for the day to their work sites, wouldn't become ill and point an accusing finger at either of them in an attempt to trace the source of the contagion. Then again, if they were sick they would keep their symptoms from Nazi detection if they were smart. Sadly, Aanya couldn't count on other people's sound judgement in the fight for survival in ghetto life.

She kept to herself during her shift at the factory, offering an expected smile or sympathetic nod here and there, but nothing more. Not that it was insisted upon. Her job was in the packaging of items: lifting heavy boxes from shelves, extracting the goods itemized on her assignment list, shoving the boxes back in place—the order and neatness of her work area were inspected hourly—packing shipping parcels and crates and affixing the correct labels so that—despite a war going on—German stores would receive their orders for their German customers without delay. If the store owners or customers were curious about where the goods came from, or who packed their orders, the poor ghetto workers never knew. There was little time to talk, gossip, or complain with her coworkers. It was just as well. She wasn't in the mood and certainly had no desire to transmit Artur's germs. Besides, she valued the isolated time to further scheme about killing the pockmarked SS man who was Laja and Lena's messenger of death. She hoped she'd remain healthy.

Part of her mind shouted out in scolding accusation. *You must hold Nazis accountable for their actions. Laja was an innocent little girl. They had no right to inflict on her this unimaginable final hardship of being taken away from her second set of parents and gassed to death. And Lena. Lena, who loved you like a mother. Lena, who knew full well what volunteering to accompany Laja wherever that sadistic soldier took them would mean. And likely, given the spreading knowledge of concentration camps, gas chambers, and crematoriums, Lena was aware of the horror she was walking into.*

On the other hand, you aren't a ruthless killer. You practice medicine, healing... you save lives. You don't promote death. You don't despise other people because they are of different heritages, or are deaf, blind, or have other unfortunate physical or mental illnesses.

But if each of them—those who were still alive—failed to defend themselves and the ones they loved, they'd be killed. Wasn't that the bottom line? But who was she? Just one woman, who could barely keep her head up in this hellhole.

Finally, fresh off of work at seven, Aanya arrived at the house. She refused to think of it as home. Yet this time, things seemed different. If she'd mistakenly walked into the wrong house, she wouldn't have been surprised. First, Artur, who usually arrived back from work before she did and greeted her at the front door—their little ritual—wasn't there to say hello. Alarm bells ripped through her mind. Was he too ill to walk back? Maybe he'd been seen retching or heard groaning and been followed by an SS soldier... and Artur dared to lead him away from their assigned housing so as not to bring scrutiny to the residence? Stay calm, she ordered herself. No need to jump to horrid conclusions. He could simply be delayed. She trotted upstairs, and wished she hadn't.

The two roommates were gone. Their belongings were also missing, as if the mother and her aunt had never existed. If this were another place or time, she might have shrugged it off and thanked her lucky stars that Artur and she would have the room to themselves. This was, however, the Łódź ghetto; they were Jews held captive under the power of the Nazi Party. Coincidence and good luck—if there were such things anymore—did not exist here.

About to run downstairs to see if Artur was approaching, she startled at the sight of one of the other women who lived in the house.

"I saw those two," she said, standing just outside the room.

"Yes?" Aanya said, aloud.

"They told me." The woman narrowed her gaze; her face flamed angrily. "Told me how they woke up in the middle of the night and saw you and your mister talking. Told me how they saw you touching his forehead." She shook an accusing finger. "You're hiding illness. Damn you both. We don't need to get sick—and we all know the consequences of getting ill in this place. Who wants that? My son went to fetch a guard—we can't have you under this roof."

"Artur's not—"

The woman swatted the air and turned her back. If she'd muttered another word, it was lost to Aanya. Just as well. After allowing the time for the woman to scurry to the downstairs apartment, Aanya reached the entrance of the house at the same time Artur walked in. Without explanation, she grabbed his hand and led him upstairs. Since the other two women weren't around to watch, and with the bedroom door shut from other observant eyes, Aanya began to sign. Artur's mouth dropped open.

"My signing is not a problem." She cupped her hands alongside his shaking head. "We don't have the luxury of time. First, tell me how you feel."

"A bit better, thanks to you," he signed.

"Good." She nodded to where the other two women had claimed their side of the room. "They saw us last night. Saw me checking you for fever. One of the children here was sent to summon a guard."

He seized her hand. Glanced around. For an idea, a solution to the madness? For a miracle to come calling with an ingenious answer? Regrets. Apologies. Confessions. This was the time to say it all, before they were seized by Nazis and escorted to a place for torture, followed by extermination. But they had mere seconds, at most.

"Artur, I love you. Love you with all my heart. I'm sorry I spent more time planning for retaliation for Laja's death instead of enjoying every precious second with you and—"

He palmed the sides of her face until she stopped her frantic signing. And kissed her, his uncontrolled emotions for her tangible, spellbinding with an unspoken promise to take her away to a safer, gentler place that would last long enough to sustain her through whatever more they might face... if they only had more days, months, one more year to live.

"I love you too, Aanya. Don't spend the next minutes thinking about wrongdoings. If we live through whatever horror is coming, I want you to promise me you'll give up this obsession of yours of avenging Laja's and Lena's deaths by killing that brute of a Nazi that took them from you. Don't sacrifice your goal to reunite with Zofia. And don't—" His signing hand dropped to his side.

"What? Sacrifice my remaining days with you?"

He peered into her eyes, and nodded.

She stared at her hand. Could she agree?

Before she could answer that question, Aanya felt the vibrations of boots on the stairs and knew that Artur heard them. He looked at her and his eyes implored her to agree before it was too late. She'd have to find another way to retaliate for the deaths of her beloved innocents. If she chose to let go of her plan for retribution, she could instead honor Laja and Lena by rediscovering the beauty of life and giving to others.

If she and Artur were to live.

"Yes, I promise to give up my plan of vengeance."

Artur kissed her deeply. The pounding was no longer of boots on the stairs, but of fists on the door. Having no other choice, he opened it.

There stood Rolf, his rifle aimed at them.

36

Rolf shoved Aanya and Artur into the back of the jeep, climbed into the vehicle after them, and kept his gun fixed at their faces as if he too had one trained on him and would die if he relaxed his guard. He remained in that frozen position as his driver took off down the ghetto street. He remained that way, weapon aimed at them, as they stopped, cleared inspection at the gate, exited the ghetto, and continued away from the stench of human decay to an unknown destination. Other than one glance at each other, Aanya and Artur didn't dare communicate with one another, nor with Rolf. No *Long time no see, buddy. How many Jews did you terrify today—did you meet your quota?* Or, *How's the killing business going?* Aanya wanted to hold Artur's hand more than she wanted to breathe, but didn't dare reach for the comfort only he could offer.

Paralyzed with fear, fighting to stay calm, she made herself look away from the hypnotic muzzle out of which a bullet could fly any second and terminate their lives. What she hadn't noticed when they'd first climbed into the jeep were the large, full burlap sacks. Were they about to stop, be ordered out of the jeep, told to empty the sacks and then lift their hands high in surrender to be executed alongside the road? Would their bodies be crammed into the bags and left to rot, if not delivered elsewhere? No, she concluded. Why would the Nazis go to that trouble when they had numerous means of torturing and killing within the ghetto? And why were they the only ones in this custom transport when they could have been packed into a train transport to Auschwitz or some other extermination center? Other ghetto residents had hidden various illnesses and been left alone. Had the others they shared the house with hoped for a larger place to live, one with heat during the winter months, as a reward for alerting the guards?

Her thoughts rocketed in different directions. Was this the hysteria a person might feel seconds before the end, if they knew they were about to die? She couldn't do it; couldn't *live* like this, even if it was only minutes more. Her mind was shutting down. But that wasn't relief enough. She wanted to shut down, entirely.

What would Zofia do in this situation? Pray for a miracle? Think of each person who had come into her life and how they had blessed her, in ways great or small? Turn her thoughts away from the savagery of war and fill the last seconds of her life concentrating on the beauty of her past, like the innocence of children enjoying a lovely spring day, like the time Zofia and she first met? Or would Zofia muse about falling in love with Jabez, making love to him, having his baby? Was Zofia—this exact second—thinking about her and Artur? Praying for their safety? Daydreaming of hosting a party when they were once again within hugging distance? The one thing she knew about her friend, whom she'd once nicknamed Pani Stubborn, was that she would refuse to permit looming disaster to sabotage the last of her joy. Well then, Zofia had christened her with the teasing but affectionate name of Pani Determined for a good reason: If Zofia wouldn't capitulate to frenzy, then she would refuse to as well.

A bump came to her ankle.

Or had she imagined it? With her mind hyperstimulated on the last surge of adrenalin needed to survive, her imagination might indeed be taking her hostage.

She looked up at Artur, and he was smiling at her. *Don't worry. It will soon be over. We'll be fine.*

He said it with his eyes, and she heard it with her heart. God knew she loved this man with all her heart, with all her life. *Life.* Sweet life.

They had been driving in silence for hours since they'd left the ghetto They stopped once for fuel and, with guns aimed at them by both Rolf and the driver, a relief break alongside the road. When the Jeep shook, Aanya opened her eyes and realized with disbelief she'd fallen asleep. They'd evidently reached their final destination—still, amazingly, alive. She blinked with the realization of a third discovery: Rolf had set his gun on the floor, and Artur and he were conversing.

Rolf smiled at her.

Artur faced her and rubbed her knee. "Ah," he said out loud. "You finally woke up. I hope your dreams were pleasant."

She switched her gaze back and forth between Artur and Rolf. Had the war ended while she slept? Were they no longer prisoners? Had a Nazi not sat opposite of them for the past five or more hours with a gun pointed at their heads? Most incomprehensible was the undeniable fact that this had been the best, deepest sleep she'd experienced since the days leading up to her wedding. Had she given up on surviving, her unconscious mind at peace with the Nazi-decreed fate chosen for Artur and her? Well then, if that meant death, so be it, albeit at the hand of Rolf, the only Nazi she had once hoped to trust. What a fool she'd been.

"Aanya," Artur said aloud, appearing to have no concern over Rolf hearing what he had to say, "Rolf and his driving pal have arranged for our departure from the ghetto—and from Poland. He'd been waiting for an opportunity to come along, purposely staying away from us since he'd first seen us enter the ghetto. Acting on the suspicion that the ghetto might be liquidated over the next few months and its people sent to Auschwitz, he took the risk of asking for a change of assignment to our section of the ghetto. Then, when he was ordered to get supplies in Bamberg, he and his friend took an even greater risk and ushered us out of the house at gunpoint."

"And the boy who was sent for a guard because you were caught sick?" she signed.

Artur asked Rolf whether a child from their house had fetched him.

Rolf leaned toward her, so close to her face she smelled spearmint when he opened his mouth. "Nein." He pointed at his chest then toward the front of the vehicle, at the driver. He continued in German and she waited for Artur to translate.

"Call it what you may—a fluke or a miracle—but Rolf never encountered a child while he was on his way to arrest us, which was a ruse." Artur rubbed his hand over his face. "And here we are in Bamberg, our new home."

As if a weight was suddenly fixed to her jaw, her mouth dropped open.

"Yes, enemy territory. We are to hide among the Germans as Herr Hans and Frau Gerda Schmidt and we already have the necessary documentation, including working papers with our new names, courtesy of one of Rolf's pals with a guilty conscience for leaving him behind in Brzeziny."

"Work?" she said aloud.

"Yes. I'm to work in the maintenance department of the Hotel Bamberger Hof. And, my new bride, because you've been injured by those horrid Jews and have lost your hearing and ability to speak, you will serve food to the patients in the Bamberg Hospital. How long we'll remain in this historic city and what will happen afterwards is beyond anyone's guess."

"Where will we stay?"

Artur tilted his head while a little grin toyed with his lips. "With Rolf's blind grandmother." He then pointed to the burlap sacks. "Those are our new possessions, courtesy of Rolf. He believes the dresses will fit you well."

She swallowed her question about whether her new clothing had once belonged to now-deceased Jewish women killed by Nazis. Her focus went to Rolf. "And you're well?"

Artur translated to German for Rolf.

Rolf replied yes, that he'd recovered a sufficient amount of hearing so no one suspected a problem. "And," he said, "I never forgot the vow I made to help my Brzeziny friends."

Aanya leaned over and did something she'd never have imagined doing: she thanked Rolf, a Nazi, and kissed his cheek.

37

After Zofia exchanged goodnights with the young woman who lived in her former Kent Street house, she pulled the collar of her winter coat up and faced the one-way street. In summertime she'd sit on the steps to this house and watch strolling couples pass by, or children playing a game of hide and go seek, but now, with the cold, damp wind blasting in from the river, she'd stand and lean against the railing of the stoop and linger just long enough to offer a prayer that Aanya and the rest of the family were safe and well. It was January, 1945. She hoped spring—if not sooner—would arrive with the fabulous news that the war has ended, and that she would be reuited with Aanya and Autur.

She peeked at her watch. Another five minutes, or ten, or until her feet grew cold, whichever came first. Then she'd go back to her Huron Street house, three blocks away, and spend the rest of the evening with Eban. At his esteemed—as he saw it—age of 13, her little boy had entered adolescence. Although he was not yet as moody and surly as some of his school pals, she needed to keep a vigilant eye on him to ensure he kept out of the mischief he tended to get into when left alone too long.

Still, it was difficult to motivate herself to return home. She couldn't blame it on her work clothes, a two-piece navy blue suit and chunky one-and-a-half-inch low-heeled boots, since she had to admit they were comfy for walking distances; nor, for that matter, could she conjure up any other excuse for wanting to delay going home.

"Mother?"

Zofia looked up to see her son. He was pale and his brow was furrowed.

"Eban! What's wrong?"

"It's Cousin Isaac."

Oh, goodness. Catastrophic possibilities from illness to accidents to death swirled about in her mind.

"He's at the house and said to get you quickly." He worked his throat several times, as if fighting sobs. "It's about Papa. But Isaac won't say more."

Bellevue Hospital, located on the east side of Manhattan, was close to Brooklyn, but not nearly close enough for Zofia's liking. Arriving there at six that evening after Isaac had filled her in on the details and then escorted her and Eban to the medical center, they made it to the ward where Jabez and other patients, mostly American soldiers, were with an hour remaining before visiting time ended.

"Yes, I understand," she'd said to her husband's physician, though she hadn't understood at all. How could she comprehend Jabez's physical and emotional state when she had such scant knowledge of where he'd been and what he'd been doing for the last several years? All she could do for the moment was accept the dismal picture the doctor had described. She nodded yes, she'd like to see Jabez, and followed the doctor down the hallway, relieved that Isaac kept Eban company in the waiting area.

She rocked back when the doctor walked right into the doorless room. She wasn't alarmed by his manner, but rather disappointed she hadn't gotten an extra minute to get herself together before seeing the husband she hadn't seen in six years.

"Jabez," the doctor said softly but firmly while Zofia waited at the room's entrance, as if awaiting a grand announcement of her name.

Foolish, she knew, but her nerves were a pile of mush. Then she thought, poor Jabez. His own nerves must also be a tangled mess. "There's a special, lovely woman who would like to see you."

"Go away," he said. His broken English, his broken voice, sounded strange to her.

"Be a good sport. Here, let me help you sit up."

Jabez started to moan, more from disgust, she thought, than actual pain. Pain he would no longer feel from a leg that no longer existed. She couldn't take his delaying a second longer and reached his bed with three strides. Three large steps that a normal pair of feet could make, an ordinary undertaking her husband could no longer manage.

"Jabez," Zofia murmured. When she glanced to her right to see the doctor, the man had already exited the room. When had that happened?

The room, actually a six-person mini-ward, each bed occupied by a wounded patient from the looks of it, had the restrictive atmosphere and medicinal smell of most hospitals. At least, with the privacy curtain drawn, she and Jabez were alone. For so long she had longed for this moment, until at some point she'd finally stopped daring to dream of it. Trying not to focus on his left leg—that is, where his left leg should have been if it hadn't been nearly blown off by a bomb to the point that doctors had to amputate the remains of it —she sat on the side of his bed and reached for his hand.

"Aren't you going to say something?" he asked in Polish. She hadn't heard her native tongue for a while. Though she lived in Little Poland, the Poles she'd met over the past few years wanted to speak English. At times, living in the United States, this new country of hers, it was too easy to let the past slip into oblivion as if it had never happened. "Why are you frowning at me?"

She refused to wilt from his accusatory words. She lifted his hand and kissed his knuckles. That wouldn't do. She leaned over and kissed him on the mouth, savoring him; her lips easily welcoming his familiar lips as if they'd only parted yesterday. "Welcome back, darling. I've missed you so incredibly much." He opened his mouth but she pressed a finger against his lips, mentally pinching herself to prove this was a delicious reality and not a painful nightmare. "Jabez, I'm sorry for the face I didn't realize I made—it's because you spoke to me in Polish. I was so thrilled to hear my native language, especially coming from your lips."

"Talk is about all I can do these days."

"I love you and refuse to believe those words." She kissed him again. "You've come home to Eban and me—to our new home in America, like we talked about."

"Nie."

He'd snapped the negative word out so fast and harshly that she did a double take. "Of course, you have, Jabez." She tilted her head and smiled softly at him. "How I love saying your name aloud, and best yet, addressing you face-to-face. These past years have been the longest ever for me, but each day I'd think about you and about when we'd see each other again."

"I'm sure you never thought of me looking like this. In many ways, I'm not the husband you used to know."

"And I'm not the same naive woman you last saw six years ago. We must catch up with each other. There will be time for that. For now, let's not worry about the past."

"Why not? It's what made me totally worthless."

"Don't say that, you—"

"Zofia, you haven't looked at me, at where my leg used to be. Haven't asked me what it feels like, how it happened."

She made herself look and held back a dry swallow. "So, your left leg is gone. I'm truly sorry, but I'm too busy being thankful that..." She dropped her gaze to the floor.

"That the rest of me is here? Is that what you were about to say? That's a convenient reply."

The doctor had tried to prepare her with information about his physical and mental injuries, and explained that his emotional healing might take longer than his physical recovery. Although he hadn't served in the official military, he appeared to be suffering from combat fatigue. He'd also warned her that not all of his patients bounced back quickly to a healthy spirit and attitude. Some never did. The days ahead—or years, even—might be long and full of anguish for every member of the family.

"Are you in pain?"

"No. Not now. After the bomb exploded, and I came to, I had no idea my leg was barely attached. It was a hot, shooting, burning pain, like I was on fire. But six months later, it's like my leg is still there, minus the pain. And I have to remind myself that it's gone, that I'm a cripple for the rest of my worthless days. You should find yourself another man."

Six months? Why had it taken him so long to arrive in New York? What had he endured? Where had he been? He must have been involved in combat to some extent to have lost a limb like the soldiers who had come home to recover and begin anew. When Jabez was under the roof of his new home, she'd find out the details. His new beginning might prove the healing he needed.

She knew what to do for her husband. She stood, closed the privacy curtain the remainder of the inch or so gap, and returned to his bedside. "I love you, Jabez." She began to cover his flesh with kisses, starting at his forehead and slowly snaking her way down his body. Midway, she stopped and looked into his eyes. "Ah, I see you're enough of a man for me, my darling husband."

38

Just as Herr and Frau Schmidt, good German citizens that they were, were resettling in Bamberg with *their* Oma Anna, having lost their home and grocery store in Leipzig, life changed again, not only for them but for everyone. The few times they'd escorted Rolf's grandmother outdoors for a walk in their Little Vienna neighborhood along the Regnitz River, past the cheese shops, the bakery with its window full of German pastries, the wedding dress boutique, and the pub, they noticed fewer and fewer inquisitive stares from strangers. Evidently, the rumors planted by Rolf about what those supposed Jews did to inflict deafness on Aanya, as well as frighten the speaking voice from her, accomplished their purpose. No one questioned her. In fact, people greeted her with the attention that they'd shower on a hero. Fortunately, no one interrogated Artur either.

On the morning of the 14th of February, Aanya woke at five o'clock for work. Her bones, her muscles, her very soul, told her that this day was different. Yet she couldn't bring herself to get out of bed to first look after Oma Anna before preparing frantically for the work day. Efficient by nature, she had never allowed herself to procrastinate back in Brzeziny. But these were definitely different times, and she was definitely a different person.

Goodness, she was no longer Aanya, a Pole, a Jew, and a Brzeziner. Now she was Gerda. A German. Born in Leipzig and living there all her life until unfortunate circumstances led her husband, Hans, and her to move to Bamberg in the hope of a better life.

She felt a warm touch on her shoulder. Artur, the early riser of the two, stood to her left. He bent down and kissed her good-morning, but she turned away. He walked to the other side of the bed so she could see him. "What's troubling you?" he signed. They used their preferred, private means of communication under Oma Anna's roof when the woman wasn't present; the old woman might have lost her eyesight in recent years, but her listening range was quite healthy. "Don't say it's nothing."

Did it make sense that she was deeply grateful for her husband, who knew her so well, while at the same time wishing he couldn't read her as easily as he could one of the books he adored?

"I'm not myself this morning."

His eyes grew wide. His gaze started to travel downward. "No, no. Physically, I'm fine. No changes." Since they hadn't made love in months—she'd forgotten when, exactly—he couldn't suspect that she was pregnant. In all honesty, during those ghetto days of sub-human existence, she had been relieved she wasn't with child.

"What about Oma?" he asked.

Oma? The woman wasn't his grandmother, nor hers. "She can take care of herself." As soon as the last word flew from her fingers, Aanya flinched. Oma Anna was so desperate for companionship and live-in help that she trusted Rolf completely when he brought them to her apartment. The bare minimum Aanya could do was to at least act appreciative for the older woman's ready compliance to participate in her grandson Rolf's ruse that Artur and she were distant blood relatives. After all, Hans and Gerda were Aryans, not Jews.

Artur knelt next to the bed and wriggled his left hand under the sheet to grasp hers. He squeezed it gently and continued to sign with his right hand. "Helping Oma is part of our agreement, Gerda."

She rolled her eyes. He knew better than to call her by that name when they were alone.

"Tell me why you're so cranky this morning."

Cranky? That was so unfair of him to resort to name-calling. She pounded the bed. "I'm not cranky. I'm contemplative... just—"

"Testy? Grumpy?"

She wanted to erase that smug look from his face. Instead, his grin, like a contagious laugh, elicited a smile from her. "All right, all right. Yes, I'm in a mood. Satisfied?"

He sat beside her and wrapped his arms around her, his warmth the balm she needed to relax. "No, Aanya. I'm never satisfied when you're unhappy. Want to talk about it?"

She shook her head, but words flew from her hand. "The guilt is blazing within me like a fever. I hate lying about who I am and who I'm supposed to be. I'm torn up with guilt for denying my heritage and my native country while well aware of how so many people have suffered illness, torture, or death, or all three, because, like me, they failed to live up to Aryan standards."

"I imagine, like me, you're also nervous about the risk of being discovered as Jews in hiding. It's not easy always having to stay on guard."

"Yes, of course. It's absurdly paradoxical that each Bambergian I've met, thus far, is quite affable."

"They've taken a liking to you, sweetheart. I can't blame them."

"Thank you for trying to cheer me, but I'm trying not to think how fast they'd change their minds about the two of us if they were to learn of our true identities and our past."

He kissed her, deeply. Delightful amazement coursed through her, not over her husband kissing her, loving her, but rather that after all they'd endured, passionate desire was stirring within her.

"I'll tell you what's vexing me. I hate lying about us. What I despise even more is socially going along with the pretense of condemning my own people for following their Jewish faith."

"I understand, but—"

"War makes us all desperate. I get it."

"Yes, desperate to survive." He sat straighter. "Aanya, don't you think many Germans also are living in fear? The world is at war with them, with their leader. Not all Germans are bad people—I didn't turn out horrible." He paused enough for her to remember that he was German by birth and that this subject must have been difficult for him to talk about. "Mind you, I'm not excusing the ones who choose not to take a stand against Nazism. At the same time, I wouldn't doubt they're also hiding truths about their families, or their faith and heritage, in the name of surviving this atrocity."

She held back a sigh. "It's like I'm a rat chasing the last bread crumb away from its pack so that I can eat it all by myself."

He quirked a brow. "You feel guilty for surviving while others have died?"

"I'll probably have to live with this guilt for the rest of my life," she signed, half-stating, half-asking. Artur and she were alive, though she questioned the definition and the quality of *living* while holding one's breath throughout each day in fear of whether the next bomb would be their ticket to heaven. But when the news circulated around Bamberg that Heinrich Himmler had ordered the Łódź ghetto *liquidated*—one of the most bizarre words she'd ever learned to sign—and the 74,000 ghetto Jews from the final transport were fed to the gas chambers of Auschwitz, Artur and she recited the mourner's Kaddish, despite not having a minyan, ten people present, to praise God despite death. They also wept in a prayer of thanksgiving to God for sparing their lives.

The morning after learning the fate of the Łódź ghetto, she'd considered telling each passerby, stranger, and co-worker the truth: she was Jewish, deaf, and an escapee from the ghetto. But what would that accomplish? It would mean death to her and Artur, and probably Rolf as well. It would mean she'd never see Zofia again in this life. And it would mean she wouldn't live to a ripe old age with Artur. And that was what she lived for, because he was the one who mattered the most to her. That was why she'd sacrificed her desire to exact revenge on the Nazi who stole Laja and Lena from her and sent them to their deaths.

So they lived in Bamberg, and Gerda Schmidt slopped spongy-looking meat and lumpy potatoes onto trays and delivered them to patients' rooms. Each time she served the sick and injured she fixed a smile on her face and resisted the urge to help treat the patients.

Hans worked long days at the hotel dusting Nazi party banners and emptying their waste cans or wiping their beverage spills while trying to ignore that Nazis and their distinguished guests were the only ones using the hotel's luxurious accommodations.

Artur enveloped her hands. She startled from her roaming thoughts.

He pointed to their bedroom door, where Oma Anna stood speaking to them. The woman had not once intruded into the privacy of their bedroom, whether the door was open or shut. Artur pressed his finger against Aanya's lips, firmly. She understood immediately. She should not say a peep, and rather, wait for Artur's instructions.

When the woman left the room, Artur began to sign. "Let's get dressed. Fast."

"What's wrong?"

"A neighbor just visited to inform us that last night, while we slept, the Royal Air Force and the United States Air Force bombed Dresden. Most of the city was destroyed, thousands were killed, and others were so severely injured they wished they were dead."

Aanya gasped. "Is Bamberg next?"

"From the talk I've heard at work, it's doubtful since there is no weapons industry here, but we can't take chances. Like everyone else in this peaceful city, we need to stay on high alert. Once again, it's time to take shelter." He stood and reached for her hand. "Hurry."

What to do first? Next? What to bring and where to go? How many times can one run?

"We can do this, Aanya. Again."

She sighed.

"Together," he said in reply to the silent question he read in her eyes. "We'll do this, hide and wait, and believe in good news to come, together." After ticks of precious seconds they couldn't afford, he extended his hand toward her, once again. "Yes, my Aanya?"

She whipped the bed sheets off, accepted his helpful, loving hand, and stood. "Yes," she replied out loud.

39

Jabez jumped at the supper table when the front door banged shut. Eban ran full tilt into the dining room with Buster following. The one-year-old black lab was a birthday gift to the then newly turned 13-year-old Eban back in January, five months ago.

"Sorry I'm late, Mother." Eban sat; Buster settled in his favorite spot—draped over the boy's feet.

Trouble was brewing. Zofia's gaze flitted from husband to son. "It's okay, honey."

Jabez flexed his fists, then wiped his palms on the tablecloth. It was a disgusting habit he'd developed, but she chose not to show her disapproval. It wouldn't help either of them.

"It's not okay, young man," Jabez said in English, the language they predominantly spoke with each other.

Eban grabbed a slice of white bread from the straw basket centered on the table. "I had to walk Buster."

"That dog of yours gets routinely walked after supper."

Eban shrugged. "He's a dog. They don't care about routines."

Jabez snatched Eban's bread from his hand. "We raised you better than to behave rudely to your parents and eat before grace is said."

"*You* didn't raise me at all." Eban glanced at Zofia, as if he couldn't bring himself to eye his father. "You weren't around. Mother took care of me. So did Babcia, Aunt Inga, Aanya and—"

Jabez pounded his fist against the table. "I'm quite aware of who lived with you at our Brzeziny house. What do you think I am—a fool? Have you forgotten about the first seven years of your life when I was home? What do you think I was doing these past few years while you played with your toys or attended school?"

"Beats me what you did, *Father*. You've never told me. You've never told us. Guess you don't want to."

Zofia narrowed her eyes at Eban and pleaded silently with him not to egg his father on. Jabez's doctor had cautioned her that Jabez's distress would, at times, raise its ugly head and appear to swallow him whole, and that Zofia needed to steel herself against taking it personally and reacting in kind. Upon Jabez's arrival home from the hospital, she'd tried to explain to Eban to 'give Papa lots of breathing room and he'll return to his old self.' When Eban countered that he'd hoped his father wouldn't return to his old self, but become nicer, Zofia was dumbfounded not so much because she didn't know how to respond, but because the family ties had deteriorated longer ago than she had suspected. Even worse—it had happened right before her own oblivious eyes.

She caught the tiny flare of her son's nostrils, the bunching of his brows, his eyes turning beady. As much as she loved her son, she couldn't deny Eban's moody, almost tetchy teenaged ways, nor the fireworks about to explode at the table. For better or for worse, her son was at an age to assert his growing independence.

Eban stood and crossed his arms. "You didn't fight in the war like my pal Freddy's pop. You never visited us. It's like you abandoned us."

Jabez pushed out his chair. Steadier now on his prosthetic leg of wood and leather, he flung his dinner napkin onto the table. "Count your blessings that we're strangers."

"Why's that?" Eban asked. "Would I tremble in fear?"

"That's enough from your mouth," Jabez said, not hiding his irritation.

"Eban," Zofia gently interrupted. "What kind of way is that to address your father?"

Eban snickered. "He's no father of mine. Some imposter. The real Jabez Badower was left behind in Polska." He stormed out of the room.

"No supper?" Zofia called out, aware he'd already left, and likely had exited through the front door he'd slammed a few minutes ago. He wouldn't starve. He'd probably visit his friend Jack and be invited for a meatloaf and mashed potato supper by Jack's accommodating eager-to-feed-every-child *ma*.

"Let him go," Jabez said. "It's obvious he wants no part of me. Why I bothered to return is beyond my understanding."

Beyond mine, as well, she wanted to say. Instead, she forced a smile. Peacekeeper between her husband and son had become her new role. Along the way, she'd lost her role of treasured wife and beloved mother. And she was beginning to forget who she was as an individual as well.

"I'm glad you came home to us," she said, her tone too quiet and flat to convince her own ears.

He swatted the air. "I'm going into the parlor to read the newspaper."

He never read the daily paper. Oh, these days, his English was perfectly sufficient to comprehend the printed pages; it was that he had no desire to read about the war's ending in Europe, with the truth about what was left of civilian life and what actually occurred at the concentration camps beginning to trickle in. And there was the uncertainty of the ongoing war with Japan. As the doctor had forewarned, it seemed Jabez didn't want to—or couldn't—communicate the hurts holding him hostage.

She'd try a different route. "It's a lovely spring day, darling. Finally! After the snowy winter, wouldn't you enjoy a walk with me? The doctor said that the more you exercise, the more you'll build up your strength and endurance."

"Don't utter the word *doctor* around me. I'm tired about hearing what the doctor advised. He has no words of wisdom for me. He wasn't with me back in Poland. Besides, endurance for what? Another sabotage mission in another war?" He took a couple of slow steps away from the table and stopped. Without peering over his shoulder, he said, "If I'm ever involved in this foolishness again, if I'm lucky, I'll lose another leg, or my head, altogether. Just think—I'd get to meet my maker." He exited the room at a good clip, a pace Zofia hadn't witnessed from him since she'd set eyes on him in the hospital, thankful he'd come back into her life.

The two males in her life were alike—hot headed. Lately, though, it was sometimes hard to tell who was the man and who was the child.

"Well, dear," she called, aware he was out of listening range. "I'm stepping out for my walk. Come find me if you grow lonely." *Lonely, like me.*

Zofia walked fast, thankful to have on her trusty flats. She passed brownstones with painted window boxes full of pink and red geraniums and orange begonias with trailing leaves, children playing catch, old men smoking cigars and playing cards on their stoops, and young lovers swooning over each other in the alleyways. Spring in New York City was a perfect time to enjoy life.

Well, at least for others it was. If Zofia couldn't bask in the glorious warmth of the longer days with their sunshine, breathe in the sweet, heady fragrances of flowers or freshly cut lawns, or smile at the animated chatter of adults and youth happy to be outdoors after a frigid winter, at least she could appreciate the happiness of others. And she'd do so on the steps of her former Kent Street house, the place she took solace away from daily tension, the place she sat and waited for Aanya. Occasionally she'd park herself on the old stone steps during the early morning hours. Often, though, it was post-dinner when she paid a visit.

She was certain Aanya would remember the Kent Street address she'd given her. If she survived the war, and if she made her way across the ocean to Brooklyn... No. One doubtful thought was one too many. God willing, her friend had survived the war. There. That was a better way of looking at things after a harrowing time in the history of mankind. Aanya would find her way to Kent Street. An intelligent woman, if she didn't find Zofia here on these steps leading up to the entrance of her former house, then she would inquire and search for her until they were reunited. At the same time, this had become her vigil of hope, of everything good that Aanya represented and Zofia was not willing to surrender.

She glanced up when she heard the familiar jingle of dog tags and the reverse sneeze of an exited Buster. "Hello, boy." She gave the tail-slapping dog a hug. "I see you're wearing your collar, but where's your leash? Did you escape from the house?"

Buster barked once. "No? Then how did you find me here?"

A throat cleared. Again, she looked up.

"Jabez? You're out with the dog?"

"I decided to take your advice and go for a springtime walk."

She refrained from asking how he'd managed physically during his first-time dog-walking event. She gently shoved Buster aside and patted the vacated space. "Care to sit with me?" After Jabez hesitated, she stood. "I'll gladly move to a lower step."

"No. That's okay. I need practice climbing stairs."

She held her breath in expectation of his grumbling. *Why I need this practice is beyond me. What's the point in regaining my strength when no one except my cousin wants to hire me? And now, my own son won't look at me.*

But no protest came as he moved beside her. When his hip touched hers, she mentally slipped back into a time—it seemed like decades ago—when they lay side by side after heated lovemaking in their bed in their Brzeziny house. A time when they had dreams of their future.

Beside him on the steps of their first Brooklyn house—though Jabez hadn't lived with her there, she still thought of it as *theirs*—she reached for his hand. "I'm happy to have your company."

"You don't sound thrilled." He groaned and dragged his palms down his face. "That didn't sound good."

That was the closest he had come to an apology. "Continue, please."

He shocked her with a little smile, reminding her of how utterly charming he could be. "What happened back home between Eban and me wasn't pretty. It shouldn't have happened. In the short time I've been home, our boy is teaching me, the adult, quite a few lessons."

Zofia's heart fluttered. *Home.* This was the first time Jabez had used that word referring to their Brooklyn residence. And to think he just used it twice. "From what I gather from my friends, fathers and sons often experience strife between them. Here's the thing, Jabez—it's never too late to make amends. Eban is our only child."

Jabez sighed. "Is that one less point for me?"

"Good grief, no." She sank her head into her hands, tempted to never remove them and see the kaleidoscope of confusion called life. "I didn't mean that as an insult."

His firm hand enveloped hers and lowered them gently. "There, that's better. One of the things I missed the most during our time apart was seeing your lovely face. Your concerned eyes, your elegant nose, and yes, your mouth that you use to speak good, wise, encouraging words."

"Jabez..." Her heart was full of words she'd held back since Jabez's arrival home. Questions that begged to be asked. Pleas for marital peace between them. Urgings to remake a solid relationship with their growing son. Suggestions on how to move forward. But she remained silent. What she wanted was for the man she married to take a stand on what he desired from this day on, choosing to embrace—she hoped—this new life of theirs.

Jabez petted the dog. Buster rewarded him with two thumps of his tail and a happy squeal. "It hasn't been easy for me. Nor, I imagine, for either of you. Especially not the way I've acted since coming back to you and Eban."

This was his first admission to having difficulties. She grasped his hand. "I understand."

He stared at the freestanding old wooden house across the street; it must have dated back to the early 1800s. "I wanted to come back to you and Eban a long time ago, but I couldn't."

"I have a story to tell you, but it's rather long, so I'll shorten it." She paused until the sting of bittersweet memory eased. "Aanya married Artur—a most decent and kind man, one you'd like. Right after the ceremony, Herszel visited, bringing the frightening news that you were missing, possibly killed. Because he wasn't sure, I didn't know what to believe."

"Lies. We fed Herszel and the other watchers at home lies in order to protect them."

"Oh? I'd like to hear about what happened to you if you want to share it with me. I think it's time to trust me with the truth."

With Buster settling down across the bottom step, Jabez rubbed both knees, though the artificial one provided no sensation. She'd never seen him do that, and it seemed like a breakthrough of sorts, as if he was accepting the reality of his prosthetic leg.

"First," Jabez began, "I want to tell you that Eban's wrong. I did come back."

She blinked as memories—Aanya's wedding, talking to Herszel, packing for the trip to America, saying goodbye—played through her mind. "You did? When? I didn't see you."

"I came back the same day, the exact moment when you left the house in Brzeziny."

"You should have stopped me. Should have—"

He kissed her. "Let me explain, sweetheart."

She touched her lips where he'd just brushed his own. "Go on," she said softly, her breath puffy.

"I wanted to witness, with my own eyes, that you left Polska. That way I could return to my assignment and face the enemy knowing you and Eban would be safe."

Contrary to the warmth flooding within her from the first kiss he'd initiated since arriving in New York, her insides turned suddenly cold. He'd *chosen* an assignment over her? Over his family? She wanted to ask if he'd seen Eban. Aanya and Artur? His mother and aunt? Rather, she looked into his eyes. "Why did you choose to leave us, again?"

"When my old military pals from the time I served in the Polish army approached me with intelligence showing proof of Hitler's advancement of Nazism across Europe, I wanted to help save Poland for the sake of our son's future. I never worked a day in Germany, Zofia."

"But you sent money home."

"My father left me funds for an emergency—"

"But you lied to me, to Eban?"

He nodded so slightly that if she hadn't been sharply focused on his face, she wouldn't have recognized his acknowledgment of her question. "It's far worse than that."

How could living a life of lies get worse? How could leaving his family be topped? "I'm not proud of what happened next," he continued. "Nor do I think I'll ever forgive myself."

A mistress on the side? Had he killed in the name of saving their beloved Brzeziny? Good God—her imagination was spiraling out of control: Had he given in to the Nazis, becoming one of them, and persecuted Jews? Made a deal with them: fight on behalf of the German army and your family will be spared?

Through tight lips, she said, "Tell me."

"I enjoyed every minute of planning, plotting, and destroying bridges and vehicles, and blowing up buildings to the point that my men—yes, I became a leader of our little resistance group—called me a killing machine. I loved everything that went into retaliating against Nazi killings by killing them or sabotaging their heinous plans. I couldn't say no. I couldn't stop." He dropped his gaze from her eyes. "I couldn't come home."

At his last four words a fresh wave of grief rolled over her. "And your leg? How did you lose it? And why were you transported to New York on an American military ship for the wounded?"

"After Germany invaded Poland, the smaller resistance groups like ours joined ranks with what was called the Polish Underground State, eventually merging with the Home Army—the AK. We thought we were helping the exiled Polish government in London, but inadvertently helped the Red Army defeat the Germans and thereby eventually gain control over Poland for the Soviets. The summer of '44 brought the Warsaw Uprising—not the Warsaw Ghetto Uprising of '43, mind you. Two different things. By that time, what I was involved in was a major war operation." Jabez's forehead furrowed. "Are you sure you want to hear about this? It's grisly."

It had taken months for Jabez to reach this point of talking to her about that horrible time, and she was grateful, no matter what he ended up revealing. She was not about to disrupt this positive development and communication between them, which she believed might prove a step toward better emotional stability for her husband. "Yes. Please tell me."

He dragged a finger across his stubbled chin. "Thousands of the AK lost their lives. Thousands were injured. I barely managed to escape and survive. Came close to starving to death. I came out of where I was hiding to save a Red soldier by throwing myself on top of him during a grenade attack. The Soviets saw me as a hero and took me to one of their medical clinics." He jutted his chin toward his artificial leg. "They amputated my leg and kept me there, not exactly as a prisoner, but not exactly as one of their own either. When they heard me talking about how my wife and boy left for New York, they packed me onto the next available ship sailing west, and here I am. What I am, Zofia, is no hero, but a man who deserted his family. I lost a leg, and my dignity, but I deserve more blows, like you leaving me and taking our son with you."

A boy stopped before them balancing on a scooter. "That's a nice pooch." He petted Buster. "My pop won't let me have one, says I don't deserve a dog."

Jabez propped his elbows on his knees. "Do you think you do?"

"Yes, sir. I get good grades and clean my room. And other stuff."

"Have you tried talking to your pop?"

"No. You think I should?"

"Definitely," Jabez said, "I have a son, a bit older than you. I'm going home and will speak with him about the things he wants."

Zofia smiled at the boy. "You have nothing to lose by talking to your pop."

"Thanks, lady. Thanks, sir. I'll go try." He pushed off on his scooter.

"I want one of those," Jabez said.

"A scooter?"

"No, I want a son that will talk with me."

She stood and offered him a hand up. "Then I think it's time for you to go home and make the first move to talk with Eban. He's a good boy, that son of ours. Smart. Forgiving, and handsome, like his papa."

"I want to be his papa again, if he'll give me a second chance."

"Second chances work both ways. I have an inkling that if you try, he'll try."

"Are you coming, too?"

"Why don't you go home and have a nice private talk with your son? You don't need me there. I'd like to stay here just a bit longer."

"I'd like to go home with my wife." He extended a hand toward her. "Don't you see what's happening, Zofia?"

As if chilled, she rubbed her arms. "I'm afraid not."

"You've waited for Aanya here so long, and practically daily, that you've robbed yourself of what home meant—should mean—to you."

"I don't understand."

"Your relationship with our son, and me, is at risk. We need to spend more time together. Don't you think it's time to make our current house a true home?"

She wrapped a curl around her index finger. "What happens if a miracle brings Aanya to this place and she doesn't find me here?"

He bent over—to kiss her again?—and lost his balance. He landed in her lap. They broke out in hearty laughter. When they calmed down a minute or so later, inches apart, they stared into each other's eyes.

"Honey, after you, your friend is one of the smartest women I've ever known. If she arrives here from Poland or wherever else she may be, believe me, she won't turn around and forget about you just because you no longer live here. Come back with me, won't you? It's time to make us a home."

Her husband was right. Zofia stood. Hand in hand, with Buster tagging along, they walked home.

40

September, 1949

Zofia sat at her bedroom writing desk. Deep in concentration, she jumped slightly when Jabez slipped his arms around her and kissed her on the cheek.

"I didn't mean to startle you," he murmured into her ear, his hot breath robbing her of her own. "You look lovely in that brown skirt and red blouse—perfect autumn colors."

"You don't think I'm overdressed for the Women's League?"

"You look lovely." He kissed her up and down her neck.

"I hate to say it, but you need to stop before neither of us is able to."

"How exactly would that be criminal?"

She loved the sparkle in his eyes and the fact that she could ignite him sensually after all these years and what they'd come through together. She made herself resist.

"I've finally decided on the right words to write."

"Another letter to Aanya?" he asked, his tone understanding.

"Yes, but it will be short." She paused, trying not to appear too dreamy to her husband. "Every day when I check the mail, I also hope to find another letter from Herta Weber."

"The woman you met on the St. Louis?"

Zofia slipped Herta's one and only letter from the desk drawer, one that offered a scant amount of details. Yesterday when she'd read it for the hundredth or so time, it was as if the dear woman and her family had left the ship with her and Eban rather than sailing back to Europe.

"Yes, she and her husband Kurt and their two daughters, Edith and Krista. I worry about them because like Aanya, they're Jewish, and who knows what has happened to them? Maybe during the war they took refuge in various strangers' homes and managed to escape the Nazis. Maybe they fled from one country to another. They might have even landed in California for all I know. But that's the thing—I don't know. I can only hope for the best, but it's so difficult after learning about so much tragedy."

"As you're fond of saying, Zofia, hope for the best. I'd like to meet Herta and her family."

"You'd like them all, I'm sure. Well, pardon me. I'm going to write this letter to Aanya, though like the others, it probably won't reach her."

"Shake that pessimism off. None of your letters addressed to our old Brzeziny house have been returned. That might be a good sign."

She gave a quick nod, sidetracked with gladness for how Jabez, Eban, and she had finally come to think of their present Brooklyn residence as a home, not simply a house with a roof for shelter. One by one, with Eban leading the way, then Zofia, and recently in the past year, Jabez, they no longer thought of the house on the former farmland just outside Brzeziny as their home. No longer did they talk about walking the cobblestone streets of town toward Market Square on Thursdays to purchase goods, or passing the world-renowned tailor shops. Still, not even a promise of millions of dollars and her wishes granted for eternity would ever stop Zofia from reminiscing about picking wild flowers with Aanya for their mamas alongside the Mrozyca River. Some things in life were worth storing within the heart, never forgetting, always treasuring.

She lifted the sheet of pastel green stationary. "Who knows if Aanya lives in Brzeziny now? From what we've heard about postwar Soviet-ruled Poland, no Jews live in our old town. She and Artur might have moved to Israel or somewhere else, and I'll never know. I just hope, whatever happened to Aanya, wherever she may be, that life's been kind to her. She deserves it."

"You're a good friend." Jabez reached for her hand and held it against his heart. "Send this letter—you'll regret it if you don't. I'll go see what mischief our son and Buster have gotten into."

She laughed. Their 17-year-old son was due to graduate from high school with honors a semester early, just in time for his next birthday. Eban had matured into a fine young man, far from the fifth-grade boy edging toward wildness. Nurtured by his close relationship with Jabez, and with an early childhood influence from Aanya in medicine, Eban set his goals on becoming a physician and would enter his freshman year of pre-med in the spring term at New York University. These days it wasn't their son who got into mischief, but rather Jabez himself with his self-appointed challenge of outdoing other men his age who had two intact legs in walking marathons. That is, when he wasn't occupied at work as an editor for *The Brooklyn Eagle*.

"Thanks, darling. I'll meet you downstairs when I'm done." She took up her pen.

Dear Aanya,

My missing you has played around with my imagination... Do you realize that in English, your first name with the letter A starts the alphabet while mine, with the letter Z, completes it? I don't mean to sound simplistic, and hope you're not giggling as you read this, but this is what our friendship is truly like. Together, you and I begin and end the letters that form the words we have always used to express our thoughts and feelings to each other. And where are words born, if not in the heart? Our friendship—and our lives, when you think about it—are complete only with each other.

. . .

She stopped when words failed her. That was when she heard the bedroom door open. She looked up and saw Jabez. "What's wrong?"

An odd expression made his face unreadable. "You may want to come downstairs right away and see for yourself."

She stood. He stepped toward her and grasped her hand, the one tightening her blouse collar that she hadn't been aware of twisting and untwisting and retwisting.

"It's okay, Zofia."

"You won't say more?"

"*Okay* is a pretty strong word when you think about it." He began to lead her out of the bedroom and toward the stairs.

"Do we have company? It would take me just a minute to change into a nicer outfit."

"You look fine. Come on."

He guided her toward the parlor. His hand had been pressed to the small of her back, but when he again took her hand, his was sweaty. Was he nervous, too?

She saw the backs of their heads first. Noted Eban's dazzled look as he sat in an armchair across from the two on the sofa. The man, wearing a wrinkled white shirt, turned first; his eyes beamed despite the drawn look on his face.

Zofia gasped. "Artur!"

The woman beside him stood and turned around, careful not to disturb her toddler, who wore a yellow dress and was asleep with her head pressed against her mama's shoulder.

Zofia's knees buckled. Jabez grabbed her elbow and steadied her. She couldn't speak, couldn't even sign, in an understandable way—not with the streams of joyful tears flowing down her cheeks.

With that uncanny sense friends have that always seems to know what the other needs, Artur took the little girl into his arms. Aanya rushed to Zofia.

"Remember how to sign?" Aanya asked aloud, in Polish, her voice glorious music to Zofia's ears.

Zofia ignored her own tears and swept her fingers gently across Aanya's face to wipe the teardrops flowing from her friend's lovely eyes. "Yes, of course," she signed.

Aanya smiled at Artur and the child. She faced Zofia and began to sign. "This is our daughter, Kasia. Translated into English it becomes Katie and means *Little Darling*, which she is to us. We wanted to come here earlier, but couldn't leave for a while. First the war, then living in displaced persons camps…" She placed a hand over her heart. "Then my pregnancy. After losing our first baby those years ago, I didn't want to risk traveling such a great distance."

"You're here now. That's all that matters to me." Zofia wasn't sure who hugged whom first. Nor did she know whether the embrace lasted seconds or a lifetime before they stepped apart. "You've come home, my friend." Deciding to speak, Zofia grasped Aanya's hands. "You've come home to me," she repeated, the words strong and heartfelt. "We have plenty to catch up on. For now, let's enjoy each other's company, face-to-face. Long overdue, yes?"

"Definitely." Aanya nodded, wiped more tears, and nodded again. "No one and nothing will ever come between us again."

One by one, Jabez, Artur with the now-awake Kasia in his arms, and Eban approached Zofia and Aanya. Like a symphony celebrating the occasion, more joyous tears, laughter, hugs, and pats on the back filled the circle of friends—of family—and Buster let loose several enthusiastic woofs.

ABOUT THE AUTHOR

Elaine Stock writes Historical Women's Fiction, exploring home, family and friendships throughout time. She enjoys creating stories showing how all faiths, races, and belief systems are interconnected and need each other.

Although multi-published in Inspirational Fiction, and a past blogger and online magazine contributor, Elaine now pens novels for the general reading audience. She is a member of Women's Fiction Writers Association and The Historical Novel Society. Born in Brooklyn, New York, she has been living in upstate, rural New York with her husband for more years than her stint as a city gal. She enjoys long walks down country roads, visiting New England towns, and, of course, a good book.

Dear Reader,

If you have enjoyed reading my book,
please do leave a review on Amazon or Goodreads. A few kind words would be enough. This would be greatly appreciated.

Alternatively, if you have read my book as Kindle eBook you could leave a rating.
That is just one simple click, indicating how many stars of five you think this book deserves.
This will only cost you a split second.
Thank you very much in advance!

Elaine.

We Shall Not Shatter is Book 1 of the Trilogy **Resilient Women of WWII**.

If you would like to read the next stand-alone volume, of this series please............

READERS GROUPS DISCUSSION GUIDE

1. The very core of the story *We Shall Not Shatter* embodies friendship and family bonds against the horrific backdrop of WWII. What would you be willing to sacrifice for your dearest friend(s) and beloved family? What wouldn't you be willing to surrender?

2. This is also a story about taking chances. Discuss how Zofia, Aanya, and Artur take chances against the odds of no guarantees of a perfect future.

3. Upon meeting the orphan Laja, Zofia reflects that the word *home* is the most "powerful" word in her vocabulary. What word is the most important to you?

4. Do you agree with Artur that it takes more effort to hate than it does to love? How do you see this in your personal life? How do you imagine love vs. hate during wartime?

5. Do you have relatives that left their family, home, and way of life to travel to another country in hope of better living conditions? Did they immigrate prior to, during, or after one of the world wars?

6. In what ways does Zofia's playful nickname for her friend Aanya, *Pani Determined*, fit Aanya well?

7. Zofia describes herself as strong but not particularly brave. Are you one or the other during stressful times? Do you think she's wrong, that one cannot be strong without being brave?

8. At what point in the story does each of the two women claim their own identity as an individual, separate from the roles of wife, mother, and daughter, and begin to take charge of their lives?

9. Have you ever lived, by your own choice, in a country outside of your native one for an extended time? For different reasons, Zofia and Aanya come to live in America. If you were in the same circumstances, what emotions might you have?

10. On a worldview level, Zofia and Aanya championed love among all peoples; on a personal level, they defended not only home and family, but especially the power of friendship between individuals. What causes and beliefs do you champion?

11. What was your reaction upon learning of Lena knowing—and covering up her awareness—of her son, Jabez's, involvement with a resistance group?

12. Bonus Question: To what degree would you defend your loved ones in a time of war?

ACKNOWLEDGMENTS

There is a cliché that circulates in the company of writers—*write the story of one's heart*. *We Shall Not Shatter* is truly of such nature. In addition to memorializing Brzeziny, it was a cathartic experience, not only in discovering buried family history but of the surprise in being reacquainted with family members who verified my heritage, filled in missing gaps, and helped to (delightfully) expand my curiosity even more. I am most grateful to David Jackson who reached out to me with his detailed Pakula Family Tree.

My gratitude also goes to my publisher, Liesbeth Heenk of Amsterdam Publishers. Thank you, Liesbeth, for giving my story a chance to be shared worldwide. Most of all, thank you for championing the true-accounts of what occurred in the Holocaust and why we should never forget this horrific time.

Thank you to my editor, Tricia, for weeding through my novel and making it shine. Your sharp eyes, patience, and encouraging comments all helped me to "save face" and I most appreciate it.

I want to also thank my first-readers for encouraging me to continue to write this story and to make it even better than what I originally had created in my mind: Megan Whitson Lee, Kay Moorehouse, and sensitivity-readers (regarding the deaf), Laurie Bickford and Jayme Bickford.

As always, thank you to my husband, Wally. Without your patience, encouragement, and zero complaints about my cooking, let alone oddities, I wouldn't have been able to write this story. I'm also in gratitude for sharing your knowledge of watches and clocks and all things mechanical.

And last, but not least, to Bonnie Lichak, who endured many conversations about my writing, our Polish heritages, and the meaning of democracy during many long walks. Your friendship and listening ear are a true gift.

www.ingramcontent.com/pod-product-compliance
Lightning Source LLC
LaVergne TN
LVHW091719070526
838199LV00050B/2469